SINNER

2

SIERRA SIMONE

Cover image: Vitaly Dorokhov
Cover Design: Letitia Hasser: RBA Designs
Editing: Nancy Smay: Evident Ink
Proofing: Erica Russikoff: Erica's Editing Services, Michele Ficht
Interior Design: Caitlin Greer

To Renee Bisceglia:
This isn't the first book I've dedicated to you, and I'm sure
it won't be the last.

PROLOGUE

With the right pen, a man can rule the world.

You wine them, dine them, flash them smiles, slip them gifts, massage them with compliments and praise and give them the old hey-buddy-buddy. You play golf or see the ballet or compare four-thousand-dollar suits and ten-thousand-dollar watches, and then you casually apply the leverage, the bladed facts against the soft underbellies, and handshake by handshake, you build yourself something new and shimmering and golden.

And when they're at the precipice, the point of no return, when they are looking behind them and see their last chance to back out—that's when you hand them the pen.

And they take it into their hands and it's solid and weighty and cool to the touch, and they uncap it to see the engraved gold nib ready to drip with the promise of money and power. And when they press the pen to the paper and the ink flows so crisp and dark, like some kind of inky, terrible blood, that's when it's done.

That's when you rule the world.

I'm not a good man, and I've never pretended to be. I don't believe in goodness or God or any happy ending that isn't paid for in advance.

What do I believe in? Money. Sex. Macallan 18.

They have words for men like me—playboy. Womanizer. Skirt chaser.

My brother used to be a priest, and he only has one word for me.

Sinner.

CHAPTER ONE

Armani tuxedo, Berluti shoes, Burberry watch.

Blue eyes, blond hair, a mouth a little too wickedly wide.

Yeah, I know I look good as I step out of my Audi R8 and walk into the hospital benefit.

I know it, the valet taking my keys knows it, the girl working the complimentary bar knows it. I give her the classic Bell dimple as I take a scotch from her, and she blushes. And then I turn and face the crowd of milling wealth, sipping my Macallan and thinking about where to start first.

Because tonight is my fucking victory lap.

First of all, I inked the Keegan deal this afternoon—which is this sexy stack of papers transferring a deserted downtown block of nothing to a New York developer—and my God, you would not believe the money these people have. It's not normal money. It's like *oil* money. It's not only making my firm a shit-ton, but it's going to anchor my position at Valdman and Associates, just in time for Valdman to retire and need someone to sit in that coveted corner office and count all the gold coins.

Second of all, *I* inked the deal, not Charles Northcutt—fuck that guy—and I would like to rub it in his stupid face tonight. I know he'll be here because he can't resist free drinks and bored trophy wives.

And third of all, I've been clocking a lot of late nights on the Keegan thing, which has severely cut into my sex life, and I'm hard up for it. I've got a few regulars saved to my phone and there's always the exclusive club I'm a member of, but tonight's my *victory lap*. That deserves something special. Something new.

I take another look around the room—Valdman's in the corner with his wife, laughing and red-faced even though the benefit's only just started, and Northcutt is right at his elbow, of course.

Fucking suck-up.

But tonight is mine, and there are gorgeous women everywhere, and maybe I'm just another white guy with too much money in a sea of white guys with too much money, but I've got the advantage. I'm a sinner with a dimpled smile and perfect hair, and I know how to make sin feel like heaven.

I swallow my scotch, set the glass down, and head off into the fray.

An hour later, I feel a nudge at my elbow.

"Dad's here. Just so you know."

I turn to see a man my age offering me another drink and giving me a convenient excuse to lean away from my current conversation and examine the room.

Sure enough, Elijah Iverson's father is across the room, surrounded by the usual cluster of hospital mega-donors and society leeches. Dr. Iverson is the physician-in-chief of the hospital's cancer center and an ever-present figure at these kinds of events, so I shouldn't be surprised he's here, but my skin tightens uncomfortably all the same, sending prickles of heat down the back of my neck. I close my eyes, and for a minute, I hear the clatter of casserole dishes and my father's raised voice. Elijah's mother murmuring pleadingly. And I can still smell all of those flowers, white and cloying and needy, funeral flowers for a funeral that shouldn't have been needed.

I open my eyes to Elijah's knowing, rueful smile. He was there that day too, the day our families went from beyond close to something else. Something cold and distant. Elijah and I had stayed close—we'd bonded over

Teenage Mutant Ninja Turtles in kindergarten, and a *TMNT* bond is a bond for life—but the rest of our families peeled apart, as if there hadn't been two decades of shared barbecues and Pictionary nights and babysitting and slumber parties and late-night card games filled with wine for the adults and as many snacks as could be quietly snuck up the stairs for the kids.

"It's fine," I say. It's only a half-lie, because even though Dr. Iverson reminds me of that day—of the awful hole my sister's death punched through my life—we're always civil and polite when we see each other, which is often enough in a city as small as this.

"Hey, the event looks great," I add, mostly to change the subject. The Iverson-Bell schism is an old wound, and Elijah's under enough pressure tonight as it is. It's his first big hurrah as the event coordinator for the Kauffman Center after leaving the art museum where he started out, and I know he's anxious for tonight to go well. And the fact that it's also the one event of the year his father and all his father's colleagues attend…I know I'm not imagining the lines of exhaustion and stress on Elijah's brow and around his mouth.

He nods faintly, whiskey-colored eyes scanning the room. With that efficient, peremptory gaze and squared jaw, he is a striking twin to his father—tall and black and handsome—although where Dr. Iverson frowns, Elijah has always been a person of smiles and laughs. "Everything seems to be running smoothly so far," he says, still assessing the space. "Except I lost my date."

"You brought a date?" I ask. "Where is he?"

"It's a *she*," he says, sending a grin my way, and then he laughs at my face, because Elijah hasn't had a *she* date since he came out in college. "I'm teasing, Sean. It's actually—"

A harried woman in a catering uniform scurries up to Elijah brandishing a seating chart, interrupting whatever he was about to say. After a flurry of whispers and a muttered *dammit* from Elijah, he gives me an apologetic wave as he runs off to put out whatever fire is igniting behind the scenes of the benefit, leaving me alone with my scotch. I glance back over to Dr. Iverson, who is staring at me. He gives me a nod and I nod back, and I don't miss the cool compassion in his expression.

I know exactly what that cool compassion is for, and a screw tightens somewhere deep in my chest.

Get yourself together and get back to the victory lap, Bell.

Except I suddenly don't feel like the victory lap right now. I feel like more scotch and some fresh air, and even with the massive glass wall overlooking the glittering skyline, I feel claustrophobic and restless—and the trilling melody of the string sextet in the corner is so fucking loud right now, expanding like gas to fill every alcove and balcony. I work my way to the terrace door almost blindly, frantically, just needing

> out
>
> out
>
> out—

The night air drenches me in an abrupt cool quiet, and I take a deep breath. And another. And another. Until my pulse slowly rambles back to normal and the screw in my chest loosens. Until my brain isn't a juxtaposed mess of casserole dishes and flowers, some from fourteen years ago and some from last week.

I wish it were just the memory of Lizzy's death doing this to me. I wish there was no reason for Elijah's dad to look at me with pity. I wish that there could be one shower, one meeting, one fuckfest with a gorgeous woman when I didn't need to have my phone close by and my ringer turned up in case of an emergency. I wish that I could just be happy that I landed this Keegan deal, that I have obscene amounts of money and a sleek new penthouse, and a nice body and an even nicer dick and hair that does a *thing*.

But it turns out there are some things money and great hair can't fix.

Surprise.

I drink the rest of my scotch, set the glass down on a high-top table, and venture deeper onto the grassed terrace. In front of me, the city rolls up a hill in a gentle flutter of lights; behind me is the stark curtain of glass and steel that marks my kingdom. Where I live, work, and play. And the air is filled with the summer music of cicadas and traffic, and I wish, just for a fucking moment, that I could remember what it was like to listen to those noises with a sense of peace. That I could stare at these lights and not remember the blare of hospital fluorescents, the beep of monitors, the smell of Chapstick.

There's hardly anyone else out on the terrace—although the night is young, and I'm certain drunk socialites will be laughing and tippling here as soon as the dessert plates are cleared away. Whatever the reason, I'm grateful for the moment of solitude before I head back into the victory lap, and I suck in one final grass-scented breath before I go inside, and that's when I see her.

It's the dress I see first, actually, a glimpse of red, shivering silk, a flicker of a hemline dancing in the breeze. It's like a red cape waved in front of a bull; within seconds, I'm Sean Bell again, victory lap and all, and I reverse direction, following the seductive glint of red silk until I find the woman it belongs to.

She's facing away from the glass and the milling rich people on the other side of it, leaning against one of the massive cables anchoring the top of the building to the terrace. The breeze plays with the silk along her body, ruffling the skirt and painting mouthwatering outlines of her waist and hips, and the city lights gleam along the warm brown skin of her exposed arms and back. I follow the groove of her spine down to where her dress sweeps over the swell of her ass and then back up to the delicate wings of her shoulder blades, which are crisscrossed by thin red straps.

She turns at my footsteps, and I almost stop walking because *fuck*, she's pretty, and *double fuck*, she's young. Not like jail-young—but maybe college-young. Too young for a thirty-six-year-old man, certainly.

And yet I don't stop walking. I take a spot leaning against the thick anchor cable next to her and put my hands in my pockets, and when I look at her, both our faces are completely illuminated by the golden light spilling out from the benefit.

Her eyes widen as she looks at me, her lips parting ever so slightly, as if she's shocked at my face, as if she can't believe what she's seeing, but I quickly dismiss the notion. More likely she can't believe how great my hair is.

Unless—do I have food on my face or something? I surreptitiously run a hand over my mouth and jaw to make sure, and her eyes follow the movement with an avidity that kindles a hot, tight heat low in my belly.

In this light, I can finally see her face properly, and I see that she's not just pretty. She's stunning, she's incredible. She's the kind of beautiful that inspires songs and paintings and wars. Her face is a delicate oval of high cheekbones and wide brown eyes, a slightly snubbed nose with a stud glinting at the side, and a mouth I can't take my eyes from. Her lower lip is smaller than her upper one, creating a soft, lush pout. The entire picture is framed by a spray of corkscrewed curls.

Jesus Christ. Pretty. What a stupid word to have used for her, what a bland shadow of the truth. Cakes and throw pillows are *pretty*—this woman is something else entirely. Something that makes me blink and glance away for a moment, because looking at her does this weird thing to my throat and my chest. Looking at her gives me this feeling like my hand is on a veil shrouding some powerful mystery, the way I used to feel looking at the stained glass windows of my church.

The way I used to feel about God.

Thinking of church and God brings with it a habitual spike of cold irritation, and it forces me to compose myself. I'm sure this woman thinks I'm nuts, coming up to her and then not even sustaining eye contact. *Head in the game, Sean*, I coach myself. *Victory lap, victory lap.*

"Nice night," I offer.

She turns her head even more, the ends of her curls kissing her bare shoulders as she does, and suddenly all I want to do is kiss her bare shoulders myself, brush her hair aside and kiss along her collarbone until she whimpers.

"It is," she finally answers, and God, her voice. Sweet and alto, with just the tiniest bit of husk to the edge of her words.

I cant my head back toward the party. "Doctor or

donor?" I ask, trying to subtly warm my way to the real question—*did you come here alone?*

Her eyes widen again, and I realize my words have surprised her, although God knows why, it seems like a normal enough question. And then there's a flash of something unreadable in her eyes before she tamps it down.

"Neither," she says, and I know I'm not imagining the guardedness in her voice.

Fuck. I don't want to spook her—but then again, I don't know that what I do want to do is that much better. She's so young, too young to invite back to my place, too young to pull up into a hidden balcony so I can drop to my knees and find out how she tastes…

God, I should walk away. Stick to my usual buffet of socialites and strippers. But even though I straighten up to go, I can't actually make my body move away from her.

Those copper-tinted eyes. That luscious mouth.

It wouldn't hurt just to talk, right?

She squares her shoulders as I'm thinking about this, lifts her chin as if she's come to a decision. "Which are you?" she asks. "Doctor or donor?"

"Donor," I say with a smile. "Or rather, my firm is a donor."

She nods, as if she already knew the answer, which I suppose she did. Most doctors have a decent tux in the closet, but let's face it, they aren't always known for their style. And I'm nothing tonight if not stylish. I reach up to adjust my bow tie, just so she can see the glint of my watch and cufflinks as I do.

To my surprise, she giggles.

I freeze, suddenly afraid I have food on my face again. "What?"

"Are you—" She's giggling enough that it's hard for her to squeeze out the words. "Are you…preening?"

"I am *not* preening," I say with some indignation. "I'm Sean Bell, and Sean Bell does not preen."

Her hand is up covering her mouth now, all long slender fingers and nails painted a shimmering gold. "You *are* preening," she accuses through her fingers. Her smile is so big I can see it around her hand, and oh my God, I want lick my way down her stomach and look up to see that smile while I'm kissing between her legs.

"You know, women don't usually laugh at me like this," I say in a long-suffering voice, even though I'm smiling too. "Normally, they're very impressed by my preening."

"I'm very impressed," she says with mock-earnestness, trying to school her face into an expression of fake awe, but she can't do it and she just ends up laughing even harder. "So very impressed."

"Impressed enough to let me bring you a drink?" I ask. It's part of the script, a response that comes from years of habit, and so it's only after I say it that I remember I don't even know if she's legal for alcohol. "Uh. *Can* you drink?"

Her smile slips a little and she drops her hand to her waist, where she runs abstracted lines along the silk. "I just turned twenty-one last week."

What's the rule again? Half my age, plus seven?

Shit, she is definitely way too young for me.

"So you can drink," I say, "but I'm too old to be bringing you drinks, which is the real problem."

She arches an eyebrow, her voice gently teasing. "Well, you are really old."

"Hey!"

That smile again. Christ. I could watch that mouth move from a scrumptious little moue to a giant smile and back again for the rest of my life.

"Anything but wine," she says, still smiling. "Please."

"Okay," I say, smiling back too. Grinning as if I'm a kid who's just gotten asked to dance for the first time at a middle-school mixer. What is wrong with me? One pretty twenty-one-year-old and my victory lap has turned into a hike through eager newbie territory. And I'm anything but a newbie.

But still, my heart is pounding fast and my cock is stirring against my pants as I go get this woman a drink. Even though she's too young. Even though I don't know her. Even though she laughed at me.

I kind of like that she laughed at me, actually. Usually I'm taken very, very seriously—in bed and out of it—and

I'm surprised at how good it feels to have to work for this girl's admiration.

That's it, I decide. That's what I want: to win her over the tiniest bit. Maybe it would be wrong to take her home, but if I can make her leave tonight wishing I *would've* taken her home, that will be enough for me. Enough to scratch the itch.

I get her a gin and tonic from the bar, asking the bartender to take it easy on the gin, and get myself another scotch, and then I return to the terrace, relieved to see her still there, staring pensively out at the skyline with her arms wrapped around her chest.

"Cold?" I ask, prepared to shrug out of my tuxedo jacket and hand it to her, but she waves me off.

"I'm okay." She takes the gin from me, taking a careful sip, then making a face. "Is there any gin in this?"

"You're young," I say, a bit defensively. "Your tolerance is low."

"Are you this protective of every woman you meet?" she asks. "Or am I special?"

"You're definitely special." I deliver the line with all the charm and panache I've collected over the years, throwing in the dimple for good measure, and then she laughs at me.

Again.

I sigh. "Is it just utterly hopeless?"

"Is what utterly hopeless?"

I take a sip of my scotch, giving her my best puppy eyes. "Getting you to like me."

She takes a sip of her own drink to mask her smile. "I think I like you just fine. But you don't have to do the charming guy thing with me."

"Well then. What thing works for you?"

She thinks for a moment, and the breeze toys with the ends of her hair, making them sway and dance. That strange feeling pulls at my chest again, as if the play of her hair in the wind is some kind of spell, conjuring up memories of stained glass and whispered prayers.

"I like honesty," she decides aloud. "Try the honest guy thing."

"Hmm," I muse, tapping my finger against my scotch glass. "Honest guy thing. I don't know if that's such a good idea."

"It's the only thing that works for me," she warns, an impish grin playing across her features. "I need complete honesty."

"I'll tell you what—I'll be honest with you if you'll be honest with me."

She sticks out her hand. "Deal."

I take her hand in mine to shake it, and it's warm and soft. I let my fingertips graze against the pulse point on her wrist as I end the handshake, and I'm gratified to see a small shiver move through her.

"You have to go first though," she says, pulling her

hand back. She narrows her eyes at me. "And no cheating."

"Cheating? *Moi*?" I put a hand to my heart as if staggered by her accusation, although I'm actually having more fun than I've had in ages. "I would never."

"Good. Because this only works if you really do it. Don't use it as an excuse to feed me some flirty line about how pretty I am and how you'd like to get to know me better."

My hand still on my chest, I drop my head forward in mock defeat. "You've got me." Because that's exactly what I was planning on saying—which technically wouldn't have been cheating. "Those things are also true though," I add, lifting my eyes to hers.

She makes a circling gesture with her hand, *yeah-yeah-yeah*, and gives me another one of those arched eyebrows. "Say something you wouldn't say to just any girl you wanted to get into bed."

"Fine," I say, and I set my glass down on the ledge next to us. "I think you're more than pretty. I think you're fucking gorgeous, and you're not impressed by me, which makes me want to work very, very hard to impress you. I want to impress you with my mouth…" I take a step toward her, my hands safely in my pockets, so she sees I'm not going to touch her. "…and impress you with my fingers…"

Another step forward, and she lifts her face up to see mine better, her mouth parted and her eyes wide and blinking. I can see the vulnerable place where her pulse thrums in her throat, the rapid rise and fall of her chest. The tight furls of her nipples against the silk dress.

"...and with every other part of my body."

We're so close now that my shoes brush against the hem of her dress, and I keep the distance just as it is—no touching, no pressing, no grinding, just my words and the electricity sparking between us. "And I *do* want to get to know you better. I want to know if you scream or if you moan when you come, I want to know if you prefer my mouth or my hands, I want to know if you like it deep and slow or fast and hard."

She swallows, her eyes searching mine in fast, dazed flicks.

"And right now I can see the V between your thighs under that dress, and all I want to do is press my cock against it. I want to see if you're sensitive enough that I can get you off through the silk, I want to see if I can lick you through the fabric." I lower my voice. "I want to taste you. I want to taste you so badly that I'm hard just thinking about it. I want to see how your little pussy unfurls when I part it with my fingers, I want to know if your clit gets hard and plump when I suck on it. I want you to feel the place my nose presses into you as I eat you out from the front...and from behind."

Her eyes are huge now, copper-brown rings around massive pools of black. "You can...you can do that?"

I cock my head a little, amused. "Do what?"

Her feet do a little shuffle as she looks down. "The, um. The eating. From behind."

Jesus. She's young, but surely not that young? Twenty-one is more than old enough to have found at least one boy who's decent in bed. And oh God, what does it say about me that this sudden revelation of innocence is *such* a fucking turn-on? That she doesn't know...that I could be the first to show her...my cock is pushing against the placket of my zipper like it's ready to burst the seams, and my skin feels hot and achy and tight. And my tongue is desperate for the satin texture of her secret place, for the hidden taste of her, and I run it along my teeth, needing some kind of sensation to quiet the rioting storm inside me.

She watches my mouth, entranced. I watch her watching me.

"Yes," I say huskily. "Yes, you can do that."

"I, ah," she says, and even in the indirect light, I can see a new rosy hue blossoming underneath the warm tones of her skin. "I didn't know."

I can show you, I want to say. *Let me take you up to a deserted balcony. Let me show you how to brace your hands on the railing and present your ass to me. Let me show you exactly how a man uses his mouth on a woman from behind.*

I don't say that, though. Instead, I lower my head ever

so slightly, just enough to make her lips part even more, and I murmur, "Your turn."

The rosy hues are even more pronounced now, spreading across the sweet skin along her collarbone and up her neck. "My turn?" she asks breathlessly.

"To be honest. Remember?"

"Oh," she exhales, blinking. "Right. Honest."

"No cheating," I remind her. "I was honest with you."

"Yes," she agrees, nodding, her eyes dropping to my mouth again. "You were honest with me."

I give her a moment, even though all I want to do is crowd her against the cable and rub my aching erection against her silk-clad dress. Even though all I want to do is bury my face in her neck and suck at the sensitive skin there as I ruck up her skirt and cup her heat in my palm.

"Okay. Honesty." She takes a deep breath and then peers up at me. "I want you to kiss me."

"Right now?"

"Right now," she confirms. There's the tiniest bit of quaking bravado in her voice, and I don't like it. I mean, I'm halfway to dropping to my knees and begging her to let me see her cunt, but the better part of me wants her to be completely ready and certain. I don't want her to fake bravery in order to be kissed—I don't want her to require bravery at all. I pluck her drink from her hands and set it next to my scotch on the ledge, then I hold out my hand for her to take.

She looks confused. "Are you not going to kiss me? I thought—after all you said—"

"I want to kiss you very much. But *right now* can be as long as we want to make it, right? Maybe it's the next ten minutes, maybe it's the next twenty. However long it is, I don't want to rush it. What if this is the only kiss I get to have from you for the rest of my life? I want to take my time. Savor it."

"Savor it," she repeats. And then she nods, relaxing. "I like that."

She takes my hand and I lead her farther onto the terrace, where a tent with a dance floor has been erected, waiting for the after-dinner crowd to come for drinks and dancing. But it's mostly empty now, and there's only a lone employee carrying out trays of waiting champagne flutes and a speaker piping in music from the sextet in the lobby.

"How about a dance first?" I ask.

She looks around the tent, and some of her earlier confidence creeps back into her expression. "Are you sure you're any good at dancing?"

"I'm *excellent* at dancing," I say, nettled. "I'm like, probably the best in the world at it."

"Prove it," she dares, and so I do. I do what I've been hungry to do since I saw her, and I slide my hand around the dip of her waist, resting it against the tempting dimples at the small of her back and fighting the urge to slide my hand even lower. And then I pull her close to me as my other hand tightens around hers.

She shivers again. I smile.

It doesn't take me long to find the music and sweep us into a simple two-step. I'm a serviceable dancer—some cousin demanded all the Bell boys take dancing lessons before her wedding, and I've managed to squeeze some use out of that exhausting experience at functions like this—and I'm pleased to find that the beautiful woman in my arms looks suitably impressed by it.

"You're not bad," she admits. As we move across the empty floor, the city glittering around us and the cicadas chirruping merrily, she meets my eyes with a look I can't read. It feels like so much, like there's so much there, history and weight and meaning, and I can almost hear the hymns in the back of my mind, taste the stale-sweet paste of a communion wafer on my tongue.

"You're not bad yourself," I say back, but they are just placeholder words, nothing-words, words to fill the air because the air is already filled with something thick and nameless and ancient and my heart and my gut are responding with a kind of keen fervor I haven't felt in years. And it scares me. It scares me and thrills me, and then she moves her hand from my shoulder to the nape of my neck in a gesture both tentative and determined, and it feels important, it feels adorable, it feels like my body is going to rocket apart from the lust and the protectiveness and the sheer mystery of what I feel right now.

"What's your name?" I murmur. I need to know. I need to know her name because I don't think I can walk away tonight *not* knowing.

I don't think I can walk away at all.

But something about my question makes her stiffen, and suddenly she's guarded again, a careful shell in my arms. "I'm about to change it," she says cryptically.

"You're about to change your name?" I ask. "Like…for witness protection or something?"

That makes her laugh a little. "No. It's for work."

"Work? Are you even out of college?"

"I'm about to start my senior year. But," she says sternly, "a girl can work and go to school at the same time, you know."

"But the kind of job where you have to change your name?" I study her face. "Are you sure it's not for witness protection? Like super sure?"

"I'm super sure," she says. "It's just a very unusual job."

"Are you going to tell me about this job?"

She tilts her head, thinking. "No," she decides aloud. "Not right now, at least."

"No fair," I accuse. "That was clickbait-y and you know it. Plus I still don't know what to call you."

"Mary," she replies after a moment. "You can call me Mary."

I give her a skeptical look. "That sounds fake."

She shrugs, and the movement makes her fingers tighten ever so slightly around the back of my neck, and it feels so fucking good I want to purr. I've been in bed with gorgeous women, experienced women, more than one woman at a time, and somehow the play of Mary's fingers through the short hair at the nape of my neck is more intense, more stirring, than anything I can remember ever feeling. I pull her in a little closer as the music sweeps into a softer, more melancholy song; the cicadas whirr along with the strings as if they've invited themselves into the sextet, loud and comforting and familiar.

"I haven't danced like this in years," Mary admits as we step easily around the floor.

"You're too young to sound so old," I tell her.

She gives me a sad smile. "It's true."

"That you haven't danced like this in years or that you're too young to sound so old?"

"Both," she says, still with that sad smile. "Both are true."

I urge her into a small spin, selfishly wanting to see the flare and wrap of her dress along her body, and when I see it, I have to trap the growl rumbling in my chest. God, those hips. That waist. Those small, high tits, braless and palm-sized under her dress. I yank her back into me, sliding my hand slowly across her back, teasing my fingers along the straps crisscrossing her spine.

She shudders at my touch, her lips parting and her

eyelids going heavy. I slow our dancing steps, releasing her hand so I can trace the line of her jaw.

"Mary," I rumble.

"Sean," she sighs, and she says it like she's been waiting to say it, she says it without hesitation, without worry, without the usual clumsiness of someone saying a name they've just learned. And the sound of my name on her lips unlocks a deep, heady need, something familiar and unfamiliar all at once, like a prayer chanted in a new tongue.

"Do you still want that kiss?" I ask her in a low voice. All of her seems ready now, there's no fear anywhere in her face, but I want to make certain, I want her to want this as much as I do, I want her to burn with needing my mouth on hers.

She blinks up at me, her eyes pure liquid heat, and when I run my finger across the plump line of that full upper lip, she shivers again. "I want it," she whispers. "Kiss me."

I bend my head down, pulling her flush against my body so that every tight curve of hers is smashed against the muscled length of me, and I am about to replace my finger with my lips, about to finally taste her, about to kiss her until she can't stand on her own two feet anymore...when a jarring bar of flattened pop music ricochets through the air.

And then suddenly Kesha is singing from my pocket.

(Yes, I like Kesha. Who doesn't? She's great.)

"Um," Mary says.

"Shit," I say, letting go of her to fumble for my phone, taking a step away as I finally manage to accept the call and put the phone to my ear.

"Sean," my dad says from the other line. "We're at the ER."

I give my arm an impatient shake to clear the tuxedo cuff away from my watch so I can see the time. "KU Med?"

"Yeah."

"I can see the hospital from here. I'll be there in ten."

"Okay," Dad says. "Be safe getting here…I mean, it won't change anything if it takes you an extra five minutes…"

He trails off, lost. I know how he feels. I know exactly how thoughts get fuzzy and stumbling after the adrenaline of rushing someone to the hospital.

I hang up the phone and look back at Mary, who is chewing on her lower lip with her brow furrowed in concern. "Is everything okay?" she asks.

I run a hand over my face, suddenly feeling very, very tired. "Uh, it's not actually. I have to go."

"Oh." But even though she seems disappointed, she doesn't seem annoyed that I'm abruptly breaking away from our moment, like some women would be. If anything, her expression is—well, it's *kind*. Her eyes are warm and worried and her lips are pulled into a little frown that I'll forever regret not being able to kiss off her face.

"If you were older, I'd ask for your number," I murmur. "I'd make sure we finished this."

"We wouldn't be able to," she says, glancing away, something vulnerable and very young in her face, and fuck if it doesn't pull at every corner of my lust and also at the bizarrely intense protectiveness I feel toward her. "This is kind of my last night out," she clarifies. "For a while, anyway."

Last night out? And then I remember that it's August, that she's a student, that she seems like the kind of woman to take her studies seriously. "Of course. The semester's starting soon."

She opens her mouth, as if she's about to say something, correct me maybe, but then she presses her lips together and nods instead.

I take her hand and raise the back of it to my lips. It wouldn't be right taking a real kiss before I dash off—something about it feels sleazy, even to me—but this, well, I can't resist this. The silky brush of her skin against my lips, the smell of something light and floral. Roses, maybe.

Fuck.

Fuck.

It really hits me that this is the last time I might ever see this woman, the one woman I've met in years that I desperately want to see more of, and there's nothing I can do about it. She's too young and she's not offering me any way to contact her anyway—and I have to get the fuck out of here and up to the hospital.

I drop her hand with more reluctance than I've ever felt over anything in my life, and I take a step back.

"It was nice to meet you, Mary."

Her expression is conflicted as she says, "It was nice to meet you too, Sean."

I turn, feeling something yank in my stomach as I do, as if my body is tethered to hers and begging me to turn back, but my mind and my heart are already racing ahead to the hospital. To the emergency room which I know far too well.

"Whatever it is," Mary calls out from behind me, "I'll pray for you."

I look at her over my shoulder, alone on the dance floor, surrounded by city lights, draped in silk, her face that intriguing combination of wise and young, confident and vulnerable. I memorize her, every line and swell of her, and then I say, "Thank you," and leave her to the glittering lights and relentless cicadas.

I don't say what I really want to say as I leave, but I'm thinking it all the way to the valet stand, bitterly repeating it in my mind as I roar up the road to the hospital.

Don't bother with that praying shit, Mary. It doesn't work anyway.

CHAPTER TWO

I used to believe in God like I believed in cancer. That is, I knew both existed in a kind of distant, academic sense, but they were concepts that applied to other people; they were personally irrelevant to Sean Bell's life.

Then cancer tore through my family with wind and knives and teeth, thundering and massive, and it ceased to be academic, it stopped being distant. It became real and terrible, more vengeful and omnipresent than any deity, and our lives became reoriented around its rituals, its communion of morphine lollipops and anti-nausea meds, its hymns of vaporizers and daytime television.

We were baptized into the Church of Cancer, and I was as zealous as any new convert, going to every doctor's appointment, researching every new trial, using every connection I had in this city to make sure my mother got the best of everything.

So yes. I believe in cancer now.

It's too late for me to believe in God.

I pull into the hospital parking garage, park the Audi, and then jog through the emergency room doors, ignoring the looks I'm getting in my tuxedo. I go right to the triage desk, and just my luck, it's a nurse I fucked a few weeks back during Mom's last stint in the hospital. Mackenzie or Makayla or McKenna or something like that. Her mouth twists into a bitter smile when she sees me, and I know I'm in for it.

"Well, if it isn't Sean Bell," she says, tilting her head up and narrowing her eyes at me. I'm suddenly grateful for the glass barrier between us, otherwise I think I might be in danger of actual bodily harm. For me, it was a desperate, needy escape stolen during long hours in the waiting room, a momentary distraction with a pretty, available body—but it had been clear after she gave me her number and her schedule that it had been more than just an escape for her.

"Hey, so my mom is here and I need to see her. It's Carolyn Bell, and I think she got in not too long ago."

The nurse with the M-name gives me a slow, insolent blink, and then turns even more slowly to her computer screen. *Click* goes an irritated press of her finger on the mouse. *Click. Click.*

Goddammit.

Godfuckingdammit. If she moved any slower, she'd be

a painting. A statue. Isn't there some kind of fucking rule about nurses doing their job no matter what former fucks were involved? Surely she's breaking some kind of nursely oath? There's a part of me that wants to go full Sean Bell on her, and either charm or threaten my way through this, but both of those things take fucking time, and I don't have time.

"Look, I'm sorry I didn't call," I say.

She doesn't even look at me. "Sure."

Oookayyy. My entire body is screaming at me to get to Mom, my chest is still tight with memories of a girl pretending to be named Mary, and now I've got this pissy nurse between me and where I need to go—and this is exactly why I've steered clear of entanglements my entire fucking life. Feelings and fucking do not mix, and Mackenzie/Makayla/McKenna is living proof of my theory.

Honesty, Mary's voice echoes in my memories. *Try the honest guy thing.*

I let out a long, silent sigh, knowing I need to fix this somehow. *Mom's more important than your pride, fucker. Just apologize for real so you can get to her.*

"Look," I say, leaning forward so that I can lower my voice and spare the rest of the waiting room my humiliation. "You're right. It was shitty of me to take your number when I didn't plan on calling, and it was shitty of me to fuck you without making it clear that a screw was all

31

I wanted. You deserved better than that, and I'm sorry."

The nurse doesn't soften, exactly, but her clicking on the mouse speeds up, and finally she looks up to me. "Room thirteen," she says, the flat bitterness in her voice slightly blunted now. "Through those doors and to the left."

"Thank you," I say.

"And just so you know," she says, still looking at me, "you treat women like shit. If you've got any decency left inside you, you'll spare the next woman you meet the headache."

"I'll take it under consideration," I lie, and then I'm striding back to Mom's room, my dress shoes bouncing reflections of cheap hospital lights across the walls as I go.

Two hours later, I'm in a surgical waiting room with my phone pressed to my ear. I'm alone because I sent Dad home to grab some things for Mom, and thank God he listened to me when I asked him to do it.

First lesson in the Church of Cancer catechism? *Thou Shalt Give Dad Something to Do.* The waiting, the bleary uncertainty, the hours of nothing-time—all of it just amplifies his fear and his agitation, and eventually he becomes a mess and no help to anyone. But as long as he feels useful, well, then, he's fine. And he's not stressing Mom and me out.

Second lesson in the catechism—text threads are sacred. After I got Dad sorted, I got the family thread updated, and now I'm in the waiting room talking to my brother Tyler.

"I thought they already fixed the bowel obstruction," he's saying in a tired voice. I glance at my watch—almost midnight on the East Coast, and knowing my brother and his wife Poppy, I'm sure they were fucking like bunnies all evening.

Lucky bastards.

"It was only a *partial* obstruction a few weeks ago," I explain, and then rub at my forehead with the heel of my palm because sometimes I feel like my entire life has been reduced to telling and retelling these condensed medical narratives. "They just kept her in to hydrate her and keep her comfortable. They thought it had cleared itself up."

"Well, obviously not," Tyler says impatiently, and while I agree with him, I also bite back a surge of my own impatience. Because he's not fucking here; he's off in Ivy League land publishing bestselling memoirs and fucking his hot wife, and he hasn't had to spend the last eight months listening to doctors and negotiating with insurance companies and learning how to flush picc lines. *I've* been the one to do it. I've been the one to bear the brunt of Mom's illness and Dad's stress, because Tyler's too far away and Ryan's too young and Aiden's too flaky and Lizzy's too dead.

Shit.

My eyelids burn for a moment and I hate that, I hate the feeling of powerlessness and guilt and loss, and I fight it back. I couldn't save Lizzy, but I can save Mom, and goddammit, I will.

"They think it's possible it got worse or that it's a complication from the radiation treatment she had two days ago," I say after I've regained control of my stupid feelings. "It's a total obstruction, so they're doing surgery now, and for whatever it's worth, they're extremely optimistic."

Tyler lets out a long breath. "I should come home."

The million-dollar question, always. What if this was *the* time? What if this was the time when everything spiraled out of control, when everything cascaded into bleak certainty? Tyler had only been seventeen when he found our sister's body hanging in the garage, and I knew that moment had scarred him as much as it had scarred the rest of us—maybe even more—and then he'd spent years serving a hollow, absent god in some sort of pointless dance of atonement. I have no doubt that the thought of missing Mom's final moments would haunt him even more than not being able to stop Lizzy's, simply because with Lizzy there was no way to know what was going to happen. But with Mom, the inevitability of her death becomes clearer with every passing day. We all know what is going to happen.

Stop it, I order myself with some annoyance. *Nothing's fucking inevitable.*

Nothing.

"If you want to come home to see her, I get it, but she's going to be okay this time. It's just a laparoscopic thing, and it will be over any minute."

Tyler's silent for a moment, and I know what he's doing, I know how easily his thoughts stray to things like guilt and shame.

"Look, Tinkerbell," I add, knowing the nickname drives him crazy, "no one blames you for having a life in another state. Mom is super proud of whatever it is you do—"

"Write books," Tyler interjects dryly.

"—And whatever it is that Poppy does in Manhattan–"

"An arts nonprofit. Do you actually even listen to me when I talk?"

"Sure don't. So don't feel guilty for not coming out, okay? If I honestly thought it was time for you to fly out, I'd buy your fucking ticket myself. But it's not time."

"My worry is that you won't be able to admit it to yourself when it is time," Tyler says carefully. "Much less tell me."

"What the fuck is that supposed to mean?"

A pause, and I know Tyler's sifting through his words,

and that pisses me off even more. "I don't need fucking kid gloves," I snap. "Just say whatever it is you want to say."

"Fine," he says, and I'm a bit pleased to hear that I've made him snappish too. "I think you haven't dealt with the fact that Mom's going to die."

"Everybody's going to die, kiddo. Or did you forget that part of being a priest?"

"Sean, I'm serious. I know you think this boils down to having the best doctors, the best treatments—the most money—but those things might not change anything. You get that, right? That you can't *control* what happens next?"

I don't answer. I can't. My hand is gripping the phone so hard I can feel the edges of the glass pressing against my fingerbones.

"There's no agenda for life, there's no itinerary, there's no strategic plan," Tyler continues. "Everything can go perfectly…until it doesn't, and there's nothing we can do to change it. There's nothing *you* can do to change it. Don't you see that?"

"I see that you've given up on Mom already, and you aren't even fucking here to actually know how she's doing."

"It's okay to feel angry," Tyler tells me quietly. "And lost."

"Don't do that priest shit with me," I hiss, pacing across the room, wishing he were here, because I'd hit him, I'd hit him right in his fucking know-it-all mouth. "You're not my fucking priest, Tyler. You're not even a priest at all anymore."

"Maybe not," he replies calmly, "but I'm still your brother. I still love you. And God still loves you."

I snort. "Then He needs to try a little fucking harder."

"Sean—"

"I've got to go. I told Aiden I'd call."

And then I hang up before Tyler can answer, which is a dick move I know, but he was a dick first, bringing fucking God into this. A god I don't believe in, a god I hate, a god who let one of his priests hurt my sister over and over again, and then instead of comforting her, let her cinch a noose around her nineteen-year-old neck to escape the pain. A god who's now killing my mother in the slowest, most dehumanizing way possible.

Fuck Tyler and fuck his god, I don't need either of them and neither does Mom.

"Mr. Bell?"

I look up to see someone in scrubs standing at the door.

"Yes?" I say hoarsely.

"Your mother's in the post-op ward now, and she's sleeping, but she's doing great. Would you like to come up and sit with her?"

"Of course." And I go to my mother, leaving all of Tyler's lectures and my anger at God behind, knowing they'll be waiting for me when I come back.

CHAPTER THREE

Harry Valdman is a selfish, greedy asshole who cheats on his wife, ignores his children, and routinely swindles people out of their hard-earned money—but he's a fairly decent boss. As long as I bring in lots of money, he doesn't care what I do or how often I'm in the office, which has been immensely helpful over the last eight months since Mom was diagnosed and I became Son in a Leading Cancer Role. I've still been nailing big deals and even bigger clients left and right, even if I'm doing most of my work now from various infusion rooms.

So I assume it won't be a problem when I leave a message with his secretary that I won't be in to the office that day, but then I get a call back from Trent the Secretary right away.

"Good morning, Mr. Bell." Trent the Secretary sounds a little nervous. "Mr. Valdman says he wants you in his office as soon as possible. Something big's come up and it's an emergency."

I look across the room to where my mom sleeps fitfully, surrounded by a cluster of poles and wires and bags and screens.

I sigh. "My mom's in the hospital right now. Is there any way it can wait?"

"Hold on, I'll ask," Trent says and I hear the electronic piano tones of a Liszt piece as I'm put on hold. Then Trent returns. "Uh, Mr. Bell? I'm really sorry, but Mr. Valdman says he needs to see you right away and that it can't wait. Should I tell him you're on your way?"

"Fuck," I mumble, running a hand over my unshaven face. I look down at my wrinkled tuxedo. "Yes, I'm on my way. I have to swing by home to change, then I'll be in."

"Yes, sir. I'll let him know."

Fuck a damn duck.

I hang up the phone and stand up, reluctant to leave Mom alone. I'd made Dad go to work—he's a warehouse manager for a small plumbing company, and his boss is not very forgiving of Dad missing work for any reason, even a sick wife—and Ryan's all the way in Lawrence, getting settled into his new off-campus digs. Aiden's at work. And obviously Tyler isn't here.

I drop a kiss onto Mom's cool forehead and she stirs, but she doesn't wake up. I find a nurse and explain that I have to go in to work, but to call me at the slightest sign of trouble, and then I leave her every number of every person I can think of in case she can't reach me, although she'll be able to reach me. Valdman will understand if I have to dash out of our meeting, I'm certain of it.

Mostly certain.

Like, halfway certain.

Shit, maybe I'm not that certain at all. I chew over this as I get into my car and speed back to my apartment, tapping my fingers anxiously on the steering wheel. It's legitimately the first time taking care of Mom has been a problem with my job, and I have to admit—even knowing that Valdman's an asshole—I'm surprised he still insisted on me coming in. Trent said it was an emergency—but what fucking investment emergency is more important than my mom's surgical emergency?

And then I feel like an idiot, because I didn't get all the money I have now by asking myself those kinds of questions. I've always, *always* put work first, at least until Mom's illness. And even after, I've done my best to give this firm every part of me not locked down by chemo-chauffeur duties and pharmacy runs. If Valdman says it's an emergency, then I fucking believe him and I need to fix it, whatever it is.

But Jesus, for real. What could it be?

I get to my place, take the world's fastest shower and jump into a clean suit without bothering to shave. I won't be seeing any clients anyway, so it's fine, although the foreign sensation of stubble abrading the fabric of a clean shirt collar is distracting. I feel unkempt, and when I glance up at the mirror to make sure my tie-knot is straight, I barely recognize the grim, scruffy man looking back at me.

Well, it can't be helped. It was a long fucking night, and not the good kind…except for the part with Mary, because I could have spent a thousand long nights with her.

Which means I'm going straight to hell.

Thirty-six year old men like me have no business wanting to see a college student's pussy. Wanting to lick and rub her until she's wet and mewling, wanting to split her legs open and mount her. Wanting to fuck and thrust and grind until she's come so many times under me that she's forgotten her name—and her fake name. And now I'm hard, which is great, *just fucking great.*

I toss all my shit into a leather satchel and run out the door to meet my boss, boner be damned. Lord knows it will shrivel the moment I get to his office anyway.

Rosacea decorates Valdman's cheeks like red, splotchy spiders, and I find myself staring at the tiny ruptured capillaries and veins as he talks, wondering if all rich white guys end up gouty and drink-ruddy and wondering what I need to do to avoid getting the Henry VIII look myself. Stop drinking probably, although I do eat a lot of kale, and that feels like it should count for something.

He's been ranting since I came in and sat down a few minutes ago, and I still have no idea what's wrong.

"—*fucked*, Sean, we're fucked, and I've already heard from two clients complaining about the bad PR bouncing back onto them. And the news—Jesus, you would not believe those vultures! They've been ringing everyone off the hook, even the fucking interns."

I force myself to tear my eyes from his cheeks. "If you'll tell me what's happened, I'll fix it. I promise."

Valdman heaves himself into his chair and reaches for the globe bar he keeps next to his desk. "You want a drink?" he asks, already rummaging for a glass and the scotch decanter.

I glance discreetly over at the clock. It's a little after nine a.m.

"I'm good," I decline cautiously. "Now, sir, about whatever's happened—"

"Right, right," he mumbles, taking a drink and then setting the scotch decanter on the desk between us. "The Keegan deal."

I'm honestly confused. "The Keegan deal, sir?"

Valdman blinks at me with bloodshot eyes, takes another drink. Waiting for me to say something.

But what is there to say? "Every version of that deal went through legal at least twice," I offer, racking my brain, trying to think of any potential snags that would have Valdman in such apoplexy. But there were *none*, seriously. Fucking none. It was a good deal—every contingency prepared for, every clause examined, every city code and sales tax bond painstakingly referenced and braided into the agreement. "And we did have to get special approval from the City Council, but that went better and easier than we ever could have planned for. And then we sent it through our legal a *final* time, after the Keegan team's legal went through it. There's nothing even close to illegal or unethical in there, I promise you, sir."

Valdman grunts. "Illegal, maybe not. But unethical? You sure about that?"

I stare at him. I know I'm wrecked from no sleep and stress, I know I'm thoroughly wrung dry from the last four weeks of late nights and early mornings trying to get this deal to paper—but my mind has always worked best when pushed like this, and so I know I'm genuinely stumped. I mean, I'll be the first to admit that in the past I've drafted some deals that nudged a few moral boundaries—the best money is made on the frontiers of morality, after all—but there wasn't even a whiff of that in the Keegan deal. No trace of anything slimy or suspicious. Just some old brick buildings that will be turned into shiny new profit centers. Hell, even as a citizen I think it's a good deal.

Valdman finally sees that I honestly have no idea what he's hinting at, and he sets his glass down with an irritated thump. "The man selling the property—Ernest Ealey? Did he ever mention anything about a lease? Tenants?"

Easy question. "Not once," I say firmly. "And we pulled every agreement logged in those three buildings for the last forty years. No standing leases, no liens, no surprise historical registry shit. It's *clean* property, sir, I promise."

"You're wrong," my boss tells me. "Because there is a lease, and there are tenants."

I shake my head. "No, we checked—"

"Ealey lied to you, son, or he just plain forgot because it was a handshake agreement done twenty years ago."

"If it wasn't disclosed—"

"I don't care about fucking disclosure right now," Valdman says. "I care about the fucking newspapers breathing down my neck."

"I'm sorry, sir, I still don't understand why the press would care about some random tenants—"

"Nuns, Sean," Valdman interrupts. "They're fucking nuns."

Of all the things he could have said, the word *nuns* was probably the farthest down on my list of possibilities and I'm still asking myself if I heard him right when he continues. "They run a shelter and soup kitchen there, and in the last year, they've used it as a place to put up victims of human trafficking."

Nuns. Shelter.

Human trafficking victims.

I blink.

And blink.

Because.

This is bad.

"Good old Ernest Ealey couldn't sell those buildings for years, so he rented them out to the nuns for one dollar a year to get the tax write-off."

"One dollar a year," I echo.

Shit, this is so bad.

Valdman appraises me shrewdly over a sip of scotch. "I see you're finally grasping the extent of the fucking problem."

Oh, I am, and here it is: it doesn't matter how legal and aboveboard the actual deal is now. Because the *story* is that an out-of-state developer is kicking a group of sweet, do-gooding nuns out of the place they do good from. The story is that a place of charity will be torn down and turned into a temple of consumerism and greed. The story is that these tiny old nuns—fuck, I can see them on the news now, with little wimples and adorable wrinkled faces—just want to feed and clothe the poor, and the big, bad millionaires are punishing them and the city's needy just to make a quick buck.

Fuck, fuck, fuck. How did I fucking miss this?

I run a hand through my hair and pull for a minute, using the pain to focus. "Do you want me to find a way to cancel the deal?"

"Fuck no," Valdman scoffs. "Do you know how much money we're making from it?"

Of course I fucking do, but I don't say that.

My boss leans forward, tapping the top of his desk for emphasis. "No, it's in Keegan's and Ealey's best interest to move forward, not to mention ours. Keep the deal, but fix this. Fix our image."

"Sir?"

"You heard me," he rumbles. "The PR is the real problem, not the deal, so you fix the PR."

"I—" I actually don't know what to say. "Sir, I don't know shit about PR."

"No, but you inked the deal, so it's best if you're the one the press sees. Plus you aren't half bad-looking, kid. Makes the rest of us look good."

I'm already shaking my head. "Sir, please—"

"It's done, Sean. I've already had Trent reach out to the nuns—"

"You *what?*"

"And they were going to send their boss or whatever to meet you, but I guess one of the sisters is sick, so they're sending a nun intern to meet with you."

"A nun intern?"

Valdman looks impatient. "You know, like she's not a

nun yet, but she's a nun-in-training or something. I don't know—you're the one with the priest brother, right?"

"Postulant," I say, surprised I still know the word. "She must be a postulant." And then I add, "And he's not a priest anymore."

His brow furrows. "But that must mean your whole family is Catholic, right? That you're Catholic?"

"*They* used to be, and I haven't been Catholic since college," I say, and something in the tone of my voice makes Valdman shut up about it.

"Ah, okay. Well, anyway, the training nun offered to come here, but I think you better go to her. Makes for a better first impression. She's expecting you around ten at the shelter."

I glance at the clock. Thirty minutes from now I'm going to be shaking hands with a nun. What the fuck happened to my day? "What's the postulant's name?" I ask as I stand. Might as well go in having as much information as possible.

Valdman glances at his computer screen. "Um, it's Iverson."

My blood jumps up a degree in temperature.

Chill out, Sean. There's probably lots of Catholics with the last name Iverson in Kansas City.

Valdman squints at whatever notes Trent the Secretary left him in the call memo. "Zenobia," he pronounces. "Zenobia Iverson."

"Zenny," I correct automatically.

Valdman looks up at me. "Pardon?"

I smooth down my jacket and grab my briefcase. My blood is hot with something between anxiety and relief. "It's Zenny. She hates the name Zenobia."

"Do you…do you know this training nun?"

"Postulant. And yes, I do."

"Well, I don't know how well she knows you. She was the one who leaked the story to the press yesterday—with your name attached."

This does nothing to settle my pulse. "Oh."

Valdman tilts his head at me. "How do you know her again?"

I answer as I'm walking out of the door. "She's my best friend's little sister."

"Careful, son," he calls after me. "Remember the deal comes first."

As if I'd have any trouble remembering that. I give him a wave as I round the corner into the hall, check my phone to make sure I haven't missed any calls from the hospital, and then head down to meet Elijah's little sister and cajole her into calling off the press dogs.

Easy peasy, right?

CHAPTER FOUR

Okay, not so easy peasy. As I get into my car, my brain starts peeling everything apart, and I have to stop thinking about Keegan and PR for a moment so I can just...process.

Little Zenny-bug is a nun?

Little Zenny-bug is a nun who reported my financial firm to the press?

My mind is in a tumult as I navigate my Audi to the Keegan property to meet with Zenny. Zenny the postulant. Zenny the soon-to-be nun. I call Elijah, and it goes to his voicemail, so I toss the phone into my passenger seat with a huff, trying to remember if he'd said anything about his sister joining a religious order.

With some chagrin, I realize we don't talk about our families much; an unspoken mutual thing, so as not to bring up anything that evokes the Great Iverson-Bell Schism of 2003. I didn't even tell him Mom was sick until after he found out about it from his dad.

And it's never bothered me that we don't talk about family, but Zenny becoming a nun seems like something I should have known, at least for Elijah's sake. His parents had been decently kind and understanding when he came out, although I knew he'd faced an unvoiced wall of Catholic discomfort about him being gay. The one thing his parents *did* voice was a desire for grandchildren of their bodies. Elijah hadn't let it bother him—or maybe he simply hadn't shown that it bothered him, I don't know, we weren't always great at talking about that kind of shit— but part of what had appeased his parents was knowing that Zenny might still give them grandchildren.

And now she's becoming a nun.

I hope that hasn't made anything harder for Elijah. I resolve to ask him about it whenever he calls me back.

I park on the street outside the property, leaving my pretty German car-baby behind with some reluctance, and then I have to poke around the block of old five and six-story buildings before I find a metal door marked simply with a cross and a local phone number. It's unlocked, and I step into a narrow linoleum-floored landing with a badly lit set of stairs leading upward. I creak my way to the second floor, and there a door marked *Servants of the Good Shepherd of Kansas City* takes me into a makeshift waiting room. It's also lined in linoleum, ringed by red plastic chairs that were definitely salvaged from a 1980s bowling alley or some shit, and dotted with baskets of well-worn toys. A dusty fake plant sits in a corner, and somewhere, incongruously, Bruno Mars is singing about Versace on the floor.

Sex and wealth—definitely the first things I think of when I think of nuns, right?

I ring the orange bell at the vacant receptionist's window and wait.

I wonder what Zenny will look like after all these years. I can't remember seeing any pictures of her floating around, but I guess it's not that surprising. Elijah always claimed he was too burned out on social media from running the museum's feeds to update his own personal accounts, and honestly, I'm too busy myself to open up anything on my phone that isn't *The Wall Street Journal* or my stock apps, so I'm pretty much clueless about anything that isn't directly related to my job—even my best friend's family.

Well, given the schism, *especially* my best friend's family.

I picture Zenny as I remember her best—as Zenny-bug, young and dimpled with hair in pigtails that ended in little dandelion-shaped puffs. I'd had to babysit her once or twice before the schism; in fact, I remember trying to slouch back to Elijah's room in junior high so we could do some Playstation and my mom making me come to the

Iversons' kitchen to hold the new baby so she could get a picture.

When had I last seen her? The day of Lizzy's funeral? Yes, yes, that had been it; I can remember the tap of her Sunday school shoes on our kitchen floor as she chased our family dog around the house after the service. The happy noise of her playing with Ryan while my dad wordlessly poured glasses of whiskey for the adults.

And me, I'd locked myself into the upstairs bathroom and gripped the edge of the sink until my knuckles went white, stared at the row of smudgy mascara tubes and half-empty lip glosses that Lizzy would never use again. I don't know how long I'd been there, staring at nothing, thinking of nothing, before I'd heard a tentative knock at the door. The soft, rain-like noise of the beads on a little girl's brand new braids clicking.

"Sean?" she'd asked. She'd been seven then, her voice just edging into a big kid voice and losing the little warbles and lisps of childhood.

If it had been anybody else, I would have roared at them to leave me alone, I would have hurled things at my side of the door until they left, but I couldn't with Zenny. She was Elijah's little sister, so I simply said, "Yes, I'm in here."

"Mom says that we're only supposed to say things like 'I'm sorry for your loss,' but Ryan and me thought you'd want to know that *Jurassic Park* is on the TV in the basement."

And miraculously—it was the only time it happened that day—I smiled. "Thanks, Zenny-bug."

"And I found a book for you to read." There was a *thunk* and papery hiss of a book being wedged under the bathroom door. "It was in Mrs. Carolyn's room, but I figured you might need it more than her. My dad always reads in the bathroom for a long time too."

I did have to laugh a little at that as I reached for the cheap paperback now being birthed from the crack under the door. It was one of my mom's historical romances, with a gold curlicue font and a guy in old-timey clothes clutching a woman's shoulders.

In the Bed of the Pirate: Book One in the Wakefield Saga

"Thanks, kid," I said. "Appreciate it."

"I'm going to go watch *Jurassic Park* now," she declared, and there was the crush of the carpet under her shoes, the plastic rain-sound of her beads, and then she was gone. The one person in the house who'd managed to stay sane through the whole mess of Lizzy's death.

I'd stayed in that bathroom for another hour, still too fucked up emotionally to face anyone downstairs and too wound up to simply go to my room and sleep. In fact, the only thing that finally calmed me down enough to leave my bathroom cocoon of pain was reading the first fifty pages of *In the Bed of the Pirate*, which was weirdly compelling. After reading the chapter where Lady Wakefield was kidnapped by the mysterious pirate king, I finally felt normal enough to go downstairs. Which was of course when I walked into the middle of the schism—raised voices, Mrs. Iverson tugging on Dr. Iverson's elbow, my mother crying, Elijah looking shocked.

And before I fully processed what was happening, I remember being grateful that Zenny was in the basement and far away from whatever ugliness was currently crackling between our families. And I'd held on to that Wakefield paperback like it contained the answers to life itself as I finished coming down the stairs and faced what would be the final, terrible gash left by Lizzy's suicide.

Fuck.

I hate thinking about that day.

I shake off the memories and ring the bell at the window again, the first tendrils of impatience snaking through me. I glance at my watch. Yes, it's definitely ten o'clock, and judging from the picture of the Virgin Mary hanging above the cheap plastic chairs, I'm definitely in the right place.

"Hello?" I call through the window. "Anyone there?"

I hear a laugh—muffled as if through a door—and a couple voices in ringing conversation, and the voices sound like they're coming closer, thank God.

"Hello?" I call again, hopefully. "I'm here to see Zenny?"

I hear a door open somewhere I can't see, I hear footsteps on the linoleum, and suddenly, I'm suffused with huge amounts of confidence. Optimism.

Because this is baby Zenny, baby Zenny who likes *Jurassic Park* and brought me a book once just so I wouldn't be bored. This is the same baby Zenny I had to push in the swings at the park and guard my popcorn from during family movie nights. This is my best friend's little sister, and this is going to be so easy. She'll see her old friend Sean and realize that this was all a misunderstanding, a simple mix-up, and then she'll step aside and let me clean this up.

Like I said before, easy peasy.

The footsteps get closer and I take a step back from the window, already pinning my best big-brotherly smile on my face as Zenny comes into view.

Except.

Except.

Shit.

It's not Zenny at all.

It's Mary.

CHAPTER FIVE

"Mary?" I say, totally stunned.

She's in a white collared shirt and black jumper, a rosary hanging from her belt and a cross around her neck—as far away from the red dress she wore last night as she could possibly be—yet it's still the same Mary. The same mesmerizing mouth, with its full upper lip pouting over the smaller bow of the lower one. The same tiny stud glinting from the side of her nose, the same eyes with their copper haloes around the pupils.

It's her. It's her, and immediately, I remember the feel of her in my arms, the tentative touch of her fingers on the nape of my neck, the silky give of that tempting mouth under my fingertip. My body responds in an instant, my cock giving a lazy jolt and thickening behind my zipper, my tongue running along the edge of my top teeth.

"Mary," I say again, and my voice has changed, just

enough to make her bite her lip, just enough to send that faint rosy hue to her cheeks.

She swallows, meeting my eyes. "Sean," she whispers.

"This was the job you wouldn't tell me about."

"Yes."

"You're a nun."

She lets out a breath. "Well, I'm a postulant. And this order is semi-apostolic, so *sister* is really more correct than *nun.* We usually use the word *nun* to refer to someone in a contemplative order."

I blink at her for a minute, willing all the words she just said to make some kind of sense. But they keep floating around in my brain, totally divorced of context and meaning. "So...you're not a nun?"

A quick, flickering smile. "I'm not a *sister* yet. I'll be a postulant for another month before I enter the novitiate stage."

"And then you'll be a nun?" I ask.

"And then I'll be a novice for two years."

"And *then?*"

The smile turns into a laugh. "Then I take temporary vows. If I still want to take permanent vows after three years, *then* I'll be a full sister of the order."

"Jesus Christ."

She laughs again. "Well, yes. He is kind of the point."

I give a not-so-discreet glance around the sad waiting room, circling back to the young, interesting woman in the window in front of me. Even in her plain postulant's jumper, even with the white headband holding her curls away from her face, she's stunning. In fact, something about the starkness of the setting, the starkness of her clothes, makes her even more beautiful than she was last night. My dick gives an insistent throb, reminding me that I never got a chance to kiss her, reminding me that I never got a chance to sling her leg over my shoulder and taste her.

And you'll never get to now, Bell. She's a fucking nun.

"Why?" I ask, trying to understand. Because why would anyone choose this? Old plastic chairs and boring routines and a life without sex? A life *without sex*, and for what? For the dubious pleasure of getting to wear a gabardine jumper? "You could do anything you wanted. You're so young, Mary. You're smart. You're in school. Why would you throw all that away?"

Her flickering smile is snuffed out like a candle. She looks away. "I wouldn't expect someone like you to understand."

"Damn right, I don't understand," I say, beginning to feel genuinely irritated.

No, not irritated.

Upset.

I'm upset that I met this girl, that I want her, that I want to kiss her and I want to fuck her and I want to dance with her again, and I can't do any of those things because she wants to offer up her life to a nonexistent deity. I mean, it's obviously not about me and it's obviously none of my business, but *still*.

"I should have known," she mutters. "You were like this when Tyler became a priest too."

Tyler.

My brother.

The words drip through my mind with slow, chilling realization.

"How do you...?"

But even as I say the words, even as she tilts her head impatiently, and even as the sun shifts behind the clouds and throws her face into a new relief of light and shadow and I see the echoes of Elijah's cheekbones and eyes and forehead—even as all this happens, I know.

Fuck me.

"Zenny?" I ask. And then again, because it still doesn't seem real. "*Zenny?*"

She doesn't answer, but she doesn't need to, because I can see it now. Not just her similarity to Elijah, but her similarity to the little girl I used to know. But shit, she's no little girl now. Fourteen years is apparently a long fucking time, which is something I know intellectually, of course, but seeing the evidence of it like this is disorienting. Unreal.

Zenny is a woman. A woman I wanted to fuck last night.

Little Zenny! And I almost kissed her, I almost—

Oh God. I clap a hand over my mouth as the real impact of it all sifts through my thoughts.

"Elijah is going to kill me," I mumble through my fingers. "Oh my God. He's going to kill me."

I see the tiniest flash of amusement in her gaze before it goes serious again. "It's fine, Sean. Nothing happened anyway."

"Nothing happened? Jesus, Zenny, I just about kissed you! I had no idea—" I turn away from the window for a moment and then turn back. "Why didn't you say anything? You obviously knew who I was—why didn't you tell me it was you?"

"You didn't recognize me," she replies calmly. There's something challenging in her eyes when she looks up at me. Or maybe it's not challenging—maybe it's...*hurt*? But that's ridiculous. Why would she be hurt that I didn't recognize her after fourteen years? "And I didn't see any reason to tell you. Especially in light of what's going on with the building."

"But you still wanted me to kiss you," I point out (and yes, I say it to be a dick). "Even though I'm the big, bad wolf trying to take your building away."

Her eyes flash again, but this time not with amusement. She walks away from the window, and next to me, I hear a door open. She stands in the threshold, looking more sweetly glamorous than any girl has any right to be, and she's gesturing me inside. "Shall we get started?"

"No! Zenny, you owe me more than that, for fuck's sake."

"I'm not talking about this with you," she says. "It's over with and it's not happening again…and nothing happened to begin with, anyway. We're past it."

I'm not past it! I'm not past the memory of her touch, the memory of wanting her—which isn't even a memory right now, it's real, it's present, wanting her is my current state of being—and how the fuck am I ever supposed to get past the fact that this is Elijah's little sister? Someone I held as a baby?

Oh my God, I'm going to hell. I don't even believe in hell and I'm going there, and what's worse is that *she* believes in hell, probably; she believes in all this stupid stuff, she's giving her life to the same church that killed my sister.

How can I still want her after all that? Knowing she's little Zenny, knowing that she's choosing the one institution on this earth that I want to see razed to the ground? But God, want her I do.

She gestures again and I finally accept her invitation, catching the smell of something rose-like and delicate as I walk past her.

"I just want you to see the shelter before we talk about anything else," she says matter-of-factly, closing the door to the waiting room and leading me down a short hallway. We pass a small office with a woman sorting through boxes inside; presumably the same woman Zenny was talking to earlier. "It's pretty quiet in the summer," Zenny continues, "unless there's a run of rainy days or we get another group of women waiting for permanent placement."

"Zenny."

She ignores me, leading me into a large room lined with neatly made-up bunk beds. "But in the winter, we're over capacity. We have a strict separation of families, men and women, but there are times when we have to let overflow guests sleep on the kitchen floor so we don't have to turn anyone away."

I glance around the sparse room, which despite its tired blankets and flat pillows, is extremely clean and smells surprisingly homey. A familiar mix of baking bread, fresh flowers and Mr. Clean. Then I look back at the young woman who's trying very hard not to look at me.

"Zenny."

She turns on her heel and walks out of the room, talking very quickly now. "And then here's the cafeteria," she says, turning into a wide doorway. "As you can see, it's pretty small for what we do, and the kitchen needs updating, but despite all that, we were able to serve close to two thousand—"

"*Zenny.*" And this time I touch her. Just a brush along

the white, artificial-feeling fabric at her elbow. And she goes still and stiff, like I've frozen her to the spot.

"Tell me what last night was all about," I say, and I know I sound bossy, I know I'm using the same low voice that I would use to tell a woman to open her legs for my mouth. I know it and I don't care. I don't think I can handle living with last night in my mind without some kind of closure, I don't think I can look at her for another second and not kiss her—I can't listen to another word without needing her to say my name over and over again. Something has to shift, something has to stop this terrible twist she's got going in my chest, and this is the only thing I can think of. "The honest guy thing, remember? How about you give me the honest girl thing?"

From behind her, I can see the lift and drop of her slender perfect shoulders as she breathes. I can see the catch of the sunlight through her curls and the tight line of her jaw as she thinks.

"Turn and look at me," I coax gently, and then oh fuck, that was a mistake, because she does turn, she does look at me, and it's like every time I forget. I forget how fucking gorgeous she is, I forget what the sight of those pouting lips does to my cock.

"Please," I say quietly, peering down into her face. "Tell me about last night."

The bright morning sun makes the copper in her eyes look molten, liquid, like her very soul is bubbling hot and

SIERRA SIMONE

waiting to be cast. She sighs, about to look down, and I don't let her, I catch my finger under her chin to keep her eyes on me. My touch seems to shock her, and it shocks me too, and in the back of my mind, I think of stained glass and the sharp taste of wine.

"I—I just wanted one last night to myself," she finally admits. "In a month, I'm professing as a novice, and aside from going to school, I'll no longer be free to…" she trails off, as if catching herself using words she doesn't want to use. "Then it will be time to seriously devote myself to the order. To this life."

"So you were going to ask just any old man you saw to kiss you?"

"You're not that old."

"You know what I meant. Answer me, please."

Another sigh. "No. I just wanted to dress up and drink and have a night that wasn't homework or cleaning shelter toilets or studying ecumenical texts. But then I saw you, and you didn't recognize me at all, and it felt terrible but it also felt…safe, I guess. Like I knew you and didn't know you at the same time. Like I could pretend to be someone else and also know that you would take care of me."

"That was a dangerous assumption," I tell her, feeling a spike of retroactive fear. "The things I said to you last night—dammit, that wasn't okay of me to do."

She arches an eyebrow. "So it was okay to say those things to me when I was just a stranger, but when you know I'm Elijah's sister, then it's not okay?"

"Well, yes. And also you're so young. And I'm not a good man. If you'd told me you wanted it, I would have spent the rest of the night with my mouth on your cunt."

Her eyes widen and I remember we're in a place run by nuns.

Sigh.

"Sorry," I concede, dropping my finger from under her chin and running a hand through my hair. "But do you see why this is a little weird to me? You're Elijah's baby sister and now all of a sudden you're a *nun* and the things I wanted to do to you, Zenny, Jesus fuck, you have no idea."

"Is this the infamous Sean Bell having a conscience?"

"We haven't seen each other for fourteen years," I say, miffed and amused at the same time. "For all you know, I'm a very principled man."

She rolls her eyes. "I talk to Elijah almost every day. I know enough to know your only principles are about money."

"Untrue," I protest.

"Really?"

"Uh, yes, really. Witness me panicking that I had carnal thoughts about you last night."

She waves a hand. "That's more about your fraternity with Elijah than actual ethics."

"I don't see a meaningful difference between the two."

"Are you still having carnal thoughts about me?" she

asks abruptly, and she asks it with that tempting combination of boldness and vulnerability that I can't resist. Like she wants to know the answer so badly that she's willing to expose her own curiosity and desire—and more than desire itself, but the desire to *be* desired. And it betrays so much about her—her youth and energy and spirit and innocence and honesty and longing, and it's potent, it's so fucking potent.

"Do you want the honest guy thing still?" I ask, because I have no problem being honest, but after I answer her, she might have a problem with it. And I want to give her the choice to back away from this conversation now, before I reveal exactly how impure and worldly a secular man can be around a holy woman.

"Yes," she whispers, peering up at me.

I open my mouth to answer her, remembering only at the very last instant that there's at least one other person here, that Zenny wants to be a nun, that it wouldn't be good for her to be caught with me whispering dirty things in her ear, and I don't want to be interrupted anyway. I need her to hear exactly what I'm going to say to her so that she understands how serious this all is.

I glance around the cafeteria to make sure we're alone, and then I take her elbow and lead her into the kitchen, which is partitioned off with a swinging door. Once inside, I let go and she instinctively takes a step back, pressing herself against the wall.

Smart girl.

I do all the good guy things: I stand well away from the door so she has a clear exit, I put my hands in my pockets, and I ask for a final time, "Are you sure you want to hear this?"

She lifts her chin the tiniest bit, and I see her nervousness, her uncertainty. But she says, "Yes, please," in a calm, clear voice.

Fine, then.

"I've wanted to fuck you since the moment I saw you today," I say, watching her blanch with surprise at my blunt lewdness. "I can't stop thinking about pushing that jumper up to your waist and nuzzling into your cunt until my face smells like you. I want to bite your tits through that white shirt. I want to see that cross necklace sliding around your collarbone as I find out if you prefer two fingers or three."

Her lips part but no sound comes out. Her eyes are wide and searching mine, and she's breathing fast, so fast that I know for sure that she's hearing and understanding every word.

"Has Elijah told you how many women I've fucked? How many women I've made come? It's a big number, Zenny, because I love to fuck. I love to make women come. I love to see their snug little cunts, I love to taste them and push my big cock into them until they stretch. I love having my hands full of their hair while I fuck their mouths. I love feeling a girl's ass clench around my finger as I tongue her clit."

She swallows.

"And I want all those things with you. Right now." I unbutton my suit jacket, parting it so she can see exactly how urgently I want it. Want her.

"Oh," she breathes, her eyes dropping to the thick outline in my trousers. "Oh."

"Yes. *Oh.*"

She can't stop staring at my erection, her teeth sinking into that plush lower lip as she looks.

"So you see the problem," I say in a businesslike tone as I button my jacket again, mostly concealing the aching hard-on that's currently dripping precum at the sight of her biting her lip. I can't stop thinking about how those lips would give and mold under my own, how they would yield to my teeth, stretch around my organ as I carefully, tenderly slid in to the back of her throat.

She struggles to drag her eyes back up to my face, and when she gets there, she finds me smirking a little. Her cheeks warm again, possibly in embarrassment or in arousal, or some combination of the two. "The problem is you being turned on?"

I take a step forward, my hands back in my pockets. "I'm a dirty man, sweetheart. I fuck strippers. I've taken conference calls with another man's wife sucking me off under my desk. You think I'm ashamed of my cock? That

I'm ashamed of wanting to fuck? Nothing's further from the truth."

Her pupils are huge now, her eyes just the barest rings of copper around massive pools of black. "Then I don't understand," she whispers.

I take another step forward, and another, until we're toe to toe. I reach up, moving slowly enough for me to catch her gaze and raise an eyebrow. *Is this okay?* I'm asking silently, and she gives me a slow, wide-eyed nod. I trace a line down the point of her chin, dropping to finger the starchy collar of her shirt. "The problem isn't that I want to fuck you. The problem is that I care about you. I care about Elijah."

"And you don't fuck women you care about?"

"No. I don't."

"That seems strange," she murmurs, her breath catching as my finger goes slightly lower than her collar and starts toying with the chain of her necklace.

I shrug. "It's how I've always done things. And…"

"And?"

I roll the cross pendant between my fingertips, keeping my eyes on hers. "And there's this."

"Is it a problem because you respect my choices and my beliefs? Or because you don't respect the Church?"

I use the cross to tug myself just that much closer to her. "Both," I tell her.

"So there's more than one problem," she says, her voice a bit breathless. "You care about me and my brother. And you don't care about God."

"Mmm," I agree. I'm watching her mouth now, the way her lips crease ever so slightly as she talks, the flick of her tongue as she shapes her words. My cock is painfully aware of how close it is to her; just a few inches more and I could press right into her belly, grind away the ache she gave me.

No. Bad.

Elijah.

Nun thing.

"I never got my kiss," she whispers. "And I'd already planned on committing that sin. What if you kissed me now and we pretended it was still last night? That you didn't know it was me?"

Fuck.

My body responds before my mind, my heart hammering quick and my memories whirring like a merry-go-round, bringing up half-forgotten feelings. Feelings of magic and mystery and *more*-ness, as if this girl holds inside her a larger universe than the one I live in, as if she speaks a language I only hear in dreams I pretend I don't dream.

She reminds me of the way I used to be. *Before.* Before Lizzy died. Before I rejected all the stupid and naïve things that had kept our family blind to the truth and her pain.

Before I made my own idol of money and ambition and $1500 neckties.

Fuck. *Fuck.*

I jerk back as I realize what I'm doing, how close I am to her mouth, how close I am to grabbing my own cock just to rub at the need throbbing there.

How the hell could temptation incarnate be a fucking nun? How fair is that?

"No fucking way," I say raggedly. "Elijah will kill me. *You'll* kill me once you realize what a bad man I am and what you let me do."

"What do you mean?" She comes off the wall, taking a step forward, her head tilted.

"I mean it would not be a good thing for me to kiss you."

"Because of my brother?"

"Yes."

"And my vocation?"

"Yes."

She takes another step forward and now I'm the one forced to take a step back.

"We're going to pretend you don't know those things yet, remember?"

"And," I say, stepping back far enough that my heel hits the stove behind me and I'm trapped, "let's not forget that I'm selfish and dangerous and far older than you. I *like* sin. I *like* corruption. You don't want someone like me to touch you."

"But I do want you to touch me," Zenny says, crowding me against the stove. "I know you're selfish and sinful, and that's why you're the perfect person to give me this. You'll give it to me and then leave, and you won't be offended that I'll never ask you for another kiss again. In fact, if anyone should understand wanting to do something for the simple, momentary pleasure of it, I'd think it would be you."

"But—"

"Just once," she coaxes, her eyes so big and pleading. "I promised myself I'd get this one last thing before I was invested as a novice. One last kiss."

"But—"

"And who better than you, my brother's best friend? I know you'll keep me safe." Her eyelashes flutter and she puts her hand flat on the middle of my chest.

And then slides it down my stomach.

"Zenny," I grunt. "*Shit.*"

My dick is practically drilling a hole through my pants, and it's like I can feel every single whorl of her fingertips through all the layers of my clothes as her hand moves down, down, down—

"Please," she murmurs prettily, and how did she suddenly get all the power here? How did she end up taking control and how did I end up trapped and feebly protesting?

And then she says, "Sean," in this way like she's said it to herself before. Like she's murmured it into her pillow, like she's doodled it in notebooks, like she's imagined what it would be like to breathe my own name back into my lips.

"Sean," she says again and the heel of her palm hits my belt and it's over, it's done, my control is snapped like a cord.

I groan.

And yank her into a searing, burning kiss.

CHAPTER SIX

The moment her lips touch mine, I'm lost. To myself, to her, to any memory of what is right or true or necessary.

Ecstasy. That's what it's called when saints experience spiritual euphoria, and I'm no saint, that's for fucking sure, but this...this is ecstasy. The small whimper she makes when I slide my hand to the small of her back and jerk our bodies close together. The hesitant flicker of her tongue against my lips. The clean, sweet taste of her, the rose smell of her skin, the satin submission of her soft mouth under mine.

The trusting way her hands lace and hang around my neck.

And the tiny noise she lets out as I make her mouth fully mine—her tongue, her teeth, her lips—I hold nothing back. I turn so she's the one backed against the stove, and I cage her in everywhere—my arms, my feet on either side of her feet—and I give in to every dirty urge pounding through me. I press my cock against her, my hands find her ass under the cheap fabric of her jumper, and I bite her lower lip until she moans. I keep it trapped between my teeth as I pick her up and deposit her on the counter next to the stove, and she parts her legs for me to step between as if we've done this a thousand times before.

The moment our bodies touch again, the moment the wide ridge of my erection brushes against the place between her legs, she lets out a gasp so sweetly surprised, so endearingly amazed, that I have to fist my hands in the skirt of her jumper to avoid doing something truly filthy, like playing with the edge of her panties. Like sliding my fingers under the elastic and finding out for myself if she's shaved smooth or fuzzed with hair, if she's wet and slick, if her clit is big and needy for rubs and kisses.

And then she grabs the lapels of my suit jacket and rocks her hips against me, seeking out the pleasurable friction again. And again. And again.

"Zenny," I mumble against her lips, some valiant part of me recognizing that this is far, far beyond the kiss she asked for, and also recognizing that I'm going to come all over the inside of my Hugo Boss suit pants if she keeps it up. Even through the clothes, I can feel her heat, her shameless rolls hinting at where she goes soft and wet between her legs.

Fuck, I want to see it. I want to see her pussy. It's

suddenly all I can think about, all I can want or crave, just one glimpse, just a peek.

"I want to see your cunt," I say hoarsely, lifting my head.

"My…cunt?" She says the word like she's never said it out loud before.

"Yeah." My voice is so ragged right now, so desperate, and fuck, I've never felt this frantic before. Like I'll actually combust if I don't get this one thing, this one small sight of her secret place.

She lets out a shaky breath, her hand dropping from my lapel to her skirt, which she slowly rucks up to her waist as I devour her lips once more, as I bury my face in her neck and kiss every sliver of skin exposed above her collar. I bite at her ear, at her jaw, my hand finding hers as it pulls her skirt up, so that I'm helping her do it, that we're doing it together, this forbidden act, this forbidden revelation.

Her forbidden body.

That word, *forbidden,* spikes through my mind, bringing with it equal spikes of lust and fear. Because yes, it's fucking hot that I shouldn't be kissing her, I shouldn't be begging to see her most secret place, my hand shouldn't be covering hers as it slides up her thigh—but it's also bad. Bad even for Sean Bell.

Bad, bad, bad.

Elijah's disappointed face flashes through my

thoughts, and I break our embrace, stumbling back a step. Zenny freezes, her mouth still wet and open from our kiss and her hand full of skirt fabric, hovering at the middle of her thigh. The long expanse of silky, dark leg gleams in the sunlight, and before she drops her skirt, I see a flash of snow-white cotton between her legs.

I swallow down a noise. I routinely fuck women who wear La Perla or Agent Provocateur, but somehow the sight of those simple cotton panties have my cock flaring and leaking all over the inside of my pants. I have to turn away from her to get a fucking grip on myself.

"Sean...?" she asks hesitantly, and when I turn back to her, there's real worry on her face, worry that's quickly turning into embarrassment.

What the fuck have I done?

"I'm sorry," I mumble. "I'm so fucking sorry. I got—I have to go."

And I leave as quickly as I can, forcing myself not to look back at the thoroughly kissed nun still perched on the counter.

Fuck.

Fuck, fuck, fuck.

I kissed Elijah's baby sister. The one who's a nun—

sorry, postulant—the one with the parents that my parents still refuse to speak with. The one who is currently causing my firm a giant PR headache, *and* to cap it off, I didn't even manage to talk to her about the deal at all.

Not even once.

Valdman's going to be pissed.

And Elijah's going to be pissed.

And now probably Zenny is going to be pissed too, and with good fucking reason.

What is wrong with me? Sean Bell doesn't do shit like this! He gets what he wants, he fucks whom he wants, and then he lives like he wants—no guilt, no ties, all the success in the world.

I run an agitated hand through my hair as I throw open the door to the Audi and get inside. I've barely even got the car started before my phone lights up.

Elijah.

Fuck. Okay. You know what? This is good, actually. This is fine. There's no need to be scared; Sean Bell doesn't get scared.

"Hey, man," I say as I answer the phone. "What's up?"

"What's up with you?" Elijah asks dryly. "You're the one who called."

"Right," I say.

Right.

"So, um…" I pull the car off the curb and into the street, trying to order my thoughts and trying to ignore the way my still-straining cock chafes against my zipper. "Your sister. Zenobia."

"Did you see her last night? I brought her with me to the thing—I meant to have you come over and say hi to her. I don't think you've seen each other in a while."

I resist the urge to bash my head against the steering wheel. "Yep. It's been a while. And I saw her."

And nearly kissed her. And then I did kiss her today and almost made her flash her pussy to me while another nun was down the hall.

"Good, I'm glad you got to see her." Elijah does sound genuinely happy, and an unfamiliar feeling of guilt crawls through me.

"Yeah, so…she's a nun now?"

"She's wanted to be a nun since she was a teenager. I never talked to you about this?"

"Sure didn't," I reply, navigating the car back to the firm. "Has it been hard with…you know? Your parents? And them wanting grandchildren and stuff?"

"Jumping right past the small talk today, I see," Elijah says, amused. "Yes, it's been hard, but it's fine now. At some point they have to understand Zenny and me are allowed our own lives. We probably should have made it easier on them by rebelling in high school instead of waiting until after we graduated, but there you are. Why are we talking about this again?"

"Uh. Well. Zenny and I are sort of working together now. Or against each other, depending on how you look at it."

Elijah is immediately wary. "What do you mean?"

I explain to him about the building deal and the Good Shepherd sisters going to the press about their upcoming eviction. And I'm about to tell him about the kiss, I really am, when he cuts in.

"Look, you know I don't see anything wrong with what you do or how you make your money, but if you do anything to hurt Zenny or her sisters, there's going to be hell to pay."

"Whoa, man, I'm not planning on hurting anyone—"

"I mean it," Elijah warns. "Zenny has wanted this for almost ten years, she's had to put up with our parents and her friends all giving her a rough time about it, she's worked her ass off to meet her obligations as a postulant while she's getting her nursing degree. Do not ruin this for her."

"I'm not going to!"

"Sean."

"Elijah."

"I know you, and I know what you do to people who get in your way, but I'm asking you for the sake of our friendship to keep her safe. Do not crush her to make more money, and do not fuck this up for her."

The guilt has teeth now, chewing industriously at

something inside of my chest. "I'll keep her safe," I promise, and I say it to atone for the ways in which I already haven't kept her safe.

"Good. Because I'll kill you if you don't."

I sigh. This is bad.

"And you are fine with her becoming a nun?" I ask. "Giving up a normal life?"

"Who gets to say what a normal life is?" Elijah asks. "The important thing is having a life with meaning. She seems to find that with the Catholic Church."

"But the Catholic Church is terrible," I counter, pulling into the Valdman and Associates parking garage. "Their meanings are all about homophobia and protecting predators and treating women like second-class citizens. How can you be okay with that? How can *she* be okay with that?"

Elijah's voice is dry again. "Because I'm gay, you mean?"

"Well. Yes."

"I get where you're coming from, and trust me, I have an entire dossier of complicated thoughts and opinions on the Catholic Church after my childhood, but watching Zenny go through this journey has reminded me that there's a lot of good people in the Church. People who believe in equal rights. People who are dedicated to helping the poor. Gay people and feminists and activists working for racial and economic and judicial justice. So maybe the

Church isn't perfect, but the answer isn't shitting on it. And for Zenny, the answer is supporting what's good about it and working to change the rest."

I think about this for a moment. "Does this mean you'll be heading back to Mass?"

"Fuck no. But it's why I'm okay with my little sister becoming a nun. Nuns can do great things and Zenny is going to do great things, and I have no doubt in my mind that she is going to help a lot of people this way. Besides, it's what she wants. That's the most important thing."

"Okay, okay." I park my car and get out. "I hear what you're saying. I still think the Church is bullshit though."

"I know you do," Elijah says. And then, his voice getting kinder, "No one's forgotten about Lizzy, Sean. No one's forgotten what you've gone through."

"She wanted to be a nun too, you know." There's a stupid ball in my throat as I say the words out loud. "It's all she talked about."

"I know. I like to think that she and Zenny would have been really good friends."

"Yeah. Me too."

"I meant what I said though. Keep her safe or I'll kill you."

"Elijah."

"Seriously. I know you've got a job to do, but do it without fucking her over."

"*Elijah*. I already promised."

"Yeah, well, I don't trust you." And then he hangs up.

Sigh.

I drop my phone into my pocket and rub at my face with both hands while I wait for the elevator. Okay, so things are not ideal right now—I've lied to Elijah (by omission though, that's not so bad, right?) and promised to take care of Zenny, and now I have to go upstairs and explain to my boss why there's not a plan in place to fix all this yet.

Sorry, Mr. Valdman, sir, it's just that she has a really pretty mouth and a way of asking for things like kisses that I can't resist.

Yeah, no. That's not going to work.

The elevator doors ding open and I go inside, thinking. Clearly, I can't trust myself around Zenny, that much is clear. And I just promised Elijah that I'd keep her safe, which almost certainly means not kissing her again.

Not begging to see her pussy like a thirsty man just craving the sight of water.

I'm a responsible human, and while I recognize that I'm what some people might call sinful and others might call an asshole, I would never force myself on a woman. I am more than capable of keeping my hands and eyes and words to myself; I'm more than capable of being around someone I desire and still acting ethically and professionally. But that's not the problem—the problem is that Zenny *asks* for things and once she asks, I can't trust myself to say no.

Because if she asks for another kiss, there's no way in hell I'll be able to stop myself. Definitely not now, not after I've felt how soft and eager her mouth is, not after I've felt the pliant mold of her compact curves against my body. If she asked for another kiss, I'd be on her before I could even catalogue all the reasons I should refuse.

And that's bad.

Badddddd.

By the time I get to Valdman's office, I more or less have a plan in place. Trent the Secretary waves me inside, and I give a cursory knock on the door before I step in.

"Ah, Sean," Valdman says. He's in a chair by the window, flipping through a file in a manner so desultory that I'm sure he's not actually reading anything inside, he just wanted to have something to look at while he drinks more morning scotch.

"Hi, sir."

"How'd it go with the nuns?"

I clear my throat, trying to muster the confidence and charm that normally come so easily to me. "Nothing's decided yet, but I saw the shelter and I think I've got a pretty good idea of how to handle this."

Valdman closes the file and picks up his scotch glass. "I'm listening."

I take a seat in the creaky leather armchair next to his. "We need to find them a new shelter. Bigger and better and at no extra cost. I don't know if we can make it happen fast enough to get in front of the story, but it will still do a lot toward repairing the image of the firm."

My boss nods. "And you've already talked with them about this?"

"No, sir. I wanted to run it by you first. But the space they are using now is cramped and shabby. If we can find them someplace bigger, nicer, someplace that photographs well and will look good on the news, then we'll be able to salvage this."

"I like it," Valdman says. "So long as it doesn't cost us any money."

"We might need to make a small donation to grease the wheels, but I'm hoping we can find an existing property that's suited to their needs and comes at no cost to us. I'm sure we can find a client of ours who needs the tax break and who already has a property that would work."

"Okay, fine," he says. "Make it happen."

I pause. This is the tricky part. "So, sir, I was wondering if it would be possible for someone else to take point on this project. At least when it comes to interfacing with the nuns."

Valdman looks at me. And doesn't answer.

"I'll still do everything else—scout the new property and liaise with Keegan and Ealey and all that. But I don't think I'm the right person to work with the nuns themselves."

My boss continues to study me, and I resist the urge to shift in my seat. *Don't show any weakness,* I remind myself. *Look confident. Look like you're ready for another victory lap.*

"You know, this is the first time in ten years that you've ever asked to be taken off a job," Valdman says. "You've handled senators, athletes, and international beer conglomerates for me, but all of a sudden you're losing your nerve? You're too soft to handle a bunch of nuns?"

"I'm not too soft," I say defensively.

"Then what is it?"

I decide on a slice of the truth that doesn't involve Zenny. "My sister killed herself because of a predatory priest. I'm sorry, but I've got too much baggage with the Church to handle the sisters directly. I'd be better off behind the scenes."

Valdman takes a drink and smacks his lips. "Well, I can't say that I'm not a little disappointed—I still think you're the best man to be in the middle of it—but I can't deny that's a damn good reason to want to avoid the nuns."

"So you'll find someone else to work with them?"

"Yes."

Thank fuck. "Thank you, sir. I promise I'll do all I can to get this taken care of from my end."

Valdman waves a hand. "I know you will. You're a good employee, Sean, and I have total faith you'll get this fixed."

I'm glad someone does, I think.

That night, after checking on Mom at the hospital, I go to the club to let off some steam and to finish the victory lap I never got to take last night. I know strip clubs are generally considered seamy places, and there's probably something so inherently dirty about transactional nudity that no amount of money can fix it, but this place comes close, because there's *a lot* of money here. It's exclusive, invitation-only, only open to members (yes, men *and* women) that clear a million a year. And besides, I like that it's inherently dirty.

I'm inherently dirty and I have no plans to change that any time soon.

I get myself some Macallan and wander out of the bar area. The club is on the top floor of a downtown skyscraper, and while the lounge and dance areas are walled off from the windows, there's a wide corridor along the perimeter of the club for members to take phone calls or simply look out over the city, which is what I do now. I cradle my glass in my hands and pick out the sharp lines of my own building a few blocks away. The lights are on in my penthouse, and I check my home app on my phone to see who the fuck is inside my penthouse, because the cleaning company should be long done for the day.

I pull up the kitchen camera feed and see the unmistakable lines of Aiden's muscled, shirtless back as he digs through my fridge. Even in the slightly grainy feed of the camera, I see sweat gleaming on his skin.

I call him and he answers with a grunt.

"Stop dripping sweat all over my clean floor," I say irritably.

"It's not like you clean it yourself," Aiden says. I hear the fridge door shutting and the clatter of a plate on the counter.

"And *stop eating my food*," I tell him. "It's fucking annoying to get home and have my fridge emptied out by a Neanderthal."

"But you also don't do your own shopping," Aiden points out.

"Don't you have your own place? With your own food and your own floors that you can get dirty any time you'd like?"

"I like the gym here," Aiden mumbles over the beep of a microwave. "Plus it's closer to Mom and Dad's and the hospital."

I don't answer, and I don't have to. Any mention of Mom is automatic ceasefire, and anyway, he's right—on one of his trademark Aiden impulses, he bought some giant old farmhouse out in the country, and it's a decent drive from the city.

"Don't know why you bought that place," I say, walking to another window so I can see in the direction of the hospital. It's impossible to pick out from here, but it makes me feel marginally better to look at it, as if I'm still keeping an eye on Mom. "It's huge and it's not like you need that much room."

"I like it," Aiden says. "It's quiet out there. You can see the stars."

"You mean you like it until you want a decent gym or until you're hungry."

"That too."

"I'm at the club. Why don't you shower and come over?"

Aiden hesitates. "I think I'm going to head home tonight. I've got a busy day tomorrow."

I frown. Aiden hasn't turned down a chance to visit the club since he got his own invite a few years back, and while I typically avoid noticing these things about my own brothers, it'd be impossible not to know that his physical appetites are as strong as mine.

"You sure?" I ask. "Might be nice to blow off some steam."

"Another time," Aiden says vaguely. "Have fun though."

SIERRA SIMONE

"Yeah. Will do."

I hang up the phone and lean my head against the glass, deciding to put Aiden's weird behavior in a box in my mind and close the lid. I simply do not have the time or the energy right now to deal with whatever's got him acting strange. And it's probably just Mom stuff anyway. All of us brothers are handling Mom's cancer in various unhealthy ways, and I guess there are worse ways to cope than random acts of celibacy.

"Hey, Sean," a low voice says from behind me. I turn to see Scarlett, a pale-skinned, befreckled dancer that I like very much. Her hair matches her name, by the way. *Everywhere.*

I give her a slow smile. "Hey yourself."

She's wearing a silk robe, but she lets the middle gape open as she walks toward me and presses her hands flat to my chest.

"How about a private dance for my big boy?" she purrs.

The city lights twinkling in from outside make her look quite pretty; even so, I can't help the way my mind wanders to this morning, to Zenny in the sunlight, to Zenny perched on the edge of the counter. To Zenny's lush mouth and copper-ringed eyes and tiny little nose piercing. To the intoxicating mix of boldness and shyness that Zenny betrays every time she speaks.

I can't help the way my body follows my mind, my

90

cock reminding me rather churlishly that it's had no relief since my episode with Zenny this morning, that it's had nothing but my own hand for the past two weeks.

"How about more than a private dance?" I say, taking Scarlett's elbow and leading her back to the hallway that leads to the private rooms. "I need to relieve some tension."

"It's extra," Scarlett tells me, looking pleased. "But for you, I'll throw in a discount."

We go inside the private room, and Scarlett pushes me onto a small couch, crawling into my lap and tugging at my tie, and I breathe a sigh of relief that has nothing to do with the fact that my neglected cock will soon be getting the attention it needs. (Well, almost nothing to do with it.)

No, I'm relieved because things are back to normal now, after this crazy day. I've figured out a way to avoid Zenny, to keep Valdman happy, to keep my promise to Elijah, and now I'm exactly where I should be—relaxing with a glass of scotch and waiting for a warm mouth to make me feel better.

I'm a fixer. I fixed the problem, and now I'm done and I can stop thinking about it.

About her.

CHAPTER SEVEN

Except I can't stop thinking about her.

I can't stop thinking about her as Scarlett kneels between my legs and makes me feel good. I can't stop thinking about her as I go back to my penthouse and clean up the dishes Aiden left in my sink. I can't stop thinking about her as I shower and fall asleep, and then the next day when I go into the office and after, when I help my mom get discharged from the hospital. And the day after that.

And I especially can't stop thinking about her as I sit in my mother's infusion room, reading aloud the most recent Wakefield Saga novel, *In the Arms of the Disgraced Duke*.

"'And what about my dowry?'" I read. "'I suppose that means nothing to you?'"

"'It's meant nothing since the day I first laid eyes on you,'" I continue, adopting the disgraced duke's deep baritone. Or at least the deep baritone I presume a disgraced duke would have.

"'Which day would that be, my grace?'" I say in the young Eleanor Wakefield's voice. "'The day I was born and my father promised me to you in order to satisfy his debts with your family? Or the night you first saw me as a grown woman at my coming out?'"

"'I don't suppose you'd believe me if I told you both?'" I read as the duke.

"He's lying," the oncology nurse says. "He didn't think of her as anything but a cash cow until the party at Almack's."

"No, no," Emmett says from the recliner next to Mom. He adjusts the blanket around his legs and sticks up a pale, knobby finger to emphasize his raspy words. "His feelings about her were always complicated, because here was this girl he was betrothed to, but she was too young to do anything but ignore for so many years. But then he lost everything and saw her again in the same week—"

"I think he always felt like he could love her, money aside," my mom interrupts, waving her bottle of Mountain Dew, "but he didn't want to fuck her until the party."

"*Mom.*"

"What? It's true."

"I know it's true, but—" I make a gesture around the infusion room, where the ten or so people inside are all my mom's age or older. "We're in public. And you know…" I lower my voice to a discreet whisper "…the *aged.*"

"Son, I fought in Vietnam," Emmett rumbled. "You think I haven't heard the word *fuck* before?"

"It's in the book," the nurse adds. "I think the duke even says something along the lines of, 'I want to fuck her right here on the balcony, dowry be damned.'"

"Sean, look at me," my mother says, and I look at Carolyn Bell. At her slightly-too-wide mouth and her dimples—just like all of my brothers and I have. At the smooth, barely wrinkled lines of her face, rendered unearthly and strange by her lack of eyebrows and eyelashes. At the silk scarf wrapped around what used to be thick chestnut hair and now is nothing but scalp.

"Yes, Mom?"

She tilts her head and very deliberately pronounces, "Fuck fuck fuck fuck fuck—"

I put both hands over my face and mumble into my palms. "Oh my Godddddd."

"Keep reading, son, I haven't got all day," Emmett says, and Rosalie on the other side of Mom grunts her agreement, even though I know for a fact she usually naps through most of Sean Bell Story Time.

For the last three months, the Thursday morning infusion crew has been listening to me work my way through the last two Wakefield Saga books. Mom and I have been buddy-reading romance novels since she caught me sneaking *In the Bed of the Pirate* back to college with me after Lizzy's funeral, and instead of teasing me, she loaded me up with the next two paperbacks in the series. Ever since then, we've been devouring books together in our little Bells-only book club, and while we like some romance novels set in the here and now, we really prefer our books with rogues and roués and castles and shit. And when Mom was diagnosed with cancer, we both knew we needed some mental comfort food, so back to the Wakefield Saga we went, to the very books that founded the informal Bells-only Book Club.

Plus it makes the chemotherapy sessions go by faster.

I wonder if Zenny knows what she started with that pirate book all those years ago.

I keep reading, ignoring the protests from literally every patient in the room and the nurse when I skip over the sex scene.

"Oh come on," Rosalie groans, her eyes still closed. "We've been waiting weeks for this."

"Guys," I sputter. "I can't read this in front of my mom."

"Pretend I can't hear you," Mom says. "You were really good at pretending I couldn't hear you when you were a teenager sneaking girls into your room."

"I'm going to leave. I swear to all that's holy, I'll do it. I'll leave you here to watch *Ellen* all day."

"If you leave, make sure you leave the book," Mom says crisply, my threats as useless as they were when I was a boy. "And then *I'll* read the sex scene out loud."

Somehow that is much more mortifying to imagine, and after the patients threaten to revolt and physically take the book out of my hands, I relent and read aloud the scene of the disgraced duke finally claiming Eleanor's maidenhead.

There is applause throughout the room as Eleanor climaxes and the duke finally unleashes his torrents of passion into Eleanor's womb.

"'It was everything I dreamed of,'" I read in Eleanor's voice.

"'But the duke winced at this," I read, and my own conscience prickles uncomfortably as I speak the words. "'He immediately felt the guilt of what he'd done, the terrible weight of it. He'd vowed once upon a time to protect this girl, and here he was tumbling her without the slightest hint of what she deserved from him. She deserved a wedding, a future, a promise of love. And all he'd given her were a few moments of pleasure and a lifetime of regret.'"

"Sean, my boy."

I look up to see the one person that I would happily see castrated and then dragged behind a team of wild horses and then maybe castrated again for good measure.

(Okay, maybe not, but I'd definitely draw a dick on his face if I ever found him passed out.)

"Don't come in," I tell the man standing in my doorway.

"I've got to say, you really know how to pick them," Charles Northcutt says, coming in. He's white, my age, possibly in better shape, although it could be that he just dresses to show it off more. He's also a pompous dick and Valdman's other favorite employee.

I hate him.

"Don't sit down," I say.

He sits down. "That nun, Zenobia, holy fuck, she's something else. I bet the body she's got under all those Jesus clothes is to die for."

The cloud of red anger is instantaneous. I look down at where my hands rest on my laptop keyboard and they're shaking. What the fuck is wrong with me? I hate Northcutt and I think he's a dog, but I've never gotten so personally incensed at the stupid shit he says—although maybe I *should* have been getting personally incensed before.

"What do you want, Charles?" I ask in a flat voice that makes it clear that I don't care. Except maybe I care a little bit if it's about Zenny; I have to push away from my desk and cross my arms so that he doesn't see how fucking furious I am to hear him talking about her that way. Which is purely because she's Elijah's little sister. And I promised to keep her safe...and Northcutt is not safe.

Unfortunately, Northcutt is not fooled by my forced nonchalance, and a new glitter enters his eyes. "So why'd you hand this back over to Valdman, eh? The nun turn you down?"

"I keep my dick in my pants when I work," I bite back, which is a lie, and we both know it. I've never crossed any kinds of lines with subordinates or coworkers, but I'm the king of the work party fuck, the convention hotel bar hookup, the entertainer of bored wives. And I've literally never cared, except right now I do care, because I don't have any moral high ground on Charles, and that's not a good feeling. I would like to think of myself as very different from him. I mean, I'm a white man myself, but the first white man to make another white man go *oh God the privilege is real* was Charles Northcutt.

"Well, whatever the reason you handed her over to me, I wanted to thank you. I think I'm going to have a lot of fun peeling the virginity off that one."

Thwack.

I'm just as surprised as Northcutt when my hand comes slamming down on my desk, but I don't stop to analyze what I've done. "You stay the hell away from her," I growl.

"Or what?" Northcutt asks, his eyebrows raised in mild amusement. "You were the one who stepped back, Sean. What did you think Valdman was going to do when you asked him to find someone else? Trust your potentially firm-destroying mistake to an intern?"

I'm pissed because he's right, and I should have known all this, planned for it and thought about it before I asked Valdman for permission to step away. But fuck. I was so messed up from Zenny and my promise to Elijah...and that broken-off kiss and my sleepless night with Mom at the hospital and—

Northcutt stands up, buttoning his jacket and giving me a smile so devoid of true human expression it could only be called sharklike. "See you around," he says, turning to leave, and I hate that I'm playing right into his hands by calling him back, but I can't help it, I'm too furious and also too scared. I don't want this shark anywhere near Zenny.

"Charles, I'll handle it from here on out, okay? If this was your way of trying to dump this back in my lap, you've succeeded. You won. I hope you're happy."

More shark teeth. "Oh, not at all, Mr. Bell. I like this girl, and I'm going to keep working this little shelter project of yours with her until I'm done liking her."

"This isn't a fucking daycare, Charles. It's not like taking dibs on a toy."

"And this isn't fucking dodgeball, Sean. You don't get to change sides whenever you feel like it, and there're real-life consequences in being shit at the game. So I'm going to fix this mess for you, look good for Valdman, and have fun while I'm doing it."

I stand up, not caring how ridiculous it is that I'm considering getting in a legitimate fistfight in my own goddamn office. "Stay away from her."

He laughs a laugh as cold as his smile. "Just try and stop me," he says as he walks out of my office.

"You can plan on it," I mutter to his back, and once he's out of sight, I kick my desk, I kick it extra fucking hard, and then I go to find Valdman.

Valdman isn't in his office, and according to Trent the Secretary, he won't be in until the following Tuesday. I have Trent forward a message that I want Northcutt as far away from the nuns as possible—for the sake of the company and the company's reputation.

Trent glances up at me as I'm dictating the message. "Are you saying what I think you're saying?"

"Am I saying that Northcutt has joked about fucking a nun? Yes."

Trent makes a face. "I hate that guy," he says *sotto voce.*

"Me too."

After Trent finishes the message, I lean onto his desk, keeping my voice low. "Can you see any of Northcutt's schedule?"

Trent gives me a slow, wary nod.

I hold up my hands. "I don't want you to do anything shady. I just want to make sure that he's not scheduled to meet with any of the Good Shepherd sisters before I can have a face to face with Valdman."

This seems to resonate with Trent's personal moral code, and he goes into Northcutt's schedule, verifying that the nuns are safe until Tuesday, at least. Thus marginally reassured, I decide to call it a day and head home, even though it's barely time for lunch. Tonight is Family Dinner, which is definitely not about checking up on Mom and extra definitely not about checking up on Dad. I've hired a company to provide all of Mom and Dad's meals while she's going through chemotherapy, which is pleasant and reassuring for a lot of reasons, but it does mean I don't have an excuse to go over early to help with cooking. If I go over now, Mom will accuse me of hovering and flap at me until I stop making her "feel like she has cancer."

No, it's better just to stay away until dinnertime.

I get in my car, think of all the eggs and kale waiting for me in my fridge, and steer my car toward my favorite greasy food dispensary, an ancient joint called Town Topic. After devouring a triple cheeseburger and fries right there at the diner counter, I decide to head home and properly sort out this nun mess once and for all. I've already found a few good leads for a shelter replacement this week; I'm going to find the perfect spot, pitch it to

Zenny (safely...like over the phone), listen to her voice light up in admiration and relief, and then I can extricate myself from this tangle.

It's as I'm driving home that Aiden pulls out from the Kauffman Center (it's unmistakably his car—a black Lexus LFA with the license plate BELLBOY and a healthy coating of gravel dust from his dumb farmhouse commute).

I lay on the horn until my center console lights up with a phone call.

"What the fuck is wrong with you?" Aiden says, by way of greeting.

"What is wrong with you? You're the one driving a Lexus covered in dirt. Get a goddamned truck."

"No."

"Or maybe move back to the city?"

"No."

"You've got probably the only LFA in this town, and you're driving it covered in dirt and rock dings, and I don't even want to know what the undercarriage looks like."

"Don't think about my undercarriage, you pervert," Aiden says, but the insult lacks his usual levity. In fact, he almost sounds...nervous?

"Everything okay?" I ask, watching the back of the dust-covered Lexus as it turns off the street and into the parking garage for his firm's office.

"Yep. Fine."

"Were you at the Kauffman for a work thing?" I ask,

and as I'm asking, I realize that what I really want to know is if he saw Elijah and if Elijah said anything about Zenny. Or, God, what if Zenny were there? What if Aiden had just seen her? And what if seeing him had reminded her of me? Or what if she talked about me? What if—

Christ. I've turned into a teenager. I've turned into a teenager because of a girl who's barely *not* a teenager, and now even the idea of seeing someone who also knows her is electric. Like her presence has infused itself into the city on a quantum level, and every place and everyone that's connected to her makes me as skittish and eager as she herself does.

Copper-ringed eyes spark through my mind as Aiden finally answers stiffly, "It wasn't for work."

"Did you see Elijah?"

"What would make you think that?" Aiden demands, and there's a sharpness to his words that makes me think we're beyond our normal brotherly ribbing.

"I don't know, because he works there, asshole? And he's my friend?"

There's a pause.

Then he says, "I've got to go." And hangs up.

God, what a fucking weirdo.

I'll see him tonight at dinner and make him explain himself. And in the meantime—the shelter. Getting this Zenny problem all sewn up so I can stop thinking about her all the time. So I can stop imagining what it would be like to kiss her again, what it would feel like to hoist her on another counter and then drop to my knees and prove to her how little oxygen I need when I've got a pussy to eat.

And now I'm hard. Just fucking great.

I park the Audi in my building's garage and limp over to the elevator, my stride hampered by my raging hard-on, and once I'm inside the elevator car itself, I can't help but to give myself a couple rough strokes through the fabric of my trousers.

Those soft lips.

Those white cotton panties.

Fuck.

I stumble inside my penthouse already peeling off my suit jacket and reaching for my cock. Just a quick jerk to take the edge off, just a few fast strokes to clear my head, I won't even think about Zenny—

That's a lie. She's all I can think of; it's her kisses and her hands trembling and clinging around my neck and her legs parting for me to step between and the small scratch of her nose ring against my own nose as I claimed her mouth...

The way she lifted up her skirt to show me her pussy...

I drop my coat on the floor and fish out my cock, as fumbling and eager as if I were about to actually fuck her, my blood pounding raw and hot and urgent, my own hand shaking with excitement as I wrap it around myself. I shouldn't be thinking of her like this, I shouldn't be imagining it's her slender fingers wrapped around me now. I shouldn't be getting off to the thought of those fingers being nervous and inexperienced. I shouldn't be swelling and leaking as I think about her showing me the cunt that she's promised to keep pure and untouched for her church.

But I am, I am. I'm hard and aching over Zenny Iverson, someone I held *as a baby*, someone I'm supposed to keep safe, someone far too fucking young and also consumed with a faith I have spent my entire adult life rejecting. And after nearly two decades of screwing all kinds of women all over the globe—women who are paid to fuck and women who fuck like it's their job anyway—I have no idea why it's Zenny who's got me like this.

Because I can't fuck her, ever? Because I actually care about her wellbeing? Because she isn't impressed by me and that makes me want to impress her?

Because she's actually a good and interesting person, and stirs up a part of me that wants to be the same?

I tighten my grip around my cock, watching the fat, dark head pushing through my fingers. Fantasizing about Zenny's fingers instead. About her pretty pussy, exposed for me and me alone—

Fuck. Gonna come.

I speed up my strokes, ready for it, ready, ready—and then there's a knock at the door.

For a moment, I consider ignoring it. I'm three strokes

away from spilling, and I need this, I need it bad, and there's no way I can spend the afternoon thinking about Zenny without needing to come, so I just need to do it now. You know, for my wellbeing.

But then the knock comes again, and reality clears up the hormone mist a little. Realistically, it's probably just a grocery delivery or the cleaning company coming early, but if there's even the slightest chance it could be about Mom…

With a pained grunt, I zip myself back up into my pants, try to arrange myself so that my boner isn't stupidly obvious (it still is) and go to open the door without bothering to check who's on the other side.

And I open it to find Zenny standing there in her postulant's jumper and bright yellow flip-flops, a nervous smile on her face.

CHAPTER EIGHT

My mind buzzes with panic.

Fucking PANIC, man.

And I shut the door right back closed.

"Uh, Sean?" I hear her say from the other side, but I'm too busy pacing in circles right now to answer. And I'm not even *thinking*, I'm just panicking, turning in circles like a dog walking into a room where the furniture's been rearranged. All of my normal confidence is gone, all of my normal contingency-thinking, all of my charm and problem solving, it's just fucking gone.

All that's left is wanting Zenny and knowing I shouldn't want her, and oh yeah, this idiot erection I have that is refusing to relent. If anything, my body and my dick are *thrilled* that Zenny is here in the flesh.

"Sean, I know your mother raised you better than this," Zenny calls through the door, sounding amused. "Let me inside, please, or I'll tell her how rude you were."

Like Elijah, Zenny was somewhat exempt from the Bell-Iverson schism, and I can't actually be sure that she *wouldn't* tell my mom about this, so I spin around and yank open the door before I can think about it any longer.

Zenny gives me a sunny smile and pushes by, leaving that delicate rose scent in her wake. I have to fight myself not to sniff the air like a wolf after she walks past me and props herself against the back of my sofa. I pick up my crumpled suit jacket off the floor and hold it in front of my crotch, a move straight from the Adolescent Boy Playbook.

You're thirty-six, not thirteen, I have to remind myself. *Fucking act like it.*

Luckily, Zenny doesn't seem to notice my odd jacket pose. Instead, she seems taken with my apartment, gazing with large eyes at the clean, minimalist space. I look around myself, seeing it as she would—the stained concrete floors and giant windows, the long, low lines of the furniture—and I feel a spike of pride. It *is* a pretty nice place, even though it's really nothing more than a convenient place to sleep and shower before I go back out to conquer the world.

"Nice, huh?" I say all cool and cocky like, and she looks back at me with an arched eyebrow that would have made a 1930s Hollywood starlet jealous.

"You know it's nice already; you don't need me to tell you that," she says. "And I was really thinking it was kind of sad."

"Sad? The two-million-dollar loft with an amazing view?"

"A two-million-dollar loft that looks like a model home. There's no pictures or books or mail on the table, nothing personal at all. It makes me feel lonely for you, actually."

Well, fuck, now I feel kind of lonely for me too.

"Anyway," she says, straightening up, "I didn't come by to see your apartment. I came by to talk to you."

Okay. Okay. I can do this.

I can talk to her—*just talk*—without kissing her and without accidentally coming in my pants. And this is a good thing anyway: I can explain to her about the shelter replacement and I can warn her the fuck away from Northcutt. This will work, it will totally work, and this conversation will end without me betraying my promise to Elijah.

I gesture her over to a seat and then I offer to get her a drink, an offer she accepts. And it's while I'm in the kitchen getting her a La Croix—carefully angling my body so she doesn't see the heavy erection still pressing against my pants—when I causally ask, "So what is it you want to talk about?"

And just as casually, she responds.

"I want you to have sex with me," she says.

Well, shit.

A few minutes later, she's drinking her La Croix and I'm sitting on the chair across from the sofa, watching the hypnotizing clench and shudder of her throat as she drinks.

She finishes drinking, sets the can down, and dabs gently at her bottom lip with her knuckle. A simple act that has my cock throbbing.

"Okay, so," I say in a choked voice. It's the first I've spoken since she dropped her giant, nun-sex bombshell. "Obviously the answer has to be no."

She looks at me, the sunlight catching those metallic glints in her eyes, the gold of her nose ring. "But why?" she asks, and God help me, it's that mixture of soft and direct of hers that I have no defense against. The headiest blend of vulnerability and confidence.

"Zenny. Be serious."

"I am being serious. Why can't you have sex with me?"

"You're Elijah's little sister," I say, holding up a finger. "You're far too young for me. And you're a nun." I add a finger to each point, until I'm holding three in the air together, like I'm reciting the weirdest scout pledge of all time.

Zenny stands up and walks over to me, wrapping my three fingers in her own, and it's so much like how I imagined her fingers wrapping around my shaft earlier that I have to close my eyes for a second. "Can we at least talk about these things?"

"There's nothing to talk about," I mutter, my eyes still closed. "Those aren't things that can be talked around."

"I don't like lying, even by omission, but if it's crucial, then…Elijah doesn't have to know."

I open my eyes.

"I'm not asking for a proposal, Sean, or even a boyfriend. I need help."

"Yeah, but sex help?"

She sits on the coffee table in front of me, her flip-flopped feet crowding against my dress shoes and her jumper-clad knees rubbing against the expensive wool of my suit trousers. "Will you let me at least explain it? Please?"

I'm so distracted by the feeling of her knees brushing against mine that I can barely speak. I manage a nod.

"Okay," she says, taking a breath and then blowing it out in a nervous huff and sending a lone curl up in the air for a moment. "So here's the thing. I'm going to become a novice soon, in about four weeks. And even though it's not the final step, it's still a very big step. Maybe the biggest. I'll put on a wedding dress and change my name. At the end of the semester, I'll move out of my dorm room and into the monastery full time; I'll start wearing the habit. It'll be the end of my life as Zenny and the beginning of my life as a bride of Christ.

"All of the other sisters—and the novice mistress and the prioress—they've told me to expect periods of intense temptation and doubt before I go through the novice process, they said it was natural and healthy even, but it hasn't happened. If anything, I feel surer than ever that this is what I'm meant to do with my life."

"I—okay. That seems like the exact opposite reason to have sex with some old stranger."

"You're not a stranger," she says, smiling—and fuck, that smile. Huge and sweet and so very, very kissable. "But I can see why it doesn't make sense yet. The thing is that I feel like I *should* be doubting, I *should* be tempted to leave, and I'm worried about the fact that I'm not. It makes me feel like I'm doing something wrong."

I can feel my brows pull together. "I mean, I personally think that anyone who believes without doubt is lying to themselves, but surely that's the goal, right? To believe without doubt?"

Her smile grows bigger, as if I've said something that proves her point. "See? That's exactly what I'm looking for!"

"Wait—what?"

"The whole 'you're lying to yourself' thing! The whole

112

'God isn't real and you're wasting your life' thing! I feel like if being around anyone can make me doubt my vocation, it's you."

I...I don't know if I like that.

I don't know why, because if you'd asked me an hour ago whether I'd like to keep innocent people from wasting their lives on a fake deity (and a corresponding religious bureaucracy that doesn't give a shit about them), the answer would be *yes*. *Hell yes*, even. But now that I'm in front of the hypothetical innocent person, hearing her say I'm good for making her doubt the things she holds valuable...I don't know, it doesn't feel so nice.

She continues, unaware of my inner struggle. "I think that a belief tested by doubt is the strongest possible belief, and my novice mistress agrees. She also thinks that I haven't had—*ah*—" there's heat in Zenny's face as she looks down at where our feet touch "—enough, um, experience to actually face what I'll be giving up to join the sisters. She thinks I need to taste more of the world before I leave it behind."

I'm still processing being Make Me Doubt Guy, and so it takes me a moment to sift through what she's saying. "Your novice mistress is telling you to have sex?"

Zenny looks up at me, and she's trying to be cool and worldly as she talks, but the shy flick of her eyes away from my own betrays her. This topic clearly makes her bashful, which is rather charming considering how determinedly and boldly she broached it in the first place. "She is kind of an unconventional woman, and a *very* unconventional nun. But being a virgin isn't a requirement for joining a monastery—celibacy is only a requirement for staying there after you've taken your vows."

"Will they still let you take your vows if you've had recent, uh, 'tastes of the world'?"

Zenny laughs a little. "Like I said, I have an unconventional novice mistress and my prioress is very, well, modern. She says she'd rather have women who choose this life in knowledge than who choose in ignorance."

I have to concede that's a fairly wise perspective on religious life—if anything about religious life can be called wise and not, you know, corrupt or pointless.

"Okay, so you feel like you haven't, I don't know, thoroughly interrogated this choice or whatever because you haven't had doubts, and your mentors have encouraged you to go fuck someone to force those doubts into being."

"Well," Zenny says, flexing her hands on her knees and looking down, "it's more like they think I'm so certain because I haven't actually confronted what I'm leaving behind. And that's not just sex. It's money and close relationships and freedom and frivolous kinds of things. I don't just want fucking, Sean," she explains, her eyes finding mine again. "I want someone to show me everything I'm going to miss. I want someone to challenge me and test me. And if I've tasted everything the world has to offer and I still want to consecrate my life to Christ, then I'll know it's what I'm truly meant to do. It will be a mature choice and not a choice made out of naïveté."

Her eyes are hypnotic, the copper rims darkening into pools so deep that I can barely separate where they blend into the onyx of her pupil. "If you really want this," I say, feeling almost dizzy looking at her, "you should find a boy your own age. Or shit, at least a boy who believes in the same things you do."

She shakes her head, and it finally breaks the spell. I stand up abruptly, going over to the window, because I can't handle looking at her, being so close to her. Not when she's asking for what she's asking for, which is something I'd fork over my own soul to give her.

Unfortunately, that would almost certainly be the price. Not my *soul* per se, since I don't believe in that shit, but you know. Whatever's left of honor and morality inside me.

"It has to be you," she pleads to my back. "I've been trying to take the Reverend Mother's advice for the last six months. Wearing street clothes instead of my uniform to school, trying to flirt with the guys in class, even saying yes to a couple of dates, but no one interested me. No one *challenged* me. In fact, most of the guys I interacted with only reaffirmed that I wasn't missing anything good. I never even got as far as kissing them, and that night at Elijah's gala—it was me saying goodbye to the whole plan. I'd have that one last time to get dressed up and drink and pretend, and then I'd give up this idea of searching for doubt. I mean, if I'd been searching for it and still didn't find it, then didn't that mean something too? That God didn't want me to doubt?"

I don't believe in a god, so I obviously don't believe in any predestination, "this is God's path for me" crap, but by dint of the situation and my vested interest in trying to maintain a semblance of control, I find myself squawking in agreement. "Surely that's the right answer. Surely you should give up this idea."

"But see, then I saw you," Zenny says, and her voice goes so soft and low that I turn to look at her. Her face glows up at me with a kind of self-deprecating helplessness, like she knows how silly it all sounds and yet she can't stop herself from just coming out with it plainly. "I saw you, and you were the first boy I ever wanted, Sean. When I was a little girl, I thought we'd get married, when I was old enough to have a real crush, I had a crush on you. When I was in high school, it was *you* that my body first wanted. And seeing you at the gala was like…like the answer to my prayers."

I'm greedy for this idea of her having a crush on me, of her wanting me with all this shy conviction over the years. The thought of it sends something spinning in my chest like a pinwheel, and I have to force myself to track the conversation. "You prayed for doubt?" I ask, hoping she can't see how boyishly flattered I am.

"I prayed for a chance. A chance to prove I was stronger than doubt—but how could I prove it if I never had the doubt in the first place? And then there you are, the first man I ever wanted, the ultimate temptation. Powerful and experienced and so hot I could barely even talk to you without stammering."

It should be shocking that this makes me embarrassed, this compliment, when I've had women call me a god or a hero or any number of insane things in order to get into my pants or my wallet. But it's not shocking because—as I'm quickly learning—everything about Zenny seems to come with a different set of rules, a different set of experiences. It's like I'm starting all over again with her, and I have no idea what to say.

Luckily, my silence doesn't seem to bother her and she keeps talking. "And it wasn't just that I wanted you, although I did. I mean, I *do*. But I know how you feel about the Church, I know exactly how worldly and materialistic you are, and what could be more perfect? *Who* could be more perfect?"

She beams up at me, like a star pupil who's just delivered a perfect answer, and I stare down at her, like a teacher trying very, very hard to suppress a boner he has for his student.

"Zenny, the answer is still no."

Her beaming smile fades into a sigh. "I thought you might still protest. It's about Elijah, isn't it?"

"And you're young. A thousand years too young. I know it's hard to see at your age, but men like me are—"

Zenny holds up a hand to stop me. "Don't give me some patronizing line about the 'depraved nature of men' or some bullshit. It's a gender theory that's about fifty years out of date, for one, and nothing more than a convenient excuse for you to avoid taking responsibility for yourself, aside from the way it neatly precludes the possibility that a woman might also be depraved. *And* aside from the obviously problematic binary construct."

I blink. Star pupil indeed.

"I wouldn't ask for this if I didn't want it, and I can assure you that I'm just as capable of sexual energy as a man. I can also say that aside from being a legal adult, I'm under no illusions about the way you desire me. You made that very clear the night of the gala."

Guilt rams through me like a railroad spike. "Zenny, I—"

"Don't apologize. I *liked* it, I *liked* your honesty. I asked for it, and I mean the things I ask for, Sean. Like right now."

She's too articulate for me to argue with, and especially when it's an argument I only halfheartedly want to win. By which, I mean that my heart feels like I should say no, while the rest of my body is throbbing with the urge to give her everything she's asking for and then some.

Not halfheartedly, then. Half-cockedly.

"Elijah, though," I mumble, trying to grasp on to some reason that she can't talk her way around. "He asked me to keep you safe."

"And what better way to take care of me than to help me when I ask for it?"

"I, uh—" Good God, where is the guy who dominates boardrooms? Who runs over lawyers and heirs and investors with sheer charm and willpower? Why can't I formulate a response? Why can't I vocalize any fucking *words*?

Zenny stands up now too, taking a step toward me. "Please, Sean. I'm only asking for a month, and I'm not asking for anything you don't want to give. I'm asking you because you're the only person who can help me, and the only person I trust to help me, and I need that. I need to trust the person I do this with, it can't be with a man like…" she waves a hand as she tries to think of an example. "Like Charles Northcutt."

Red.

Furious, jealous, protective red. Everywhere, in my eyes and choking my throat and tightening my fists. "Stay away from him," I manage. "He's a bad man."

I'm so twisted up in my sudden fit of jealous fury that I don't see her reach for me; I only feel it as she puts a gentle hand on my arm. "I can tell he's a bad man," she says matter-of-factly, "and I have no interest in him anyway. I'm saying that men like him are exactly why I want a man like *you* to help me with this. You're all the things being a nun is not…but I also feel safe with you. That's a very rare combination."

I look down at her hand, slender and dark and tipped with chipped gold nails. There's the unmistakable streak of pink highlighter across the back of one pinky finger, and if I'm not wrong, a faint remnant of a list made across the back of her hand in Sharpie.

It's the hand of a college student, the hand of a woman fresh out of youth, nothing like the chubby dimpled hand of a baby girl I once held in a friend's kitchen. It's the hand of a woman who's still learning herself, who's sometimes forgetful and sometimes daydreamy and sometimes bored. It's the hand of a woman who needs to be kissed and caressed and loved down so thoroughly that she will never forget how to appreciate her own body and the feelings it can give her until the day she dies.

And the shitty thing is that I still know all the reasons I shouldn't say yes; they are banging and parading around me like a marching band. But I still want to say yes.

Fuck, do I want it.

I close my eyes and that's when she moves in for the kill. A soft, tentative kiss against my lips, sweet and teasing and then gone.

My eyes pop open. "Shit," I say hoarsely.

"Please, Sean," she whispers, and she's so close to me. So very close, and if I wanted, I could pull her into my arms, I could bury my face in her neck and bite like a vampire, I could make her feel every hard, dangerous inch of why this is such a terrible idea.

And I think about how I still don't *know* her, not really, not like I should. I don't know anything about her except the barest biographical facts gleaned from Elijah's random mentions of her...and of course, that she's an almost-nun looking to find out what she'll miss after she goes into those cloisters of hers.

"I need a day to think about it," I say, taking a stumbling step back, away, my body immediately kicking up a fuss at the distance between us. "I'm not going to pretend I'm a good man, but this is something even I have to think about."

She nods, and she doesn't seem surprised or upset, and I realize she expected this. She expected me to need to think about it, and I'm a little relieved by that. Even if I am Make Me Doubt Guy, at least she wasn't lying about feeling safe with me, about trusting me. She clearly thinks that I have a moral compass of some sort, and I'm weirdly proud of that, in a way I don't want to examine too closely. In a way that whispers to me how much I already care what Zenobia Iverson thinks of Sean Bell.

"I understand," she says. "Can I expect you to call?"

Even if it's a stupid idea to see her in person again, I can't bear to discuss something so personal and important to her over the phone. "Dinner here. Tomorrow at seven. We'll talk again."

"Dinner," she says, a tiny smile pulling at her mouth. "Okay."

"Okay."

And she walks over to the door and I walk with her, telling myself that tomorrow I'll find a way to let her down gently, that I'll find a way to say no to this insane scheme of hers. There's no way she's going to come to dinner tomorrow and I'll say yes.

I tell myself that and then I watch her ass under her modest jumper all the way back to the elevator.

CHAPTER NINE

For the first time in eight months, I almost flake on Family Dinner. Aiden and Ryan are incorrigible dinner skippers, but me, I've always gone. Every week. Not even work has kept me away—I'll go to dinner and then go right back to the office if I have to.

But after Zenny leaves, I'm in a strange, restless limbo. My thoughts are running in circles. My boner is back and demanding attention. And the unfamiliar sensations of guilt and integrity chase each other in circles like dogs.

What is the decent thing to do?

Trust that Zenny knows herself and is capable of making decisions and choices? Help her on her quest for a deeper, richer relationship with her deity?

Or is the decent thing to interrupt her relationship with her deity, given that the deity is fake and also that the fake deity's church killed my sister?

I stand at the window for a moment, then mutter a quick *fuck it* and unbelt myself, giving in to the need to tug on my cock again. The flesh is straining and aching and a dark, angry red, and I brace a hand against the window and smell the air as I start yanking on myself.

I smell the faint hint of rose.

I smell Zenny.

There's nothing but the wild need to come jolting through my body as I imagine Zenny's hungry, innocent kisses and the tight curves of her body and the inviting arch of her throat. Nothing but untrammeled lust coursing through my veins as I imagine the flash of her white panties, like some kind of sick "best friend's little sister" fantasy brought to life. I imagine how her pussy would taste against my lips, how she'd smell, how she'd shiver when I circled my tongue around the dark rosebud between her cheeks after I suckled on her clit.

I'm nothing but a beast, a man possessed with the need to fuck.

So why is *You were the answer to my prayers* the last thing to run through my mind before I come?

"Is Mom okay?"

"Mom's okay, man. Sorry to worry you."

A few minutes later, I'm changed into different pants and a fresh shirt, cum wiped off the concrete floor, and I'm sitting in my home office, staring blankly at my bookshelves, which are about half the kind of businessy crap you see popping up on the non-fiction bestsellers' lists and about half historical romance novels, categorized by subgenre (Regency, Victorian, American West) and then shelved alphabetically by author.

Oh, and I called my brother. Because I'm currently freaking the fuck out, and he's the only person in my life that I trust to give me any kind of advice when it comes to clerical vocations and sex.

I can practically hear Tyler relax after I tell him Mom's not back in the hospital. "What is it then?" he asks. "I know you wouldn't call unless there's something dire going on."

It's true, for better or for worse, and I'm not sure why. I like Tyler, but he's never needed me the way that Aiden and Ryan do...the way that Lizzy did before she killed herself. And so I've gotten into the habit of being the de facto caretaker of the Bell boys—making sure Aiden gets some sleep occasionally, helping Ryan enroll in college classes and hunt for apartments, reminding them both to visit and call Mom—but Tyler's exempt from my bossiness. When I trust and respect someone, when I value their time and their judgment, I'm more than content to let weeks go by without talking, because I know they'll be just fine without me. Tyler falls into that category. Flaky, impulsive Aiden probably never will.

"Well, it's a little embarrassing to ask," I admit, "but I need advice. Uh. About a woman."

"Do I need to remind you about that time I was a priest?" Tyler asks dryly. "I'm probably not the best person for dating advice."

I stand up, feeling fidgety. "Well, she's Catholic."

"That's hardly an alien race to us, Sean. In fact, I think Mom still has your 'Best in Old Testament Trivia' award from Vacation Bible School somewhere."

That sends an automatic scowl to my mouth. I don't like thinking about that boy, the one I used to be, the one who believed in God and spent Vacation Bible School gluing Popsicle sticks together and teaming up with Elijah to tease Lizzy and her friends on the church playground. And for the first time, I realize—like really, fully realize—that spending time with Zenny means that I'm going to have to remember that boy. If I'm going to coax Zenny into the land of doubt, I'm going to have to remember why I ever occupied the land of belief.

"Is she some kind of weird Catholic?" Tyler asks. "Like one of those pre-Vatican II people?"

"I'm annoyed I still know what that means," I sigh. "And no, she's fine with Mass in English and all that—at least I think so. More like, she wants to be a nun."

I blurt it before I can hesitate any longer, but the

awkward silence that ensues makes me wish I hadn't said it at all. "You know what, never mind. I—"

"Sean," Tyler interrupts, and I hear him walking into another room. A door closing. "I need to know before we go any further if you're exaggerating. Be serious for once."

I run my fingertip along a line of Sarah MacLean paperbacks. "I'm not exaggerating. She becomes a novice in a month."

A long, long sigh from the other end of the line. "What have you done?"

"Look, I haven't done anything—"

"Sure."

"I swear. It's more like…I need to make sure that I keep not doing anything. Or if I do something, that it's the right something."

I'm only asking for a month.

I'm not asking for anything you don't want to give.

I'm asking you because you're the only person I trust to help me.

I scrub my fingertips through my hair, trying to gather my thoughts. My feelings. My wayward cock cravings.

"So you've met a girl," Tyler prompts after I don't speak for a bit. "Met a nun, I mean."

"Well, the word *met*," I say, turning to lean against the bookshelf and stare at a wall lined with diplomas and academic awards. "That implies we didn't know each other before."

"Sean."

Just tell him.

"It's Elijah's sister," I force out.

"Zenny? But she's only—"

"She's not a kid anymore, Tyler. She just turned twenty-one, it's her senior year of college. And before you ask, no, Mom and Dad haven't reconnected with the Iversons."

Tyler grumbles something on his end that sounds like, *well, they should*, which I ignore. Maybe, when looked at rationally, the Iversons weren't to blame for the schism, but no one was thinking rationally the day of Lizzy's funeral, and after the fallout, it seemed safer not to touch the still-smoldering pieces. Safer just to side with my parents and keep my friendship with Elijah separate from all the pain and alienation. Tyler had been the lone voice of dissent in the Bell clan, being the Mr. Conscience that he was, and it hadn't changed a thing, it only made life harder for him.

That's what having a conscience will get you.

Which is why it's super inconvenient that I've grown one now.

Before Tyler can spin off into Lecture Mode, I explain to him about the gala and then about the issues with the Keegan property and the Good Shepherd shelter. And then, in a voice that is more faltering and faint than I care to admit, I tell him about her visit today. Her situation.

Her request.

Tyler listens quietly through it all, and it gradually becomes easier and easier for me to talk, and I have a moment when I wonder if this is how his parishioners felt when they gave their confessions. If he made it this easy for all people to talk to him, to stumble through their messy thoughts and lusts and regrets. I could almost resent him for it, except right now I'm nothing but grateful. I need this, I need the unloading and confessing and just to *talk* about it, because I can't with anyone else.

"So then I told her I'd think about it and that we'd talk over dinner tomorrow night," I conclude.

Tyler takes a breath. "Wow."

"Yeah."

There's more silence on the other end, and I'm done with the silence, I'm done with the uncertainty. It's only been an hour since Zenny left, and I think I'll be ripped apart from the sheer insanity of it all if I don't find a way to fix it.

"So what do I do?" I ask impatiently.

"Well," Tyler says carefully, "it sounds like she was able to neatly shut down all of your objections."

"Yeah. It was humiliating."

"Never argue with a budding theologian," my brother laughs. "We like being the smartest one in the room too much."

I snort at my wall of degrees. I used to think I was a

pretty smart guy, but this afternoon proved that I've got nothing on Zenny.

"What do *you* think you should do?" Tyler asks. "Maybe that's the best place to start."

"I should say no," I say after a minute. "I should stay far away from her."

"Why?" Tyler asks.

"What do you mean, why?" I say in my best *isn't it obvious* voice. "She's young, she's Elijah's sister, and she wants to be a professional non-sex-haver."

"Twenty-one is hardly jailbait, Sean, and also I imagine that your connection to Elijah is precisely why she feels safe with you. As for her vocation and how it intersects with sex, I would suggest that you're looking at the intersection with the wrong lens."

"Are you going into Lecture Mode?"

Tyler ignores me. "You might think that you're so liberated from the trap of Catholic morality, but you're still acting like a man who thinks sex is dirty. Like a man who believes in the concept of purity."

"I don't think sex is dirty," I sputter. "I fuck literally all—"

"—all the time, I know, but listen to me: you can still fuck a lot and unconsciously believe these things. You can smugly think you're better than all the people trapped in repressive paradigms, but still believe, deep down, that you have the capacity to taint another person with your cock."

"I don't think that," I say, not at all convincingly.

"Tell me, Sean. Do you fuck strippers and socialites *only* because they're conveniently around? Or do you fuck them because you feel like they're already impure and you won't hurt them with just a little more impurity of your own?"

I don't have a ready answer to that. And I don't like what I'm finding in my mind as I search for answers, which are the clammy skeletons of half-forgotten beliefs and sermons from hypocrites. I thought I'd thrown away all that shit years ago.

"Okay, let me ask you this," Tyler says when I don't answer. "When's the last time you fucked someone you cared about? When's the last time you fucked someone and hoped to God you never had to stop holding them?"

I swallow. "A while," I lie.

Never is more like the real answer.

"Okay, last question," Tyler says, and his voice is kind. "How much of that do you think is about Lizzy?"

I nearly jolt off the bookshelves at the mention of her name, shock and grief sizzling through me. "It's fucked up to bring her into my sex life, man."

"Think about it. How can sex be anything but ugly, anything but perverted and twisted, when it took our sweet, happy sister and killed her? How could we not have the idea that she was pure, innocent, and the thing that destroyed her was a man's predatory desires?"

"I know it's different," I whisper, closing my eyes. "I know it is, I know it is."

"The place where you know that is not the same place where your fears come from. And until you untangle your fears—that you are like the man who hurt our sister, that you have the capacity to harm someone innocent—you're not going to be able to untangle your beliefs about sex."

"I—" I take a breath, my eyes still closed. This is too much to think about, God and Lizzy and all the ways that those two people have wormed their way into my adult identity without my permission. "Did you have to untangle anything?"

"Yes," Tyler says after a minute. "Yes, I did. I thought by being a priest I could atone somehow, that I could erase all the scars Lizzy had left. And the way I wanted sex—I felt fucked up about that too. I wanted it rough and raw, and what if I hurt someone when I was like that? What if I was like that with someone who'd already been hurt?"

"So how did you get around it?"

"There's no getting around anything," Tyler says, and I hear the rueful tiredness in his voice. "There's only getting *through* things. I had to admit to myself that I didn't fully understand my reasons, I had to shine a light into very dark corners and just *look*. Just *see*. See myself, and all the ways fear and guilt had trapped me.

"And I came to understand something while I was going through it. To be fully human is to be fully sexual, and while that doesn't mean having sex or even sexual desire, it does mean being fully in your body. It means recognizing that there's nothing any less holy about your body than there is about your soul, that as long as your body is treated with consent and respect and affection—and that you treat the bodies of others in the same way—there's nothing inherently sinful about your flesh. About its desires or lack of desires. About what it does or does not do. You do not have the ability to tarnish her or yourself; that right isn't given to any mortal person. She'll be no more or less holy for sex; the same goes for the lack of it."

"Try telling her Church that last part," I mutter.

"Abstinence is asked of everyone at some point in their lives. Maybe a partner is not emotionally ready for sex, or maybe they temporarily aren't able, like with Mom and Dad right now. And for some people, celibacy is not a struggle, just like fasting isn't the same struggle for everyone...or giving up money or giving up spare time or giving up sleeping in late or—*or, or, or...*do you see what I'm saying? A life consecrated to God is a life where you give up personal desires to serve God instead, and there's nothing more or less special about celibacy than there is about poverty or seclusion or sleep.

"And," my brother adds, "it's not always easy to discern God's desires for us. Because He or She wants us to be fully human and love each other as fully human, and that takes as many different forms as can be imagined. You can consecrate a life to God and have sex seven times a day. You can consecrate a life to God and go live in a cave for the rest of your life. No way is any holier than another, because our bodies are holy no matter what, and our lives are holy no matter what. Monasticism and lay life are just different ways of loving the same God and showing His love to the world."

"This is not an answer, Tyler."

"I know."

"For real."

"It's because there's not an answer," he replies. "Not one I can give you at least. I do have some advice, though."

"How can you possibly have more to say after all that?"

"Ha. Ha. But here it is: don't make Zenny part of your story with Lizzy, okay? It's not fair to her and it's actually not fair to you, either."

I want to argue with him, I want to tell him that of course I'm not doing that, that of course I'm not dragging my Lizzy baggage into this—but I can't speak the words.

Because they're not true.

This is a world apart from what happened with Lizzy, and yet there's a young woman—a little sister figure, even—and the Catholic Church and sex involved, and I can't pretend that my reflexive fears of hurting her or discovering something monstrous about myself aren't tied up in what happened with Lizzy. I never did therapy after Lizzy's death; I was young and stubborn and certain I didn't need it. Instead, I buried the pain and anger with drinking and sex and chasing after money.

And surprise, surprise, now it's coming back to bite me.

"Okay," I finally agree. "Okay. I won't."

"Good. She deserves to be treated like herself. Not as a proxy for a girl who died fourteen years ago."

"Ugh. Stop being such a know-it-all."

"I told you not to argue with a theologian."

"Yeah, yeah."

We say goodbye and hang up, and then I glance at the clock and see it's time to go to Family Dinner. I text Aiden to make sure he's coming and then I head out the door.

CHAPTER
TEN

Sean—

Hi. It's Zenny. I don't know if you have my number yet, and so I didn't know if you'd know who this was, and I...um, I'm rambling now, sorry. I was actually kind of relieved when you didn't pick up the phone because it's easier to talk into the void, as it were, than to talk directly to you, especially when your voice does that thing. You know the thing? Where it goes low and rough and the tiniest bit hoarse, almost like you're already in bed. Do you do that on purpose?

Uh...this is not why I called. To talk about the voice thing.

I called to talk about me.

When I got home this afternoon, I started flipping through my prayer journal. It's something my novice mistress has me keep, and for the last year, I've kept it faithfully. But even though I've been detailed and diligent with it, I realize there's something missing.

Openness.

You know my family, you know my parents. Dad is Dr. Jeremiah Iverson, physician-in-chief at the city's top teaching hospital, and Mom is the Honorable Letitia Iverson, and they wanted me to be whatever I wanted to be when I grew up...as long as it was a doctor or a lawyer.

So when I chose nursing and midwifery—and then when I decided I wanted to be a nurse-midwife for God— they were so upset. The private schools, the Jack and Jill meetings—it was all supposed to a make a certain kind of young black woman—and the young black woman I wanted to be was something different.

I knew I'd be disappointing them, and I guess it made me a little stubborn. Defensive. But it's the first time I've ever chosen things for myself, you know? When it came to school and clothes and even my first boyfriends—it was all to make them happy, to earn their approval, and it wasn't until I was staring at the Spelman application my mom gave me that I realized how limited my choices had become. Mom went to Spelman, so I should go to Spelman. Dad studied abroad his sophomore year, so that's when I was going to study abroad. I would have one year to pick pre-law or pre-med, and I would date a boy from Morehouse, and I would be Catholic but not too Catholic, and I would volunteer for one charity and one political campaign, but it had to be a national one—

Do you see? Can you feel it? It was like my entire life was decided for me before I'd even lived it, and I was suffocating under the weight of the future Zenny, the Zenobia Iverson everyone wanted me to be. But then I realized that there was one person who wanted differently for me, who would want me to find my own path and find something that made my soul sing with excitement.

I know you don't believe, so I won't say much about that moment except that it was maybe the moment I became truly aware of God. God wasn't just a word anymore, a reason to get up every Sunday and sit in the first row. Not just a theory behind the all-girls Catholic high school I went to and the charity events my parents helped organize. He or She became real. I could feel Him or Her or Them—or whatever the best pronoun is—I could feel God's presence like fingertips across my own fingertips. I could hear God like whispers from another room.

Except that changed somewhere, and I don't know where, just that it did. I'm going through the pages of this journal and I'm seeing someone say: I'll do anything for God...as long as it's what I want too.

I've refused to be open to possibility. To God's whispers.

Anyway, none of this substantially changes what we talked about this afternoon, but I wanted you to know and to hear why this is so important to me. I have to make sure that I'm listening for God everywhere and I want to make sure that I haven't made an idol out of my own Future Zenny the same way my parents did.

I want to be my own Zenny. And I think this is how I do it.

Okay, this was long, way longer than I thought it would be. Um, I'm excited and hopeful about tomorrow and I hope you're having a good night, and I'm just going to hang up now because I have no idea what to say next. Goodbye, Sean.

CHAPTER
ELEVEN

I've never been more nervous than I am right now.

Never.

Not before my basketball championship game senior year of high school, not before I got up to read the eulogy at Lizzy's funeral, not before my interview with Valdman. Not even during that terrible doctor's appointment after Mom's first scan when they said *here's how bad it is, here are the few options we've got left.*

Even though I usually keep my kitchen stocked with efficient and nutrition-dense options, I don't want to serve Zenny grilled, skinless chicken breast and chard. I want to give her something stylish, something good, something that says *you thought Sean Bell was awesome before, well, look at him smoldering at you over the fancy dinner he just made.*

Yes, I said *made*. Because even though I don't do

relationships and never really have, I know enough from my mom and Tyler talking about Poppy to know that ladies like it when you cook for them.

Plus, given the topic of our discussion, I figure it's best if we avoid a restaurant tonight. I want Zenny to be comfortable. *I* want to comfortable. And I could order something in, yes, but like I alluded to earlier, I want to impress her. All that trust and affection that she has for me that I don't deserve? I want to start deserving it.

The only problem? I don't really cook. Like ever.

But I've got two things going for me:

One—I know my way around a kitchen decently well after years of sous-chef-ing for Mom. So even though I may not have a cooking *instinct*, per se, I know how everything works.

Two—I watch a lot of *GBBO* (that's *The Great British Bake Off* for you uninitiated) and by now I can recite the ingredients for most different kinds of pastry, bread, and biscuit by heart.

So to that end, I decide on a curried chicken pot pie topped with homemade puff pastry and some expensive cheese imported from somewhere. I'll serve with a couple craft beers, since she's probably sick of wine, and *voila*.

Cue impressed admiration.

Except when Zenny knocks on the door at seven o'clock, there's nothing to be impressed about. I'm covered in flour, my vegetables refuse to brown up in the roasting tray like Alton Brown said they would, and I've forgotten how many times I've folded the puff pastry. I think it's only two—Mary Berry says in her cookbook that I at least need three folds—but I drank a couple of the craft beers in nervous desperation before Zenny could get here, and now time and previous pastry-folding events are all fuzzy.

What the fuck is wrong with me? I'm worth twenty million dollars! I've snapped companies in half like kindling over my knee, and yet I can't even be cool for one dinner? For long enough to make a fucking pot pie?

But when I open the door and Zenny catches sight of the flour dusting my Hugo Boss suit pants and the steaming wreckage that is my kitchen, she laughs so hard she has to slump against the doorframe, and that laugh makes it all worth it. Her laughter is light, happy, still the tiniest bit girlish, and her smile is like a shot of sunshine right to the heart.

I start laughing too.

"What happened?" she finally manages to ask, her eyes roving over me again. Except this time they linger not on the dusty smears of flour, but on the tapered lines of my waist. On the places where my sleeves are rolled into crisp, straight rolls, showing off the forearms I pay an ungodly trainer's fee for.

Watching her drink in my body is headier than any eight-point-five percent beer, and I have to remind myself to focus.

Dinner. Pastry folds. Right.

"I'm cooking," I say with dignity, closing the door behind her. "And it's going very well."

"I can see that," she says, and when I turn, she lifts her eyes to my face very quickly as she blushes.

She was just checking out my ass.

The knowledge sends hot blood south, and my fingers are burning with the need to touch her, hold her, yank her into a kiss.

I walk toward the kitchen as quickly as I can...away from her and her sweetly roving eyes. "Would you like something to drink while I finish up?"

"A sparkling water would be nice."

She comes to sit at the large island in the middle of my kitchen, pulling up a tall chair and sitting across the work surface from me as I hand her a LaCroix and go back to rolling out my piecrust. I'm giving myself a silent pep talk, trying to run through all the decisions and phrases that I've decided on in the last twenty-four hours, when she breaks the quiet with one of her determined yet vulnerable questions.

"So are you going to do it?" she asks.

I pause the motions of the rolling pin, looking up at her. She's in jeans and a worn St. Teresa's Academy T-shirt; no headband or scarf today, just curls everywhere. She looks like a college student. She looks young. And the expression on her face—hopeful and nervous and filled with shy attraction—it's not doing anything to help either my conscience or my stiffening cock.

"Do you mean, am I going to have sex with you, Zenny?" And once I say it, I hear it—the voice thing she mentioned in her message. My words have gone all husky and a little dangerous. "Am I going to fuck you like you asked me to?"

Her tongue peeps out to lick her lower lip, pink and wet, and she breathes hard. "Yes," she whispers. "That's what I mean."

And here we come to it, the *thing*, the reason she's here tonight and the reason I couldn't sleep after Family Dinner and the reason I spent today punishing myself in the gym and later in the office.

I don't know what a good man would do in my shoes.

I can only guess at what an unafraid one might do.

I walk around the island to her, taking the back of her chair and turning it so that she's facing me. I brush the curls away from one side of her face so that I can cup her cheek and lean close. "Yes," I breathe against her lips.

"Yes?" she repeats in a trembling voice, as if she doesn't quite believe me. She pulls back the tiniest bit to search my eyes. "Really? Yes?"

"Yes. For the next month, my body is yours."

"Oh, Sean," she murmurs, throwing her arms around my neck. Her lips are against my cheek now, impossibly soft, impossibly tempting, and my cock surges against my pants, reminding me that I'm only a half-step away from being able to grind against her inner thigh. Against the place where the denim seams meet right in front of her precious pussy.

"Thank you," she says, kissing my cheek. "Thank you, thank you." And then she turns her head and finds my mouth with her own, and my world catches fire and burns into a shrinking nothing; her mouth is all that's left, her yielding lips, her searching tongue, her sweet taste.

It's so very, very cliché, but kissing Zenny makes me feel younger, reminds me of the incendiary kisses one gets as a teenager, when every touch, every lick and caress is so fucking charged with excitement. As an adult, kissing can fade into something perfunctory, the prologue, the necessary foreplay to get a woman wet and squirming for what I really want—but as a teenager, I lived to kiss. Lived to make out. Even came in my pants once making out in a movie theater with a girl named Giana Saviano.

I'd forgotten how fucking incredible just kissing is.

God. I want to scoop her up and carry her to my room and kiss her there forever. With her body nestled against mine and my arms around her and our legs tangling. Just kiss and kiss and kiss—

My cock is not getting the *just kissing* memo, though, nudging against my pants and aching with the need for attention, and if I keep kissing her, I'm worried I'll push us too far too fast, that I'll spread her out on top of all this flour and fuck my fist while I eat her pussy and then we'll have jumped right into this without doing what needs to be done first.

Which is talk.

Reluctantly, I pull back, surprised at how hard and fast my pulse beats through me. Zenny's body makes my own feel like it's running a race, all hot and breathless and ready to sweat.

"What is it?" she asks, her nervousness creeping back in. "Do you not want to…you know, is kissing not on the menu of things we can do?"

"It's on the menu," I growl. "Everything's on the fucking menu."

She visibly relaxes.

I touch her lower lip with my thumb, then move to trace that slightly plumper upper lip. "This mouth. I want to eat it and fuck it and worship it and abuse it." I let my hand slide down, brushing my fingertips over the pebbled stiffness of her nipples. She's wearing some kind of flimsy bra that allows me to pluck at the sweet furls. "In fact, that's how I feel about all of you."

Her lips are parted now and she's not looking at me, she's looking at my fingers teasing idly at her nipples through her T-shirt, as if she's never imagined such a thing, as if she's never known the sight of a man's hand big and knowledgeable against her body.

"But," I say, dropping my hand and nearly losing my

load at the sound of her disappointed whimper, "we have to talk first."

"Talk?"

I step back. I step back again. Each step away from her perky tits with their firm little nipples is killing me, but it has to be done. "Talk," I confirm. "I almost said no, Zenny, and the only reason I can say yes is because I promised myself I'd do this right. So please let me do this right."

She nods. I don't miss the little squirm she makes in her chair though, like she's trying to relieve an ache between her thighs, and I almost run back over there and relieve it for her. Just two fingers would be all I need, right down the front of her jeans. Two fingers and two minutes, and I'd make her feel so much better.

Bad Sean. Focus.

Pastry folds and conversation.

"So is this going to be like a business negotiation?" Zenny asks. "We hammer out the fine print?"

I pick up the rolling pin again, mostly to give my hands something to do other than rub Zenny's cunt until she gasps out my name (although I do distantly remember that dinner is still in various, messy stages around my kitchen). "A business negotiation was my first thought," I admit to her, rolling the piecrust dough. The way her eyes watch my forearms as I work the rolling pin and the dough is *not* helping my self-control at all. "But the thing is that business negotiations are kind of shitty, when you think about it. It's all about what you can get from the other person while keeping what you want to keep. And that's not how I want this to go between us."

That seems to touch something inside her thoughts, because she looks up at me and there's trust shimmering in her eyes while the rest of her face goes slightly guarded. Her contradictions—trust and armor, bold and shy— they're like catnip to me, yanking at parts of my mind that I didn't even know I had. Pulling at something in my chest that I can't identify.

She fucking fascinates me.

"So not a business meeting," she says.

"No." I roll the piecrust over the rolling pin and it promptly tears in half, which makes Zenny laugh. I give her a playful glare as I try to arrange the dough pieces in a casserole dish. "No business meeting. How about a palliative care appointment instead?"

She tilts her head a little, waiting for me to elaborate, which I do.

"Obviously, we're not here because we're dying, but when my mom went to visit her doctor, the way they talked really stuck with me." Vegetables finally roasted, I set the dough-lined casserole aside and start mixing together the filling. "I thought Mom would go in and they'd have this transaction about pain levels and side effects and stuff like that, but instead, they talked about Mom's goals and priorities. What was important to her in her last days. How she imagined her death."

I pour the filling into the casserole, top it with the maybe-underfolded puff pastry, and slide it into the oven. Then I face Zenny, who is watching me attentively.

"Was it hard for you to listen to?" she asks. "Your mom talking about her death?"

I can still remember the doctor's office—not an appointment room, but a true office, lined with books and pictures of his family. *I just don't want to be in pain*, Mom had said, her voice cracking as my father put his face in his hands. *That's all.*

"Yes," I answer. "It was hard. But worthwhile. And I promise I didn't mean to derail the conversation into sad cancer talk, because this is about us and much more fun things."

"So which one of us is the doctor and which one of us is the patient?"

I start cleaning off my counter as I talk. "I think we're each both. Both things at once. We need to figure out what's important to each of us, what our priorities are. And also we need to talk about boundaries—what we won't do and we won't give up—and also all the practical stuff, mechanics and schedules—all of it. It's going to be awkward and feel kind of intimate for two people who don't know each other very well, just like with the palliative doctor and his patient, but that way we start out with all the important information on the table."

"Okay." She gives a nod of approval, which is belied by how hard she's chewing on the inside of her cheek. "You go first."

"Me first. Okay." I look at her, my hands still scrubbing at the counter. "Keeping you safe is the most important thing to me," I say. "I promised your brother I would, and beyond that, I...I couldn't live with myself if I hurt you. I can't deny that I want this—and I want *you*—but it can't come at any price that you have to pay."

A pause. Her eyes glued to mine, her pulse jumping in her neck.

"Okay," she finally whispers.

"Zenny, I need to know as we move forward...are you a virgin?"

She blinks up at the ceiling. "Sort of?"

I finish cleaning, toss the sponge into the sink and lean forward onto the granite, bracing myself on my elbows. "Explain *sort of.*"

"Well, I do feel like I should mention that I think virginity in general is an arbitrary construct designed by men as a system of control and fear. *And* it's heteronormative. *And* limiting, because why do certain sexual acts preserve virginity and some destroy it? What if I fucked a dildo every night, but I hadn't fucked a man? Why doesn't anal sex count? And what if I was with someone and penetration wasn't an option, for any number of biological or emotional or identity reasons—

would that make our sex *less* somehow? I'd be a virgin forever?"

I open and close my mouth, completely at a loss for an answer and feeling a little ashamed that I'd actually never even considered the concept of virginity that deeply.

"But for the purposes of our conversation, it means that I had a boyfriend in high school, and I decided to try intercourse with him. I changed my mind in the middle of the act, he stopped, and that was it."

I don't miss how easily she can toss around words like *fuck* when she's talking in hypotheticals, but when she's talking about herself, about real life, it becomes *intercourse* and *the act*. I mentally file that away as I say, "Was it consensual?"

I don't like the way she hesitates before she nods, but she does nod. Slowly.

"Can we talk about it more? I won't push if you'd rather keep it in the past, but for the purposes of your 'exploration,' it could be helpful to know what's new or what has a negative association for you." My words go up at the end, lilting like a question, because I really *don't* want to push her. But I also want to take care of her and I want to show her all the delicious things she's been missing—which means it would help to know what's in her past.

Zenny blows out a breath, but she looks determined, not troubled. "Yes, we can talk about it more. It's just awkward, like you said."

"I want to hold and touch you while we talk about it. Is that okay?"

She bites her lip, suppressing the flicker of pleasure that moved across her face. "Yes," she says quietly. "That would be okay."

I come around the island and step between her legs again, but this time I don't stay there. I scoop her up by her thighs and carry her with her legs wrapped around my waist to one of the sofas.

She squeals in surprise when I do it, but her legs tighten around my waist and her hands lace around my neck, and suddenly, I want very much to keep holding her forever, just like this. With her thighs bracketing my torso and her face slightly above mine, laughing down at me.

I arrange us on the couch so that she's on my lap but perched far enough back that I'm not nudging her with my erection. And I do it so that we're close, in something that could be called a cuddle, where I can hold her and speak to her and support her, but she's above me and she can easily change position. Easily gain space.

"Is this how couples talk?" she whispers, gazing down at me with the laughter still fading from her face. "Is this how you talk to all your women?"

I reach up and run a finger along her jaw. "I don't know if this is how couples talk," I say. "I've never been in a couple. And no, I never talk to women like this."

One of those film-star eyebrows again. "Is that because you don't talk to women period?"

"Smartass," I say, giving her bottom a teasing pinch, and the breathless giggle she gives has me regretting not peeling off her jeans before parking her on my lap. I could make her smile so much more if I didn't have all this denim in the way. "I talk to plenty of women. I even talk to the women I fuck. Although generally if I've got a woman in my lap, she's doing something else instead of talking."

"Something el—" Zenny catches herself.

I grin up at her. "I'll be happy to show you all the things other than talking you can do in my lap, sweet girl."

SEAN BELL. FOCUS.

"But first," I say. "We talk about the awkward stuff."

"We talk about the awkward stuff," she agrees.

"Tell me why you decided to go to bed with this guy in high school," I gently ask. "Why him? Why then?"

She looks down at her hands, which are now resting atop her thighs and rubbing restlessly at the fabric. She seems to be gathering her thoughts. "On paper, he was the right guy for it, you know? He went to Rockhurst, I went to St. Teresa's. He had great grades, he was star of the track team, he did all this volunteer work, we were in Jack and Jill together as kids...my parents adored him. And he wanted to have sex. And I wanted to have sex."

"And what had you done before this? With him or any other person?"

She shakes her head. "Just kissed. I'd kissed a handful of boys by the time I met Isaac. And Isaac and I had made out several times. It never went further than that because we were always in my basement and Isaac was terrified of the Honorable Letitia Iverson coming downstairs and dragging him by the ear to jail or something."

I have to smile at that; I definitely didn't make it out of my own childhood unscathed by Mrs. Iverson's fiercely maternal style of justice. But back to the topic at hand. "So wait, he hadn't even given you head by this point? What about fingering? Dry humping?"

My frank use of the terms seems to embarrass her a little, but she rallies. "Um, he touched my breasts once while we were kissing, and that was it," she says. "But he kept asking for more, asking if we could find a place to be alone, if we could just try it—so I said yes. We told our parents we were staying with friends, and then we snuck into the youth center at church because I had a key from volunteering. And like I said, I didn't like it and I asked him to stop. He did. That's it."

There's something about the way her gaze darts away from mine, about the way her shoulders draw up and her voice goes brittle that makes me think there's more to the story.

"Did you say yes because you really wanted to? Or because you liked him and you wanted him to keep liking you?"

"I really did want to, Sean, I promise. But I was nervous and I think...I think if he hadn't kept asking, I would have wanted to wait. But it seemed stupid to keep telling this boy no when there was nothing *wrong* with him, you know? He was smart and handsome and everyone liked him—why wouldn't I do it with him? And what if we didn't do it, and then I regretted it later?"

I'm about to reply when she puts a finger over my lips. "I know now that I didn't owe him sex," she says, and I exhale in relief. "And maybe I knew it then too. My reasons for saying yes, while complicated, weren't coerced."

"And the sex itself? How did he prepare you?"

Her eyebrows draw together. "Prepare?"

"To get you ready," I say. "To get you wet."

She stares down at me, eyebrows still furrowed. "We took off our clothes and he told me to lay down, so I did. Then he put on a condom and put his penis inside of me—what?" she says at my face. "What's wrong?"

I'm furious as fuck is what's wrong. "Did it hurt you?"

Her chin dips low and she looks away. "How did you know?"

I rub my hands along Zenny's arms, trying to find a way to explain. "That would hurt any woman, shoving inside without her being ready, but a virgin? I'm impressed you ever wanted to consider sex again after that."

"I didn't know," she says, her hands fiddling with her

jeans again. "And he probably didn't know either. It just hurt so badly and I started crying, begged him to stop. He did—but there was a moment when I thought he wouldn't. Just a second, really, and it was nothing he did or said, but it was this moment when I realized that I had nothing but the decency of a now-pissed-off teenage boy protecting me. He did the right thing, but—" her voice catches and she swallows again. "I'm sorry, I'm not that upset, it's just so embarrassing."

"Go on."

"He said it was supposed to hurt the first time, and that it would have felt better if I would have been patient. He broke up with me the next day. Said he wanted to be with a girl who really liked him and wasn't 'just pretending.'" Zenny pauses, looking at where my hands have curled into fists in the sleeves of her T-shirt. "Sean?"

"Keep going," I say, remarkably calmly. "I'm just keeping the lid on some mild rage here."

A tilted smile. "It's okay, really. That's about the worst of it."

"About the worst of it?"

"Well," she says, taking a breath. "There was this thing on Twitter for a while. The Rockhurst boys—his friends—all started a hashtag. #ZennytheNun. If they could only see me now, eh?"

"Jesus Christ. Zenny."

"What?"

"You had the worst first time possible. You were incredibly brave and stood up for what you needed in the moment...then you were dumped and subsequently bullied for it."

"It's not—" she stops, thinks, starts again. "It sounds traumatic when I lay it out, and yes, it stings to think about sometimes, but even in the moment, it didn't gut me. It didn't wound me. It sucked, but it sucked like a broken toe. It happened, it hurt, but I was fine and I *am* fine."

I take her hands in my own, trying to read her expression. If I were going to trust anyone about their emotional inner life, I suppose it would be easiest to trust a nun—and the clear-eyed way Zenny's looking down at me doesn't betray any secret pain—but I have to be sure. If I'm going to take her to bed, I have to be able to keep her safe in every way possible.

"Honest girl thing? You really are fine?"

A soft smile. "Yeah."

I don't think she'd hold back after I asked for honesty, and so I move on. "And then no sex after that?"

"I kissed a couple more boys after, but it never went further. And by the time I was ready again, it was impossible to find someone, the right person. Until you."

It's a lot of pressure. I don't say it and I don't show it, but knowing what a shitty experience she had the first time ups the stakes. It transforms this into something more than just a doubt experiment, an exploration, and it makes me feel like I've been given some kind of cosmic task to undo the wrongs of someone who came before me. To cherish this woman who deserves to be cherished, who deserves to know what good things a body can feel and do.

Of course, I don't believe in anything cosmic, so that feeling has to be all in my imagination, right? And the way my skin tightens as I look up at this brave, vulnerable girl and silently vow to give her everything I know how to give. That's nothing spiritual, it's just biology…

Right?

"What about you?" she asks, shyly. "What have you done?"

"Just assume I've done everything," I answer.

"Everything?"

"Well, okay, there's a few categories on Pornhub that I haven't dabbled in, but for the most part, everything."

"And girlfriends?"

"I've never had a serious girlfriend, and I haven't even casually dated anyone since college."

"Why not?" Zenny asks. "Isn't that normal? To date?"

I shrug. "Don't have the time, mostly. And well, I'm a little bossy, as you may have noticed. Women like it in bed, but I have trouble turning it off in real life."

"Bossy how?"

I think for a moment. Then make a decision. "You really want to know?"

I'm not imagining the widening of her pupils as she says, "Yes."

"If we get through talking over everything, I'll show you."

"Like a reward?"

"Yes, darling. Like a reward."

She tries to hide a smile when I call her *darling*, and I decide right then and there that I'm going to call her every endearment in the book if it makes her so fetchingly happy.

"Back to the talk," I say, and there's a new quickness in my voice because *fuck* I'm hard. I want to get through this and get to dinner, and then, you know.

Rewards.

"Boundaries," I say. "I need to know yours."

This kind of straightforward talk seems to put her back in her comfort zone, and her voice settles back into its usual, clear tones as she rattles off a list of things she's clearly given thought to. "No spit, blood, or third parties. If we do anything kinky, we have to discuss it first and we both get safe words. And obviously, I can't risk pregnancy or disease. I've been taking birth control to help control migraines for a few years, but I still want to use condoms."

"Of course."

She looks surprised that I don't argue more about the last thing.

"I always use condoms," I tell her. "You've got nothing to worry about there. And everything else we can easily manage."

"Okay, good," she says. "And this can't cut into my studies or my volunteering, so we might have to be creative about scheduling."

"I can handle that."

She squeezes my hands. "What are your boundaries?"

I'm glad she asked because I've spent the last twenty-four hours trying to find the right limits to this arrangement—any ethical loophole, any technicality that I could hold onto and think to myself, *I'm not a bad man, I'm doing this to help her, here's how I'm keeping her safe while giving us a taste of what we both want.*

"I have one boundary and one caveat," I tell her. "The caveat is that whatever happens with the Keegan property is separate from this. What happens in bed has no impact on me trying to find a new shelter—or on you slandering me to the press, if you wish to continue to do so."

That makes her eyes sparkle. "Deal."

"And the boundary—you don't make me come."

Record scratch.

Zenny sits up, letting go of my hands to cross her arms across her chest. "I'm sorry, I don't follow."

"I want to do this with you…for you…but I don't want to take advantage and I don't want to use you. I don't want there to be any doubt that I'm doing this all for you."

"So you're not planning on coming when we're together at all?"

To be honest, I haven't really thought that far ahead. I'd only gotten so far as to decide I couldn't actually, in good conscience, erupt inside a nun's mouth. "I don't know. I—"

"Because I don't accept that," Zenny interrupts. "You said everything was on the menu, and that's a part of everything that I refuse to compromise on." She pauses, and then forges ahead. "I need you to come too. If you don't, I don't know, but it makes me feel like I'd be missing something important."

"It's not that special, sweetheart. It's cum."

She shakes her head, not having it. "It's special to *me*. I only get a month of this, and I won't miss any part of it."

I rub at my jaw, trying to bring my brain around to find some way to convince her, but my God, all I can think about is how much she wants to see me spill.

"How about," Zenny says, "you come when we're together, but I won't be the one to finish you off? It won't be my hands or my mouth or—you know."

"Your pussy?"

"My pussy," Zenny echoes and we're staring hard at each other now, thinking of the same thing. Thinking of me coming deep inside her, giving her everything.

"Deal," I say hoarsely.

She leans down and kisses me—gently at first—then

eagerly as I kiss her back, and she scoots forward on my lap so she can rub herself against my angry, needy cock. "Are we done with the talking yet?" she asks against my lips. "Please say yes."

I smile at her eagerness and shake my head, giving her a final, soft kiss before I say, "One last thing."

She groans.

But it can't be ignored and it can't wait. I take her hands in my mine again and brush my lips across her knuckles. "Zenny, I don't want to move forward without…I mean, I want to be aware that there's…"

Dammit. I can't find the right words. This is just as awkward and intimate as talking about sex, and I'm fumbling around for ways for this to come out right and coming up short.

I start again, peering up at her. "You're young. You're *so young*. Elijah…he asked me to protect you, and I'm pretty sure this is the exact opposite. I've never done this before—dating or fucking someone I care about or fucking someone I'm supposed to take care of, and I'm terrified of hurting you. Of getting this wrong."

Those copper eyes search my own, shimmering and serious and sharp. And then she nods. "Okay," she says simply.

"Really?" I ask, feeling clumsy and guilty for reasons I don't entirely understand. "I want you to know that you always have the power between us, Zenny. To say stop or to say go. To tell me what you need from me. To tell me I'm an asshole."

That last earns me a little smile. "I'll never be afraid to tell you that," she says. "And I trust you, Sean. That doesn't change reality, but I'm willing to navigate it with you."

The weight of her undeserved trust sits heavy on me, and I shift underneath her, still worried, still guilty.

"And it's only for a month, remember?" she adds. "It's not like we have to figure out how to raise children together."

"Right," I say, except now I'm suddenly wondering what our children would look like, and I've never wanted children, never ever, no sir. But damn. Zenny and I would make cute babies. And I can picture her belly swollen and tight with my child, picture her sitting in a glider in some quiet room, nursing our baby while I sat by her feet and stared up at her adoringly.

Happiness.

That's the feeling unfurling in my chest right now, fragile and easily blown apart, and the sensation of it is so strange that I'm rendered still, staring at Zenny as if she's the only thing in the world.

She misinterprets my stillness and laughs. "I was only joking about the children, Sean, don't panic."

"I—"

"In fact," she continues, oblivious to my fantasy and the unfamiliar excitement blooming inside me, "I'm surprised you didn't give me some speech about how I can't fall in love with you while we do this."

"I don't think that will be a problem for you," I murmur, kissing her knuckles again so that she can't see my face. I hadn't forgotten about the possibility of emotional entanglement—in fact, almost every other book in the Wakefield Saga had a speech to that effect in there somewhere whenever the characters first get together. *I'll pretend to court you for a season, but we mustn't fall in love,* or *since I'm a widow, I can teach you how to please a future wife in bed, but of course it will end between us the moment you get engaged.* That sort of thing.

But I don't need it with Zenny. The way she talks, the way she lives her life—I'm never going to be able to compete with her God for love. She'll fuck me, use me to whatever purpose she needs, and then go back to her church with a deeper faith than ever. I don't doubt that for a second.

It's weird though, how quickly that thought wilts my happiness.

"Is that smoke?" Zenny asks, and I turn with some alarm to see a steady white plume coming from my oven.

"Ahhhh shit shit shit." Zenny slides gracefully onto the sofa and I leap to rescue the pot pie, which I already know Mary Berry would declare "overdone" and our awkward discussion comes to a sudden, smoking stop.

CHAPTER TWELVE

The pot pie is only barely burnt, and I make sure to sprinkle lots of the expensive cheese over the worst parts, and then it's fine. I dish it out, crack open the beers, and soon Zenny and I are sitting at the small table by the window, looking out over the darkening city.

"It's strange," Zenny says, after blowing on a forkful of pie to cool it off. "Even though it was uncomfortable to talk like that, I feel really good right now. Like I've just exercised or something."

I was very busy staring at the little creases in her lips as she put them together to blow, and it takes me a minute to answer. "I agree. I'm glad it didn't scare you off."

"I'm not easily scared," Zenny says as she takes a bite, and I watch the slow slide of the fork's tines between her lips, the flutter of her eyelashes as she savors the food.

"No, I don't think you are," I murmur, knowing

distantly that I should stop watching her so intently, but damn, the girl's fucking gorgeous. I think I could happily sit and watch her balance a checkbook or browse through *Consumer Reports*, she's that arresting to watch.

And she's right. The air between us feels good. Clear and charged with all the right charges.

"This bossiness," she says.

"Yes."

She sets down her fork and studies me, a daring glint in her gaze. "So far I'm not all that impressed by it."

I study her back. "Is that a challenge?"

"Maybe."

"I haven't started yet." I pause. "It's not one of my finer traits, Zenny. But it's hard for me to turn it off for people I—" I stop because a very incautious word almost slipped out, and I'm scared at how *not* scared I am to say it in front of her.

"—people I care about," I say instead.

"People you care about."

"My brothers. My mother," I say. "My sister, when she was alive…much good that it did her," I add with some old, tired bitterness.

"What do you mean?" Zenny asks, and she asks it without playing into my obvious self-pity. She asks like she'd ask about the weather or about who tailors my suits.

"I mean that I was over-protective and stubbornly in her business all the time. School, boyfriends, what parties she was going to and if her cell phone was fully charged and if she remembered the mugging classes I begged her to take before she came to KU. And the whole time she'd been carrying this wound, this shame, years and years of what this man had done to her, and I had no idea. I had no idea that I'd failed to protect her until it was too late."

"So you are bossy to take care of the people you keep close," Zenny says, "but there was a time once when—in your eyes—you failed. And you haven't let anyone new into that circle since."

"I—" I break off because...well, she's not wrong, actually. The people in my life—my parents, my brothers, Elijah—they were already there before Lizzy. I suppose I haven't let myself get close to anyone new since she killed herself because getting close would mean feeling responsible for them and taking care of them.

And Lizzy's suicide proved how inept I really was at keeping the people around me safe.

"I don't know how you manage to do this," I say, taking a quick swig of beer to hide my discomfort. "Make me talk about all kinds of depressing shit."

Zenny reaches across the table to touch my hand. "Sean."

"Yes?"

"It's only a month between us," she says quietly, "and I'm not your sister."

I think of Tyler's words yesterday, of his warning.

"I know that," I tell her.

"Good. Because I want this month to feel *real*. That's the whole point, for me to feel everything I'll leave behind, not just the sex, but the companionship and friendship too. We are friends, right?"

"Yes, Zenny," I say, watching how the city lights sparkle in her eyes. "We're friends."

She beams. "Good. Then that means it should be easy for you to be bossy. We're friends and you're going to fuck me, and that's basically like being my boyfriend."

I haven't thought of it like that, and the surge of fierce pleasure at the thought of Zenny being my girlfriend, being *mine*, is impossible to ignore.

"That's how I want us to be until this is over," Zenny goes on, ignorant of the stormy happiness thundering through my veins. "I want to feel what a woman of yours would really feel."

"I've never had a woman I called my own," I say softly. "You're the first."

"Really?" She tries to hide her smile at that.

"A lot of things are new with you, Zenny. Even for me." And I mean it. I may have done almost everything there is to do in bed, but I've never done those things with a woman I really cared about. A woman I could pretend was mine.

"Let's start right now," Zenny says, straightening up and pushing her plate back. "Say I'm your girlfriend. How would you act?"

I straighten up too. "First of all, you need to know that I'll stop with the bossiness at any moment. Just say the word."

"Is the word 'asshole'?"

I grin. "Yes."

"I can do that." She wiggles a little in her seat, like a cat waiting for a string to move across the floor. "Seriously, Sean. I'm starting to think you were bluffing."

"I don't bluff, sweetheart. It's why I'm so good at business." I take a breath, because this is new to me, letting my natural inclination to control spill into a relationship that's not familial. But it feels good, it feels nice, and I've been fighting the urge to take care of Zenny in all sorts of ways since the gala—allowing that urge out to play feels delicious.

And of course with Zenny, it takes a very different shape than it usually does with my family, the lust and affection and protectiveness twining and twisting into something new. Something I've never felt before.

"To start, I want you to finish what's on your plate."

Zenny's eyebrows furrow, and I can tell she wasn't expecting me to say something so ordinary.

"Eat your dinner, Zenny. I won't tell you again."

Eyes narrowing, Zenny picks up her fork and starts to eat.

"You want to call me an asshole yet?"

She swallows a bite. "Not yet."

I smile. "Good. Take off your shirt."

Her fork clatters to the plate. "What?"

"You heard me," I say silkily. "I want to see you while you eat. I want to know the color of your bra, I want to see the shape of your little nipples as they pucker up, all cold and needing to be sucked warm again."

She swallows again, and this time it has nothing to do with food. "Jesus," she whispers, and I can't tell if it's a swear or if it's a prayer. It doesn't really matter either way; she's tugging her shirt off as fast as she can, tossing it behind her.

I rumble in approval, leaning forward to get a better view. She's wearing a pale lavender bra, a sweet color against her warm brown skin, and I can see the dark circles of her nipples under the thin fabric. I can see them hardening, pulling up tight.

I can also see the faint shadows of her ribs laddering down her sides and a faded mandala-like doodle spiraling out from her hip.

A college student who sometimes forgets to eat.

A college student bored in bed while she studies and draws idly on her own skin.

In classic Zenny fashion, she is a mix of fearlessness and uncertainty, squaring her shoulders and hiding nothing from my hungry gaze while she bites nervously at her lower lip.

"Perfect," I rasp, and I see how my praise affects her. Good. I plan on praising her lots over the coming month. "Now finish eating while I look at you."

"I—what?"

"Finish eating. I know you went to the shelter after your classes today, and I'm going to guess that you haven't put anything in your stomach since maybe some coffee you had this morning."

The corner of her mouth twitches. "Maybe."

"And how often is that the case? That you're doing so much between school and the shelter that you miss your meals?"

One of her hands comes up to rub at her shoulder as she looks away. "Often," she admits.

"That ends tonight," I say sternly. "Eat."

There's a moment when I think it's coming, the inevitable *asshole*, the moment she tells me to stop. She doesn't need some white guy playing Daddy with her, she definitely doesn't need someone treating her like she's not capable of caring for herself. But Carolyn Bell was a social worker until her cancer diagnosis, one Bell brother was a priest, another Bell brother burns a candle at both ends like his wick will never run out. I've seen what happens to busy people, and I know it's much, much easier to justify losing a night's worth of sleep for the cause than it is to justify taking ten minutes to make a sandwich. The most selfless people, the most driven people, they *need* permission to take care of themselves, they need someone who will put them first, because they won't do it for themselves.

The word *asshole* never leaves her lips. Her eyes flash with irritation, then they shimmer into some internal struggle that leaves her lower lip trapped between her teeth and her hand hovering over her fork.

After a short silence, she picks up the fork and takes a bite. And another. And another, until her plate is clear. I watch her the entire time, stretching out in my chair and thrilling in this new feeling that's a potent mixture of desire and a caveman-like satisfaction at tending to someone's needs. The combination of seeing her eat the food I provided and the promise of all that smooth skin slowly pebbling into goose bumps.

She pushes her plate back and sets down her fork, giving me a look that says *well?* And also giving a little shiver of anticipation, because she thinks that was it, that I had my bossy fun and now we'll move on to the part where I fuck away her sort-of virginity.

I do really, really want to do that. But I have plans first. Because if she really were my girl, there's a certain way these things would unfold *and* since I've officially committed to Project Doubt, I'm going to give this experiment everything in my considerable power. Seduction, affection, bossiness, fun—everything.

I stand up, not bothering to adjust the thick penis

pushing against my slacks; I've been hard for so long tonight that I've stopped caring if it shows. Zenny's eyes follow my body as I clear the table and set the dishes in the sink, and more than once, I see her gaze linger over the ridge of my erection.

I resist the urge to smirk, but only just, coming back after washing my hands and helping her out of her chair. Then I trace a finger down her belly, circling her navel until she shivers.

"I'm going to unbutton these jeans, Zenny," I tell her. "I'm going to unzip them. Then I'm going to slide my fingers inside your panties and play with what I find there. Yes?"

"Yes," she breathes, her stomach quivering under my fingertip, and I make good on my word, slowly working the metal jean button through the buttonhole until it pops free.

Zenny gives an answering exhale—shaky but determined. I keep my eyes on her face as I tug the short zipper down, keeping tabs on her expression, on her comfort. Some embarrassment is normal, nerves are to be expected—but there's a razor-fine balance I need to maintain between giving her what she wants and pushing her too fast. A month just isn't enough time to do this properly, to cultivate and tend to her blooming lusts. To awaken her body.

If I could ask for anything right now, it would be a year

with her. A year of tutoring and teasing and bossing and savoring her.

Even a year wouldn't be enough.

That thought pings through the rest of my musings, loud and resonant, and I'm not sure where to put it, so I ignore it for now. I need to focus on what's important, which is the girl trembling all pretty and eager in front of me.

I run my fingertips along the scalloped line of her panties, which match the color and the filmy material of her bra. I know without asking that this is probably the most daring lingerie she owns, and despite how modest it actually is—there's no straps or mesh or cut-outs or any of the usual trimmings that makes women's underthings into confections of fun—it makes the entire effect more delicious somehow, more sinful. My sort-of virgin, my almost nun, trying to be naughty and instead looking more innocent than ever.

I look down to where my fingers toy with the top edge of her panties, then back up to her face.

"Are you nervous, baby?"

"Yes," she confesses, her hands going up to my shoulders and fisting in the shirt there.

"Fun-nervous or bad-nervous?"

She thinks for a minute, which I appreciate, because I need her to be sure. *I* need to be sure. I wasn't bullshitting her when I said I was worried about our age difference, because the things I want to do with her are not just dirty, but like, *dirty* dirty. The kinds of things you don't admit to wanting in the harsh light of day, the kinds of things that make even a man like me blush.

Keep her safe.

"Fun-nervous," she says. "If you would—" she stops.

"Tell me, Zenny."

She takes a breath, pins her eyes on mine. "I'm ready for more. I'm nervous, yes, but it's excitement, not fear."

"Good."

"So," she swallows, "give me more. It's fun and I like it, and I'll call you an asshole when I'm ready for you to back off."

It's my turn to swallow. Her green-lighting *more* in that signature combination of careful and bold is almost enough to make me throw all my plans out the window and just kiss the hell out of her until we end up on the floor in a hungry press of hips and mouths. To fuck the soft split between her legs until I've fucked away this fierce infatuation, the alarming affection and possessiveness I already feel for her after such a short time.

Sean, I scold myself. *Fucking stop it.* I was the one who was all *I'm doing this for you* earlier, and I'll hold myself to that if it kills me.

this is for her
this is for her
this is for her.

"Okay," I say, finally gathering myself. "I'm trusting you to call me out on being an asshole. Now take off your jeans, darling. It will make it easier for me to play with you."

She kicks off her flip-flops and wriggles out of her jeans with a perfunctory kind of shimmy, and I find myself strangely drawn to the sight. I've paid lots of women lots of money to undress for me, I've fucked society wives determined to show off every expensive stitch of their La Perla or Agent Provocateur—but I've never seen a girl undress like this, artlessly and quickly, without performance. It feels intimate, somehow, and it makes me wonder what else I could get hard watching her doing. Brushing her teeth or putting on lotion. Tying shoelaces.

Then she's in front of me, all bare skin and thin silk. Her nipples are begging to be sucked, her belly is tight, and her hands twist together in front of her panties, as if she wants to hide herself from me and is trying not to.

I step forward, deciding to give her hands something to do. "Hands on my shoulders like before," I tell her. And then I add, a little sternly, "No hiding from me. You're fucking beautiful and I'll stare at every inch of you until I get my fill."

She puts her hands on my shoulders again, a little smile playing across her mouth. I can guess why.

"You like being called beautiful?" I ask, brushing my lips across her forehead. Then across her cheeks. Her eyelashes flutter in girlish happiness and I both curse and thank every man that came before me who didn't give this woman every compliment and tender word she deserved. It's ridiculous that she's twenty-one and she's never been properly petted and praised, and yet thank God, because otherwise I wouldn't be the one in front of her, here and now, with my fingers tickling gently along the top of her panties.

"You are beautiful, Zenny," I say with my lips still against her cheek. My fingers slide beneath the elastic border and her belly tenses even more. "Your face is stunning, your body is a work of art. But it's *you* I can't stop thinking about, how you ask for things and how you argue, how you tease and how you rant and how you glow when you talk about what matters to you. When I say the word *beautiful*, sweetheart, know I mean it."

She nods, about to answer, when the pad of my middle finger brushes against a narrow triangle of short curls.

"Oh Zenny," I say, my cock giving an abrupt, painful throb. "Oh baby."

"What is it?" she whispers, tilting her head to meet my eyes.

"On the couch," I say hoarsely, pulling my hand from her panties and giving her ass a little swat. "On your back."

She moves backward, turning uncertainly toward the living room as she does and giving me a view of her perfect ass. Firm enough to curve, soft enough to bounce a little as she walks, sloping into strong thighs and up into hips made to have my hands curled around them. I can already imagine the heart shape her ass will make when she's bent over for me.

Fuck. Me.

With a stilted breath, she lowers herself onto the sofa, dark curls like a halo around her head on the cushions and her bra and panties pulling tight against her skin as she arranges herself. And I prowl up to her like a cat, like a predator, like a hungry man coming to a banquet table.

"Should I take off my—" Zenny's thumbs hook in her panties, but I still her movements with a steely look.

"That's for me," I say. "I want it."

"You want to be the one to take off my underwear?" Her thumbs don't move, so I squat down beside the sofa and give one little nip with my teeth, which sends her hands up to her chest. And then I keep my mouth at her hip as I speak, letting my breath warm and tickle the skin there.

"I'm not going to take off your underwear. I'm going peel this silk off you like the skin of a fruit, and then I'm going to eat you. I'm going to suck on you like a plum. I'm going to unwrap you like a Christmas present and then you'll see what a happy boy I am."

She's breathing hard, her copper-tinted eyes dilated and dark on mine.

"But first," I say, turning my lips to drop a real kiss on

her hip, flicking my tongue along the edge of her panties, "there are some things you need to know."

A flicker of impatience across her face; an involuntary press upwards with her hips. "Sean, we've been over this–"

"No," I murmur, moving my mouth closer to her navel, which silences her. "This is different. I know you trust me, you know I trust you. And now it's time for me to show you what I would do if you were mine, my own sort-of virgin."

Her belly quivers under my lips. "Yes," she says, her voice dry until she wets her lips. "Yes…I…I want to be that. Yours to do with as you like."

"You are, darling. You are." I chase a finger up her thigh until she gasps and jerks underneath me. "My little virgin. That boy before, he didn't do a good job with you, did he? He didn't know what a gift he had in your body, in your sweet little cunt."

My finger gets to the edge of her panties where her thigh meets her body, and her legs part of their own accord. "He didn't tell you all the things you need to know."

Her back arches as my fingers skate over her center, light as a tickle, and to the other edge of her panties. "N-no, he didn't."

I *tsk*. "He should have known such a smart girl would want to know everything first. He should have known that you would have wanted to hear about your cunt. And about the parts of him that would hurt and ache until you made them feel better."

Her breath hitches and her eyes go glassy. "Are you going to tell me?"

"Oh yes, sweetheart." I can see the pout of her cunt through her panties, the tempting secrets underneath. And when I run a finger straight up her middle—fuck, yes— she's wet, wet enough to leave a sweet little spot on her panties as I press them against her flesh. "I'll tell you everything."

CHAPTER THIRTEEN

I start stroking her pussy again over her panties and she inhales instead, trying to move toward my hand.

"This is your cunt, sweetie, and it needs to stay happy. It needs to be licked and kissed and petted. Doesn't it ache now? Doesn't it need something?"

I see the moment she decides to play along with my little teacher game—a flash of thought, chased by an eager bite of her lip. She nods at my question, parting her legs even farther.

My fingers slide up the silk-covered folds to the swollen tip of her clit, which I then give a firm circle. Her back bows off the cushions as her mouth gapes in a silent moan.

"This is your pretty little clit, isn't it?" I say, circling it with the kind of pressure that sends her toes curling. "It needs to be played with when it gets stiff and needy like this, baby. It needs to be rubbed."

"Yes," she swallows, eyelashes fluttering. "Oh God."

"And all that wet—you feel it, don't you?" My fingers echo my words, finally sliding beneath the edge of her panties.

She gasps. "Y-yes."

I play with her for a minute, running clever fingers along the slick skin. "When it gets wet like this, that means it needs attention. It needs to be fucked."

I pull my fingers out—relishing her whimper of protest as I do—and then I wrap my hands around the sides of her panties and tug them down. "I've been dreaming of this cunt since the gala," I tell her roughly, my eyes on the vee between her legs that's appearing as I peel off the silk. "I need to see it now. It's all I can think of, it's the thing I wake up wanting—"

I break off because I've worked her panties down her thighs and to her knees, and once the silk is past her feet, she's all mine to see. All mine to look at and to play with and to taste and to fuck, and Jesus, that feeling is so heady, like a slug of whiskey, like a shot of morphine, burning up my veins and blurring my vision.

Her knees are back together from helping me ease off the last of her modesty, and I take a deep pleasure in sliding my hands up the lengths of her legs, my thumbs finding that sensitive spot above her knees and just on the inside of her thighs. There's a moment when I see it—see *us*—see my hands being the hands of a thirty-six-year-old man with a too-expensive watch glinting on his wrist. See her legs being the smooth and slender legs of a woman barely budded into womanhood.

It's wrong to be turned on by that. Wrong to notice it in a way that makes me hungry for more.

But I can't help it. It's like every reason I shouldn't do this—her age and her impending vows and the fact that she's Elijah's little sister—makes it more and more undeniably arousing.

I push her legs apart and finally see what I've been mad with wanting.

"Oh Zenny," I say in a choked growl. "Oh darling."

"Sean," she says, and that's it. Just my name.

Every part of her quivers.

I take my time looking at her, committing every single curve and fold of her to memory. The curls kept short and neat, the cleft itself shaved bare, revealing all of itself proudly. And when I run my thumbs up her thighs to caress her outer lips, I feel for myself how fucking soft and silky she is. My cock feels like the skin will split it's so fucking hard; a jut of painful need throbbing in my pants. It's getting so difficult to remember why I wanted to follow this little plan of mine, especially now when I can see the rich, wet opening waiting for me. And—oh *fuckkkkk*— when I part that opening with my thumbs, I can see her most secret place. The place that blushes into wet and pink and tight.

I groan and close my eyes. And then I open my eyes to see her gazing up at me with an expression of pure, liquid trust.

It melts me. Renders me into something both less and more than a man.

"Your pussy is the most beautiful thing I've ever seen," I inform her. And then before she can argue or laugh or respond, I bend down and give that sweet cunt an inaugural kiss, taking my time to taste her, to lick her, to find the satin skin under her opening with my tongue, the needy little nub at her apex.

She lets out something that sounds like the cross between a laugh and a wail—an inelegant noise that comes right from her belly—all surprise and longing. I grin against her pussy, because I've heard so many women issue the kinds of practiced moans they think men want to hear, scheduled gasps and *oohs* and *oh you're so good*. But I'd take Zenny's laugh-wail over those other noises any time.

I kiss her pussy thoroughly, deeply, taking advantage of my armless sofa and moving between her legs—knees on the floor, wide shoulders folded in between her thighs, my hands sliding greedily under her ass to lift her to my face.

As with everything, she is a contradiction. Artless and deliberate, embarrassed but driven past caring. I feel it in the way she jolts and squirms the first time my tongue laps at the pleats of her asshole, in the way her feet confidently rub at my back while her hands cling desperately to my wrists, the squeeze of her fingers asking questions I know she's too proud to voice.

Do I taste good?

Do you like it?

Do you like me?

My tongue and my hunger answer for me. Yes, she fucking tastes good, a clean kind of sweetness with that rich undertone that seems calculated to drive men like me mad. Yes, I like it, I'm starving for it, starving like a mortal who's tasted fairy fruit and now can never eat anything else again.

Yes, I like her.

I like her too much. A worrying amount.

"You taste so sweet," I grind out as I pull back for a breath. "So fucking sweet. And you smell—" I bury my nose in her and breathe it in, which makes her squeeze her legs together in embarrassment. I let her, because it only accomplishes locking me in closer, tighter against her, and then I take my time smelling, deliberately running my nose along the outside folds and to the tip of her clit and then down between her cheeks, which makes her jolt in panic.

I place a firm hand on her tummy to keep her still, splaying my fingers so they can stroke her mound as I keep her pinned where I like. "Stay still for this," I tell her. "Stay still for me."

Her eyes are so hooded that I can see the shadows of her eyelashes on her cheeks and her chest heaves with short, needy breaths. Through the lavender silk of her bra, her nipples are plucked out into proud little points. "It feels so good," she whispers. "I just worry…I've never…"

"I know you've never. That's why I'm practically fucking the side of the couch while I smell you and stare at you."

Her lips part in an expression of undiluted lust. "Are you really?"

"Sit up on your elbows and look down at me."

She does, and I know what she sees—my body bent over the couch, my hips grinding mindlessly into the cushions.

"You're that horny?" she murmurs. "Because of me?"

"Because of you."

She blinks, as if she can't believe it, which is insane to me. Yes, the nun thing, but she's gorgeous and fascinating and smart and effortlessly captivating—surely she's had men desire her like this, crave her like this.

"Zenny, I've been stroking my cock all week thinking about you. Every day, I have to pull myself out and beat off, just so I can see straight. This pussy is all I've been thinking about for a week, and it's even prettier and tastier than I dreamed of. I want my fill of it."

"Okay."

"I want my fill of *you*."

A long shuddering exhale. "I think I want my fill of you too."

I give her a wicked grin. "That's the plan, isn't it?"

She smiles back, a smile that flickers into an adorable look of concentration as my finger probes her folds and slowly teases at the wet, soft border of her entrance. And then tenderly, carefully, I push in to the first knuckle, watching her face the entire time. She's so goddamn tight, so goddamn small, that even with all her wet coating me, the tip of my finger still feels like a huge invasion.

I have to swallow when I think about how she'll fit around my cock. She'll stretch around me, grip me, fit me tighter than a glove.

Jesus Christ. I'm about to blow inside my pants again.

"This is how I'll get you ready to take my body," I explain in a kind voice, trying to focus on what we're doing and THE PLAN, SEAN, THE FUCKING PLAN, which involves us going to bed together in a certain kind of way and does not involve me shoving my hand down my slacks and tugging on myself.

At least not at the moment.

I slide in to the second knuckle and watch her furrow her brow, as if she can't decide if it hurts or it feels good. "I'll stroke you from the inside, tickle you there and play with you, until you open up like a flower," I continue. "Until you feel how empty you are. Until it hurts more to have me on the outside of you than on the inside." I crook my finger up to press against that special spot on her front wall—I do it gently, gently, gently—and the light glints off her nose ring as she tosses her head back and forth.

"Sean," she says, and there's the first sparkle of sweat on her forehead and chest. "That feels...I..."

"Like you have to pee?"

"Yes," she says, throwing an arm over her face. "Oh my God, I'm so embarrassed."

I don't stop what I'm doing. "It's normal. Just let the feeling pass, darling. Ride it out. Ride it out on my fingers."

Her legs move around me, her bare toes squeezing and digging into my sofa, as I carefully work the inside of her, and then just as I see her belly relax and her body-panic transform back into pleasure, I lower my mouth and trace the point of my tongue over her stiffened clit.

"Oh," she breathes. "*Oh.*"

I alternate long licks and flickers of my tongue, my finger doing its work all the while and rubbing the inside of her wet little cunt, and then my skittish sort-of virgin starts panicking again.

"I—" she can't find words, but her body is fighting itself, seeking release and also scared of the immense wall of sensation roaring ever closer, and I decide she needs a little persuasion to get all the way there. I take the entire bead of her clit into my mouth and suck.

The response is immediate, gratifying, electric. Something like a keening whimper echoes off the stained concrete and glass of my apartment as her feet dig deeper into the sofa and she arches her body, her inner thighs and belly going taut as a drumskin. And then the first rolling wave hits her, sending my name out of her mouth like a prayer, sending images of stained glass and gold-stitched cloth through my mind, sending spasms and butterfly flutters around my finger and against my tongue as she comes for the first time with me.

It won't be the last. It won't even be the last time tonight.

I coax her through the final waves with my mouth and my finger, watching her gorgeous face over the rise of her pubic bone and the planes of her stomach, watching how her eyebrows pinch together in something almost like worry, how her lips work around silent words, how her eyes stare down at me in glazed wonder. And then with a final kiss on her clit, I straighten up and slide my finger out of her, sucking it into my mouth to lick it clean.

Her eyes widen a little, as if she's never imagined something quite so carnal as a man licking his fingers after touching a woman, and I smirk at her.

"I get a lot dirtier than that, darling. So buckle up."

CHAPTER FOURTEEN

Zenny stares hazily up at me, languid-limbed, redolent of sex, and in a stunningly lovely sprawl that I wish I could look at for the rest of my life; the way her legs are parted easily now, her well-pleasured cunt available to view. The slowing, sated breaths of a woman coming down from orgasm.

"How did you like being eaten, sweetheart?"

"I like it a lot," she murmurs. "Will you do it again, please?"

I laugh, pleased by her eagerness. "Any time you want. I believe I once promised you that I would show you how I can eat you from behind."

Her mouth twitches up in a smile. "You did promise that."

I'm on my knees at the edge of the sofa still, running soothing hands up and down her legs, trying to ignore my cock, which also wants a soothing hand up and down it. "How often do you masturbate?"

There goes that arm over her face again. "I don't know if I can talk about this."

I make a noise that would be called a scoff in a Wakefield novel. "Zenny Iverson, the girl who marched into this same apartment and demanded sex, is too shy to talk about masturbation?"

"It's different," she says into the crook of her elbow. "Completely different."

"It's all sex. And you might as well tell me about it before I make you do it in front of me."

The arm moves and she looks at me with a blend of intrigue and alarm. "People do that?"

"People have thirty-person orgies and fuck themselves with dildos shaped like Thor's hammer. I would think masturbating in front of a lover is one of the mildest things one can do."

That makes her smile again. "Am I your lover?"

"You're *mine*," I say simply, crawling up onto the couch and over her body.

"For a month," she corrects.

"For a month," I repeat. "Until you marry Jesus or whatever." Details, details.

I settle between her legs, groaning when my clothed erection makes contact with her mound and ducking my head down to nip at the tip of her breast before I slide my arms under her shoulders, prop up on my elbows and stare down at her. "Now. Tell me how you touch yourself when you're alone and how often you do it."

She turns her head away, but with me on top of her like this, there's no escaping my gaze, my words.

"Do you use a vibrator?" I ask her, dropping a kiss on the sharp line of her jaw. "Or your fingers? Or do you put a pillow between your legs and rub against it until you feel better?"

My words have the desired effect, making her redden faintly at the rounds of her cheeks and making her breath quicken. "I've never used a vibrator," she whispers. "But a pillow..."

"Yes?"

"And a stuffed animal...this teddy bear I got for my high school graduation. He's on my bed in my dorm room. Oh God, I can't believe I'm telling you this."

"I can't either. I'm going to beat myself raw thinking about this for years to come, darling. How do you use the teddy bear? On your side? Do you lay on your belly and grind on him from the top?"

"I straddle him," she says, closing her eyes, her face still turned away. "I put him between my legs and move on top of him while I'm on my knees."

"Shit," I groan, my face dropping to the rose-scented curve of her neck. The image of Zenny in her dorm room rubbing her needy pussy against a teddy bear is almost too much to hold in my mind. And I'm going to hell for imagining her in knee socks, surrounded by girlish posters, a barely matured girl overwhelmed with these big womanly needs...

"What?" she asks uncertainly. "Is that really fucked up?"

"It's really fucking hot is what it is," I mumble into her neck. "And I'm having a really hard time keeping it together right now."

"Really?" she asks, turning her head back to me. "That turns you on?"

I take her hand and guide it down to the indisputable evidence of my being turned on. "Feel for yourself."

Her slender hand traces my cock through my slacks, any clumsiness outweighed by her eager curiosity. "I've never..." she clears her throat. "That time with Isaac, I never really got to see him. I've never been able to see this part of a boy."

I give her a long kiss, parting her lips with my own and chasing the silky feel of her tongue until she's panting and twisting underneath me. Then I get up onto my knees. "You showed me your pussy," I say. "Now it's my turn to show you something."

She scrambles up to her elbows, excited. "Are you going to have sex with me now?"

Fuck, I wish. "Not yet, baby. We're still in Sex 101 right now—and intercourse is a senior thesis at the very

SIERRA SIMONE

least. Get on your knees in front of the couch."

Together we move, so that I'm standing directly in front of the couch and she's kneeling in front of me, peering up with these big schoolgirl eyes. She's sucking on one corner of her mouth, and I can just picture her in a classroom with this same expression—wide-eyed, concentrating, poised to raise her hand at any moment.

"Have you ever unbuckled a man's belt before?" I ask, already guessing the answer.

She shakes her head slowly. "No."

"Unbuckle my belt, Zenny. Leave it in the loops when you've finished."

If I thought she looked schoolgirl before, it's nothing compared to now, when her eyebrows pull together and her forehead wrinkles the tiniest bit in concentration. She reaches for me with the focus of a surgeon, visibly trying to steady her hands as she works at my buckle with precise, careful movements. And then she looks back up at me as she finally manages the glossy leather, as it slides through the metal with a distinct hiss.

It's the only sound in the room, followed by the muted clack of the buckle piece falling free to the side. It's such a familiar sound that my dick gives a Pavlovian lurch.

"Now you unzip me," I instruct. "And you take care with me as you do."

She does take care, my little honors student, her slender fingers parting the placket of my zipper, the worn

194

gold polish on her nails adding little flashes of color to the show as she finally manages to angle the slider down and tug it over the teeth of the zipper. The noise of it affects us both—it's a noise of promise, a sound so unmistakably sexual that even a nun recognizes it for what it is.

Then the zipper is down, and the placket parts under the weight of my heavy cock, still clad in the soft jersey of my boxer briefs. Her eyes flicker between my face and the Very Obviously a Penis outlined in my underwear. It throbs visibly under her attention, and her tongue darts out to lick at her lower lip.

I groan.

"Sweetheart, you can't look at me like that or I won't make it."

"Really?" she says, all curiosity and a little flattered smile. "Just from me looking?"

"With you, looking is as dangerous as fucking." I pause. "Well, nearly. Hands in your lap now."

"Okay," she whispers, and her breathless readiness nearly makes me breathless myself as I pull off my shirt in preparation to show her my cock. I toss the shirt onto a nearby chair, and I nearly have a heart attack when I turn back to her.

Little Miss I'm Too Embarrassed to Talk About Masturbating is now slanting sideways on her knees, searching for the right angle to grind her pussy against her heel, her eyes like hunger itself as they trace over the lines of my stomach and chest, over my bare arms and shoulders.

I run a slow hand down the ridges and furrows of my belly, and she whispers, "You're preening again," but there's no heat in it, no judgment, no injunction for me to stop.

"Hell yes, I'm preening," I tease. "I'll do whatever it takes to keep you looking at me like that." And I mean it; as a young man, I worked for this body because I craved the pride that came with it, I craved the admiration and the petting I earned from women delighted by my shape. But over the years, as with any kind of dopamine hit, the pleasure of being admired faded, and so I kept in shape for duller reasons. I was used to being in shape; staying in shape had become indelibly tangled with my daily routine; it seemed like at this point it would take an effort of its own to stop.

But my God. The way Zenny's looking at me now, stunned and rapacious, I remember how it felt the first time a girl ever looked at me. The first time I'd ever felt the bolt of lust that came from being wanted. I'm feeling it now like I did then, all this electricity and awareness skittering over my skin, which suddenly feels too tight to contain all the things I'm feeling. Too tight to contain my wanting her, which right now is as big as a prairie storm. Big as the prairie. Big as anything, certainly bigger than what my body can hold.

She reaches up tentatively, and I nod my head, yes, she can, she should, I'll make her if she doesn't, because now that she's reached for me, the thought of *not* having those curious fingers on me is close to pain.

"Touch me," I say. "Touch me. Touch me."

She touches me.

The moment her fingers—slightly cool and delicately shaped—whisper across my stomach, I nearly buckle. The touch zings through me, reverberates like music, up and down every nerve pathway I have.

All from her touching my stomach. God help me when she touches my cock.

"You're so hard," she says, a bit wonderingly, her hands sliding up to my chest. She has to lift her ass off her feet to reach my chest, and I can see the wet spot she left on her heel. Jesus.

In fact, I'm so distracted by her distraction over me that I forget to make a joke about the word *hard*, I forget to do anything but stare down at her while she probes and pets at every plane on my stomach, every line and band of muscle on my back. When she touches my back, she does it by sliding her arms around me, and despite my insistent erection, despite my simmering blood, the feeling of being held and embraced by her is almost more potent than anything else. I want her to hold me forever; I already hate the thought of not having her arms around me.

Her curious hands finally find the band of my boxer

briefs, shy at first with little strokes along the edge, then braver and braver as she starts sliding her fingers underneath the fabric. I let her find her own way, summon her own courage. Not out of laziness on my part, or even indulgent amusement (though I can't deny how heady that feeling is on its own, *indulgence*, the state of wanting this girl to have whatever she wants, of letting her take it; I'm dangerously close to wanting her to take everything). But honestly I'm doing it because I am suddenly just as nervous as she is, as excited, and also as scared of what lies over the horizon of my own nakedness.

Moving is impossible, coaxing her to any other pace is unthinkable. Any faster and my heart will beat itself right out of my chest in terrified lust; any slower and my blood will overheat with desperation and I'll die.

There's only going as she moves us, at this uneven virgin's pace, and I wouldn't have it any other way.

Finally, either courage or impatience (so often they are the same thing) takes hold of her, and I'm treated to the sight of her face as she peels down the front of my boxers. She's rapt, greedy—and then confused.

My erection has sprung free, bobbing down and then bobbing back up, throbbing, urgent, an angry red. I've been so hard for so long that the flared tip shines with pre-cum, and I've left a sizable smear of slick near my hip. The fresh influx of cool air across it nearly makes me shiver, and then I *do* shiver at the sight of her hands wrapped around the waistband of my underwear. But I have to laugh at her expression.

"Not what you expected?"

A glance up at me that I can't interpret, although if I had to, I might say it was somewhere between saucy and rueful—a look only Zenobia Iverson could pull off. "I don't know what I expected," she admits. "But it's so *bumpy*."

"I think the word you're looking for is big."

She rolls her eyes. I've got the prettiest sort-of virgin in the world on her knees in front of me, my dick in her face, and she's rolling her eyes. My ego wilts a little.

My cock doesn't mind though.

"No," she says slowly, "bumpy. Like here." She runs a gentle finger up the line of one vein on my shaft and I let out a wounded hiss.

She looks alarmed. "Did that hurt?"

"No," I manage. "Keep going."

The finger returns and starts tracing a maddening path around all the places I'm ridged and swollen. She draws a map of my veins, she navigates the sensitive shoals of my frenulum. She meanders around the crown and over the leaking slit at the top. Her fingers drop down to my root, circling the base to measure me, and I register a nice swell of masculine pride when I see the tips of her fingers and thumb can't meet around me—although the pride is still largely secondary to the feeling of her touching my cock because *holy fuck, she's touching my cock*.

SIERRA SIMONE

"I want to see all of you," she says, oblivious to the effect she's having on me. Her eyes are on my body, on my abs and my cock and the places where my open pants strain around the muscles of my hips and my ass, and I have to say, her seeing all of me sounds amazing, the best idea anyone's ever had.

"That can be arranged," I say, pulling her to her feet and leading her out of the living room and into my bedroom. I don't bother with lights out of habit, but Zenny flips them on and then gives me a shy smile when I glance back at her. "I need to be able to see," she says with a little shrug.

"Anything you like, darling." I wouldn't miss her exploring my body for the world. For seventy times seven worlds. And I am almost unbearably unworried about how infatuated I am with this girl—I've never felt like this about anyone else...but then again, I've never met someone like her before, so perhaps it's not shocking. Perhaps I'd been programmed at birth only to want this one person, and there's this tiny thing in my mind—not a thought, not even the seed of a thought, but like the frozen root of some dormant plant that might one day years from now drop a seed that can become a full-blown thought—that I can almost remember feeling this way about God once upon a time. That years ago, there used to be a Sean Bell that loved without restraint and reluctance and fear.

She reminds me.

I make to ease myself out of my pants, and Zenny helps me. I allow it, because there's no sweeter feeling than having an eager woman tearing at your clothes, and also the sweet clumsiness of it is both endearing and so fucking hot.

"Okay," she says matter-of-factly once we've finished and I'm naked. "On your back."

I comply, lacing my hands behind my head after I arrange myself, watching her move around the foot of the bed and take off her bra, which she drapes carefully over the footboard. She looks good here, naked in my room, the city lights moving in gleams and glitters across her skin as she walks past the windows and her hair trailing cascades of corkscrewed shadows across the floor and over my bed.

Then she crawls onto the bed and I forget everything else. There's only her, only her utter lack of artifice and complete ignorance of seduction as she moves to my side and then sits crisscross like a kid. Just her curious fingers and nervous sucking on the corner of her mouth and her avid gaze roving over me.

She pets my arms and caresses my stomach. She runs her hands along the swells of my thighs and chest. She asks me the names of the muscles hugging my ribs (serratus) and if I'm ticklish (yes, but only on the soles of my feet). She strokes down to the hyper-aware skin near my cock and she fondles my sac—not to stir me, but to weigh and to measure. And then when she sees how my body responds to being touched, she seems to make an experiment of it all. Silently measuring how much I twitch when she brushes up along my underside, how much I moan when she circles me, how much I gasp and seize when she slides that circle up the length of me.

I groan when she moves her attention elsewhere, but I'm grateful—beyond stamina and pride reasons, it feels just as good to have her exploring the rest of me. It's hot to see how new everything is to her—my feet and hands, for example, so much bigger than hers. Or the hair along my thighs and calves, rough and distinct against her silky legs. She spends what feels like hours running her fingers along my happy trail and I have to fist my hands in the covers to keep my back from arching off the bed; she rakes those chipped gold fingernails over the flat discs of my nipples and I have to grit my teeth and close my eyes to keep from grabbing her.

"Turn over," she whispers, and I do.

Hands roam up my thighs, over the tight muscles of my calves and down to my feet, where she discovers for herself that I didn't lie and am indeed ticklish. She finds the furrow of my spine, the broad spread of my shoulders, and the place at my nape where my hair threatens to curl when it's left too long without a trim.

Then I feel her straddle my thighs, bracing her hands on my hips as she does, and I make a noise into the bed. The extra weight pressing my cock between my body and the mattress is amazing, in the worst way.

Or it's terrible in the best way. I can't tell.

She runs both her hands up my back and then back down to the tops of my glutes, plumping them with those measuring, probing touches that seem calculated to drive me mad with lust. She squeezes my ass cheeks, scoots farther back on my thighs, and then does something that makes my toes curl.

She spreads my ass apart and sends a curious finger down the seam.

I make another noise into the bed.

"Are you okay?" she asks. "Should I not...?"

"No, no, you definitely should."

"Do you like having this part of you touched?" She's touching me again, this time swirling the pad of her finger along my rim. Sensation flares everywhere, and I feel fucking dirty, so fucking dirty.

"I don't know," I manage, my voice muffled by the blankets. I'm so hard I might die, and I'm consumed with the need to fuck. To come. "No one's ever touched me there before."

Zenny makes a studious kind of *hmm*, like she's my own personal anthropologist, the first person to discover and survey Sean Bell, and I can feel the strain of staying still everywhere in my body. I want to flip over and yank her to my chest, I want to crush my mouth to hers, I want to wrap her legs around my waist and push deep into that wet, sweet well between her legs.

"I can't believe no one's touched you here before," she says, a finger pushing against my entrance while her thumb strokes pensive strokes along my perineum. "You've had so much sex—how is that even possible?"

There's no way to describe to her how it comes to be that way. How the same three or four acts simply get put on a tired merry-go-round, made different only by the person you're with, and how the journey becomes tainted by the destination. I'm a generous lover by most accounts, but it's only because pussy gets me hot. It's a selfish thing, really, and all my sex is selfish. I've just justified it to myself by having sex with equally selfish people.

Anyway, I can't describe it because all my words are gone, they've been driven out by waves of painful need, and even if I could describe it, I wouldn't want to. I don't want Zenny to know how banal sex can be, I only want her to know sex as a revelation. As the kind of epiphany that rivals all religion.

But still I need to answer her, so I say in a joking voice—or as close to joking as I can get with my body on fire, "Oh, you know. People get bored and they just want it to be easy. Get it over with."

She doesn't joke back, her fingers trailing down my ass cheeks to rest on my thighs. "How could anyone ever get bored with this?" She's quietly incredulous. Faintly accusatory.

I assess the quiet wonder I feel at the warmth of her on my legs. I can't even see her, I'm not touching her with my hands, my cock is nowhere near her body, and yet this is the most profoundly sexual I've ever felt.

"I don't know," I finally say. "I don't know."

We continue in silence for a few more minutes, and I stay there, stretched and straining and still, all so she can pet and explore me, so she can satisfy her curiosity.

"On your back," she says after a while. "I want to see your…" a shy pause. "Your penis again."

I don't tease her for the Latinate language. I'm past teasing. I'm starving, I'm dying. I roll over and expose my aching cock to the cool air, and I know I said I wasn't going to let her make me come—and I meant it—but I just want her to touch it again. Just once, just a little bit.

"So when you're not…erect…it's not this big?" she asks. She's moved so that she's perched on her knees between my legs and her hands slide up my thighs to bracket my balls. Her thumbs meet in the tender place right below my testicles and my cock jolts like it's been hooked up to a car battery.

"No," I say, my voice so raspy it's barely a voice any longer.

"And then it gets—"

"Hard," I supply, trying to nudge her past the textbook terms.

"Then it gets hard," she soldiers on, "whenever you're turned on?"

"Yes. That's when it needs to fuck."

"And when you don't have anyone to fuck? What do you do?"

I show her by circling a hand over my cock and tugging upwards. Pleasure spears deep into my groin as I do, and I have to remind myself that I'm showing her, that she's exploring, that this is part of the plan, and I can't just jack myself right over the edge like I want to.

I go slowly, so she can see the places that send me squirming, so she can see the steady rhythm I like, the grip. And then there's the way she looks at me as I do it, her gaze hot on my tensed stomach and bunching biceps, on the swollen tip that emerges from the end of my fist over and over again.

"Can I try?" she asks in a voice both timid and inflamed, and my God, it's the sexiest thing I've ever heard, ever, ever, ever.

"Yes, baby. You can try."

I release my cock and watch her grip it, a bit uncertainly, stroking up with a hold too loose for any real friction.

But it's still too much. Her determined face, with its pouty mouth screwed up in concentration, which makes the piercing in her nose wiggle and glint as she wrinkles her nose. Her hair brushing the ends of her shoulders in uncountable dark spirals, her tits with their nipples in tight little beads, her ribs and stomach quivering with breathing she can't quite control.

I throw my arms over my face so I can't see her, because even her clumsiness is fucking hot, everything about her is so much, too much, and I should be worried, I should be terrified that she has this power over me, but I'm not, and maybe that's the scariest part of it all.

I let her experiment with rhythm and pace and tightness, I let her try stroking the lower part of the shaft and squeezing and caressing the head, I let her try whatever she wants and I just do my best to hold on, to keep my promise not to come at her touch.

It's fucking agony though.

Agony.

Finally she finds the killing zone, that sensitive underside right under my crown, and within seconds she has me arching and panting. When I dare to peek out from under my arms, I see her lower lip tucked into her teeth and her eyes glued to my steel-hard dick, fascinated. And her other hand rubbing idly at one breast, as if she can't stand not to touch herself as she's touching me, as if she doesn't even know she's doing it.

I'm going to come if she doesn't stop.

"Enough," I growl, sitting up and grabbing her fast enough to surprise her, to send a cute little squeak out of her mouth.

"But I want to see you come," she says from the cage of my arms. "You promised I could see you come."

She's too perfect not to kiss, so I kiss her. I drop my mouth to hers and I fuck her mouth with my tongue the way I want to fuck her pussy. "You'll see me come, princess," I murmur against her lips. "You will."

She's dazed by the kiss, melted and boneless in my arms, sharing breath with me, tentatively sliding her tongue against mine, her hands flexing and fisting at my bare chest like a kitten kneading her paws. "I want you to come now," she finally manages. "Now."

"One thing first." And if I enjoyed having this body because of the way Zenny looked at me before, I extra enjoy it now, being able to effortlessly move with her cradled in my arms, being able to drape her over the edge of the bed with her face down and her ass and cunt available for me to eat.

And then I show her the thing I promised on the night of the gala.

She squeaks again at the first lick—right up to the pleated aperture between her cheeks—and I have to band an arm over top of her hips to keep her still. She squirms and gasps, one of her legs kicking up at me in an instinctive move to hide herself.

"Sean," she pants. I can actually hear the scratches of her fingers against the covers. "It's…I'm…"

I know what she is. I stop eating her, running the tip of

my nose in the divot between her cheeks, very close to that entrance that she's embarrassed of. "Don't worry, darling."

"I know, but you can see everything like this," she protests, a hand reaching back as if to block me.

"I know, and I can smell and taste everything too. That's why I like it." I catch the hand and guide it to my hair instead. "Here. Whenever you think you can't bear it, you pull my hair instead of trying to pull away."

She gives my locks a gentle yank. "I don't want to hurt you."

"It would be worth it," I say and then lean forward again, letting her feel it all—the bump of my nose against her ass as I devour her cunt, the stubble of my jaw as I work, even the light scrapes of my teeth. It's messy and delicious and she's all over my lips and my face, she's on my tongue, she's the slick combination of sweet and salt and earth. She may be shy, embarrassed, inexperienced from her navel up, but down here, she is all woman. Her cunt knows what it needs, growing wetter and softer, her clit getting plumper like a little needy berry, and even as she still makes noises of flustered, uncertain pleasure, her hips grind back into my face and her legs spread more and more, letting me deeper, lower, letting me suckle on her clit. Her hand still snatches at my hair; like a good student, she's done as she's told and pulled on my hair whenever the surge of shame or awkwardness rolls over her. But the yanking has changed from the simple tugs on my hair to practically tearing at it to get me closer to her, to get my mouth on her harder, faster, more—

"More," she gasps. "Oh my God, more, more, more, *more...*"

Shit, I want to fuck her right now. Right here, bent over my bed, with her so wet and begging. I'd squeeze into that tight hole and show her how good it feels to come around a cock.

In fact, I even get so far as standing up before I remember myself, before I remember THE PLAN, SEAN, THE FUCKING PLAN, and instead I smooth a gentling hand up her back and press a single finger inside her. I easily find the spot that drove her so wild before, and I press down in massaging caresses that make her moan into the bed. I lean my body over hers, savoring the feel of her smooth legs against my hair-rough ones, the delicate wings of shoulder blades against my chest. The firm plumpness of her ass against my hips as I replace my finger with my thumb and start rubbing at her clit with my middle and pointer fingers together.

She cries out in jumbles and moans, she arches and bucks under my body, and it's so delicious, so very delicious, especially hearing my name in those jumbled noises, *sean oh sean oh God keep going keep going more more more sean more*—she's an ocean whipped into a restless froth, storming and pitching and nothing but a tempest ignic with lightning and electric tension. I kiss everywhere as I coax her over the edge; I bury my face in her curls and smell her hair, I nip at the nape of her neck, I drop my lips on her cheek and the shell of her ear and the edge of her jaw. And then as I kiss and suck on her neck, she comes underneath me, an ocean out of control, a tempest beyond reckoning. A noise tears out of her throat, something like keening, something delirious and violent and helpless all at once.

All her bucking and rocking under me has me in agony, not only because it's insanely hot, but because her ass is grinding hard against my cock. I can still smell and taste her, and her pussy is all flutters and clutches in that addictive way that pussies flutter and clutch when they're happy. And it takes a superhuman act of strength to keep from pressing harder against her ass and coming right then and there—screw chasing snakes out of Ireland and stigmata, this is an *actual* miracle, that I'm able to keep myself sewn together while Zenny rides out her joy on my hand.

By the time she's finished, she's utterly limp, goose bumps everywhere and a faint sparkle of sweat misting her forehead. Her eyes are closed and her breathing slowly evens out, and I take the opportunity to scoop her into my arms and crawl back onto the bed so that I'm sitting with my back against the headboard with her nestled snugly against my chest.

I kiss her head and leave my lips there because it feels

nice, because I want to kiss her forever, and she reaches up to trace idle shapes on my chest, eyes still shut. The lashes are long and thick and curved against her cheeks.

"It's your turn," she says sleepily.

"I'm fine, Zenny-bug." It's a lie, I'm dying, but I also feel like I might die if I have to stop holding her, so maybe it's not too much of a lie. I'd be content to stay here forever too.

She wrinkles her nose at the childhood nickname. "I'm not a kid anymore, you know."

"Oh, I'm aware."

She opens her eyes, her hand sliding over the bevel of my collarbone and up the corded length of my neck, and curving to fit the cut of my jaw. With her peering up at me with those copper-ringed eyes and her hand so warm and lovely-feeling against my face, I can't help but to want to taste her mouth again, and we kiss for a long moment before she sits up in my arms.

"Seriously, though," she says impatiently. "Your turn."

There's a moment when I almost feel guilty, but it dies as soon as it's born. Or rather, it dies the moment Zenny arranges herself at my left side and puts my right hand on my cock. I wrap an arm around her and snug her close, and she rests her head on my chest as she watches me fuck my own fist. There's something strangely erotic about having her cuddling me as she watches me beat off; it's different than the normal performance these acts usually turn into. It's intimate and real. Nothing but itself—which is frenzied, near-painful release.

Her fingers wander over my happy trail as I pull on my cock, she makes maddening little circles around the base and then down to my balls, which are drawn up so tight that it almost hurts.

"When you orgasm—"

"Say come," I say breathlessly, roughly.

"When you come," she corrects herself, looking up at me. "Where will it go? On your stomach? Your hand?"

My head falls back against the headboard in sheer defeat. She's too much, far too fucking much, sexy and innocent and daring—

"Watch," I say and with a grunt, several hours of need finally, finally erupts. My body breaks in half, every part of me from my toes to my chest to my thoughts twist into a knot and then snaps, and I'm there. *There.* Plummeting right into the abyss, static creeping at the edges of my vision and heat hooking deep into my groin and spilling out of me in thick, big ropes.

They shoot onto my stomach—hot, white splatters like paint, all across my abs and into my navel, catching like thick pearls in the hair leading down to my cock and finally spilling out onto my hand, and I keep beating myself through it all, a long groan tearing out of my chest as my balls drain and I'm blissfully wrung out to the last drop.

Until I'm empty and panting and completely, completely spent.

Zenny absentmindedly drags a finger through the mess on my stomach and lifts it to her mouth. My softening cock gives a painful throb as I watch her suck the finger clean.

She makes a cute little face. "It's bitter."

I laugh. "Yes, I think the general consensus is that cum tastes terrible. Usually people go to great lengths not to taste it."

A little shrug against my chest. "I don't want to miss any parts of you," she says. "Even the parts other women haven't wanted."

I don't answer that. I can't, because there's this sudden and unfamiliar tangle in my throat that keeps the words down. Instead, I pull her tight to my chest, and we stay there for a long time, quiet and sticky, all while I register the fact that I'm feeling things an old man like me has no right to feel about a young woman like her, and I'm not sure at all what to do about it.

CHAPTER FIFTEEN

"We should shower," I finally say, with no small amount of reluctance. "And then we can go to bed."

She stirs against me (I'm pretty sure she was nearly asleep or totally there) and her curls brush against my jaw in the most amazing way when she lifts her head to look at me. "You want me to stay the night?" she asks, like I just asked her to donate a kidney.

Bossy Sean rears his head. "You're not driving home this late. It's not safe."

Cue eye roll.

It's adorable, but I still playfully pinch her ass. "Hey, I'm serious. I don't feel good sending you out this late when I've got a perfectly good bed right here. And I'm an excellent snuggler."

"I drive home from the shelter this late all the time," she informs me. "And I live in some pretty sketchy dorms.

I can handle myself."

I swallow down my first seven reactions to this. "Sorry. Did you say sketchy? As in unsafe?"

She sighs. "Please don't be like my parents. It's perfectly safe if you know what you're doing."

I swallow down my next seven reactions. "Are you moving after you take your novice vows? After the semester ends?"

She nods. "It's why I wanted something cheap and small before. There's no point in me wasting money on a huge place I'm just going to leave. Plus I feel like it's good practice for living in the monastery, you know? Basic. Economical."

I come to a spontaneous and insane decision. "Stay with me."

"I guess class isn't *that* early tomorrow—"

"Not just tonight. For the month."

Zenny sits all the way up and faces me. "Pardon me?"

"Sleep here, study here, be here between the shelter and class." The more I talk about it, the better it feels. The more obvious it seems. "Think about it—you were worried about scheduling and finding time to be together before, and you want to see all the things you're going to miss— what's bigger than getting to live with someone? Sharing their bed all the time, eating with them, showering with them, seeing them always?"

She blinks at me slowly, her lashes going down and then up, her expression unreadable. "That's not...I mean, we don't—"

"You've known me literally your entire life, Zenny. You can't say we barely know each other, because it's not true. You can't say it's too soon because we only have a month." I take her hands in mine. "I want you here. Say you'll do it. Say you'll stay with me."

Her lips part, as if to speak, and then they close. "I have to think about it," she finally says.

"Are you tempted to say yes?" I ask, searching her face. "Do you want to?"

The sweet middle of her mouth wrinkles slightly as she holds back a smile. "I can't deny that there's a certain logic to it."

"Fuck logic," I say, because I am. Because it might make sense on paper, but even if it didn't, I'd still be begging her to move in with me. Because I want her, and the wanting her is sharper and bigger than anything else.

Because the idea of her leaving me tonight sends something clawing through my chest, and the idea of her leaving me every time we fuck leaves me in nothing but tatters.

Zenny seems to come to a decision. "Tonight. You can have tonight."

"And then?"

"I said you can have tonight, Sean. Then I'll think

about the rest."

"Meanie."

Her hand darts out, fast as a flash, and yanks a sizable chunk of my leg hair hard enough to make my eyes water. It's a childish move, and I respond in kind, flipping her onto her back and tickling her until her own eyes leak tears and her cheeks must hurt from laughing so hard.

I'm hard again, because of course I am, because I'm tickling and grappling with a supple, happy virgin, and I don't bother to hide my hardness from her as I lean down to kiss her. "Did you bring a change of clothes?" I ask. "You're more than welcome to wear my things, you know." And I have a vision of Zenny curled up on my couch in my sweatpants and my T-shirt…and then one of her wearing nothing but a single Charvet tie of mine…

"I did bring a bag," she says, and she says it like she's admitting something she doesn't want to admit. "I wasn't sure of the etiquette, and I wasn't even sure you'd say yes to this whole thing, but I thought it's better to be prepared, you know, just in case—"

I'm already dropping a kiss on her cheek and rolling off her to reach for my pants. "Is it in your car? Where are you parked?"

"In a visitor's spot in the building garage," she says, and I make a note to get her a parking pass for my building, along with her own set of keys. The happiness I feel at the idea of her having keys to my apartment is impossible to hide or handle with a cool expression, and I keep my head ducked down, so she can't see the carousel of near-giddy smiles as I try to wrestle back the unfamiliar sensations.

"I'll be back fast," I say and make an escape, grabbing her keys and going down to the garage as quickly as possible. And once I get to her car, I brace my hands on the hood and force myself to take several deep breaths.

I've lost my mind.

I've lost my mind and I haven't even fucked her yet.

I've lost my mind and I don't even care.

I realize I'm smiling like an idiot at the dented hood of a 2005 Hyundai Accent and I try to stop, but I can't. It's like whatever mechanism controls my mouth has stopped interfacing completely with my brain. And it's the same with my heart, which is hammering like I've just gotten done fucking, like I've just closed a huge deal, and all I've done is asked her to move in with me.

I'm not Mr. Brooding Romance like Tyler and I'm not Mr. Impulsive like Aiden, and the disconnect between the man I am with Zenny and the man I always thought I was is jarring. Jarring...and pleasant. One night in and I'm like a fucking convert to the Temple of Zenny.

But then there's the moment I unlock her car to find her bag and see all the shit piled in her backseat.

Boxes and bags, all neatly labeled with colorful Sharpie. *Baby clothes - Shelter*, says one box.

Pads/Tampons - Shelter. Used Paperbacks - Shelter. New Bras - Shelter. There's a bag of brand new stuffed animals from a local toy shop, the donation receipt tucked neatly inside. A bag of deodorant sticks and shampoo, also with a donation receipt inside. I must have known, vaguely, that shelters like Zenny's ran on these kinds of donations as much as they did monetary ones, but seeing this backseat full of what must have been hours of picking up and dropping off and phone calls and emails and glad-handing, I see the scale of Zenny's dedication to helping people in need. It's one thing to write a check here and there, but I know the shelter's budget from this whole Keegan fiasco, and I know they're operating on less than a shoestring.

There's twenty sticks of deodorant back there. How long does that last at a shelter like Zenny's? A few days? A week? How long does a box of infant formula last? Or giant box of toothpaste? The need is so huge, so vast and unending, and the shelter doesn't have the money to keep up, and so they must go pleading to businesses and other charities on behalf of their needy. They have to beg for the beggars.

This...this *work*, this thoughtfulness. This kind of relentless holding back of a tide of need...

It takes faith. Faith of a magnitude that is hard for me to comprehend.

When I grab the backpack out of the front seat, my smile is gone. I've remembered what I already knew but had conveniently forgotten in the rose-smell of her skin and the soft pout of her mouth, which is that I'll never be able to compete with her god. With her mission and vocation.

I'm losing my mind over her, but for Zenny, I'm merely a stop on the road to sainthood.

I'm quiet when I get upstairs, but Zenny is quiet too, giving me a small smile as she takes her backpack and disappears into the bathroom, shutting the door firmly behind her. After a few minutes, the shower starts running.

I spend a long moment with my fingers playing over the handle, my skin thrumming with the ache to be in the shower with her. I want her slippery skin, I want her eyelashes threaded with water droplets, and her body loose and warm against mine as I lick water from her lips and her collarbone and her neck…

But I also feel strange about the evidence of her indelible goodness in the car, strange because it makes me feel bad and selfish and clumsy, because it makes me worry that I was right all along and I'm dangerous for her, that I'm polluting her. And strange because I like her beyond all reason and she is the first woman to spin me up like this—and also the one woman I can't keep.

I also distantly recognize that she might need some space. We didn't fuck tonight, but we moved through a lot of firsts, not to mention candidly discussing things usually left unsaid. And I did manage to convince her to stay the night, so if she needs to shower alone to get her head on straight, it would be boorish of me to intrude.

I drop my hand from the handle and go clean up the kitchen.

Thirty minutes later, I'm also showered and I come out of the bathroom in a towel, brushing my teeth. Zenny's in a tank top and Winnie the Pooh sleep shorts and it looks like...like she's unfolding a pillowcase?

I squint at her, willing the scene to come together in some kind of logic, because I'm like ninety-nine percent sure I've got pillowcases. I'm not Suzy Homemaker or anything, but I have accomplished "pillowcase" level of adult. And they're really *nice* pillowcases too. I told my assistant to pick out something expensive, and he pretty much found the most expensive linens money can buy.

Oblivious to my presence, Zenny takes a pillow off the bed and gently wiggles it out of its pillowcase, replacing it with her own.

"What are you doing?" I ask through all the toothpaste, confused.

She turns to face me and looks down at the pillowcase in her hand. "It's a pillowcase from home. It's satin," she adds, as if that explains everything.

"Well, mine are Egyptian cotton," I say, using my toothbrush to gesture at the bed. "They're imported from Paris."

"Yes, but your Parisian pillowcases won't work for me." With a few deft shakes, she has the pillow neatly inside her satin case.

I squint at her again, very confused, and decide this is too complex to be a toothbrushing conversation. I go to spit, rinse and dry off my face, and then I come back out. "Should I buy new pillowcases?" I ask. "Did I buy bad ones?"

I get the sense that I'm missing something when she holds her pillow in front of her mouth to hide her smile. "No, I'm sure they're very nice pillowcases. But they'll dry out my hair."

Dry out her hair?

A slow-dawning horror washes over me. "Do they dry out *my* hair?" I try to surreptitiously catch my reflection in the decorative mirror behind her, wondering if my hair has been slowly drying out over the last year and everyone has been secretly judging me for it.

My vanity has Zenny outright giggling now. I walk up to her, still wearing nothing but a towel, and a low growl builds in my chest when her eyes rove all over my bared, still-wet chest and her smile grows shyer and also hungrier, in that Zenny way. I want to crush her to my chest and kiss that contradictory smile until we're both dizzy and panting.

"It's *my* hair," Zenny finally says, but she can't drag her eyes up from my abs. "Black girl hair. The satin keeps it from getting too dry or frizzy while I sleep. My guess is that all this noise is fine with the pillowcases you have."

All this noise means *my* hair, which she says as she runs her fingertips through the wet strands, tousling them over my forehead. Her pupils dilate as she watches drops of water roll over my cheekbones and down to drip off the line of my jaw.

My stirring cock is threatening to nudge off the towel currently tucked low around my hips, and I take a step closer to her, close enough that I could lean in and kiss her.

"But satin is better for wrinkles, for everybody, so really everyone should have a satin pillowcase," she says. "Or a silk one, but silk is more expensive. Although I guess you wouldn't mind that." I get the feeling that she's reaching for something to say right now, that she's very close to babbling nervously, which is very unlike Zenny.

Which means she probably is nervous.

Fuck.

This is so goddamn hard to figure out. Normally I wouldn't care if the woman about to climb into my bed was nervous—for one thing, I never have a woman crawling in my bed to stay the night, because my hospitality extends only to a shower and a car service home. (A gentleman always pays for the ride home—

224

remember that, ladies.)

For another thing, if I get the slightest wave of apprehension off a woman, it's game off, right away. I'm not interested in coaxing a reluctant woman to bed, for a host of ethical and I-don't-want-the-emotional-aftermath reasons. And I'm not interested in being with a woman who's only pretending to have a good time.

I can do all that because I don't normally care about the women coming in and out of my bed; I can find a new one who's enthusiastically consenting before we even finish our appetizers. But I *do* care about Zenny, which means I care about whatever is upsetting her, and I'm going to make it better.

Trusting that she'll call me an asshole if I push her too hard, I scoop her up and toss her gently onto the bed, crawling in after her once I drop my towel. Her eyes are glued to the erection swinging heavy and dark between my legs, and I take my time reaching for the light switch and turning it off. Then I gather her to my chest and simply hold her, ignoring the throbbing bar of heat pressed against her warm thigh.

At first, she's tense. Rigid and holding herself still, breathing carefully, like her tent is being circled by a bad-tempered grizzly ready to maul her for her empty potato chip bag.

But slowly, slowly, as the dark settles into a hazy golden glimmer of city lights through the window, she

SIERRA SIMONE

relaxes against me. Her breathing goes even and easy, and her hands tentatively find places against my shoulder and chest.

"Everything okay?" I ask quietly.

"Yes," she answers. It doesn't feel like the entire answer, though.

"Honest girl thing?"

"Honest girl thing."

I stroke her arm, long sweeping strokes just so I can feel her skin again. "You're not going to scare me off, Zenny-bug. I'm not going anywhere." *Ever* is the next word I want to say.

I don't say it.

"I guess—" She clears her throat, plucks at the sheet. "I thought you were going to have sex with me tonight. Like we'd climb into bed, and that would be it. And I was ready for it, but I suddenly felt so stupid and immature. As if you'd want to fuck me in my Winnie the Pooh pajamas, and maybe you'd even changed your mind after we'd done all that tonight, maybe I'd done something wrong or I tasted bad or I should have—"

I silence her with a kiss. A long one.

"I'll prove you don't taste bad right now," I murmur against her lips. "I'll spend the entire night with my mouth on your cunt."

"But—"

"Do you honestly think there's anything you can do to

make me *not* desperate to fuck you? I practically came as you told me about your teddy bear friend. I'm dying to fuck you in your little college-girl pajamas, I want to fuck you in your dorm room, I want you clumsy and new and inexperienced. I want you as you are, Zenny, and one of the things you are is young. I'm going to hell for it, but that's the way it is."

"Oh," is all she says. But I think it's a good *oh* because she's currently rubbing her pussy against my thigh like a needy cat. I don't even think she knows she's doing it.

I'm not going to survive this, I think. It's Night One, and I'm already about to have a heart attack from how fucking sexy she is.

I continue. "We're waiting to fuck because you're mine—"

"But only for a month—"

I growl at her words, and she shushes…and then rubs herself against me harder.

"Because you're mine," I repeat firmly. "And because you're mine, I want to take my time with you."

"That's what you would do if this were real?"

If this were real…already I'm hating every single reminder of what this is. Project Doubt. A stop on the road to thoroughly interrogated sacrifice. "Isn't it still real?" I ask, and I hope with everything I am that she doesn't hear the vulnerability in my voice.

Her hand finds mine in the dark. "It's real enough."

"Then you're mine, Zenny-bug. And we'll do as I say."

"Okay," she whispers. "I trust you."

And I decide that's wholly enough talking for now. I disappear under the sheets and take care of the part of her she'd been so cutely rubbing against my leg, and afterwards, I hold her until she falls asleep, a newfound contentment staggering around on coltish, weak legs inside my chest until I too fall off into slumber.

CHAPTER
SIXTEEN

"This is ridiculous," Zenny says. "And bad for the environment."

It's the next morning and I'm driving Zenny to class. I glance over at her, eyebrow raised. "I know you're not referring to my beautiful German car."

"I'm referring to this insane plan of you driving me to class and having someone drive my car down to my dorm room parking lot for me...*after* you have them drop off those supplies at the shelter."

"I was running out of things for my assistant to do anyway."

She sighs, but when I sneak another glance, I see the reflection of the smile she's fighting off in the window.

I don't bother to fight off my own smile.

"We decided it's real, remember? This is what happens when it's real. I don't want to be away from you a minute more than I fucking have to."

Now she can't hide her smile, although she keeps her head ducked away. "You're ridiculous," she repeats.

"I am. And you know what you are?"

"What is that?"

"Mine, Zenny-bug. All mine."

Now she looks at me, her eyes more copper than usual in the August morning light. "Yes," she says softly. "I am that."

This morning, we woke up and made out for a solid forty-five minutes, grinding like teenagers until she came against my thigh. And then she watched me with huge, sleepy eyes as I peeled off her fuzzy pajama shorts, wrapped them around my fist, and fucked my aching cock into them. After I shot thick ropes of ejaculate all over Winnie the Pooh and his hunny pot, she begged me to put my fingers inside of her, and she came like a champ after only a minute.

And then with my fingers still coated in her, I handed her a pen and paper and sternly ordered her to write down her schedule, along with a list of what she needed from her dorm room so she could stay the month with me.

"You're being bossy again, aren't you?" she'd said as she'd taken the pen. She was naked from the waist down, her nipples hard and her thighs quivering from her last orgasm.

"Would you like to call me an asshole right now?

Would you like me to stop? I will the moment you say so, darling."

She'd shaken her head, her expression full of disbelief. "God help me for saying it, but keep going, Sean. I like it. And consider me your new roommate."

Even Charles Northcutt sitting in my office when I walk in can't ruin my mood, although it gets pretty fucking close. I *really* hate him.

"Happy Friday," he says. He's sitting behind *my* desk, just to be a jackass. "I just wanted to let you know that my assistant heard from Trent that you were sniffing around my schedule."

Goddammit, Trent. Loose lips sink ships.

Northcutt gives me the kind of smile I imagine a logging executive gives a stand of redwoods before ordering them sawed down. "That wouldn't have anything to do with a pretty little nun, now would it?"

I drop my leather satchel on the short client sofa across from my desk and then walk over to Northcutt. "You're in my seat," I say calmly.

"Valdman already put me in charge of the nuns, Sean. You can't control that."

I regret ever showing him an ounce of interest in the

sisters; it's the only reason he wants to work with them, with Zenny. Just to fuck with me. Just to prove that I'm not made of the right stuff to sit in Valdman's office after he retires from day-to-day.

"You're in my seat," I repeat, and into my voice, I pour every schoolyard match, every drunken Irish boy brawl, every fight I've ever won. Northcutt is the kind of man who thinks holding someone's head down a toilet in fourth grade has acquitted him as some kind of badass, and I would welcome the chance to show him his mistake by smashing his teeth in.

Unfortunately, Northcutt seems to sense I'm past the point of playing, and he gets out of my seat.

"I'll let you know how my meeting goes with them next week."

"You're not meeting with them next week," I say through gritted teeth.

"It's not up to you," he answers with an evil smile, and finally leaves me the fuck alone.

I stare at my hands for several minutes afterward, willing them to unclench, and then once they do, I shoot off a quick email to Valdman, asking him if he got my earlier message about Northcutt and the Keegan deal, and then I calm down by sending my assistant an email asking him to buy five or six sets of satin sheets by tonight. All that taken care of, I finally get to work.

The day passes quickly, although I'm beginning to feel Zenny's absence like a palpable thing, physical and awful. But I've got several contracts, memos, and client calls to catch up on, plus several returned inquiries for new shelter properties, and by the end of the day, I've done a hell of a lot and I'm ready to drive to the shelter and scoop up my sort-of virgin and bring her home where I can spend the evening with my face between her legs.

Sadly, she won't be done with her shift at the shelter until after ten o'clock tonight, so instead I gather my things and drive to Mom and Dad's house in Brookside.

The family house is a modest cream-colored Colonial from the 1920s with sage-green shutters and a giant oak tree in the front yard. The shutters have changed colors at least eight times in my life; the tree has changed not at all. It's not a big house—at least it never felt big with five of us Bell kids jostling for space inside—but it's well maintained and it's got all the stuff people like in older houses—the wood floors and big staircases and big fireplaces. So obviously, a plumber and a social worker could never have afforded it on their own. It came to my parents after my father's mom passed away when I was a baby, and it never escaped my notice as a kid that my parents felt slightly illat-ease in the upper-middle-class neighborhood.

Even now, at thirty-six and several years after acquiring some substantial wealth, I can't suppress my habitual satisfaction at driving to their house in my R8, at pulling into the driveway that I paid to replace, seeing the fresh siding and roofing that I pay to maintain. For so long, the Bells were the poorest family in the neighborhood, but now Mom has the kitchen of her dreams and my father has the best television money can buy to nap in front of. And maybe it makes me a materialistic dick that I noticed being poorer than my peers growing up, maybe it makes me a dick that I still care now, but making enough for Mom and Dad to never worry about money again is the best fucking feeling in the world and I refuse to give it up.

I pull into the driveway, averting my eyes from the garage out of habit as I walk to the front door and let myself inside. Dad doesn't seem to be home yet, but Mom is in the kitchen, slowly putting away dishes, pausing between each and every plate to catch her breath.

Seeing her like this is like hitting a funny bone but everywhere in my body—my chest and my throat and even my hands ache with anger and frustration and stupid, terrible grief.

Carolyn Bell used to be the definition of energy, of smiles, of *doing*, a whirlwind of dimples and dark hair and sharp wit. She was the mom that made other moms feel inferior and ungenerous with how much she gave of her time: she worked, she volunteered, she was the Girl Scout Troop Leader and the Boy Scout Den Leader, she babysat and shuttled any and all nearby kids to games and meetings and slumber parties. She read voraciously, she adored throwing parties, she loved my dad like he was still the same nineteen-year-old boy who swept her off her feet. Growing up, I thought she was the most beautiful woman in the world.

I still do, although now she's tied with Zenny for the honor.

"Mom, let me help," I say, shooing her away from the dishwasher, and I'm irritable. I'm irritable because I'm upset, and I'm upset because she's dying, and she's dying because I haven't found a way to fix her yet.

I slam the rack back a little bit too hard and my mother winces. "Sean. I can do it."

"I wish you'd let me get you more help around the house. It's really not—"

"It's not about the money, sweetheart," she says gently, putting a hand on my arm. When I look down at it, it's dry and trembling and the back of it is mottled with blood-draw bruises. "I like to feel useful still. Normal."

"You need to focus on getting well," I say. "You need to rest."

"All I do is rest," she says, dropping her hand. "It gets stale, you know. Doing nothing."

There's no arguing with her when she's made up her mind, so I redirect the conversation. "At least let me empty the dishwasher. Can you make me a cup of coffee while I do it?"

"Oh, of course," she says, and there's relief all over her tired face at being asked to do something real and useful. "Coming right up. Sure you don't want a Mountain Dew instead?"

I make a face. It's my mother's elixir of youth—the beverage that powered her nonstop working-mom-perpetual-volunteer lifestyle for all the years I've been alive. But I can't stand it.

I finish the dishes and together we take our drinks into the living room, where Mom's got HGTV on. She sits in her recliner in the corner, a corner that's become something of a cancer nest of heating pads and giant hospital cups and fuzzy blankets. I help her get into her nest, tucking a blanket around her feet and making sure she's got the remote nearby and her cold Mountain Dew within reach.

A fresh romance paperback is on the end table, and out of habit, I tilt it toward me to see if it's one I've already read or one I'll have to steal from Mom once she's finished, but the movement sends something hard and small sliding off the end table. A pile of beads.

A rosary.

I blink down at the thing, the crucifix shining against

the matte leather of my shoe, the beads in a familiar curled pile by my sole. I blink like I've never seen a fucking rosary before, but I have. I've seen them too many times, but why is one here on my shoe, why did it fall off Mom's table, why was it near her chair like she's been using it?

I look up at her, and her too-wide mouth pulls into a sad smile. "Sean."

"What's this?" I say, which is a stupid question because I know what it *is*. What I mean is why does she have it, why does she need it? She doesn't need some fake god, she has me, *me*, her oldest son who's been moving fucking heaven and earth to get her the best treatment money can buy.

"Sean," she says again. "Sit down. You're shaking."

I don't listen at first, and I bend down to pick up the rosary. I pick it up like I expect it to sizzle against my skin like acid or bite at me with an electric shock, but it does neither. It's just an inert pile of cheap metal chain and glass beads. It's not alive, it's not magic. It's nothing but an object.

So why am I still shaking when I stand up? Why don't I let it go as I sit down on the couch next to Mom's chair?

"You said," I say carefully, trying to keep my voice even, "when all this started, you said you didn't need God. You said you didn't want him around, and you didn't want to be like every other cancer patient who got super religious in the face of death. You *said those words*." I

SIERRA SIMONE

realize I'm accusing her now, my fist clenched around the rosary beads, and the fist is clenched in anger, but when I look down, it looks like I'm holding the beads in fervent prayer. It's a jarring sight.

"I changed my mind," Mom says simply, like that's all there is to it, like there's not a window behind her that looks out onto a haunted garage where my sister killed herself.

"You changed your mind," I repeat, incredulously. "*You changed your mind?*"

Anger flashes through her eyes, the quick Irish temper that she gave all her boys. "I have a right to that, Sean," she says in a sharp voice. "I'm the one dying. Not you."

I clench the rosary even tighter because I can't snap back at her, not after she's played the cancer card. "But why?" I say, betrayed. "I thought we were in this together. I thought we felt the same way."

She reaches over and puts her bruise-splotched hand over mine. "I'm still furious with God over what happened to Lizzy. But I realized being furious with Him was not the same thing as wanting Him out of my life."

"God isn't real," I whisper, searching her eyes. "None of it's real. How can that comfort you at all right now? How can you want to hold on to make-believe?"

She's shaking her head. "That's not…" She sighs. "This is my fault."

"What is?" I ask, feeling now doubly irritated at this

238

betrayal and at the idea that I'm making her feel guilty. I don't want her to feel guilty, I just want her to explain herself, explain *why*, after all this time and after what He's done, she thinks God deserves her attention.

"Your anger. Your hurt. After Lizzy's death, your father just shut down about it and everything around it. It's what he had to do to survive. But I never could hide my anger and my pain, not after her death and not when Tyler took his vows..." She looks away from me. "I worry sometimes that you came to your beliefs not because you genuinely believe them, but because you were young and in pain, and you saw your family in pain too. And you closed the ranks of your heart more out of some kind of tribal loyalty than out of personal conviction."

"That's not true."

She tilts her head, still looking at the floor. "Maybe not. But the reason it scares me is that I would never ask you to reconfigure your beliefs to fit mine."

"I know."

"So then please don't ask me to do the same for you," she murmurs, looking up at me and squeezing weakly over my hand.

What can I say to that?

Nothing.

Nothing at all.

CHAPTER SEVENTEEN

"Why do you believe in God?" I ask as I get into my car. We're at the curb in front of the shelter; I'm picking Zenny up at the end of her shift, and I've just kissed her senseless and then helped her into the passenger seat.

She drops her backpack with a thump on the floorboard and twists to buckle her seatbelt. "I see you're not wasting any time in challenging me." Her voice is mild, a little wry maybe, but when I look over at her, I immediately feel like shit. She looks fucking exhausted, and she smells like cheap tomato sauce and infant formula. The lumpy backpack between her feet is clearly stuffed with textbooks and there are dark smudges under her eyes that speak to how late I kept her up last night.

My dick fusses at me, but I decide the minute we get home that I'm tucking her into bed.

"That was thoughtless of me," I admit, starting the car

and heading the handful of skyscraper-filled blocks home. "I had a weird conversation with my mom tonight, and it's fucking with my head. But that's not an excuse."

"The conversation was about God?"

"Yes. I found a rosary on her table, and I just…" A tight anger fuses in the knob of my throat. I feel like a parent discovering a bag of meth in a teenager's room. "How could she?" I burst out. "After what happened to us? After what happened to her only daughter?"

Zenny's quiet for a moment, leaving us with the echoes of my outburst. I try to swallow it down, I try to reel everything back in, but I can't, I can't, I can't.

"How do you think she could?" she finally asks.

"I—wait, what?"

"You asked a rhetorical question, and I'm asking the same question, only not rhetorical. Place yourself in her shoes, with her memories and her life, and then ask yourself how she could pray the rosary again."

"The thing is that I don't *know*," I say, frustrated. "How can she forgive God for letting that happen? Lizzy loved God *so fucking much* before she—" I stop, full of the same wounded anger I felt the day after her funeral, when Tyler and I got into my car and her stupid Britney Spears CD had started playing. Neither of us had realized she'd been the last one to drive it, and we'd crawled in—me drunk as fuck and Tyler hung over—and then we'd heard it. The music that Lizzy had loved, had sung badly in the shower, had saved up babysitting money so she could go hear live in concert—it came spilling out of the radio at full volume, and I'd lost it. Just lost it, like a fucking maniac, kicking the shit out of my dash until I'd finally smashed something crucial and made the music stop.

I still can't listen to Britney Spears. Not without that memory howling up inside me. Not without feeling like I want to tear apart the world with my bare hands.

My baby sister. My annoying, funny, nosy, and earnest baby sister. Gone.

All these years later and it still won't stop fucking hurting. And it's God's fault.

"There's a story Elie Wiesel tells," Zenny says, and her voice anchors me back, away from the screaming drunk boy and to the man I am today, and I feel my chest loosen the tiniest bit, my hands relax on the steering wheel. I can breathe again.

"It's about the Holocaust," she continues. "Wiesel says in Auschwitz a group of rabbis decided to put God on trial. They charged God with crimes against His creation, and it became a real court, a real case. They found witnesses. They presented evidence."

In the distance, lightning stitches across the sky and wind buffets the car. There's going to be a storm. And still I find myself settling, easing to the sound of Zenny's rich alto, to her story.

"The trial lasts several nights," she says, "and at the

end of it, they find God guilty."

"Good," I mutter, as the first drops of rain splatter the windshield.

God *is* guilty. God deserved this trial.

"And then do you know what the rabbis do next?" Zenny asks, gathering her backpack into her lap as I pull into my parking garage.

"What do they do?"

"They pray."

I park, turn the car off. And then I turn to look at her.

"They find God guilty and then they pray," she says again, her eyes and her voice and her *everything* soft and full of something I don't understand. But it reminds me of the way I used to feel as a child, falling asleep as a music box chimed the notes of "Jesus Loves Me."

"What are you trying to tell me?" I ask.

"Just that you can do both, Sean. You can do both."

There is some fuss regarding my bossiness about bedtime—Zenny wants to play our new bedroom games and pouts so magnificently after I order her to ready herself for sleep that I almost reconsider—but I only have to look at the exhaustion around her eyes to remember to hold my ground. I ask her, as always, if now is the time she'd like to declare me an asshole and have me back off, but she shakes her head with a huff and stomps off to the bathroom to brush her teeth. But I know I've done the right thing when she's swaying on her feet while she waits for me to get ready.

"Get in bed," I say after I rinse my mouth. "I'll be right after you."

She zombie-shuffles into the bedroom and then I hear a sleepy, happy squeal from her.

"Satin sheets?"

"And satin pillowcases," I say, changing into a pair of drawstring pants that hang off my hips. She's not so tired that her eyes don't gobble up the sight of my bared torso and hips—and again, I almost reconsider Plan Tucking Zenny Into Bed. But her health is more important than fun, and I climb into bed myself to set a good example. She looks disappointed, but the moment I flip off the lights and gather her into my chest, she turns into a sprawl of tired, heavy limbs.

"I can't believe you got new sheets for me," she says.

"I'd get new anything for you, Zenny-bug. New everything."

"Sometimes you are just too smooth," she says and I know there's got to be a smile on her face from the tone of her voice. "But it works somehow."

"All part of the Sean Bell charm, I assure you."

Her hair tickles against me as she nods, and I stroke

her arm until I feel her breathing relax and drop into a steady rhythm.

"Theodicy," she murmurs dozily.

"Um. What?"

"It's called theodicy. When people try to explain how God can still be good when bad things happen."

"Oh. Okay?"

Her lips press against my chest in the sleepiest kiss ever and then she rolls over onto her pillow, wriggling backward into the cradle of my body. Despite the serious God talk, my cock surges happily against her.

"Some people think it's a bad idea, trying to justify God's goodness, because it distracts us from what's important. It tangles us up in intellectual knots, when intellection isn't the point. We have philosophy for that. Religion is for ritual, for practice. For moral action."

"So it's more important to pray than to figure out God? That seems backward to me. How can you pray to something you don't understand? To something that might not be *good?*"

"*Credo ut intelligam,*" Zenny says. "It means: I believe so that I may understand. But *believe* is a tricky word in English, and so the meaning of the phrase has gotten slanted over time. The Latin *credo* came from *cor dare*—to give one's heart. What St. Anselm was saying was not 'assent blindly and uncritically to these intellectual positions about a deity,' but rather that the intellectual positions were less important than the practice of living a moral life or a spiritual life. He was saying, 'I commit so that I may understand.' Or 'I engage with this because it is the kind of thing that can only be understood by engaging with it.'"

I turn this over in my mind.

"Your mother is like St. Anselm," Zenny goes on after a short, cute yawn. "She's willing to engage in a spiritual practice while coexisting with a host of complicated ethical and metaphysical questions. A comfort with doubt concurrent with a commitment to living a spiritual life— that's amazing."

It occurs to me that it's Zenny's goal to live like that. That somehow in the midst of tragedy and impending death, my mom has found a relationship with faith that could make even a nun envious.

It's a curious thought.

"Tyler's middle name is Anselm," I say, apropos of basically nothing, but I don't have any response to her insights. She's too smart and I'm still too close to the howling boy kicking his car open in a fit of drunken pain.

"See then?" Zenny murmurs, and I know she's very close to sleep now. "I bet she already knows all this."

I snug my little nun in close and stare at the lights outside as she sleeps in a temptingly sweet burrow against me. I think about God on trial and my mother's rosary until my thoughts blend into unhappy dreams, dreams I can't remember when I wake the next morning.

It's a Saturday, and Zenny has a clinical rotation today—her first—and she has to stop by the shelter afterwards to help with dinner. I practically gnash my teeth in frustration, because after being so twisted up over God and Mom last night and after my (very noble and very stupid) insistence on sleep instead of play last night, my cock is approximately the hardness of a carbon dwarf star, and the gravity of its need is insane. My thoughts, my hand, everything feels like it's pulling toward my aching organ, and I just want to fuck it all away, I want to ride Zenny until my chest stops hurting and my thoughts are clear again.

But I won't, not even when I get her back tonight, because of the plan. The stupid fucking plan that I can't let go of. Although as much as I'd like to fuck her, I am pretty excited about tonight.

We're going on a date.

I have to call in a favor from Aiden (sigh), but even that can't dampen my excitement as I get everything ready.

"Sixty dollars," Aiden's saying as I finish up a few odds and ends in my home office before I get Zenny from the shelter.

"*Sixty*? Are you insane?"

"Oh, like you're not good for it," Aiden says dismissively. "And are you going to tell me who this girl is or what?"

I think for a minute. Aiden's not exactly what I would label "trustworthy." Once, right after college, he promised to help me move a couch into my apartment, and then moved to Belize the next day. (He came back a month later with a sunburn, a fresh hatred of tequila, and a vague story about a girl named Jessica.) Last year, I spent God knows how many hours touring lofts and condos with him, examining minute differences between exposed brick and stained concrete, and then he up and bought a creaky farmhouse in the middle of nowhere without a word.

The nice word for Aiden is *spontaneous* and the less nice word is *flaky*, and either way I slice it, I'm not sure that I can trust him with a secret like this. For all I know, he'll meet another Jessica and somehow end up at the Vatican telling the Pope about Zenny and me.

But also I have this adolescent need to talk about her. I want someone else to know how fucking smart she is, how fucking pretty, how fucking sweet and tart all at once. I want to talk about her contradictions and her layers, I want to talk about the things she dredges up inside me—these old sensory glimpses of churches and rituals—about the version of Sean I remember when I'm around her.

I want to talk about how much I want her, how much I

need her, and how much that doesn't scare me.

"It's Zenny Iverson," I say quickly before I can change my mind. "Zenobia. Elijah's sister."

A silence yawns on the other end.

"Aiden? You still there?"

He doesn't answer right away, but when he does, his voice is strangled. "Elijah's sister?"

"Yes."

"The nun?"

How does he know about that when even I, Elijah's best friend, didn't? "It's a long story," I say.

"You're taking a nun on a date," Aiden says, as if he's a teacher laying out a remedial logic problem for a student to solve. "You're dating a nun."

"Not...*exactly*," I hedge. "It's complicated."

"Oh my God," Aiden says. "Elijah's going to kill you."

"Elijah is not going to know," I say firmly. "Because Zenny and I won't tell him."

"But—" Aiden makes a fretting noise.

"There's no buts, man. It's not like *you're* going to see him to tell him, and no one else is going to tell him, and it's going to be fine."

Aiden is still making agitated sputters.

"And anyway, we should be talking about you. I notice you haven't been raiding my fridge the past few days; I wondered if you'd died or something."

"I'm just busy," he says, and there's a note of evasion

in his voice. But with Aiden, evasion is sometimes par for the course. He's Belize Boy, after all.

"Okay, fine. I won't pry. Just tell me if you're dating a nun too."

That earns me a laugh. "I'm not as bonkers as you."

"Yet," I warn, and I do mean it as a joke, but it does come out with a prophetic sort of ring and hangs in the air as we finish making plans for tonight and wrap up the call.

CHAPTER EIGHTEEN

"Where are we going?" Zenny asks. "And why is there sixty dollars tucked into your console?"

"You'll see. And there's sixty dollars because it's a fancy date, Zenny-bug." I'm kidding, obviously, because I could easily spend tens of thousands of dollars on a single night with her—and I considered it, I really did. I thought about whisking her away to St. Bart's or Paris or the Seychelles, but somehow I knew that wouldn't impress her.

And I do want to impress her. Or more accurately, I want her to have *fun*, I want her to be happy, I want her to feel what it's like not to have the world on her shoulders. I want to see her smile and laugh. I want tonight to belong to her, not to her nursing degree, not to her shelter, not to her family's subverted expectations. Nothing gets to claim her tonight but laughter and bad pizza.

Zenny misses the humor in my tone though, because

she rubs her hands uncomfortably on her jeans. "Should I change?"

I glance pointedly down at my own clothes—jeans and an artfully rumpled button-down. "You're dressed perfectly."

"Okay," she says, and then makes a noise that is somewhere between nervousness and self-deprecation at said nervousness. "Between the new nursing scrubs and the jumper, sometimes I feel like I forget how to dress for the real world. Not that I know *where* we're going in the real world," she adds pointedly.

I don't take the bait. It's going to be a fucking surprise. I shift gears as we merge onto the interstate south, and then I ask, "So you'll wear the habit all the time after your vows, but you don't have to wear the postulant's uniform all the time now?"

Zenny leans back against the headrest and props her sneakers up on the dash. It's such a young thing to do, such a *college* thing to do, and it makes me smile.

"Every order has their own rules about dress," she says, not seeing my smile. "With SGS, when and where the postulant wears her uniform is determined between the postulant and the prioress. In my case, the Reverend Mother wants me in street clothes more often than not, because she's concerned about my youth. We agreed on the shelter and at monastery events, and that's it for me.

But I've seen some postulants wear their uniforms all the time."

I think about this for a minute. Come to some important conclusions. "I still want to fuck you in your postulant's uniform."

This earns me a lip bite and a very studious examination of her sneakers. "Okay," she murmurs, and I don't miss the way she squirms in her seat.

My smile gets bigger.

On the way to our date, Zenny guesses all sorts of places we could be going, all of them wrong. She guesses restaurants and movies—which I scoff at like a cynical Wakefield pirate—and then suggests other things I almost wish I'd thought of, like the arboretum or the local improv club. But no—we're going to a place less classy and far more juvenile than an improv club, and I tell her that, which puzzles her for a long time.

I finally exit the highway on one of those indiscriminate suburban exits, the kind that have a hotel for no reason and a McDonalds and a chiropractor's office, and navigate a few turns to our destination. Then I park the car and turn to face her.

"Well?" I say.

She gives me one of those Hollywood starlet eyebrows. "Are you actually taking me to a skating rink?"

"Yes, I am, Zenny-bug. Your skates are in the trunk," I say as I grab my things and open my door.

"Wait…my skates? I don't have any…" she trails off as she follows me outside the car to the trunk and sees that she does, indeed, have a pair of skates.

"I didn't want to take a chance on them not having rental skates available," I explain as I lift our things out of the trunk and shut it. "So I noted your shoe size and had my assistant order some skates."

She stares at me a moment and then shakes her head in incredulity. Her face is crinkling up into an amused smile, however, so I know I'm not in too much trouble.

"Okay, rich boy," she says.

"This is *not* a rich-boy date," I protest, offended. "This is exactly the kind of normal date normal people go on."

She laughs. "With their custom-ordered skates and their Audi R8 parked outside?"

"Well, I'm not going to compromise on *everything*."

She tucks an arm into my elbow, glowing up at me. "I have to admit, this is exactly the kind of date I'd want to go on if this were real. Let's do it."

And we go inside, pay our six-dollar admission fees, and stroll into the dimly lit, badly carpeted lobby. Top-forty pop music blares awkwardly through the mostly empty space, and the smell of stale popcorn permeates the air, and Zenny's *if this were real* chafes at me. I'm starting to have the uncomfortable feeling that I'm in a Wakefield novel myself, that I'm the hapless hero or heroine who starts to fall in love even though I know better, even though I know that's not the arrangement, even though I know I'll have my heart broken.

But I can't stop. It's like watching a tornado carve up a prairie field, like watching hail tear through leaves and roofs and dirt. It's happening, and all I can do is take shelter.

Zenny's skates fit perfectly, and so do my new blades, and she gives a delighted little clap of her hands as I pop up and skate backwards around the table. The light pings off the stud in her nose, and she's so fucking hot, so fucking young, and I want to fast forward to the end of the night and what I have planned, but I manage to keep myself under control. As soon as she has her skates on and she's stowed her shoes, we roll out to the rink itself, a wood-floored affair crowded with disco balls and scores of teenagers too young to do anything more interesting with their Saturday nights.

"I didn't know you could skate like this!" she exclaims, as I move in circles around her.

"Elijah and I played roller hockey, remember?" I say, moving in front of her and skating backwards as she tentatively skates forward.

"I was a baby," she points out in playful exasperation. "Of course I don't remember."

"Oh yeah," I say. And she's right. In fact, Elijah and I both quit roller hockey the year Zenny was born—me because it was not one of those sports that netted lots of attention from girls, like basketball or football, and Elijah because he was so busy with his ten trillion other extracurriculars that he had to start dropping things to make time for the activities he really wanted to do.

A quick bite of shame follows the realization. Because what am I doing with this girl, really? Who do I think I am? There's got to be a special hell for men who fuck their best friend's sister, especially when their best friend's little sister is much, much too young for the kind of fucking I like to do.

I execute a few figure eights around Zenny, trying to push these thoughts away, and my antics earn me more clapping, which only makes me peacock more. I know I'm thirty-six, but it feels really good to show off sometimes, okay? Even on rollerblades.

It only takes Zenny a few laps for her legs to remember how to move on skates, and then we settle into a nice pace, holding hands and talking to each other over the music. I feel like a kid, like a teenager, electric that she's holding my hand, stealing glances at her tight ass moving under her jeans. The breeze created by our movement plasters her T-shirt against her body, and under the thin, worn-through cotton, I can see the divot of her navel, the smooth cups of her bra. I can see the place where her hips flare out from her narrow waist, the outline of the button of her jeans. A button that I plan to have unbuttoned very soon.

I adjust myself subtly as we skate, and sneak a look at

my watch. Twenty more minutes and I'll be able to put my sixty dollars to work.

"See something you like?" Zenny asks dryly, noticing my gaze and my not-as-subtle-as-I-thought handling of my cock.

"Just reading your T-shirt," I pretend to lie, knowing she'll see right through it and not caring. I want her to know how much I look at her, how much I want her. I want her to have me at full force, full desire, not only because it's what she wanted out of this arrangement, but because I don't know if I can actually hold myself back. It might kill me to pretend to want her less.

"Uh-huh," Zenny says, in a voice that conveys that she's clearly on to my lecherous ways, but she glances down at her shirt anyway. It's a mission trip T-shirt from several years ago, with the words *Maison de Naissance* printed underneath the picture of a cross superimposed on the outline of Haiti.

It rings a bell, and I manage to fish out a fuzzy memory of Tyler's wife talking about *Maison de Naissance*.

"That's a birthing center, isn't it?" I ask, nodding at her shirt.

"It is," she affirms, looking a bit impressed that I know that. "Do you speak French?"

"Only enough to order good food."

"Ha. Well, it's actually a place that provides prenatal and postpartum care to women and babies. We went there for a mission trip—it was my first mission trip ever—and I just fell in love."

"With the babies?"

She spreads her fingers in my hand, gesturing. "With all of it. Every part of it. Mom and Dad had pushed me toward medicine or law, and growing up, I thought that's what I wanted too. But there was something about medicine that always felt—I don't know—sterile, I guess. Impersonal. But when I went to work with the nurses and midwives down there, a part of me came alive. It was so necessary, so intimate, so...*human*. To be with these women while they carried their babies and labored them into the world. And to know what huge differences small interventions could make—it felt magical. There's no glory in it, there's no money, but the magic is better than both those things."

"And that's when you started thinking about becoming a nurse-midwife?"

She nods. "Dad was so upset. Of course, he'd rather I'd chosen something like surgery or oncology, but at the very least couldn't I compromise and study obstetrics? But I guess I know too many doctors, and I felt that choosing obstetrics over midwifery would limit me. I didn't want to be a doctor at all, I didn't want to be wearing a white coat and playing God." She sighs, and the sound is mostly lost in the whirr of our wheels over the wood floor. "It was a hard fight. But there was no changing my mind."

"So what happens after you graduate? Will you ever get to practice midwifery if you've taken vows?"

Her face lights up, as if I've asked exactly the right question. "I'll still have two years of midwifery school after I graduate with my RN next spring. But the Reverend Mother and I have plans. See, so many of the people who come into our shelter are in some stage of needing maternal care—either they're pregnant or they're about to deliver or maybe they have a young infant and they're struggling to breastfeed—and most of them don't have access to healthcare. Some of them are afraid to go to a hospital, even when they're in labor, because they're undocumented and they're frightened of being arrested or deported. Some people simply can't afford it. So what if we opened up our own birthing center? Here in Kansas City? There's a huge need for it, and by the time I finish my midwifery degree, we'll hopefully have enough money and all the right permissions to launch it. We could help so many people, Sean, from all walks of life. We can really make a difference."

I'm captivated by the passion in her voice. I can't remember feeling this passionate about anything, about any cause, any vocation, ever in my life, and the gap between us in this is both humbling and absorbing. I feel like I could spend the next year thinking about it and only just begin to unravel the rift between the kind of woman Zenny is and the kind of man I am.

Zenny saw suffering and it made her want to engage and change things and invest her life in helping. The literal only time in my life that I've seen and felt real suffering—Lizzy's suicide—my response was to reject everything. To disengage. To scorn.

For the first time, I begin to understand why Tyler went back to the Church. Why he became a priest.

And suddenly I feel strange about my own choices, about my own convictions. They feel flat and callow next to Zenny's lively, energetic zeal. I'm not used to feeling that way about myself, and it's rather uncomfortable.

"If I hadn't brokered the Keegan deal, how were you planning on fitting a birthing center into the shelter? You're already crammed into that space just doing normal shelter stuff."

She gives a shrug. "We would have asked the owner for more space in the building, since it was empty anyway. Or found an off-site location. We have faith that something will open up."

I'm about to say that she doesn't need faith, that she has *me* and I'll make sure she gets the best fucking space available in this city, but my conversation with my mom is still rattling around my head, a loose ball bearing denting up my thoughts. It's like no one cares about what I can do when they have *faith,* and I find that's making me rather surly.

Instead, I check my watch and see that it's time for my

sixty dollars to find their new home.

"Be right back," I say, giving Zenny a quick kiss and then dashing off toward the front desk of the rink, dodging teenagers as I go.

And when I come back, she's leaning against the railing on the outside of the rink, watching the clumps of youths skate around.

"Everything okay?" I ask, because she looks very pensive right now, and not a little sad.

"Oh, yes," she assures me. "I'm just thinking about things."

I lean next to her, bumping her hip gently with my own. "What kinds of things? More about the birthing center?"

"I wish. It's more like thinking about the birthing center made me think about that first mission trip, and that made me think about being a teenager again...like, I just—" She stops, and I get the feeling she doesn't want to tell me. Or that she does, but doesn't think she should. Finally she just lets it tumble out. "I'm not much older than the people in the rink, but I already feel like I missed out on so much. I didn't have Saturday nights to goof around—if I wasn't doing homework or volunteering or at a debate tournament, it was a dinner party with my parents' friends or some society event we needed to be seen at. My teenage years were spent trying to make myself into the perfect Iverson daughter, and after I rejected all that, I felt like I had to work even harder. I had to be the best nursing student, the best postulant, to make throwing all that away worth it, and—"

I let her find her thoughts, her center. She's twisting her fingers together as she talks, and twisting them hard enough to make her knuckles go tight. I don't like that she's hurting herself in her agitation, so I slide behind her and cup her hands with my own, forcing them to relax.

She sighs and melts back into me, her hair tickling irresistibly at my neck.

"I guess I just worry that I've thrown away the last three years too, trying to prove that I can succeed like this. Like, maybe this whole time I wasn't working hard for just myself; even if it felt like I was doing it to spite my parents, in a way, it was still *for* my parents."

"Are you saying you're having doubts?" I ask, unable to quell the happy little spit of excitement kindling in my chest. "You can stop trying to prove your parents wrong and stop this nun thing and just marry me instead?"

She shakes with laughter in my arms. She thinks I'm joking.

Wait, I am joking right?

I'm definitely joking. Totally. I'm just joking that I want to see Zenny at the other end of a church aisle in a gorgeous white wedding gown, her nose ring glinting mischievously from under her veil. Or that I want to spend every night for the rest of my life kissing that delicious mouth and watching her sweet belly slowly grow with our children and cradling those tiny babies in my arms as I watched them coo and chirp and blink themselves to sleep.

Of course I'm only joking that I want to spend the rest of my life with the most beautiful, fascinating, sexy woman I've ever met. It's all a joke. Ha ha ha. Hilarious.

Oh my God, I'm so fucked.

"Sean? Are you okay? You went all rigid and quiet all of a sudden."

"Totally fine," I lie, but unfortunately, my voice is all knotted and tight, and it makes it patently clear how *not* fine I am. I feel like I can barely breathe, because I don't even know who Sean Bell *is* anymore, and all I want in the fucking world is to be close to this girl, but even having my arms around her doesn't feel close enough. I'm acutely, painfully aware that she'll never be mine. She'll always be God's.

But before she can call me out on my obvious upset, the DJ's voice comes over the PA system, silencing all the chatter across the rink.

"And now we have a very special couples' skate tonight. This song goes out to Zenny, from Sean."

Zenny swivels in my arms, and there is no way to tell if she's amused or alarmed because the expression on her face is very much both of these things.

"Zenny, Sean says you can make this sinner change his ways," continues the DJ, and it's actually a lyric from the song I picked, but he delivers it with such oozing smarminess that it really sounds like something a lover would say, and for a moment I wonder if I *would* say it. I already want to marry this girl—what else about my old sinner's ways is going to change from being around her?

Bruno Mars' "Locked Out of Heaven" starts playing as the lights dim and the disco balls start spinning. (Sixty dollars at work, everybody, sixty dollars that are now in the possession of the assistant manager—an assistant manager who also happens to be an old frat brother of Aiden's.)

"I love this song," she says, and it's the most warily anyone has ever said those words in the history of the world.

I laugh and tug on her hand to pull her back onto the floor. "I know," I tell her. "I did some research before we came here tonight." I don't tell her that "research" involved me scrolling through her Instagram like a lovesick teenager.

The DJ chides all the non-couple skaters off the floor, and soon it's just pairs of awkward teens, and then me and Zenny, the only adults. And despite her initial wariness, Zenny warms up to my little gesture, holding my hand tightly and singing along with the words and looking so deliciously kissable that it's everything I can do to keep skating and not swing her up into my arms and dash away with her like some kind of rollerblading caveman. And at the end of the song, she even allows me to tug us into a slow-rolling kiss in front of everyone, letting me nibble and taste at her lips until the rink breaks out into whoops and applause and she pulls away with a bashful smile.

"I'm sorry you missed out on so much teenage fun," I say, as the song changes and we start skating again. "But you have to admit that some things are more fun as an adult."

She gives me a naughty little smile. "Oh really? Show me another thing, then."

"Is that a dare, Zenny-bug?"

The eyebrow goes up. "Are you up to the challenge?"

I make an arrogant boy noise and tug her off the rink floor, onto the bad carpet and toward the skate rental counter.

"Sean? Where are we—*Sean!*" My little rule-follower is panicking as I look both ways to make sure no one's around and then duck under the counter, pulling her with me.

"Shhh, it's okay," I murmur. "I paid off the manager on duty."

"You what—"

But then I'm skate-crowding her behind the walls and walls of rental skates, into a dark nook that's hidden from view. I brace my hands on either side of her shoulders and pin her against the wall with my gaze. "Now, let me show you something a man can do better than a teenage boy."

Even in the dim, weirdly-shadowed light, I can see her

pupils go big, and even over the music, I can hear her breathing change. "Yeah?"

"Yeah." I lean in, trace the line of her jaw with my nose. As always, she smells delicate and floral, like roses on the wind. "You see, if I were a teenage boy, I'd be so excited to have a girl as gorgeous as you back here that I wouldn't be able to be patient. I'd be shoving my hand up your shirt and mauling at your tits. But I'm no boy, Zenny, and I know how to take my time."

She shudders as I move my face in the graceful curve between her neck and shoulder and I breathe her in.

"I know that girls need special little kisses," I murmur, kissing her neck softly. "Special little touches." And then my hand drops to the outside of her thigh, and I run my fingers up the seam of her jeans until I find a belt loop. I hook my fingers in the loop and gently tug her hips forward. Our bodies are almost pressed together now, and she's arching to me, trying to get closer, seeking out pressure and friction.

I don't let her yet, returning my attention to her mouth. To those perpetually pouty lips, which I brush my own lips over until she opens for me. Until I can slide my tongue against hers in a soft, warm dance. God, that tongue of hers, with its tentative flickers and hesitant flutters. I can't stop the growl in my throat as she bravely reaches up to my neck and pulls me tighter against her, deepening the kiss.

And the thought of her inexperienced tongue making those same little flickers and flutters on the head of my cock drives me near mad, sending a rush of need so violent through my blood that my hand fists itself around her belt loop and I growl into her mouth.

My noises make her pant and break away just enough to speak. "What else do girls need?" she asks breathlessly. "Show me what a boy couldn't."

My other hand trails swirls over the collar of her T-shirt, make teasing tracks over the cups of her bra, giving her enough sensation to titillate, but nowhere near enough to satisfy. "You mean you want a man to please you? You want me to put my hand down your panties and make this awful, little ache go away?"

She nods eagerly, her eyes big and her lips parted and her hips squirming. "I need your help," she whispers. "No boy my age knows how to make me feel better."

The game is morphing a little, edging onto a dangerously pitched slope, and then Zenny goes ahead and hurls us over the edge. "If I were still a teenager," she says, her eyes finding mine, and fuck they are so dark and hungry there's no way I'll be able to say no to anything she wants. "And you were still a man…"

"It would be wrong," I manage to say, although any judge able to look at my thoughts right now would send me straight to jail.

"Seventeen," she says. "Almost to eighteen."

"Unethical."

Her hips finally make contact with mine, grinding against my erection. "So close to legal."

My cock surges, and I'm shamefully hard. "Jesus Christ."

"Four years ago," she persists. "I'd be almost eighteen."

"I'd be thirty-two, Zenny."

"And what if that's when you saw me again? What would you do?"

"I'd—" Fuck. I can't think straight.

"If you saw me, and I told you I needed help? That my body felt all strange, and I knew only you could make it all better?"

"Zenny," I say, I plead. She's done that thing again where she's flipped the control, stolen it away and left me dazed and staggering, even though I'm supposed to be the expert and she the virgin.

She takes the hand still plucking at her bra cup and guides it down to her jeans button. "Just pretend," she murmurs. "It's just make-believe. I know you wouldn't, but now I am an adult and we can pretend that you would."

"I—"

"What if I showed you where it hurt?" she asks, now guiding my hand to cup her pussy. It's hot to the touch, even through the denim. She presses my hand against her harder, rubs against it. "If I begged and begged and begged? If I said, just this one time, just this once, teach me how to make my pussy feel better?"

Teach me how to make my pussy feel better. Jesus, I can't resist that shit. I let out a wounded, hitched breath and she knows she has me. A triumphant smile plays over her mouth.

My hand drifts up to the button of her fly and works it open with practiced ease. We're both looking down at it now, at the view of my hand framed by our roller skates and jeans, and her old T-shirt and my too-expensive watch, and it feels very, very easy to pretend right now. And then when I've worked her jeans open and slid my fingers down her panties and I've felt how fucking wet she is, all the pretending goes out the window.

"Baby," I whisper, wrapping one arm around her waist to hold her steady as I tickle over her slick folds. "My little nun is so wet for me."

She whimpers the moment my fingers find her opening. "Is this what you need, sweetheart? For me to finger this virgin pussy?"

She gives a desperate little nod, gasping out a *please* as she tries to push against my fingers. Her skates make her move and buck and the only thing anchoring her is my arm on her waist and the two big fingers circling her entrance. My hand in her most secret place is tender, capable, working her open by degrees as my palm cups her clit.

"You think you're ready for two fingers?" I ask.

"I—" Her head is rolling back against the wall. "Yes, God, please."

"That's good," I tell her. "You need to learn to take more fingers if you're ever going to grow up and take my cock."

My shameful, forbidden words have her eyes fluttering closed and her hands fisting at my shirt. "Yes, please, please," she moans, and I slide both fingers home.

She's so fucking tight and so wet that my hand is coated in her, and she's so gorgeous like this, so lovely and sexy and mine, my bold sort-of virgin, and it's so easy to forget that she's going to leave me, that it's not really me she wants but my body and my experience. It's easy to pretend she actually wants *me*, bossy, flawed Sean, and that when she starts letting out my name in these breathless, air-starved bursts as she rides my hand, it's because she's feeling the same thing I'm feeling: this keen, jagged edge of longing.

"It feels so good," she manages. "Oh God, Sean, it feels so good, it feels so good—"

She thrashes and thrashes and still I tend to her sweet little pussy the way it needs, petting the spots inside that make her moan and rubbing at her clit, and then I bury my face in her neck and breathe in the sex and rose smell of her as she lets out a low cry and clenches hard around my fingers. More of her wetness soaks over my skin and her pussy seizes in long, luscious pulses, and I'm so fucking hard, but I think that I could almost give up my own satisfaction if I got to give Zenny pleasure like this every day. It's heady, almost as heady as an orgasm of my own.

The pleased, affectionate—and yes, proud—glow I feel as I slide my hands out of her panties and slowly button her up is more potent than anything I've ever felt. I lick my fingers clean like the animal I am as she watches me with hooded eyes, and then I say, "That isn't even the beginning of what I had planned for this pussy tonight."

And this time, she's the one to grab my hand and yank me away, right to our shoes and socks, and she's the one to herd me, impatient, giggling, warm-faced, back to the Audi so that I can get us back to where we both want to be.

CHAPTER NINETEEN

"Are we going to have sex tonight?" my impatient girl asks in the elevator. "I did so well with your fingers."

"Darling, two fingers isn't even close to my cock," I inform her smugly. But seeing her disappointment, I assure her, "But we're still going to have lots of fun tonight."

"I want to have sex," she complains.

"Now, Miss Intercourse Doesn't Define Sex, I thought we agreed that I'd set the pace. And it's all sex, remember?"

She sighs, looking a bit forlorn. "Yes. I remember."

"Good. You're mine to treasure, sweetheart, and I want to savor each and every part of you as you flower open."

I mean all those words, but I am secretly pleased that she's growing hungry for sex. I'm starving for her too, but not even starvation will drive me past making this amazing for her. And amazing things take time.

Once we're inside, I give her five minutes to get herself ready for me, and then I want her naked on my bed, a request that's met with an eyebrow.

"Then you have to get naked too," she says. "That's only fair."

"Okay," I agree, and she looks suspicious at my easy acquiescence, like it's a trick somehow. I laugh. "Zenny, I'm happy to get naked for you. It gets me hard knowing you like my body even half as much as I like yours. Now hurry up, so we can start playing."

She disappears into the bathroom, while I get the bedroom ready, turning off the overhead lights and flicking on a corner lamp, arranging tonight's props on the bed. I wasn't kidding about how her obvious lust for me gets me hard, and my cock is heavy and rigid as I unfasten my jeans and pull off my shirt and toe off my shoes. I'm naked except for the jeans—my cock a dusky, thick pole jutting out from the open zipper—as she opens the door the bedroom. The bright light from behind her limns her body in glowing gold, glowing over those long, lithe legs and that taut belly and those pert little tits, currently tipped with hard, tight buds. Her hair is a soft, dark halo, and with the light angled like this, her eyes shine like stars. A naked angel. My naked angel.

My cock throbs and I have to swallow to find my voice. "On the bed," I whisper, nearly cracking open with need as she walks toward me and the shadows melt away from her body. Every inch of her is perfection personified, and I can't believe that of all the men in the world, she's chosen me to share her body with. Her smiles and her worries and her time and her trust.

How did I get so fucking lucky?

And how will I bear it when it ends?

"I changed my mind," Zenny says, a bit huskily. "You can leave the jeans on."

And I realize she likes this, seeing my need for her framed so obviously, so painfully. I give her a playful little bow. "Whatever milady desires," I say.

"You say that now, but I know you're about to get bossy again—" She freezes when she sees what I've got laid out on the bed, and I study her face and her body as she takes in the toys. "Sean?"

I come up behind her, holding her hair away from her neck so I can trail comforting kisses along the curve of her shoulder. The tip of my cock brushes against the dimples at the small of her back, and we both shiver at the same time.

"You said you'd never used a vibrator," I murmur, my lips still moving across the warm skin of her shoulder. "I thought it would be fun to try it out."

"Oh," she says. "I—I didn't realize they were so *big*."

I slide one of my hands down her arm and over her hand, and I guide her fingers to the wand vibrator that has her so spooked. "This doesn't go inside you," I promise, letting her examine the toy. "It's big because it's so powerful. And this one—" I move her hand over to the much smaller one "—is made for your G-spot. See the flattened knob at the end? You slide it inside and let it tickle you from the inside out."

Her hand moves on its own to the small jeweled plug at the edge of the towel the toys are laid out on. "And what's this for?" she asks, picking it up. The light prisms around the scarlet-colored jewel and gleams along the fat bullet of the plug's body. Zenny's voice is all innocent curiosity. "Is this for inside me too?"

"Yes, baby. We make it all slippery, see, and we get you all squirming and dirty-feeling, and then I'll put this in your ass, and it will make you feel better."

Her breath catches. "It will?"

I nuzzle her. "I know it sounds scary, and we're not going to do it tonight. But I wanted you to see it, to hold it, to start getting used to the idea."

"I—I don't know about anal," she admits, but she's still holding the plug in her palm, stroking along the cool metal with her other hand. "It always seemed like something that was more for the man to enjoy than the woman."

"Too many men have been selfish with it," I agree. "But have I ever been selfish with your body in a way you didn't also enjoy?"

She makes a thoughtful *hmm*. "I suppose you haven't yet."

"And you trust me?"

"I trust you."

"Then I want to try it with you. Anything we do, from anal to sharing a coffee mug in the morning, I'll stop the minute you ask. And so if we try it and you hate it, we'll stop and move on to the next thing. There's so many other things to do, Zenny-bug, that we won't even notice dropping this one by the side of the road."

She turns in my arms, which now traps my cock against the softness of her belly. I heroically resist the urge to start grinding into her navel.

"But you really think it will feel good?" she asks.

"I do," I tell her warmly, pressing my forehead to hers. "I'm going to say something that isn't true for every woman, but I think it's going to be true for you."

"Oh?"

I let my hand play over the curve of her hip, dance over the soft bed of curls between her legs. "Once I fuck you," I say, my voice kind and instructive like a teacher's, "you're going to start to feel an emptiness deep inside your cunt."

I press the blunt pad of my fingertip to her clit and rub at the swollen bud until she spreads her legs and bucks against me, like a needy little kitten. I slide my finger

SINNER

down, pleased to feel that she's still so incredibly wet, and then I gently breach her entrance with my finger. "Here," I explain, going deeper, pressing against her inner wall. "Right here, baby. It's going to pout and whimper when it's empty. And when your pussy gets wet and your clit begins to stiffen, you'll feel this new hollowness too. You won't just need pressure and friction. You'll need fullness."

Her hands are flat against my chest now, the metal plug warming between her palm and my skin like a promise. "I will?" she says, her eyes flicking up to me. I gently rub at the inside of her, and I swear if she were a cat, she'd be purring right now.

"You will. And fullness will feel good. And with a plug in your ass and my cock in your cunt, I promise you'll feel so full that you think your heart might break from it."

"Okay," she whispers. "I'll try it."

I kiss her as I finger her, kiss her and play with her pussy until her hands are doing that cat's paw kneading at my chest again, fisting and flexing, fisting and flexing. I slide my finger free and then bring it up to Zenny's mouth, and she sucks it without prompting.

I groan. "Are you sure you're really a nun?"

The only response is more suction, more tongue flutters against the pad of my finger, and I can't even see straight. My vision is fucking blurring. From her mouth on my *finger*.

"That's how you taste, baby," I say as she sucks. "Isn't

it so good? So sweet? Fuck, I can't wait to eat you out again."

That makes her eyelashes bat in surprise, and I smile, pulling my finger free and pulling her hand away from my chest. I pluck the anal toy out of her hand, give her palm a quick kiss, then tell her to climb on the bed.

"Which way?" she asks, all her finger-sucking bravado melting into self-consciousness. "Should I lay down, or be on all fours, or…"

The idea of Zenny on all fours nearly gives me a heart attack, so in the interest of my health and mortality, I say, "How about on your knees to start, by the headboard. That way you can grab on for balance."

By the time she's arranged, her body is all tension and uncertainty, and when I turn on the wand vibrator and it makes a deep, thrumming purr like a car engine, I can see the moment she nearly bolts.

I'm behind her in an instant, kissing her neck, running soothing hands all over her tummy and breasts and legs. "I'm right here, baby," I croon in her ear. "I'm right here."

"It sounds like so much," she says, and I can hear the effort she's putting into making her voice sound calm.

"It is so much, but only in the best way. Do you want to be my brave girl now? Let me touch you with it?"

She nods, blowing out a breath. "Of course." I watch, amused, as she braces her body like I'm about to sprinkle spiders all over it or something.

"It's just a vibrator," she mutters, more to herself than to me, "I don't know why I'm so—*eek! Sean!*"

I've put the wide head of the wand against the delicate sole of one foot, tickling her. She shrieks with laughter, and I hold her still against me, only relenting on her foot once she's nothing but smiles and joy again, until all her apprehension has melted away under the laughter. And then I make a slow, lazy path from her foot to her calf, from her calf to her thigh, keeping the toy far away from any erogenous zones. And she stays melty and relaxed, even slumping forward against the headboard and humming happily as I use the wand to massage at her back and shoulders and neck.

"My grandma used to get these catalogs," she says, "that had 'personal neck massagers.' You know the kind of catalogs that also have things to hide a spare key in and novelty cupcake tins?"

"Mmm," I say, more interested in the way Zenny's back ripples with pleasure as I massage the tension away.

"I just realized that those 'personal massagers' were vibrators," Zenny says, and I make a noise indicating how adorably cute that is. "*And*," she adds, "I guess if my grandma can handle it, I can too."

"I'm glad to hear that, babydoll. Spread your legs a little."

She does, and I'm happy to see that she doesn't seem nervous anymore. I still go carefully, gently, moving from her shoulders to her arms, from her arms to her chest. And there, I lightly, deliberately, graze the head of the wand over one erect nipple.

The effect is immediate and deliciously gratifying. She lets out a needy gasp and arches to its touch, trying to bring it back. I oblige her, giving each tight little tip all the attention it deserves. And then when I have her arched and breathless and her hips moving and seeking relief, I move the wand down her tummy.

"Oh," she breathes, and her head comes back to rest against my shoulder. "Oh."

The wand buzzes playfully around and around her navel, dipping to buzz at the soft curves of her inner thighs. And just when she's twisting and turning, trying to chase the buzz with her hips, I give her what she needs. I spread my hand over her tummy, tuck her close to me, and then nuzzle the head of the wand against her clit.

"*Oh*," Zenny pants out, her voice incandescent with surprised pleasure. "Sean, that—it feels so good…"

I chuckle, arranging one of her perfect thighs so that I can angle the vibrator better against her. "That's the idea, Zenny-bug. It's not supposed to feel *bad*."

"No," she mumbles, her body a hot, sinuous writhe against mine. "Not bad. Good."

I grin, kiss her ear, and then have her brace her hands on the headboard again. I love playing with her like this, with her back to my chest and my arms around her, but all that movement against my dick is going to have me spending my seed in no time, and I don't want that. I want this to be about her, only about her.

And so after she has her hands on the headboard and she's raised slightly up on her knees again, I slide the vibrator under her from behind, so that she can control the angle and the pressure, so that she can ride it, and my girl takes to fucking herself against the vibrator like a champ, finding a slow, rolling rhythm that leaves her sweaty and trembling after only a few moments.

I watch the show in front of me, enthralled, hypnotized, my cock past human levels of hardness and into mithril or adamantium categories of hardness. And my balls are already drawn up so tight, and some jagged ache is already scissoring so deliciously deep in my groin, and she is just so beautiful like this, her head hanging between her shoulders, as if she's overwhelmed with the pleasure, and with every lovely, firm line of her back and waist and ass available to view. Moving her pussy so well over the toy, and I'm so proud of her, and I tell her this. I tell her how brave she is for trying something new, and I tell her how much her trust means to me, how much I treasure it, how much I want to deserve and deserve her. I tell her how beautiful she is, how good her ass and thighs look as she circles her cunt over the toy, how strong and how sweet she looks.

And my words make her moan even more, her body

rippling with pent-up need as she gets closer and closer to the edge, and then she accidentally moves herself too far forward and instead of rubbing her pussy against the vibrator, the blunt head of it slides back against the firm eyelet of her asshole.

A shudder runs through her entire being, all the way down to her toes, and then she does it again.

On purpose this time.

I am frozen on my knees, holding this wand for her, watching as this virgin nun rides a vibrator against her ass, listening to her dirty moans and whimpers as she gets closer and closer, and then it happens. Not with the vibrator against her clit or her G-spot or even a nipple. No, my best friend's little sister comes in a toe-curling, groaning climax with the vibrator against her anus, and I've got the best seat in the house.

And with a ragged grunt and a release I can feel jerking at the muscles of my stomach and thighs, I erupt all over her legs and her ass and the bed. I erupt without her touching me, without even touching myself, just from fucking watching her, and I spill everywhere, in huge, hot spurts that lace her skin and my wrist and the wand and basically everywhere, and the fuck of it is that I'm still hard when I've finished, and when Zenny turns around, dazed and still quivering, she whispers, "Do it again, show me, show me," and I do, I show her. I drop the wand and grab myself, and I've never done this already messy and sticky from myself, and it's shockingly filthy, even for Sean Bell, to use my own cum to jack myself off with, but that seems to be the way with Zenny, that she nudges me into the new and the depraved when I thought there were no more new depravities to be had.

In any case, the memory of her firm ass moving against the wand is still painfully, sweetly fresh, and her expression now—avid curiosity and blatant lust—and her hands rubbing up and down my stomach, smearing more cum everywhere—

Well, it doesn't take long. I come again, this one more powerful and more vicious than the first, tearing through me like a tornado, and Zenny hums with approval as I do, her hands dropping down to squeeze my thighs as I pant and spurt my way through it.

"Jesus Christ," I manage, after my body is finally drained completely dry. I feel like I've been hit with a truck. But a sexy, amazing truck I want to be hit with every day for the rest of my life. "What are you doing to me?"

"Making you very, very…" her voice is a seductive whisper as she leans close enough to my face to kiss me "…very, very…*sticky.*"

The next week passes in a tightrope walk of longing

and release. I refuse to allow myself to be the reason Zenny falls down on any of her responsibilities, and so I drive her to all of her clinical rotations, classes, and shelter shifts to make her life easier, and I make her do her schoolwork at night before we get to fool around, sitting at the kitchen table with me as I work on contracts and review client emails. It's agony to miss her all day and then to be so close and still need to keep my distance, but it also assuages some of the guilt I feel about our unusual arrangement. I feel like I'm helping her, supporting her and taking care of her, and feeling that way about a woman I like the way I like Zenny is beyond addictive.

But sometimes Elijah's face will flash in my mind, like a big *YOU'RE AN ASSHOLE* warning, and then I'm not sure whether it's a good thing or a terrible thing that I'm so addicted to Zenny.

"Am I big brothering you too much?" I ask over breakfast.

Zenny looks up from the nursing textbook in her lap, blinking. "Explain," she commands.

"Making you move in. Driving you places. Making sure you finish your homework. Fixing your coffee in the morning." I bring said coffee over to her to punctuate my point.

She accepts her coffee with a grin. "It *is* very, very terrible having a sexy millionaire play personal barista, personal chauffeur, and personal orgasm attendant with me."

I sit down in the chair across from her, leaning forward on the table and wrapping my hands around hers, which are currently wrapped around the warm mug.

"I'm serious, Zenny-bug," I say.

"Alright," she says and seems to give it some thought. "Okay, well, I *chose* to move in here for the month, and yes, that was under the influence of many orgasms, but I don't regret it. I actually like that my success matters to you as much as it matters to me. I'm used to—" her hands flutter under mine as she searches for the right words "—going it alone, having to be the best but also having to make it look easy, you know? I get tired, and it's nice to feel like someone's in the game with me, like it's not all on my shoulders anymore. Which it still is in a practical sense, but at least it feels easier. At least it's less lonely. And a lot more fun."

I perk up. "Really?"

"Really."

"I just…" Why can't I get over this? "You're so young."

"Hmm." When I look up, she's got her head tilted and her lips pursed as if this is an academic problem and not a deeply personal one. "Well," she asks, "I suppose the question is if you'd be like this with any other woman you cared about?"

I think of my lovers in the past, and while I've slept with women all across the range of race, religion, and age, there's a problem with that question, and it's a simple one. "There are no other women I care about like this," I explain. "You're the first, and frankly, given my age, I think you'll probably be the only one."

Her mouth parts but she's not breathing, as if I've said something monumental or something insane—or something monumentally insane—but I haven't. It's just a plain statement of fact. And it's a fact that I thought she already knew.

She finally takes in a breath and averts her gaze to the window. The morning light plays across her face, burnishing the bridge of her nose and her cheekbones with the faintest luster of gold. "Sean, I don't know what to say to that."

My eyebrows furrow in puzzlement. What does she think she needs to say? It was just an objective truth, like the color of the sky or the reading order of the Wakefield Saga novels. It doesn't need a response.

But then I realize that perhaps she thinks I would like her to respond in kind, to make some kind of declaration about her feelings in turn, which of course I don't expect...

I mean, I definitely don't expect it, and it hadn't occurred to me before, but now that it *has* occurred to me, I can feel this thing inside my chest, a gap. It's almost like a physical space, and somehow I know that if she said something back to me—that she liked me, that she cared about me, anything—it would fill up that mysterious chink, and somehow that would make me feel better.

"Back to my age," she says, and I nearly let out a bleak laugh. We've ventured into strange territory indeed if our massive age gap feels like a safer topic of conversation.

"Yes?"

It's her turn to cup my hands now and she gives me a smile, one of those Zenny smiles full of contradictions, because I can tell she's trying to be reassuring but that she's also troubled about something. I don't like this, any of it, the troubled smile or knowing I've made her uncomfortable, but I also can't bear to take back what I said about her being the only one for me.

"I appreciate you checking in with me, and while there might be some women in my position who would feel stifled or patronized, I'm okay with it. I like it, actually. I feel rather, well, *doted* on, and it's nice. And I also trust that if I ask you to back off, you will."

"Anything. Anything you say or want, and I'll do it."

"I believe you," she says, and I wish that she didn't look so worried as she said it.

Three weeks left, I remember. Only three weeks left.

As the days go by, she's growing bolder and bolder in bed, using those words I like: pussy, dick, come. Fuck.

She's growing antsy for my cock, which is exactly what I wanted, for her to be peeling apart with lust, bursting with it, aching and heavy and ripe with it—and tonight's the night I'll finally give her what she's so eager to have.

But two things first.

First order of business: I think I've found a place for the sisters, a renovated warehouse sitting empty on the north end of downtown, with an owner who's desperate for any kind of tax relief on the vacant property. It would need a kitchen and dormitory space, but not only is it centrally located to bus stops and interstates, but it has ample room for a birthing center in an adjoining property that the owner is willing to lease out as well.

I take some time out of my afternoon to tour it personally, politely listening to the owner chatter on about all his financial woes since taking the property on and how hard it is to find commercial tenants in this part of town and—

Okay, maybe I'm not so politely listening to him because I ignore the rest of what he says. It's irrelevant—I've seen his financials and I know that the write-off that the nuns would bring would give him a huge boost. We leave on a handshake deal and I call my assistant to see if he'll arrange a meeting between me and the prioress.

He calls me back a few minutes later.

"So the prioress says that she already met with Charles Northcutt. Well, she and Zenobia Iverson met with him.

Before lunch."

Roaring red flames my vision, making everything crimson and hateful.

I'm.

Going.

To.

Kill.

Him.

I call Zenny immediately, but I know she won't answer because she's in class and she's one of those nice humans who silences her phone in those situations. I fume for a minute—not at her, never at her—but at Northcutt. At whatever he's done.

And when I get back to the office, surprise, surprise, he's nowhere to be found. Probably left early to get his devil horns sanded down before the fundraiser tonight.

Which brings me to the second order of business: there's a fucking fundraiser tonight, and it was supposed to be glamorous and fun and the perfect prelude to finally taking my little nun to bed, but unfortunately now it's going to have to be the scene of a homicide. Northcutt-icide.

I'm going to kill him.

CHAPTER
TWENTY

I can hear Zenny's breath trembling over the phone. "This is for me?"

"It's for you," I confirm. I pin my phone between my shoulder and my ear and glance around the dull-ass country club. Valdman is supposed to meet me here, and I've encountered several Valdman-*like* men, paunchy and white and entitled, but no actual Valdman. Just lots of polo shirts and huffing laughter.

"Sean, I…this is beautiful. Thank you."

I scrub at my perfect hair in frustration. I was supposed to be there right now, I was supposed to be there with Zenny surprising her with the gorgeous gown I bought for her, helping her change into it, dropping teasing hints about when I'd peel the dress back off her body. I'd made big fucking plans about every detail of tonight—Zenny hadn't even known I was taking her to this fundraiser, it was going to be a little surprise—and now it's been ruined because I have to see Valdman about Northcutt before he does any more damage.

"Nothing's too beautiful for you," I tell her seriously. "I'm so upset that I can't see you right now."

She laughs. "You'll see me soon enough. What time is this party again?"

I look at my watch and stifle an impatient groan. "Ninety minutes. Look, I have to meet with my boss, but I'll—"

"I completely understand," she says, although she doesn't exactly. I haven't spoken to her about Northcutt yet because I want to have everything fixed before I ask her what happened and what inevitable shitty thing he did or said during the meeting. I want to be able to pull her into my arms and croon that Sean's taken care of everything, that everything is going to be okay, and that Northcutt is going to be castrated for his crimes. "You've got a job. A big fancy job. I get that and I'm a big girl, Sean. I can handle dressing myself." She sounds amused.

"Okay, well, there's a car service planning to pick you up in eighty minutes in case I'm running too late to get you myself. I'm not sure how long this thing with Valdman will go."

"You do remember who my parents are? I've been to hundreds of these parties. They're all the same, and I know what to do."

"I know, but—"

"Sean," she chides. "I'll be fine. Don't worry about me."

I worry about her.

It's almost an hour later that I pin down Valdman wandering in drunk from the golf course, a young woman who is definitely not his wife petting his arm and asking about dinner. And look, generally I've never cared that Valdman is a garbage person because he's good at running his company, and there didn't seem any reason to care about the first when the latter seemed more important.

But I don't know if it's Jesus-osmosis or working more closely with the shelter or hearing Zenny speak so passionately about her callings, but I'm actually kind of grossed out by Valdman right now. Embarrassed for him...and then embarrassed for myself, because I'm honestly not on track to be any better than he is.

He stumbles to a table, dismissing the woman with an impatient wave of his hand...and gesturing over a waiter with the same hand once she's gone. He orders a scotch and then looks at me through narrowed eyes.

"I thought you were going to be at the fundraiser representing us tonight."

"I am," I assure him, although an irritable part of me wants to remind him that I'd already be there if he just would have met with me on time. "But I've got to know that we're keeping Northcutt away from the Keegan deal."

"I've gotten your messages," Valdman says, accepting the scotch glass that comes his way. "But I don't understand, Sean. You were the one who wanted off the deal in the first place."

I wish that I could tell this red-faced old fuck the truth and have him care, but I know him too well, so I spin the truth so that he'll actually care. "Look, we both want this thing to get fixed and get fixed quietly. And Northcutt is a recipe for an unsavory news story. If he says or does something to those sisters, they are not the type to stay quiet about it. And that's not the kind of press we or our clients want."

Valdman considers this, and I press on, sensing a victory. "Yank him off anything to do with the Keegan deal. You can trust me to keep my nose clean and get this swept up."

I don't mention, obviously, that I'm planning on fucking one of the nuns tonight, and that's probably the exact opposite of keeping my nose clean. I'm different from Northcutt, what Zenny and I are doing is different and fun and good.

I think.

I mean, I hope I'm different from Northcutt. And

Valdman.

I look down at my hands as Valdman takes a drink, and I have a moment of real doubt all of a sudden. Why am I working with these people? Why have I made it my goal to *be* Valdman? Do I really want to be a gouty lecher with no meaningful relationships in my life when I get older? Is there any amount of money that's worth such a hollow life?

"I'll tell him personally to back off," Valdman says finally. "You have my word."

"Thank you, sir." I shake his hand and leave the country club. I'm going to be late to the fundraiser, and all I can think about is Zenny alone, waiting for me in her pretty new dress, at the mercy of the wolves.

My biggest fear when I stride into the hotel ballroom is that Northcutt is already here and he's causing some kind of mayhem with Zenny, but once I get into the event itself, I don't see him anywhere in the room. Thank God. It takes me a heart-poundingly long minute to search out Zenny, but once I find her, that strange new gap in my chest expands and contracts with enough force to make my breath catch.

She is magnificently, indescribably, painfully beautiful.

The dress I bought for her is a delicate shade of blue-green—seafoam is what the girl at the store called it—and it gorgeously sets off the amber-brown of her skin and the copper in her eyes. And then there's the way the chiffon flutters and kisses along her body—over her perfectly curved shoulders and teardrop breasts. Along her narrow waist and then over that sweet ass. She's living, walking art. And she's mine.

For the next three weeks, a hateful voice in my head adds, and that hollow in my chest starts to physically ache.

I go straight to her, not even bothering to make eye contact with the people telling me hello as I pass, and then I pull her into my arms. And for a moment, the ache eases.

"Hey you," I murmur, nuzzling against her hair.

"Hey yourself," she says back, smiling. "Glad you could finally join me."

"I'm so sorry," I say, still nuzzling. "Dumb boss. Dumb meeting. All I could think about was you in this dress."

"You like it?" she asks, suddenly shy.

I pull away enough to look at her, to run my hands over her waist, and then I pull her back into me so she can feel where I'm getting hard. "You look like something out of a fucking painting. Like a princess. I can't wait to do very un-princesslike things to you when we get home."

"A princess? Really?" she says, but I can tell she's pleased.

I nod, pressing into her belly and running my lips over

the shell of her ear. "The kind of princess who ends up bent over a bed with her gown up over her waist while a prince kneels behind her and kisses her pretty cunt."

"Promises, promises," she replies, her voice hitching with undisguised arousal.

I want to tell her that tonight is the night that I'll do more than kiss her cunt, that tonight is the night I'll finally give her what she wants so much, but then she pulls away and I realize her phone is ringing.

I make a grumbly noise as she pulls it out of her clutch, wanting to be pressed against her and murmuring dirty words into her ear once again, but it's someone from the shelter with a question, and I understand when she has to duck out of the party to take the call. I do some discreet adjustments to my body and find a drink, suddenly feeling very grouchy and restless without her, my Zenny-bug, and that hateful voice pops up in my head again.

Less than three weeks left.

Less than three weeks.

"Sean Bell!" a stupid voice says nearby, and I turn and try to look polite, because it's not this person's fault that they aren't Zenny and therefore aren't interesting to me. "It's been ages! It's Hayley, remember? And this is Sophia, Todd, Katelyn, and Jeremy. Sophia, Sean used to work with Mike, before Mike moved into consulting."

And before I know it, I'm swallowed whole by a cluster of stupid people and their stupid chatter.

Introductions are made—apparently I used to work with "Mike," although if it's the Mike I'm thinking of, Hayley needs to get a divorce and take him for everything he's worth. (At the office, we used to call him Cocaine Mike, until a fuzzy and very illegal night involving a park bench and an escort earned him the new nickname of Double Condom Mike.)

Ugh. I can't believe I ever hung out with that guy. Or anyone like him.

Why am I spending my time with these people? I run my gaze over the group currently gabbing at my face, and all I see are entitled, self-absorbed faces honking like geese about their entitled, self-absorbed lives. I feel the same wave of discomfort I felt earlier with Valdman, but even stronger this time.

I don't like this, I realize, and the realization is like a leviathan circling my raft. *I don't like these people and I don't like this life.*

It's a terrifying thing to consider, because I've spent every year since graduating college working to be *here*. Working for the money and the parties and the hilarious-but-disgusting nights with guys like Double Condom Mike. I thought it was what I wanted; I thought it made me strong; I derided anyone too weak to see the world for what it really is, which is a fish tank of angry eels. But now I want out of the tank, and I really, really want away from the eels.

I want what Zenny has. And Tyler and my mom and everyone else in my life who's actually *good* and not a human dumpster fire.

It's while I'm processing this that I register a lull in the conversation, and I see that everyone in the group is looking at me. Well, not actually at me, but at someone behind me. I catch a blessed glimpse of seafoam chiffon and a crown of scrolled, luscious curls, and turn, ready to yank Zenny to my side and nuzzle her some more. Or maybe I'll simply take her hand and lead her back to the car, because now I can't even remember why I thought this would be a fun idea. Her parents are so involved with Kansas City society that surely she's been to enough of these in her life to be bored by one, and I'm definitely bored here, and this was a dumb idea.

Yep. I've decided. I'm going to lace my fingers through her slender, perfect ones and then we are going to my car, and then we are going home and I'm going to let her claim my body the way she's been aching to claim it all this time.

I get as far as reaching for Zenny's hand and finding it, which is then that Sophia (or Hayley, I'm not sure which) says casually, "I'll have another glass of champagne."

There's a silence, and I'm completely lost as to why the hell Sophia (or Hayley) is telling us this, and then she adds, "Actually, make it two. And you can take this one." She holds out an empty champagne glass into equally empty air, as if she expects someone to take it.

As if she expects Zenny to take it.

Zenny's hand feels carved from rigid stone inside of my own, and the world seems to slow down, time accordioning out, as the absurdity of what Sophia or Hayley is saying starts sifting through my mind. Because of course Zenny isn't going to take the glass, of course she doesn't work here—obviously she's dressed as a guest, obviously I know her because *we're holding fucking hands*—and then everything sifts lower and oh my God, this isn't just Sophia or Hayley being stupid (well, yes, she's also being stupid) but it's something else on top of that, something worse—

"No, no," one of the guys interrupts. "That's Jeremiah Iverson's daughter." There's a resounding chorus of *oh yeses!* where it becomes clear that she must be Dr. Iverson's daughter and it also becomes clear that nobody knows her name but it's definitely, definitely his daughter and they all love Dr. Iverson and the Honorable Letitia Iverson and does everybody remember that time Judge Iverson pardoned Hayley's parking ticket, because Hayley does, Hayley remembers it.

They're talking about Zenny like she's not even here, and there's a small intake of breath from next to me, and I realize I'm squeezing her hand too hard. I give her a gentle pump in apology, and then turn back to the group of garbage geese people ready to rip them apart.

Which happens right as Sophia or Hayley says one last

terrible thing. "Oh, so you're a *guest* here!" she says, reaching out to give Zenny a playful tweak on the shoulder. "You should have said something!"

"Get your hands the fuck off her," I say, in what I think is an admirably calm voice, given the situation. Because it's finally become clear to me exactly what dynamic is at play, and I'm beyond angry, I'm beyond furious, I'm something else altogether. I'm biblical, I'm Jehovah finding Israel worshipping false gods, and I'm going to smite these motherfuckers, I'm going to unleash plagues on them and watch their bodies be eaten alive by sores and fires and famine.

And locusts. I'm going to kill them with locusts too.

"Um, what?" Sophia/Hayley laughs nervously, thinking surely she misheard. Surely.

"I said," I say (again, in a voice that I think is graciously calm, given the circumstances), "get your hands the fuck off my date. And don't you ever fucking insinuate she doesn't belong somewhere ever the fuck again."

The silence that follows is appropriately deep, and I straighten up a bit, feeling slightly better, although still very smitey, and then Sophia/Hayley laughs. "Oh my God, Sean! You are so funny!" And her friends laugh along with her, bleating, oblivious idiots, and I'm so confused.

Unless…

Unless it makes more sense to them that I'd be joking, pulling one over, rather than actually telling them not to insult the girl holding my hand. A girl who happens to be black.

And that—well, that makes me want to breathe fucking fire.

The hell of it is that if you'd asked me just this morning what racism was, I'd have given you an answer that involved slurs and bus seats and throwing rocks, I would have said that I'd never personally seen racism, I might have even said something about how we live in a post-racial world and racism is over.

And the extra hell of it is that, based on words alone, you could almost make a case that everything was fine, that this was just an awkward misunderstanding. But it wasn't. Because I was here, and I heard the subtle condescension in that woman's tone, I heard the layers and layers of assumptions she was making about Zenny in just a handful of careless words. It's dangerous because of how subtle it was, how insinuating. Almost hard to pin down, and then once you have it stabbed wriggling and wormy to a board to examine, it tries to morph, it tries to shapeshift, it tries to hide in plain sight.

And the extra, extra hell of it? There's this gross, almost instinctive part of me that wants to make some kind of excuse for Sophia/Hayley, that wants to justify or defend her, and as soon as I recognize that impulse for what it is, self-loathing roils violently in my gut.

I open my mouth to say more, to set these people the

fuck straight, but before I can get a word out, Zenny is flashing a smile at everyone and tugging me away. "So sorry, I need to have a word with Sean, one second."

And before I know it, I'm in some strange giant hallway outside the ballroom, tucked behind a plant where I can't smite anyone. Before Zenny even says anything, my eyes are on the ballroom doors, because I'll be patient and let her tell me whatever it is that's so urgent, but then I'm going back in there and I'm killing everyone, killing them and then stomping their corpses into the parquet floor until they're flat enough for Zenny and me to dance on.

Then I'll calm down, I decide. Once I'm waltzing on their corpses.

"Stop being an asshole," Zenny says, and it's not at all what I expected her to say, and also over the past week I've become painfully attuned to that word—*asshole*—latching onto it as our safe word of sorts and marking it in my mind as a signal to back off.

And so I tear my eyes away from the ballroom and focus on *her*—on my Zenny-bug, who is beautiful and who also looks like she's a combination of angry and amused and annoyed and...pitying, maybe?

I take a deep breath, trying to harness my fury, because it's not directed at her and I don't want her to think for a second that it is. "Zenny, they were saying—"

"I know."

"They were acting like you—"

"*I know*, Sean. I know."

But how can she tell me that she knows and still act like she doesn't want to pour boiling oil over everyone in that cursed ballroom? "Zenny, they were acting like that because you're—" and here I falter, because I'm still so angry, and saying the bald truth out loud feels like having a nest of hornets in my mouth. "Because—"

"Because I'm black," she says. "They assumed I was working the event because I'm black. They saw me, a black woman, in what they think of as 'their' space, and to them it was a logical assumption that I was the help."

"But…that's shitty," I protest.

"I know."

"Because why *wouldn't* a black woman belong in there? Why is it more likely that you were a server than that you legitimately belonged there?"

"I know, Sean. You don't have to tell me."

"And that part about you belonging only after they realized who your dad was!" I fume, barely even listening to her now, so lost in my own anger. "That almost makes it worse, like, oh, now it's okay because we've vetted your parents?"

"Sean," Zenny says, holding up a hand. The first edge of bitter impatience lines her voice. "Please. I know all of this."

"But," I splutter, "then why are you so calm right now? How can you live with it?"

This strikes a nerve; I see it in the copper flash of her eyes. "This is my life, Sean. I deal with this every fucking day. What am I supposed to do? Not live? Not go anywhere ever? Not talk to anyone ever?"

"But then why aren't you *angry?*" I demand.

"Because I can't get angry!" Zenny bursts out, her words loud and shaking with frustration. And then, clearing her throat and glancing around the empty hallway, she says again, "I can't get angry. If I get angry, then I'm the Angry Black Woman. If I admit to having my feelings hurt, then I'm being too sensitive. If I ask for people to treat me thoughtfully, then I'm being aggressive. If I joke back, then I'm being impertinent or sassy. If I cry, then I'm hyperemotional. If I don't react at all, I'm intimidating or cold. Do you see? There's not a way I can react where I win. *I can't win.*"

Her words gouge at me, at the space in my heart that's cracked open just for her in the last week and they also gouge at my mind, where my admittedly flawed concepts of fairness live. I hurt for her, I want to bleed for her, I want to fix it—

I want to fix it

I want to fix it

I want to fix it

"Okay," I say. "But *I* can get angry—let me go back in there and—"

"Sean," she says sharply. "Stop. If you go back in there

304

and do anything else, the headline is not going to be 'Noble Sean Bell Heroically Defends Young Woman.' It's still going to be 'Black Girl Causes Scene.'"

"But—"

"It will reflect back on me. And," she adds in a defeated tone, "it will reflect back onto my parents. I can't risk that. I can't risk their standing and their livelihoods just so that *you* feel better. Please tell me you understand this."

And all at once, I feel like seventeen emotions are collapsing in on me. Rage and righteousness and concern for her and the need to protect her and—ugh, defensiveness. Shame. I don't like admitting them to myself; they're such gross feelings to have right now, when all of me should be focused on Zenny, but they're there.

And I realize those flashes of shame and defensiveness are there because I'm just as guilty as Sophia or Hayley. Maybe not tonight, maybe not in the exact same ways, but I'm still guilty. Of assumptions and careless words. Of unkindness and disrespect. Not once ever in my entire life have I been put in a position like Zenny was tonight—a position that she's put in every day—and with deep, ugly regret, I recognize times that I've been on the other side of it. The times when I've been the garbage goose person, the one casually spraying a room with my entitlement.

I'm not innocent of harm and the thought is painful.

"Zenny, I've—I think I've done shitty stuff like this

too." I want to reach for her but I don't let myself. I don't deserve it. "I mean, I know I have."

"I'd be surprised if you hadn't," Zenny says. "You're a straight, cisgendered white man from the Midwest."

"I—" I stop, because I still feel a swell of defensiveness, because I can't *help* those things, I can't change them—but in light of what just happened in the ballroom, I can't deny that they've given me blinders, that they've shaped how I see the world, and probably not for the better.

"Even good people can do or say racist things. Even white boys with an actual, literal, black best friend." She cracks a small smile as she says the last part, and I huff out a self-deprecating breath.

"It's stupid of me. I always knew Elijah was black, that you were black. It's not like I didn't know, but it never seemed like something different, not when we had so much in common. I just never thought outside myself enough to consider what it might mean for you..."

"It's okay," she says, and she takes my hand. "I mean, not *okay* like I'm absolving anything, but *okay* like...you're learning. And learning is good."

I search her lovely face, which looks sad and tired and still all the lovelier for those things. "How can you want to hold my hand after all this? How can you want to touch me?"

She puts her hands on my chest, and then slides her arms around my waist in a full hug. I can't stop myself; I crush her tight against me, bury my face in the crown of her hair. "I'm sure there's something smart and insightful I could say about human interactions within the locus of marginalizing social constructs, but I can't think of it right now," she says into my chest. She tightens her slender arms around me. "All I can think of is that I still trust you. I still like you. I still want you."

That doesn't change reality, but I'm willing to navigate it with you.

That's what she said the night we discussed *us* and what an *us* would look like, and here we are. Navigating. I thought it would be only about our age, about our shared connection with Elijah, but here it is about something else entirely.

I remind her of what she said, and I can feel her smile into my chest.

"You've missed your calling as a prophet," I say, and she sighs against me. Not a sad sigh or a happy sigh. Just a sigh.

"It doesn't take being a prophet to know these things will happen," she says.

Which stirs me up all over again. "I want to build a tower around you, and then build a castle around that tower, and then dig a moat around that castle, and then I want to guard you like a dragon. Burn anyone who tries to hurt you into ash and then scorch those ashes a second time."

She doesn't answer in words, and simply burrows her face in my chest. And together we stand, arms tight, breathing in harmony, her cheek to my heart and my lips pressed to the top of her head.

"I'm getting makeup on your tuxedo," she mumbles, but I don't let her move.

"Fuck the tuxedo."

Finally, she tilts her head to look up at me with liquid eyes. "Take me home," she says.

And I take her home.

CHAPTER
TWENTY-ONE

My apartment is nothing but moonlight.

I open the door for Zenny, and after I lock back up, I don't bother with the lights. I don't bother with anything, actually, except coming up behind where she stands at the window and kissing along her neck. She smells, as always, faintly of roses, and her skin is so soft and delicious. I can't stop kissing her neck, her shoulder, the secret hollow behind her ear. She sighs back into me, a sigh of contented desire this time, her hands reaching up and back to lace in my hair and keep my mouth against her neck. That small act alone has me hard beyond belief, throbbing with the need to fuck.

"Tonight?" she asks.

"Tonight," I confirm, and scoop her easily into my arms, carrying her like a bride to my bedroom. She moves her arms around my neck, and it's so good, so very good.

She's all I want, all I'll ever want, and I almost don't want to put her down when we reach my bed.

"Is this still what you want to do?" I ask her instead, still holding her tight. "Am I still the one you want to do it with?"

"Yes," she says simply. "And yes."

"Are you sure? I know you've said one part of sex doesn't matter any more than the next part, and I know that's technically true, but it just feels like this is different—"

"Sean," she calmly interrupts. "If you don't shut up and start taking my clothes off, I'm going to scream."

And I pause, because even as she says it all bold and daring, I feel her shiver of nervous excitement, I see the shyness hiding in her eyes.

"Honest girl thing?" I check one last time. "Fun-nervous?"

"Honest girl thing," she says clearly. "Fun-nervous. *Please*, for the actual, literal love of God, make love to me."

I don't bother to correct her adorable sex phrasing—I didn't know people actually still said the words *make love*—and she'll see soon enough that I'm not the kind of man to whom words like that apply. Instead I set her gently on the bed and crawl over her, moving in a slouching, slow prowl so that I can absorb every single detail, memorize every single part of this beautiful, trembling girl laid out in front of me.

Her parted lips and her hooded eyes. Her nose ring glinting in the dark and the shadows swirling like fog in the hollows of her collarbone and between her breasts. The gleaming skin of her legs and arms and the tempting swells of sweet, innocent curves underneath the flirtatious chiffon. And her high-heeled feet moving nervously against the bed and her hands twisting fretfully at the fabric of her skirt—both things at odds with the expression on her face, which is one of pure, aroused fascination.

Nervous and bravely wanting—even now, Zenny is a puzzle of feelings, quivering like a virgin sacrifice but looking at me like I'm her next meal. It's endlessly enthralling, and I drink down every part of it. I've fucked an untold number of women, but this is something different, something much different, and it's all to do with *her*. All to do with this strange cavity she's carved out of my chest and left empty and keening.

I'd dreamt of this night since the gala—exactly how I would unwrap her body, in what gradual stages I'd uncover her nakedness and kiss and lick at her skin. Exactly how I would seduce her already willing body and introduce her to my own body and its needs. But before I can execute any of my careful plan, Zenny reaches up for my face and pulls me down for a long, lingering kiss, a deep one of shared breath and parted lips and silky tongues. Between us, my cock pulses like a living iron bar. I try to hold it up from her, which she notices.

"Be yourself. Don't baby me," she says against my mouth, and I remember all the times Elijah and I were trailed by a pigtailed Zenny, demanding the same thing. *Don't baby me.* I'm the boy who once tied her shoelaces and helped her find her missing Barbies, and is it reprehensible or some kind of fucked-up destiny that I'm the one to initiate her into these things now that she's grown?

"I've never fucked a virgin before," I admit. I'm over her, braced up on my arms, and still tuxedoed, and the flowing skirt of her dress is everywhere, tangled around my dress shoes and half-rucked up around one of her thighs and spilling around our knees like a sea of tears.

"Really?" she asks. "Never?"

"Never," I say, ducking my head to nip at her breasts through her dress. "You're my first."

"What would you do if I weren't a virgin?" she asks curiously, her words studded with gasps as I bite teasingly at her. "Would you do anything different?"

"Some things."

"Like what?"

I shift my weight to my knees and elbows so that I can find her hands with my own. "Well, first," I say, leaving her breasts to kiss at her neck and jaw, "I'd pin your hands over your head, like this." And I do as I'm narrating, stretching her arms over her head and keeping them locked there with one of my hands around her wrists.

"Oh," she says underneath me, and she gives a shivery kind of wriggle. A happy wriggle.

"And then I'd reach under your dress and check your pussy, to see if you were wet for me." And I do that too, finding the weightless hem of her dress and sliding my hand up her warm thigh, my thumb brushing across the bare, slick skin of her snatch. She lets out a low whimper, her legs falling completely open and her back arching the tiniest bit underneath me.

"No panties?" I ask in a growl, rising up to my knees and yanking her dress up to her waist to see for myself.

"No panties," she agrees. And sure enough, that cunt I'm so obsessed with is naked and exposed, a velvet split between her legs. The revelation that she was bare all night like this, that I could have pulled up her skirt and tasted her whenever I wanted...

I groan at the very thought, leaning down to smell her.

"Sean!" she says, her voice embarrassed as I press my nose and lips to her cunt and breathe her in deep. Why she hasn't accepted the terminal thing I have for her pussy yet, I don't understand. I love everything about her cunt; I love to smell her and to taste her and even just to look at her, which is what I do now. I spread her legs, and in the moonlight, I stare at the welcoming, wet seam; I use my thumbs to part her folds and see the tight, pink place I'm about to fuck. And very suddenly, it's not enough to be only looking at her, I need more, more, more, and I settle between her thighs for a long kiss on her pussy, and I stay there for several more kisses, enjoying the delicate scrape of her high heels along my back, the tangle of her skirt around my head, and her taste. Fuck, do I enjoy her taste. Sweet and intimate and all her.

"Sean," she says again, but her tone has changed, and now she sounds like she's been running, like she can't quite remember how to breathe. "Sean, oh, oh God—"

I've added a finger now, and then another, and she's unraveling into a sheer sensation, all twisting limbs and panting breaths and that delicious dress tangling everywhere around us, and then her first climax rolls through her like a storm, sending her tightening around my fingers and grinding against my face.

I love it.

I'm ready to do it again.

But then Zenny comes down from her peak and reaches for me, and I reluctantly come up from between her legs, torn between kissing her cunt to another climax or crawling into her arms. But it's worth sacrificing the chance to give her another orgasm to have her hold me, to hold her again, to kiss her and let her lick her own taste off my mouth like some kind of curious kitten.

It also makes me nearly wild with need, and enduring her kissing me like this is something close to madness.

"You're shaking," she whispers, pulling away from our kiss to search my face. Her eyes are metallic, her mouth is wet. Jesus Christ.

And I am shaking. I'm shaking because I need to fuck, I'm shaking because the woman I need to fuck is a woman I'm feeling insane things for, I'm shaking because I'm going to fuck a woman I'm in love with for the first time in my life.

I'm shaking because—*wait*.

Wait.

Am I *in love* with Zenny?

The idea stuns me even as the truth of it thrums down to my bones, and it floods every part of me as we kiss again, as she wraps her legs around my waist and pulls me close. I love her. I love Zenobia Iverson, and maybe I have since the moment she knocked on my door, asking me to make her doubt. Since our first kiss, even. Or the night at the gala, when I met her as an adult and red silk kissed her skin in all the ways I couldn't.

"Teach me now," she breathes, oblivious to the earth-shattering awakening I'm having, oblivious to the real source of my trembling. "Do the thing where you teach me?"

I move my lips away from her mouth and kiss her ear. "Is that how you want to do this?"

"Yes," she says. "It makes me feel...special. Safe."

And how can I argue with that?

I yank at my bow tie as I rise up on my knees, unknotting it and shucking my jacket. I'm in the middle of unbuttoning my shirt when she gives a little whine.

"What is it, baby?"

She bites her lip and then says, "We're going to have lots of sex, right?"

"Lots and lots."

"Then save all the tenderly undressing parts for later. I want you to fuck me *now*." She sounds a little grouchy, and I have to laugh.

"Such a demanding little virgin," I murmur, leaning down to nip at her jaw. "I thought I was supposed to be the teacher here, hmm?"

"As long as you teach me fast," she says huffily. And after I untie the dress's halter at the back of her neck, I rise up to look down at her. Her skirt is a puddle of blue-green around her hips, her thighs are spread revealing a wet and kiss-swollen pussy. The bodice of her dress is now drooping off her chest, revealing her upthrust breasts with their furled, needy tips. A demanding little virgin, indeed, all the traces of nervousness now melted away and leaving only unselfconscious desire in its wake.

I let my hand drift over her tummy and find a place holding her hip still as my other hand goes to my fly. Pinning her like this as I one-handedly get my cock out feels filthy, on just this side of wrong, and judging from the way she squirms and chews on her lip as she stares at my hand working open my pants, she feels the same.

The breath she lets out once it's free actually eclipses

my own, as if she felt the discomfort of my trapped arousal as acutely as I did, and then I take her hand and guide her to me, guide her into handling and stroking me. I grunt with pleasure at her still-uncertain handling of my cock.

"You feel how hard it is, baby?" I ask. "It's like that for you."

She makes a low purr of satisfaction, her eyes not on my face but on the crude thickness of my erection in her hand.

"Here," I say, taking her hand and wrapping it around the head of my cock. "This is where I'll start. Just with the tip of me. I'll find where you're wet and tight, and I'll begin to push in. It'll feel big, Zenny, so big at first, like I'll split you open, and just when you think you can't do it, I'll push in a little bit more." I circle my hand over hers and push it down, just a little, so that she's gripping me around my shaft just under my tip. "I'll be stretching you to take me, and I'll be petting you and rubbing you the entire time so that the stretch feels good, it feels like what you need."

"And then?" she asks in a whisper, looking up at my face.

I guide her hand all the way down to my root. "And then I'll be all the way inside you. And it will feel so good, baby, so full, full like you've never felt. Then I'll start to move, start to slide—" I coax her hand into mimicking the motion. "—that's when I'll be thrusting. That's how we'll fuck."

"Yes," she says, looking a little dazed and a lot excited. "That's how we'll fuck."

I lean over to my end table and fish out a condom, handing the packet to her once I have it, patiently waiting as she fumbles to get it open.

"This way," I say kindly, showing her how to start it with the pinch and the roll, and then letting go and allowing her to roll it all the way on. Seeing her like this, eager and clumsy, is painfully arousing, and I find myself breathing in deep, shaky breaths to keep from tackling her and fucking her bare. I've never fucked a woman bare, and it's never been something that I've thought much about before, but God, the image of my naked cock pushing into that sweet, tight cunt…

Fuck. I want it. I want it and I'll never be able to have it.

"There," Zenny says, sitting back and admiring my shining, sheathed penis. She looks proud of her handiwork, and it's really quite charming. She's sitting in a pool of unbound chiffon, mussed and well-pleasured, and she's looking at my erection like a term project she's just gotten a good grade on.

"Such a good student," I praise. "Such a good girl."

She looks pleased.

"It's time, sweetheart. Lay back."

And she does, spreading her legs without me telling her, and I praise her for that too, for being so smart, for being so perfect. I lean forward and tuck a pillow under her head, and then I give her a quick kiss on the lips. "Watch," I tell her, and with the pillow behind her head, she can and she does. She watches as I kneel between her legs, as I brace myself over her, my loose bowtie dangling between us. I should tear it off, but both my hands are occupied and I honestly can't bring myself to care right now.

I'm about to fuck the woman I love, and that's all I can ever care about.

I take myself in hand and caress her entrance with my cock. The head of me is blunt and fat and wide, and much, much bigger than the tiny seam it's currently rubbing against, and she stiffens the moment I make contact, the moment she feels for herself exactly how big the cock is that wants inside her pussy.

And so I lean down and croon in her ear about how brave she is to take me, how sexy she is, how good I'll make her little cunt feel if she'll let me. And as I say all this, I keep pressing and rubbing and gently pushing until finally, finally, my tip squeezes inside of her.

She arches underneath me, letting out a stung noise, and I'm letting out the same noise, because it's so tight, God help me, it's so tight. I'm only barely inside her, and already I can feel my groin clenching hot and deep with the need to release.

"Stay with me," I murmur, dropping my forehead to

hers. "Stay with me."

She nods underneath me, her hands coming up to lace around my neck in a gesture that conveys pure, unsullied trust. Trust I don't deserve, but I'll do everything not to betray.

"It's going to pinch," I tell her. "But it shouldn't hurt, because you're nice and wet and ready for me. But if it does hurt, tell me and I'll fix it."

She nods again. "Okay. I—" she gives the most tentative of movements with her hips, and I nearly come from that alone. "It feels better now. Put more inside me."

I lift my head so that she can lift hers and continue to watch as I push in another inch. The stretch of her around my cock is the filthiest thing I've ever seen and also the sweetest thing I've ever felt, and then I give her another inch. "You're so tight here," I mutter, and I can feel sweat starting to bead along the muscled furrows of my back and stomach. My bracing arm is trembling—my entire body is trembling, actually—with restraint.

"You're shaking again," she says.

"It's because of you."

This earns me a kiss. "More," she commands, like a little queen.

"Darling, I'm going to have to push," I say, my voice as shivery as my body right now. "It's so fucking tight, I can't—"

"More," she says impatiently, and so I press my hips

forward and slide in deeper, regretting every bit of force it takes to wedge in deeper.

She's been watching me as I feed my cock into her pussy, but with this last thrust, she falls back, her eyes squeezing closed.

I freeze. "Zenny?"

"It doesn't hurt...exactly," she assures me, eyes still closed. Except her words aren't very reassuring. I start to withdraw and her hands fly from my neck to my hips.

"No," she begs. "Stay. Keep going. I'm breathing through it and...*oh.*" This last comes as I rock in and out the tiniest bit, giving her a little taste of what it will be like when I fuck her in truth.

"It doesn't hurt," she says again, but this time her words have a faint wonder to them. "It feels good."

"Yeah?"

"Yeah."

"Halfway there, baby," I soothe her. "Halfway there."

I look down at where we're joined myself and groan. *Fuck me*, but she's tight, and the stark visual of my thickness spearing her virgin pussy is nearly too much. It's only the barest shred of my control that keeps me from piercing the rest of the way home in one, sure thrust. Instead, I go slowly, agonizingly slowly, until finally at last, I'm all the way inside. I'm finally able to let go of my cock, and I brace myself on my elbows so that I can cradle her face in my hands.

"How are you doing?" I ask her, searching her face. "Okay?"

"Yes," she says, and her hands move to pet at my stomach and chest. "Very yes."

"I'm going to start moving now, and I'm going to play with your cunt as I do. We're going to go slowly at first."

And that's how we begin for real—in slow, succulent movements, with her running her fingers along my abs and me braced on one arm by her head, my other hand splayed near her hip and my thumb working soft circles around her clit. And I'm murmuring more teacher words to her, telling her how good she is, how clever and how curious, telling her to move her hips or to hug my waist with her thighs. It takes all I have to be a teacher right now, all of my threadbare control, because she's fitting me like a tight, hot glove, she's so wet and everywhere she is so beautiful, so perfect, so *Zenny*. Even the tangle of chiffon around her hips is her, even the unpracticed catch of her heels on the bed. I love her and I'm fucking her, and I see now why she used those words earlier, *make love*, because that's what this is. It's still dirty, it's still raw—I'm still gloating over the way her virgin cunt feels on my cock, I'm still biting at her breasts like an animal—but how I feel about her is a shimmering, golden thread through it all. It's electric, sizzling everywhere, ionizing everything, transforming everything into something more than just biology.

I can't explain it because I don't understand it. I don't understand *myself*, even.

I only understand that I love her.

"Sean," she moans, and her head is flung back again, but this time not in pain, definitely not in pain. "I'm going to come again, oh God, oh my God—"

With a cry, she buckles and seizes around me, going so tight and so delicious, and the difference in this orgasm from her first is stunning, momentous, like it's eating her alive and she can't get enough of it. Her cries echo through the room, and she writhes and twists under my body, even as I keep her pinned in place with my hands and my hips. Impaled on my dick, she squirms and whimpers her way through it, finishing at last with an almighty shudder, and the sensation is so carnal, so vulgar, to have another person use you so baldly for their pleasure—and then for that person to be a gorgeous virgin who currently looks stunned, as if she never knew something could feel so good, as good as your cock inside her—

"Shit, shit, shit," I mumble, because I'm coming, I'm going to come while I'm in her pussy, and I can't, I promised her I wouldn't, and I slide out of her cunt just in time. We both watch in crude, animalistic interest as my cock juts glistening and heavy between us, and then with several vicious throbs, fills the condom.

"Oh my God," she breathes, "Sean, oh my God," and then her hands are all over me as I finish grunting and pulsing my way through it, the condom finally full and my body drained.

"Shit," I say again, but it's probably the most reverently that word has ever been uttered.

Then my demanding newly-not-virgin sits up and says, "I want to do it again."

CHAPTER
TWENTY-TWO

I'm amused at her eagerness, but I'm an unmoving wall of aftercare, which earns me a charming little tantrum.

"I'll fuck you every time you ask me," I promise. "But I need to make sure you're doing okay first."

"I'm okay," she pouts. "Now come over here and do it again."

I'm over at the bathroom door; I've just finished with the condom, and also with a ten-second staring session in the mirror where I stared at the face of a man who's in love.

I've never been in love before.

It's gutting and disorienting and dizzying—and *joyful.* Like a roller coaster careening wildly around corners, like a car punching into top gear as the highway streaks away underneath you. Like standing in a prairie summer storm—the blowing rain soaking your skin, lightning sawing across the sky, the wind a part of a song that you knew a long time ago but have since forgotten.

It's too soon, but I love her.

She's Elijah's little sister and much too young for me, and she only wants me for sex, but I love her.

And she's going to leave me for her God, but I love her.

I go back to the bed, and I undress her, I undress myself. I make us shower, flicking water at her from the spray while she stands just outside pulling on her shower cap and wrinkling her cute little nose at me. I spend a long time washing and soaping and massaging her, petting her and spoiling her and telling her how much I want her, how grateful I am, how perfect she is.

I don't say that I love her. Not because I doubt it, not because it's new, but because I honestly think it might spook her given her reaction to my *there are no other women I care about like this* comment the other day. I don't want to scare her away, not when I've just gotten her, and also—is it even fair for me to tell her this? She didn't explicitly say *and we can't fall in love* when we were negotiating our arrangement, but I'd felt it in the air nonetheless, hanging like a heavy fog.

I don't think she wants that from me.

And it might even be cruel to burden her with it in the looming face of her vows.

So I stay silent about that part, and after we're toweled off, I spend another long time rubbing her with lotion and she rubs me with her lotion so that I smell like roses and I don't even care. I want to smell like her always, I want to carry roses with me wherever I go. And I use the lotion as an excuse to check the bite marks on her breasts, to gently test her clit for soreness. I'm hard, and I'd love nothing more than to burrow inside her soft heat once again, but I refuse to hurt her. I couldn't stand it if I hurt her.

But gradually she convinces me that she's not sore, not hurting, and we go again, completely naked this time. She wants to try being on top, and she pierces herself on my offered-up cock in a slow, anguished slide. She's shaking as she sinks home, and I murmur reassuring words to her, run gentling hands over her flanks and hips. I tell her how hot she is like this, perched above me like a goddess, how sweet her tits look, how hard it makes me to see her pussy stretched around my base, as if I barely fit. I *do* barely fit, and the thought is inflamingly coarse, sinfully vulgar.

So of course I share that with her too.

She rides herself to a whimpering, shaking orgasm— one I endure marginally more stoically than the last time— and when she's finished, I make to pull off the condom.

"No," she insists, dismounting me as if I were her steed, her stallion.

(God, that thought shouldn't be as erotic as it is, but fuck me, I can't help it.)

She puts her hand on my wrist. "Come in the condom again," she says, her eyes gleaming in the dark. "I like to watch it."

"Your wish is my command," I whisper, and as she kneels next to me, my little anthropologist once more, I wrap my hand around my Zenny-wet cock and jerk off.

Strictly speaking, jerking off through a condom is not something I'd normally enjoy, but it doesn't matter now. With Zenny next to me, her perfect tits hanging forward as she leans in for a better view, and her lovely, fascinated face in profile with her button nose and long eyelashes, it doesn't take much. I only need to pull on myself a handful of times before my erection swells inside the condom and starts pumping out my release.

It's raw somehow, raw and almost unclean feeling— which is surprising given that it's perhaps the cleanest sex act one can perform—but it's something about how it traps my cock inside its own leavings, something about how much it puts my grunting, rough release on display.

It's enough to make a man hard again.

Which is how we end up having sex a third time, this time tangled together on our sides, one of her legs over my hip and my arms tight around her. It's slow and languorous and when she comes, it's nearly silent: a caught breath and then the telltale contractions on my dick.

I jack off a final time—yes, into a condom once again, I really can't refuse Zenny anything—and we clean up and crawl into bed like two tired children coming home from a theme park. Exhausted physically, exuberant mentally, sleep a fuzzy, earned embrace waiting for us the moment we close our eyes.

"Thank you," Zenny murmurs, tucking herself into me. "It was everything I wanted. More than I could have wanted."

"No, thank you, darling."

And I almost don't ask, because the night has ended so perfectly, so sweetly, but I have to. "Zenny, what happened with Northcutt today?"

She yawns, and I relax the tiniest bit because I don't think she'd yawn if something terrible had happened. "He met with me and the Reverend Mother, tried to convince us to issue a follow-up statement to the news outlets that Valdman and Associates has been nothing but helpful, it was all a misunderstanding, yada yada. We said no."

Relief rolls over me at the same time as delight. "You told him no? Just like that?"

"Well, the Reverend Mother did. And he started to be shitty and then she asked him to leave her office and he did. She's very intimidating when she wants to be."

I picture the scene, with stupid Northcutt fleeing the office with his tail between his legs, some old lady in a giant winged nun's hat scolding him as he goes. It's a very nice scene to imagine.

"So you're okay? She's okay? I was so fucking worried

when I heard."

"We're okay," Zenny says sleepily. "Believe it or not, we can take care of ourselves without Sean Bell coming in to save the day." She pats my chest as if I'm a tamed bear who thinks he's ferocious, but is only a harmless old lump instead.

"I know, I know…I just want you to be safe, is all. I—" *wrong word, Sean!* "—care about you."

"Mmm. I care about you too. And I like that you care about me."

She says it simply, dozily, and it's the last thing she says before she falls into sex-exhausted sleep.

But me? I stay awake for a long time, my brain still spinning and reeling with this new thing, this new love. This new love that I can't ever, ever keep.

The next week passes in a blur of sex and work. We find a rhythm that feels impossibly right—sex in the morning, then work for me and classes and rotations for her. In the evening she has her shelter shifts and I start going with, because I can't stand to be apart from her (of course, I don't just get to hover around her and steal kisses when no one's looking; she puts me to work in the kitchen). And then we come home and fuck late into the night. Her curiosity knows no bounds, it makes her brave, and she tries the jeweled plug for the first time and loves it. We fuck in every position she wants to try, every position I can think of, we sneak a fuck in my office and one in the corner of an expensive restaurant. We snuggle and watch movies and I burn with this secret love for her and it chars me up inside, it sears me and cracks me. I can't get enough of it.

I try to make her doubt in earnest.

It never works.

And it's a stinging thing to note that even as I try my hardest, even as I throw every reason I ever hated God or despised the Church at her, I can't crack her faith the way her love cracks me. I can't carve away her connection with God the same way she's carved a gap into my heart that she refuses to fill.

I can't bear to tell her I love her. It feels manipulative somehow...and also I'm frightened. I don't think I'll survive it if I tell her and she dismisses it. Dismisses me. I can even imagine it, in my worst moments, the way her mouth will soften in pity and her eyes will shine from compassion.

Sean, I'm flattered, she'll say, and she'll do something mortifying, like pat my shoulder. *But you know I don't feel the same way. You know I never will.*

God, the fucking irony of a sinner loving a nun. It's agony. I'm dying. And as I'm both alight and aflame with loving her, these splashes of thought keep coming out of nowhere, like raindrops on a sunny day.

Raindrop number one: I'm jealous of Zenny's relationship with God—not only jealous like a lover watching his beloved with someone else but jealous that she has it. Jealous that she's mature enough to be angry about all the pain in the world and to accuse God of not doing enough, and then in the same breath, work to change that pain in His name.

Raindrop number two: Zenny reminds me of the things I loved about God. A sense of curiosity, a bravery, a turbulent emotion bundled close with the deepest peace. Things I felt about God once upon a time, and felt about myself.

Raindrop number three: if loving Zenny is even close to the way she loves God, I understand why she's choosing this life.

I realized being furious with Him was not the same thing as wanting Him out of my life. That's what my mom said the day I found her with the rosary. What if that were true for me too? Is hating God the same thing as not believing in Him? Can you hate a thing you don't believe in?

And when I say I hate God, what do I mean? Do I mean that I'm angry about Lizzy, angry that humans who were supposed to serve goodness were actually monsters, and that it's all His fault? Do I mean I never want to think about Him again? Or do I mean that I want to rage at Him, to howl and pace and scream, and have Him listen? Have Him witness and hear and see my pain?

And one night, in the dark as Zenny sleeps, I send up a thought like a balloon.

I still hate you, I think up to the ceiling. *You let us all down and I'll never forgive you.*

Nothing happens. The ceiling remains a ceiling, my room remains quiet save for the soft snores of the little nun at my side. There's no burning bushes or shimmering prophets poking their heads out of the walls.

Except when I tell Zenny about it the next morning, she gives me a knowing smile and eyes full of compassion.

"Sean," she says. "That was a prayer. You prayed."

It's like looking up and seeing a green sky, this thought.

It haunts me for days.

CHAPTER
TWENTY-THREE

Two weeks left.

CHAPTER
TWENTY-FOUR

I stare at my phone for a minute before I slide it back into my pocket. The property owner is ahead of me, talking in over-bright tones to the Reverend Mother and Zenny, gesturing around to windows and load-bearing beams. I should be up there with them, and I will be.

In just a moment.

It's another bowel obstruction, Dad had explained. *They don't know if it's the old site flaring up or something new—new mets in her intestines, maybe. Adhesions from the last surgery. They did a suction on her stomach to relieve the pressure; she's about to go in for a scan now.*

It's funny how quickly everything can fall apart. Only last week she was putting away dishes and arguing about God...and now we're back in the hospital, possibly facing another surgery.

I glance at my watch. It's 4:13 now, and Dad thinks

Mom will be done with her scan and back in her room before six. That should give me plenty of time to finish the tour and drop Zenny off at the shelter and the Reverend Mother back at the monastery.

Maintain, you idiot, I chastise myself. Because my hands are shaking, and for a dumb, terrible minute, all I can feel is this kind of stale fear and even staler exhaustion. Because I know once I get to the hospital, it will be the triple duty of comforting Dad and handling the doctors and keeping Mom company. I love my father, but he can barely be strong enough for her—he can't be strong for himself. Or be counted on to ask hard questions and to chase down nurses and to demand every next step Mom needs.

It has to be me.

I take a breath and catch up with the group.

"And here, we can easily build in an office for you," the owner is saying.

The prioress is nodding thoughtfully. "And the expense?" she asks.

"Well, ideally…" the owner trails off as the prioress studies him. She's in her mid-seventies, black, short and stout, with massive glasses and wrinkled, expressive hands. They're folded over her belly now as she waits for him to finish saying whatever stupid thing he's going to say.

He wisely reconsiders. "I'd be happy to do the renovations myself."

"Oh, how kind," the Reverend Mother says. "That would be a lovely gift."

She says it in a way that's genuine, that even *I* feel, and I think she *is* warmly grateful. But I also recognize as a businessman that she's getting exactly what she needs from him, and all it took was a silent look. I wonder if she gives lessons.

And then it's done. The prioress approves the site, both parties sign a provisional contract I drew up, and then I'm driving the women away from the property. I can't kiss Zenny goodbye at the shelter with the Reverend Mother waiting in my car by the curb, but I do get out and walk her to the front door and tell her things that have her lashes fluttering until she disappears inside. And then I climb back into the car, preparing to drive the Reverend Mother back to the monastery, which is a sprawling old house in Midtown.

"So you're the man having sex with Zenobia," the Reverend Mother says before I can even get my seat belt buckled.

My hand fumbles for a minute on the belt; a thousand awful, awkward scenarios roll through my mind, the worst ones featuring Zenny exiled from this vocation she holds so dear and the least worst involving unwelcome lectures about chastity and propriety.

It occurs to me, in a racing shadow of desperate expediency, that I could lie to her. I could say that I'm simply helping with this shelter move and trying to make up for my part in the Keegan deal. I could say that Zenny's an old friend, that what I feel for her is nothing more than older-brotherly, and I'm merely looking out for her for Elijah's sake.

But right after the shadow comes a quick slant of light.

I can't lie.

Not only would lying to the Reverend Mother be—I suspect—quite futile, as she'd see through it immediately and be understandably unimpressed with my deceit, but I can't help but feel that Zenny wouldn't want me to lie. That she'd want me to be honest no matter what the consequences were, because she would do the same in my place. Because she has lived honestly, even when it came at the cost of her identity as the model Iverson daughter, even when it brought her parents' disapproval down around her ears. Here I am, a thirty-six-year-old millionaire taking courage from a college student, but there you are. When the college student is Zenny, you'd be foolish not to use her as an example.

And—cheeringly—I realize that any lecture can only last as long as the drive to Midtown, which is about fifteen minutes in the afternoon traffic.

I finish buckling, start the car, and glance over at the prioress. She's staring serenely back at me, knobbled hands folded in her lap, the stark framing of her wimple around her head making her eyes behind their glasses look even bigger, inescapable.

"Yes," I say. I don't know what else to say after that, though, so I turn back to the road and shift into gear and we pull away.

"And?"

Well, that was definitely not what I was expecting. Does she want some kind of report? Or am I due for a lecture and she wants to start with me accounting for my actions like a schoolboy?

"And what, ma'am?"

She makes a noise—it's the noise old people make when they think young people are being deliberately obtuse. "How is she? How is she feeling? Where does her heart wander? I might be her mentor but you are her lover—surely you know these things."

My hand opens and closes on the gearshift as I search for words. Trying to describe Zenny in some kind of bizarre moral report—and within such a short time as the drive allows—is an impossibility. Zenny defies simple observations, simple explanations. It's part of why I love her so much.

"Try," the old nun says, seeing my struggle.

I don't like talking about Zenny like this—when she's not here—so I decide to talk about her only in the most abstract and broad strokes, so as not to accidentally betray any confidence.

"She's magnificent and fierce and smart," I say. I think

of the roller-skating rink, of our nights together at the shelter, and then say, "She cares more than I can tell you about the people in the shelter and becoming a midwife for the needy; she speaks about God with reverence and balance. She told me she wanted to take this month to make certain of her path and her upcoming vows, and all I see from her is ironclad certainty." I give a smile that I mean to be lighthearted but it twists bitterly on my mouth instead. "She's more committed than ever."

"Ah. You love her."

What's the point of denying it? "Yes," I say, helplessly. "Yes, I love her."

"And you don't understand why she chooses this path."

I shrug with one shoulder as I shift gears. "I understand it better than I did two weeks ago, but...you're right. I still don't understand. Not all the way."

The nun is silent for a moment, and I get the impression she's more comfortable in silence than she is in words, and it's not as awkward as I would have thought it might be, sharing a car with someone who prefers quiet.

It's actually quite soothing, the silence not heavy or demanding or smothering. It's restful, and everything takes a kind of bluing, quieting hue like this. Zenny and my unrequited love for her, my mother in a hospital bed right now, getting scans and tubes and medicines.

Images of empty sanctuaries flit through my mind, the

kind of reverent hush that comes with a sacred space. The calming way candles flicker and dance along the edges of the room.

"Zenny told me about your sister. It was a terrible thing that was done to her. A terrible, evil thing."

And suddenly, like a key turning in a lock, I trust this woman. I trust her because she didn't give me some blandishment about God's will or how Lizzy is "in a better place" (although even the last phrase was only sparingly handed out following Lizzy's suicide, given the uneasy Catholic attitude toward self-destruction and its implications for the immortal soul). The Reverend Mother didn't offer up an empty apology or murmur something about praying for our family or Lizzy's soul.

She simply said the truth. And having the truth acknowledged feels like an embrace and comfort all on its own. I thought of the night last week when I prayed; when I decided to believe in God just long enough to accuse and censure Him, when I realized I wanted Him to sit and listen to me roar and scream until my voice was hoarse. Because having God listen to the truth, to really *hear* it, to really *see* it, was the only thing that could heal the sister-shaped gouge in my soul.

I'd tried disbelief, I'd tried scorn, I'd tried every kind of nonbeliever's stance and sinner's trick, and I tried them for a decade and a half, and still there was this ragged, infected wound somewhere inside me. The only thing left to try was going back to God and informing Him of the mess He'd made.

"It was terrible," I echo. My voice is barely there when I say it.

"And so you wonder how anyone can believe in God after that? After what She let happen?"

That catches my notice. "*She*?" I taunt, gently. "That's not very devout."

The prioress smiles. "Biblical metaphors for God include a laboring woman, a breastfeeding mother, even a mother hen. And man *and* woman were both created in God's image, were they not? Why use Him and not Her? In fact, why even say God instead of Goddess? Both Him and Her are not enough to contain the fullness of God, who is outside the construct of gender, who is so much more than the human mind can conceive."

I smile too, because if this is a sample of the Reverend Mother's mentoring style, I can see why Zenny is at home in her order.

"I don't know what to think about God," I say, going back to our earlier thread. "I used to know exactly what I thought, I used to know exactly how I felt. But I'm more confused than ever. It feels like going backwards, going from being *sure* to not sure at all. Going from all the answers to none."

The nun nods, as if I've said something wise and not just confessed to my own muddle-headed stupidity.

"Isn't that bad?" I follow up. "Not to know *anything*? And then I look at Zenny and how she is so comfortable with what she doesn't know, and that scares me too. I'm worried getting comfortable with not knowing means surrendering something crucial."

"Sean, faith and belief are the practices of committing a life in the face of no answers. God is and always will be outside of human comprehension. And loving Her is an *act*, it's not stubbornly repeating creeds and trying to force Her into modern expectations or rational paradigms. She'll never fit in the same boxes we apply to science and reason; She's not meant to. And to try to force it only breeds spiritual violence in the end."

"Okay," I concede, although the things she just said are all things I'll have to think about later. "That's God. But what about the Church then? Can't Zenny—or you or any of the sisters—do these same good works without pledging away your free will?"

"Our free will?"

"Obedience is one of the vows, isn't it? Obedience to the Church? Obedience to the men who run it?"

The old woman snorts, and I look over in surprise. "I'll be obedient to those bishops the day I die and not a day sooner." At my expression, she huffs again. "I'm obedient to God and to my conscience and to the poor. I'm obedient to my fellow sisters."

And then under her breath, she mutters, "Obedient to *men*. Hmph."

"But they're the entire administrative structure of the Church."

"For now. But the Church belongs to us as much as it belongs to them." And then she nods her head at her own words.

I want to protest this—there's still so much I can complain about, ways that the Church hasn't changed since the abuse scandals for example—but then she adds, "We make a place for people to meet God and for God to meet Her people. A place that is safe and free of corruption."

And I can't argue with that. In fact, it's the perfect counterargument to my complaining about the evil hierarchy of the Church—the nuns have carved out a place separate from the bishops and the bullshit and the bureaucracy, a place where they can put their heads down and get on with the work of serving the sick and the poor.

Of course, I understand that it's not that simple—I've heard Tyler talk enough about the troubles between the nuns and the Vatican to know that the men still frequently try to take the women in hand. But the sisters, as the saying goes, persist.

I notice the Reverend Mother shivering the slightest bit and turn down the AC. "So that sorts obedience," I concede. "But what about chastity?"

"I'll admit, I'm less strict about it than many Reverend Mothers—as you well know. But we ask chastity of our vowed nuns not only as a trust and sacrifice to God, but also so that they live lives free of other obligations. Our sisters are free to serve the poor completely because they don't have children and families of their own. Because they don't have needy men taking up their time."

Well. Fair.

"It just seems like so much to give up," I say.

"It is." The prioress doesn't argue with me. "It is."

We turn onto a street of large old houses; the monastery sprawls over a shady corner, marked only with a hand-painted wooden sign by the porch stairs and a Virgin Mary statue in the semi-neglected flower bed.

When I park the car in the driveway, the Reverend Mother turns to me once more. "So you love Zenobia. Are you certain she does not love you back?"

I think of her confession on the day she asked me to do this with her. That she'd always wanted me. And then I think of her laughter at the skating rink when I mentioned marrying her, of her troubled face when I told her she would be the only woman I cared about, of my messy and imperfect reaction the night those people were shitty to her at the gala.

It's only for a month. It's not like we have to figure out how to raise children together.

"I'm certain," I say tiredly.

"Have you told her?"

I shake my head.

"Tell her," the old nun commands, unwinding her fingers from one another so that she can poke one in my direction. "She deserves to know."

"Isn't it…kind of cheap to fling that at her now? She has so much to think about already, and it feels like I'm trying to sabotage her moment."

"I like your awareness, but in this case, you're using it as an excuse." She nods to herself again, the starched fabric of her wimple brushing roughly along her shoulders. "Are all those muscles just for show or are you actually strong, my son?"

And with that, she unbuckles her seat belt. I scramble to help her out of the car, and we don't say anything else as I walk her to the door, but the look she gives me before she goes inside is very loud with all the things she doesn't say.

Tell her, the look says above all else, and my heart gives a hopeful and ugly lurch at the very thought.

Mom has a NG tube coming out of her nose, and she hates it. She can be patient about IVs and ports, but the moment there's something on her face, she gets irritable—and in this case, the thing is *in* her face, not just on it.

I do my Sean Bell thing when I get there, the Oldest Child thing, all the rituals and little sacrifices made to the Church of Cancer. I see first to Mom, then to Dad, who is, as always, a fraying shell of himself in these circumstances. After Mom is asleep, exhausted from the pain and the procedures, I manage to find the charge nurse and doctor on rotation, and avail myself of every detail of the day.

All that sorted, I send Dad out to get us some real dinner—not cafeteria dinner—and sit in Mom's room and try to work from my laptop.

Aiden shows up a few minutes later, his suit and hair rumpled, like he spent the day sleeping (which I know for a fact he didn't because he emailed me no less than three times this morning about a puppy he wants to adopt). He flings himself on the small, hard couch next to me.

"She doing okay?" he asks, running his hand through his messy hair. He's breathing hard too.

"Yeah. I mean, for now. We don't know yet what's causing the blockage, and I guess the suction got messy and difficult, so that's not great."

"Oh," he says.

"I texted like three hours ago. Where were you?"

"I just got your message," he says vaguely. "I was almost out to the farmhouse. Had to turn back."

Hmm.

I give him a more careful once-over. His tie has been hastily re-knotted, the laces on his dress shoes are untied, and there's something about his face, all flushed and swollen-mouthed.

"You were having sex!" I accuse, sitting up.

"Shh!" he hushes me frantically, glancing over at Mom, who's still deep in a morphine nap.

"Don't *shh* me," I say irritably. "You think Mom doesn't know you're a total fuckboy?"

Aiden looks very annoyed at my lack of quiet. "That's not true."

I roll my eyes. If Aiden were a Wakefield Saga character, there would be all kinds of words for him. Rakehell, scoundrel, cyprian, cad, libertine, lothario. He's barely better than Double Condom Mike, and I know a lot of the trouble he's gotten in because I was right there next to him. In fact, until he started acting weird last month, I would have put good money on him having more sex and with more women than me.

"I don't *care* that you were having sex, dummy," I say. "Mom wouldn't either. It's just a dumb reason not to be here."

He sighs. "I know. I honestly didn't look at my phone until after though. I came as soon as I saw your text."

"Fine. Was she good?"

Aiden looks puzzled for a minute, like he can't quite track this turn in conversation.

"The fuck, Aiden," I clarify, exasperated. "Was she good?"

He opens his mouth. Closes it. And before he can ever make the words come out, Dad is walking in with Indian carryout, and we all fall on the plastic bags like a pack of starving wolves.

The next five or six days pass in a blur. Between Zenny's life and mine, all we get together are nights and mornings. Sometimes a phone call during the day if we're lucky.

I never do work up the courage to say what the Reverend Mother wants me to say, but also, it's so hard to do when our quiet moments of snuggle and talk have been robbed from us, and all we have are stolen, sweaty hours in the dark and the ensuing bleary-eyed mornings.

I'll vow to do it tomorrow, and then tomorrow comes and I vow to do it the next day, and on and on it goes, until I almost feel like telling her is an impossible task, a Holy Grail-style quest that God has set before me and I'll never be pure and brave enough to complete.

It's maddening.

Towards the end of the week, Mom starts developing pneumonia. It makes a godawful wheezing when she breathes, and things start to change in the predictable comings and goings of the nurses and doctors. There's more bustle around the bed, more bags being hung, more tests and X-rays. Conversations start taking a more somber tone. Mom is given a cannula and antibiotics. I finish reading *In the Arms of the Disgraced Duke*, and we speculate about the next Wakefield novel, which comes out next week. We watch HGTV on the hospital television and make fun of the tiny house people.

I tell Valdman I'll be working remotely for the week. It doesn't go badly, but it doesn't go well. He's annoyed with me, annoyed with how much I'm willing to let my family interfere with making him money. His displeasure is the kind of thing I would have cared about before, but now…

Now, I couldn't fucking care less.

And then somehow this week is gone, this precious week, one of the two I have with Zenny, and I have nothing to show for it. Not a healthy mom, not a confession of love, not even a boss who likes me as much as he did at the beginning of the week. It's hard not to feel like something is slipping away from me, time or something as vital as time, and the harder I try to grab onto it, the more elusive it gets. A quick fish in the water, a ribbon in the wind.

At night, my dreams are of empty arms and white flowers propped against fresh dirt.

I will myself to pray again, even if it's just to scream obscenities at the ceiling, but nothing comes. Even my anger has ribboned away in the wind.

CHAPTER
TWENTY-FIVE

One week left.

CHAPTER
TWENTY-SIX

There are clouds in my mother's lungs.

Dr. Nguyen and I are bent over his iPad in the hallway, looking at the X-rays, while my father paces behind us.

"This was yesterday," Dr. Nguyen says. "And this is today." He swipes on the tablet, bringing up the most recent image, which shows a sprawling fog of white along my mother's lower left lung. "My best guess is that there was some aspiration into her lungs when we were suctioning her stomach. It's not an uncommon complication in these scenarios. Unfortunately, I'm not seeing the response I'd like after three days of antibiotics."

I run my hand over my mouth. *Not seeing the response I'd like* is a polite way to frame the state of the woman in the room behind us.

"See, I'm looking at this effusion in the lungs and I'm looking at her respiratory rate and the oximetry readings, and I'm thinking that we need to move upstairs." Dr. Nguyen looks up at me with apology in his eyes. "She needs the ICU."

My dad makes a noise from behind me, and the Sean Bell who Gets Shit Done, who's a priest in the Church of Cancer, makes note of it, shelves the noise away as a reminder to touch base with him later. But for now I make myself talk through every step of this with Dr. Nguyen, every option, every variation. Steroids, different antibiotics, CPAP, BiPAP, draining, not draining, pain management—all of the puzzle pieces are laid out and considered. Dad distantly agrees to what the doctor and I decide on, and then Dr. Nguyen goes off to make it happen. Within an hour, Mom will be moved upstairs. I try to remind myself that people move back downstairs from the ICU all the time; this isn't a one-way street, this isn't a cascade of dominoes. The dominoes can be picked up again, straightened and reset. It will be fine.

I still call all the other brothers and let them know.

Back in the room, Mom is awake, blue-lipped and ashen. She looks staggeringly unbeautiful like this, frail and strangely flattened, every line and wrinkle in her face thrown into sharp relief. And yet, I can't remember my chest ever stitching with so much love and pride for her.

She tries to say something to me, and she can't find the breath to do it. I touch her arm. "It's okay, Mom," I say. "You don't have to say anything right now."

"Need...to," she pants.

"Okay," I say, taking her hand. "What is it?"

"You..." she manages "...look...like shit."

I burst out laughing and when I also start crying, she doesn't say anything. Simply gives my hand a weak squeeze.

"We're going up to the ICU tonight," I say after I can speak again. I wipe my face with my sleeve. "They need time to try some more antibiotics, and they're going to give you an oxygen mask to help you breathe while they do that."

She doesn't respond for a minute. Then she says, "Will it hurt?"

"They said the mask might be uncomfortable, but otherwise, no."

She looks like she wants to say something more, but she can't catch her breath. It's only as the nurses come in to start readying her bed and IVs for the transfer that she gets it out.

"Go...home...few hours," she says. "Not going to die tonight."

I go home.

I shower and I do some laundry and I consider shaving

for about three seconds before I decide I don't have the energy. I've gone from "sexy stubble" to actually scruffy over the course of the week, but there just hasn't been time to do anything more than wash my body and brush my teeth in between the hospital and Zenny and trying to keep a handle on work.

So instead I yank on an old henley and some jeans and crack open my laptop to get some shit done in the quiet of my kitchen before I go back to the hospital. Before I go up to my mom's new room in the ICU.

Except.

Except now that I'm home and things are quiet, it's really hard to drown out the lingering hospital feelings. I can hear the beeps and the murmurs, I can see Mom's face, that uncomfortable combination of sick-sunken and steroid-swollen. I can hear Dad crying softly to himself in the lounge, see the steam curling off the free, oil-black coffee as the respiratory therapist talked us through how the BiPAP would work.

And now that I'm alone, now that I don't have to be strong for anyone or take notes or take charge or anything else—everything crashes into me like a train from nowhere.

Not going to die tonight.

But she is going to die, isn't she? Maybe not tonight, maybe not even this time at the hospital, but she's going to die and I failed her. I threw all my money in all the directions I could, I barely let her out of my sight, I spent every waking minute trying to get her well—and I failed.

The knowledge of it rolls through me, those prairie storms I'm always thinking of, vast and charged and ready to tear through trees and chew through houses.

You failed

You failed

You failed

She's going to die

She's going to die she's going to die she'sgoingtodie—

With a vicious gesture, I slam my laptop closed and grab my keys, trying to escape the clouds roiling black and electric in my mind.

"Sean!" Zenny squeaks as I wrap my arms around her from behind. "You scared me!"

"I'm sorry," I say, nuzzling her neck. "I couldn't wait until you were done with your shift. I needed you."

She's in the shelter kitchen, finishing up with the dishes. Now that the meal is over and the supply pantry of fresh clothes and toiletries has closed, the shelter is emptied out. Zenny's told me before that it's common during the warm nights of summer; people will come in to shower and to eat, but prefer to be on their own afterwards.

"Maybe some of them feel awkward about the charity," she'd said when she was explaining it to me. "And some of them are suspicious of us, think that we'll try to preach to them."

And in a way, I can understand. Sometimes freedom is worth the discomfort.

My hands find the hem of Zenny's jumper and gently ruck it up to her thighs, and I give a masculine noise of distress when I discover that what I thought were leggings are socks that end just above her knees—some kind of schoolgirl fantasy and nun fantasy fused together into one.

"Fuck, baby," I say, my fingertips playing with the edge of her socks. The skin above is soft and smooth and warm. It tickles her where I touch. "Are you trying to kill me?"

She giggles, breathless and happy and also trying to protest. "Sean! We can't do this here!"

"There's no guests at the shelter tonight," I say, nipping at her ear. "And Sister Mary Theresa just left. It's just us and the front door is locked."

"Oh," she says, her tone of protest giving way to something more...intrigued. "We're alone?"

"We're alone. And I want to play a little game."

"Yeah?"

"It's called Sean Finally Gets to Fuck Zenny in her Nun Outfit."

She lets out a surprised laugh, which quickly turns into

an intake of breath as I spin her around and crowd her against the counter, my cock pressing rough and needy into the soft stretch of her belly. I shape my hands to her pert little tits, moving my thumbs over her nipples, which are hard and budded even through the layers of shirt and jumper between us.

"Remember our first kiss?" I ask, brushing my nose against hers. "Right here?"

"Yes," she breathes.

"Let's pretend we're there again."

"Yes," she agrees.

And so I kiss her. I kiss her like I did that day, a hard, searing slant of lips and tongues. A bite on her lower lip, my hands around her waist, lifting my little nun doll up on the counter and stepping between her legs. And this time when I growl, "I want to see your cunt," there's nothing holding me back, nothing left to make me shy away.

This time, I help her shove her skirt up to her waist, and I get to see those sweet cotton panties for real. She spreads her legs and I step back, my cock throbbing in time to my heartbeat.

There's those light blue knee socks, there's those firm, curved thighs. There's the innocent cotton of her panties and not-so-innocent rumple of her skirt around her waist. There's that plain white headband holding her curls away from her face, throwing the high curves of her cheeks and the graceful sweep of her jaw into lovely relief. And there's the cross around her neck and the rosary at her waist, and they dredge up every suppressed feeling in me—fear and anger and shame and still more fear—and yet there's also a comfort at seeing them that I can't name. Like familiarity, but more profound.

I don't pretend the cross away as I drink in her body. It's here, just as we are here, and it's a flickering, inconstant revelation to think that God could be here too, in the same way. That sex isn't apart from God, it's not separate, that somehow the God that's prayed to and sung to and served by charity and love can also be a god that's inside of sex and exists just as much inside fucking as He does inside a prayer or a nap or a meal or anything else a human might do in a human body.

And, like a dancing candle flame, the revelation gutters and hides itself once again.

"More," I say hoarsely. "Show me more."

Zenny gives me a look that's the swirling crossroads between mischief and virtue, and then she spreads her legs wider and pulls the crotch of her panties to one side.

I groan at the sight. She's all soft and small there, with the tiniest glimpse of where my cock will go and with an obvious glisten along the tight line of her folds.

"Your cunt is wet," I say.

She nods, giving her kitty a little stroke with her other hand. She shivers at her own touch.

"Was it wet last time we did this?"

She nods again, squirming on the counter.

"Did you have to go home and use your teddy bear? Did you have to rub your poor little clit until you felt better?"

"Yes," she confesses, her head dropping down. I realize she's looking at herself, taking in the picture the hiked-up dress and cotton panties make, and I take in the picture she makes as she looks at herself—the gold stud glinting from her snub nose, the aroused part of her lips, the long sweep of eyelashes against her cheek.

"Tell me," I say, stepping closer, running my hands up her thighs. "Tell me what you did."

"I—I—" She shivers again. "I needed it so much. After you left, I went straight back to my dorm. My roommate was out and I just…" She's squirming with the memory.

"Did you pretend it was me?" I ask, letting my thumbs play against the wet silk of her cunt. "Did you pretend you were riding me?"

"*Ah*," she gasps because one thumb has started circling her clit while my other thumb has plugged her opening. "*Yes*. I pretended it was you. I pretended that you never stopped; that you took one look at my pussy and knew you had to fuck me right then and there."

I nip at her jaw and then reach in my pocket for my wallet, digging out a condom.

"This time, I will," I say. "This time we don't stop."

I tear at the condom wrapper with my teeth, tear at my

jeans, and soon I'm rolling the sheath over my erection and feeling the Pavlovian pulse of excitement as I do. I'll be inside her soon, I'll be fucking that tempting pussy, I'll have a nun speared on my cock and writhing in pleasure.

"It never gets old watching you do that," she whispers. Her eyes are on my cock, which is hard and dusky-red and shining with latex. "It's so sexy."

I step between her legs again and both of us look down. All fucking is carnal, of course, but there's something extraordinarily carnal about this sight: both of us still dressed, her knee socks and her innocent panties held to the side for me, her postulant's uniform shoved up around her waist. My cock, hard and rude and male, demanding to be taken between her legs.

But Zenny's innocence will always be tangled up in her boldness, in her fearless ability to *want*, and she takes the aching part of me in her hand and rubs me against her pussy. I let her use me however she likes—the blunt, round crown against her firm budded clit, long sweeps through her folds, the occasional shy brush against her taut asshole—and then when I'm shaking with the effort to hold still and let her play with me, she finally wedges me at the source of all her wet and whimpers for me to push in.

I do.

It's shocking how tight she is. Every fucking time. I mean, all women are—I've never met a pussy that didn't feel good on my cock—but Zenny's is some magnitude of heaven I've never felt before. She holds me like a glove, tighter than a glove, and when I get so deep that the tip of me is in her belly, she flutters and grips me tighter. And when I slide out, her body tries to hold me in, greedy and hungry for my organ.

I cup her ass in my hands and start fucking her cunt in earnest, and her hands leave her panties and go everywhere—to tangle in my hair and to rub against my beard and to fist up my shirt so she can see my stomach muscles working to fuck her.

"Sean," she says. She says it possessively, like it's her name to say, and it is, it is, I want my name to belong to her for the rest of my life.

"Yes, darling?"

"Harder."

I go harder, making sure to drag my cock out at just the right angle, making sure to rub against her clit as I sink all the way in. I relish the feel of her ass in my hands, the blue glimpse of her schoolgirl socks out of the corner of my eye. The awakened, happily agitated look on her face as she stares down at where I move between her legs. The cross necklace sliding and jumping along her chest as I thrust.

"Does this little nun need to be fucked?" I murmur to her. "She's gone too long without it and now she has to have it?"

"Yes," she squeezes out, eyelashes fluttering as she

looks up at me with eyes the color of treasure and earth. "Oh, yes, Sean—oh, *oh*—"

"I'll fuck you anytime you want, little nun," I say into her ear, my arms cradling her back and head as I drive into her down below, picking up the power and pace and letting her feel my strength. "Anytime you want."

And it's as she's coming with a bowstring-tight cry that I hear what I just said, and what I just said slices a gash of hope right across my open heart. Maybe we don't have to end with her vows, maybe she'll interpret the vow of chastity as loosely as the radical sisters around her interpret obedience. Maybe I can be her lover still, a cicisbeo to a bride of Christ.

She salts the hope-gash within seconds of it opening; as she comes down from her climax, clinging helplessly to my shirt, she murmurs, "I'm going to miss you so much."

It's said in a gauzy, fuzzy way, the kind of careless words that slip out in the unguarded softness after orgasm, and I can tell by the way she continues to cling and sigh as I chase my own release that she doesn't know how that simple comment has gutted me, how it's punctured something vital and now I'm bleeding everywhere between us.

She's going to miss me.

She's going to leave me.

And I'm going to die when she does.

"Come inside me," she says into my chest. "Come

lots."

"Can't," I grunt. "Can't."

I pull out, my wet erection resting on her belly and then it happens. I come lots, making a few short, staccato strokes along her stomach as pleasure hooks hard in the pit of my belly, and then I fill the condom with a ragged breath, pulsing heat while my cock throbs right above where her womb is inside. The thought makes me come even harder, like a primal caveman eager to spend inside a woman and plant his child there.

But there will be no child, and there is no claiming.

God claimed her first.

I keep her close until the last jerks have settled, and when I pull away, Zenny coos appreciatively at how much I've given her, which sends a jolt to my flagging dick.

"Can I throw this away in here?" I ask, nodding my head to the condom.

Zenny laughs. "It won't be the first time there's been a condom in the shelter trash."

I tie up and clean off, but when I'm turning back to Zenny as I'm tucking myself away and zipping up, I find her completely naked and leaning against the counter with not a single stitch of clothing left on her body except those damned knee socks.

"More," she says simply. "I want more."

I prowl to her, a growl rising in my throat. "More of me?"

"Yes," she says, her tongue running along the top edge of her teeth.

"More of these things you'll miss?"

If she hears the bitterness in my voice, she doesn't let on.

"Yes."

I trap her naked form between my arms, bracing my hands at the edge of the counter around her hips. "And what will you miss, Zenny? When you become a nun, when you marry God?"

"Your cock," she says bluntly. As unhappy as I am with the turn her thoughts have taken, I'm proud of her for using the filthy words I like. I'm proud of her boldness.

"It's yours. Anytime you want it. What else?"

"Mmmm, your mouth," she says, and I take my cue to chase kisses all down her neck and between her breasts and along the firm skin of her belly. I sling her leg over my shoulder and open up her sweet cunt to my mouth, and then I show her all the tricks and twists and hungry sucks that will make her miss my mouth all the more.

Her hand tangles hard in my hair and yanks, I can hear the rasp of her knee sock against the waffle-weave of my henley and it drives me crazy, I swear to fucking God.

"I'll miss your fingers," she moans, as my hands get to work.

"The scruff on your jaw," she says, as I leave her rough scruff-kisses on the inside of her thighs.

"The way you look at me when you're eating my cunt, like you want to eat my heart." And sure enough, I'm looking up at her from between her legs, making sure she sees how wet my mouth is every time I pull away for a breath.

"What else?" I rasp against her flesh. "What else?"

She hesitates and then plunges ahead. "Feeling you come inside me. For real."

That makes me pause. Think. Stand up.

"Keep going," I order.

"Wondering if you made me pregnant." Her voice drops to a whisper. "Being pregnant."

Oh my God, this woman. This woman and my poor, aching cock, hard all over again for her. Because of her.

I splay my hand across her tummy, low and insistent and selfish. "My baby here?" I ask, in a dangerous purr. "You'd miss feeling my baby grow inside you?"

"Yes," she confesses. "Wouldn't you? Wouldn't you miss it?"

"Of course I would. Of course I do." I keep my hand large and demanding at her belly while I kiss her until she can barely breathe. "I think about it all the time. Every waking moment and then it's in my dreams too. You carrying my baby. You nursing my baby."

At the word *nursing*, I pluck gently at one of her nipples, and it's as if I've struck a gong somewhere inside her. The tiny movement seems to reverberate through her body, sending goose bumps hurry-scurry all over her flesh.

"Fuck," she mumbles, and I have to smile because she sounds like me. I bend down and lick at the furl I've just touched, opening my mouth and running my tongue along her areola, across the tip of her nipple in gentle flickers.

Then I stand up. "What else?"

"Marrying you," she whispers, and then she looks away like she can't bear her own words.

My heartbeat is threatening to vault right out of my chest. Could she actually love me back? Babies and marrying—those are love actions, love words, surely she means that she misses the chance to do them with *me* and not just in general—

I'm going to tell her. Right now, when our hearts are full and honest and raw with appetite. I'm going to tell her.

But she beats me to speaking. "I want you to fuck me," she says, voice growing shy. "…back there."

I'm so tangled up in practicing my declaration of love that I very nearly miss this. "Pardon me?"

"I mean…anally," she says, and the kitchen light is too dim for me to see the reddish hue at the apples of her cheeks, but I know it's there. "I want to try it at least once before…"

Before she leaves me.

God. How can that idea still hurt so much? How can it hurt more and more and more, like a train rolling over you, like being stretched on a rack, like being crucified?

Tell her now. Tell her so she knows.

I open my mouth again, but she is already taking my hand in hers, guiding it over the firmly plump curve of her ass. "Please," she murmurs. "I don't want anything left undone. Not a single thing."

My heart hammers at my chest and my objections hammer at my skull and my cock—well, my cock is just as hard as a hammer, pushing against the teeth of my zipper like a cellmate trying to break free.

"I—"

"Sean," she begs, spinning in my arms and leaning forward on the counter. The act turns her body into a buffet of tight curves and narrow lines, showing the clear dip of her waist and the edible swell of her hips. It also displays that firm, sweet ass. And the shadowed well between her legs.

Reasons why I should tell Zenny I love her right now:

1. I love her.

2. She needs to know.

3. She likes the honest guy thing.

4. An old nun told me to.

Reasons why I should wait to tell her:

1. She's bent over a sink.

And really, I think, as I smooth interested hands over

her waist and ass, I'm going to love her even more after we do anal, so what's the rush? It can wait.

It can wait.

Except.

Sigh. Huff. Grumble.

"Zenny, we can't do this here," I explain softly. My hands are still everywhere on her, fondling and caressing and loving, despite my words, because fuck it, I can't help it. Not when she's like this, bent over and peering back at me with a daring kind of half-smile.

"Why not?"

"Because it's a fucking kitchen," I say, giving her sides a quick tickle as I say it.

She giggles at my touch, but then pouts at me. "I don't want to wait," she says. "I want to be able to look back and say I was spontaneous, say that for once I didn't care about what anyone else thought, I didn't do something to be the best at it. That I did it just because I wanted to. Just for me. I could barely make myself choose this in the beginning but now…" she gives me a shy smile. "Being with you has made it easier. It feels easy to demand the things I want. Good, even."

Ugh, I hate all this casual talk of looking back, this implication of her future life apart from me…and yet at the same time, pride burnishes a warm glow inside my chest. Pride for her. If I couldn't have my wish of worshipping her for the rest of my days, then this would be my second wish—that she'd grow into her own needs. That she'd find a balance between pouring her love into the world and loving herself.

But, be that as it may… "That makes me glad, sweetheart. I promise it does. But I don't want to hurt you, and anal is, well, *delicate*, at the best of times."

"Can't we at least try?" she asks, wriggling her cute bottom at me, and it's absurd that I, Sean Fucking Bell, am trying to talk a woman *out* of anal, but that's what Zenny's done to me. She's unbuttoned me and shaken me out all over the ground and now I'm just a mess of jumbled pieces, nothing resembling the arrogant know-it-all I was just a few weeks ago.

"I don't have toys to warm you up—"

"Use your fingers, then. Are you Sean Bell or what?"

"—or lube come to that—"

"It's a kitchen! I'm sure there's oil in here somewhere."

"Baby, I can't use a condom and oil. It will break the latex."

There's a pause, and I watch Zenny's teeth dig into her lower lip. I think for a moment—with a rueful sort of relief—that she's finally conceded, that she's finally accepted that it's bananas to have kitchen-sink anal, and then she says, "Then don't wear a condom."

This would be a good time for me to remember how to pray.

"Zenny…" I breathe. My hands are still on her body,

rubbing circles and lines along her silk-soft skin. I know I should say more, I should resist, but being bare inside her…even if it's just once…

"You're clean, and so am I. And it's not risking pregnancy," she says, and then—sensing my weakness—"Teach me how it can feel good, Sean. Please."

Fuck. I can't refuse the teacher game and she knows it. I curl over her body, defeated, my willpower melted away like a snowflake on a tongue.

"Okay," I mumble into the delicate bird-wing of her shoulder blade. "But you have to let me do it the way it needs to be done."

"As long as you hurry up," she says, wiggling against me. Fuck.

It takes me less than a minute to source a mostly full bottle of vegetable oil—I'm very motivated—and then I'm covering Zenny's body once again with my own. "Are you sure about this?" I say, kissing her ear. "Very, very sure?"

"Very, very," she says impatiently. "Why is it when I want to speed up, you want to slow down—and then when I want to slow down, you want to speed up?"

I'm straightening now and unscrewing the bottle cap. "When has that last ever happened?" I ask, amused. "You've never wanted to slow down a minute in your life."

"Not with sex. But with…other things. Feelings." She stops, as if hesitant to say more.

The furrowed-out space in my chest aches with her

implied meaning, aches more at the thought of telling her I love her. Would it be wrong to? If she has just said she wants to slow down with the feelings?

This is not ass-talk, I decide. Ass first. Orgasms for Zenny first. Then we talk.

"I'm just rubbing oil on you now," I explain to the little nun in front of me, shoving my feelings to the side and focusing on her. Her pleasure. "I'm not going to press inside just yet."

"Okay," she says, and then hums a little as my finger brushes against the sensitive pleats, spreading oil warm and plenty over her.

"Now inside. Just like the plug, baby, you'll push against me." And then I gently, as gently as it can be done, work my finger inside the tight aperture. Inside, she is a furnace. A fucking furnace. A snug ring of muscle and a smooth sheath of heat behind it. My blood goes on fire, all at once, burning me up from the inside.

"Okay, this part you'll help me with," I say, taking one of her hands and guiding it to where my finger is burrowed inside her. "You're going to replace my finger with yours...and then add a second one as soon as you're comfortable. Yes?"

"Yes," she says eagerly, already pushing at my hand to replace it. I let her, drizzling some more oil for her, and then while she fingers her own ass, I quickly toe off my shoes and tear off my jeans and shirt. She adds a third finger without me telling her to, and I abruptly lose the ability to breathe.

"Jesus," I mutter, liberally glazing my palm with oil and wasting no time fucking my oiled-up hand as I watch her. "Jesus Christ."

I step closer, the view impossibly intimate, impossibly carnal, and then I run my hands all over her ass and flanks. "Are you ready, sweetheart?"

"Ready," she sighs out, withdrawing her fingers with a noise that would make God Himself sympathize with all my decisions. I move myself behind her as she braces herself on the edge of the sink, and I feel her shiver when the broad head of my dick nudges against her rim. It's much, much bigger than anything she's taken before, and I run a soothing hand up and down her back.

"Relax and push out against me. Think of how full you're going to feel. What a dirty girl you're going to be with my cock in your ass, hmm?"

My words have the desired effect, dispelling her apprehension, and then when I reach around to massage her clit, she melts even more, humming her tuneless happy hum once again.

And so I begin.

I forge ahead slowly, tenderly, letting her find her breath when she needs it and giving her a much-needed break after my head pops past her first ring of muscle. I don't pull out, but neither do I keep cramming in—I wait and let her breathe around the huge invasion, playing with her clit as I do.

Gradually, inevitably, the discomfort becomes something more complicated, the more complicated thing then in turn becomes a new kind of pleasure. I wait until I see this transformation ripple through her body, until her limbs go from a taut wariness to seeking me out. A hand reaches back for me, her feet part and open up her ass even wider, and most tellingly, her hips move back against me; she's ready for more.

I impale her with care and love. I pierce her with affection and attention. I stretch and invade and stroke into her with every iota of emotion I've ever had for this girl—protectiveness and love and amusement and respect—it seeps into everything, and when I finally have her stretching around the base of me, I am barely holding it together. Trembling, sweating, my vision going dim around the edges.

"How are you?" I manage to say through the pleasure-fugue. "How are you doing?"

"I'm—" She's shivering too, covered in a thin layer of sweat, and I can hear her pounding heartbeat in the threadiness of her voice. "I'm good. Strange. But good."

"I'm going to move now," I say in a hoarse voice. "I'm going to fuck you."

"Yes, please, I—" I've started massaging her clit in earnest now and her words fall away into a moan. I slide carefully out, all the way to the tip, and then slide back in.

There are no words for it.

There are no words.

And I'm going to come embarrassingly fast.

"I've never been bare with a woman," I mumble, my eyes glued to where my cock powers in and out of her. My naked cock, and fuck, if I'd known how good a naked cock could feel inside a woman, I don't know that I would have been such a saint about wearing a condom. It's slicker, just *more*, and her ass is the tightest, hottest fucking tunnel, and knowing that when I come it will touch her, it will be inside her—

No, I can't do that, I promised, I promised—

Fuck, fuck, why did I ever make such a foolish declaration? Because now it's all I want, all I ever want, and it feels like if I can't do this, if I can't have this one thing, I'll die. I'll simply die.

"It feels so dirty," she whispers. "You being back there."

"You like it, baby? You like me back there?"

"Fuck—yes."

"Filthy girl," I growl, banding an arm around her waist and raising her up to near-standing, keeping her upright as I thrust with an arm against her chest and a hand around her throat. My other hand continues to rub her pussy, tease fingers at her sopping wet slit. "You're wet all over my hand. You get so wet for me, don't you? So wet to have my cock in your ass?"

My words and my hand have her squirming and tightening and her hands flying backwards to grab at my shoulders. And then, with me buried deep inside her, stretching her virgin asshole, she climaxes with a slow, rolling cry, low and earthy and long. My name comes out, so does God's, but mostly it's that long cry, a cry that could be a hymn unto itself. A cry I memorize like a prayer.

She is everything around me, not just the slick massage squeezing my cock, but the nubile press of skin and warmth in front of me, the rose scent in my nose, the sweet taste of her cunt still on my tongue. Her laughter still in the air, the evidence of her passion and devotion all around us. Her clever words and her contradictions and her bravery and her vulnerability and her determination—

The jagged lurch just behind my cock almost warns me too late, and I jerk myself outside of her right as I start ejaculating. Cum goes everywhere, thick ropes of it, and like the animal I am, I'm pressing her cheeks around my spurting cock and fucking the cum-covered cleft until the climax finally wrings itself out and my body relaxes by degrees.

We are sticky and slick with oil and cum, Zenny laughing weakly as she comes to standing and wipes a hand across her sweaty face. I know I look ridiculous completely naked, with a still-wet cock and moonstruck expression on my face, but none of that is enough to stop the stupid words from coming out. I'm just so *happy* and I feel so *good*, and she's smiling and stretching like a cat, and I love her I love her I love her.

"I love you," I say.

And the world comes to a crashing halt.

CHAPTER
TWENTY-SEVEN

Zenny turns to me, her face frozen.

"What did you say?" she whispers.

I'm reaching for a handful of paper towels to wipe off the oil and...other things. "I said I love you. Now hold still for me, please."

She bats my hand away before I can start trying to clean her. Her smile is gone, her eyes are wide, and her entire body is tensed—a frightened deer, ready to flee.

"You...love me?" She says it like I just confessed to fucking microwaved melons in my spare time; her words are filled with horror and near-revulsion.

"Zenny." But before I can think of anything else to say, before I can even get a handle on the blistering, wailing hole in my chest—*the hole that she made*—she keeps going.

"You said, when we started this, you said we wouldn't fall in love!"

"Let me clean you up first."

She backs away from me. "You *said*," she accuses.

I sigh and settle for extending the paper towels to her. She takes them warily. "I never said that," I tell her. "You said that I hadn't brought it up. And then I said I didn't think it would be a problem for you."

Something wounded flashes in her eyes, bounds away faster than I can trace it to its source. "And do you want it to be a problem for me?"

This feels like a trick question. One I should be old and wise enough to answer, and yet I can't answer it safely, because I'm *not* wise. Everything with Zenny has been new from the start, and this is the newest thing of all. Loving her.

"What's that supposed to mean?" I ask carefully.

She scrubs at her body without meeting my eyes. "You know what it means."

She's not baiting me, I know she's not, and yet I can't help but feel hurt. Hurt in the kind of way where you've made yourself vulnerable and someone else has made you feel foolish for it. And extra hurt because I knew better, *I knew better,* I knew I shouldn't have forced her to hear this thing that only makes her life harder. And on top of it all, I know it's stupid to have done this and then to pull the *I'm a sad boy* routine on her.

And then I see that crushed look on her face again and her trembling chin and she's so young. So, so young.

"I don't want you to have any problems, not a single one, not even me. When I told you I wanted to be your dragon outside of the castle, I didn't mean it like…like I'm the only one who gets to keep you hostage. I meant it like I wish I could burn everything bad away in your life so you can do whatever you want."

She looks down at the used paper towels in her hands, and I hate how cheap this moment feels, how tawdry. "Honest guy thing, Sean. Do you want me to love you back?"

Desperation crowds inside me, murders of flapping ravens' wings in my chest.

There's no right answer. I can lie and say no—a lie she'll see through, and a lie given when she's asked for truth. Or I can say yes, and lose her trust anyway.

I don't know what a good man would do in my place. I can only guess at what an unafraid one might do.

"Yes," I let out in a long rush of breath. "Of course, yes."

"Which means what exactly?" she whispers, and she finally looks back up at me, her eyes full of tears. "I leave the order? I don't take vows? Surely you don't mean that you'll be content to hang around the sides of my life, wearing my favor to tournaments and writing me poetry? Because I can't give you *anything* after my vows—not my time or my body or my heart. It will all belong to God."

God again. Stepping in and claiming everyone in my life with His jealous demands.

I close my eyes, trying to hold back this wall of—I don't even know what. Fear and loneliness and anger and love, just so much fucking love. But the wall is there, it's looming, it's crashing down on me.

"Yes," I finally let out. "Yes! Dammit, Zenny, why shouldn't I want you to stay with me? Why shouldn't I want you to love me back?"

"Because loving you back would mean giving away myself," she whispers.

Cold silence follows her words, and we both stand naked, awkward, still damp with each other. *Let it go, Sean,* my better nature cautions me. I've read enough romance novels to know that it never goes well for the hero when he pushes the heroine, and I've absorbed enough human decency to know it's not my place to ask her to give up anything—especially not something she's risked her family's approval and all her time and energy to work for. And I know enough about myself to know I'm feeling anger and grief over my mom, another person God is taking, and that's not Zenny's fault.

I know I'm not being fair. I know what I want is not as important as what she wants.

But.

But but but—

"I don't think that's true," I say, letting the wall crash down on me, crash down on us both. And I've just fucked up everything by saying that, so I keep going, keep burying us in the rubble of my selfish wants. "You know what I think? I think you're frightened. I think even the *possibility* that you might not be suited for a nun's life terrifies you. I think you're still worshipping an idol of that Future Zenny, because not worshipping her means all the pain and hard work you've done has been for nothing."

A tear spills out one eye, tracking slowly down her cheek and along her jaw, where it drips onto the used paper towels. "You're just like the rest of them," she says thickly. "Just like my parents. Just like my teachers. You want me to have any other life than the one I've chosen."

"I just want there to be some kind of middle ground," I say, stung that she'd lump me in with the other people in her life who've held her back. "Look at my brother! You can still serve God and—"

"And what? Be your whore at the same time?"

"Shit, Zenny," I say, really hurt now and really furious. "Is that all you think I want? Does my love seem that cheap to you? I want you to be my fucking *wife*."

"No, Sean," she says, fully crying now. "You just like having sex with me. You think that's love, but it's not."

I take the paper towels out of her hand and throw them away because I'm sick of looking at them, sick of looking at my cum-rags in her hands.

"Maybe I don't have any experience with love, but here's what I know. You are the most interesting person I've ever met, and I want to spend the rest of my life with you. And if you told me right now that I could never fuck you again, I wouldn't bat an eye because it's not your body I want—it's *you*."

I come back, and I can't stop myself from reaching for her because those tears, those tears, but she steps back again, not letting me touch her.

"Come here," I say in a low voice.

"You don't get to do Bossy Sean right now," she says. "Not even a little bit."

Something claws at the pit of my stomach. "I wish I could," I say fiercely. "I wish I could tell you to stay."

"You don't get to control me," she seethes back immediately, her hands curling into determined fists at her side.

"And you don't get to throw me away just because I admitted something you must have already known!"

"I can't do this," she tells me, tears blurring her voice, shining on her face. "I'm not going to choose you, Sean. I can't. It's not the plan."

"Right," I bite out bitterly. "Who am I compared with God?"

She bends down, jerkily grabbing at her clothes. "This was a mistake," she says. "This whole month was a mistake."

"So now you're just writing me off? You're just going to quit me because it's gotten hard?"

She whirls on me, eyes blazing underneath her tears. "I've never quit a fucking thing in my life because it was hard. I'm *cutting you out* because you're hurting me. Because I thought you were the one person who knew me and understood what I wanted, and now I know you're only thinking about yourself!"

"You asked me to do this precisely because I don't understand why you're doing it," I retort, leaning in. "You can't be upset that I still don't understand."

"No," she whispers, her voice fading. "The problem is that you understand, but you still want me to be something different. And that's worse than not understanding at all."

That silences me faster than a hand around my throat.

She pulls her shirt and jumper on and steps into her sneakers. "I'm going to swing by your apartment tonight to get my things. Please don't be there."

There's a moment, both grossly selfish and possibly righteously hurt, when I think about my mom in her new ICU bed—and then I realize Zenny doesn't know. I didn't tell her this afternoon; there wasn't a good time and I didn't want to weigh her down with it, and I just feel like there has to be a rule against having your heart broken while your mom is dying.

Except when I open my mouth to say that, nothing comes out. And it shouldn't. I don't want Zenny to stay with me out of pity. I don't want this heartbreak hanging over my head like a sword of Damocles while I wait for my mother to get better. No, it's better if she doesn't know Mom's in the ICU, it's better that she's able to be honest here, no matter how much her honesty drills right through my guts.

"Zenny, please," I say. I beg. My voice is strangled. "Wait—"

"It was going to end next week anyway, Sean," she says, not meeting my eyes. "We might as well do it now."

"It won't change it," I say. "That I love you. Just tell me, please, before you go—do you love me? *Could* you ever love me?"

For a fleeting moment, I think she's going to answer. Her eyelashes flutter and her breathing catches and her face is all delicate longing and hope and pain.

But then it shuts down, snuffed out like a candle. She pushes past me without answering, and I'm left in the kitchen, naked and alone and—for the first time in my life—utterly heartbroken.

CHAPTER
TWENTY-EIGHT

Aiden's farmhouse is mostly dark when I pull up, with only a single bedroom window upstairs glowing faintly against the night. Everywhere else there are stars. Stars and stars and stars, and as I park my car and climb out into the warm summer air, I think I can almost understand why he likes it here. It's like another world, and right now, another world is exactly what I need.

My hands are shaking as I try to hit the lock button on my key fob, and I make myself stop, take a moment to drag in a long breath of air. It smells like grass and wind and Kansas.

No city.

No roses.

No Zenny.

I finally succeed in locking my car and make it onto the porch, letting myself inside with the key Aiden keeps under a planter filled with dead plants. It might be ridiculous that I've driven almost an hour outside the city just to use my brother's shower and steal some of his clothes, but Zenny asked me not to be at the apartment, and Sean Bell that I am, I still don't feel comfortable sitting in my mother's ICU room smelling of sex and used vegetable oil.

So shower and fresh clothes it is.

It is literally the only thought I've let myself have since Zenny left me naked in the shelter kitchen. The only decision I've allowed myself to make. I'm buried in the rubble of my own making, the destructive wall of my anger and love and need, and I can't breathe. I can't live.

Just get to the shower. Shower and then go to the hospital. Don't think about her don't think about her don't think about her...

"Aiden?" I call out, tossing the key onto his coffee table. The man makes a lot of money but he's too scattered to do things with it, like furnish his house properly. His coffee table is made from nailed together wood crates, and his couch is a stained lump from his college apartment. His walls are still the basic farmhouse white they were when he bought it.

"Aiden?" I call again, getting ready to go up the stairs. I saw his car in the driveway, but with Aiden those usual signs of human behavior are completely useless. He might have decided to Uber to Canada or go cow-tipping a mile down the road, there's simply no way to tell. And just when I think for sure that he's not here, a light flicks on and he comes skidding out of his doorway, still yanking up some pajama pants. A penis definitely flaps around in the process.

"Aw, Jesus," I say, throwing my hand up over my eyes. "Why, man? Why?"

"What do you mean *why*, you—you cat burglar!" he splutters, stomping down the stairs to me. "Haven't you heard of fucking knocking? I don't know, calling maybe?"

I drop my hand, assuming it's safe, and then Aiden pauses on the stairs, looking at me.

"Have you been crying?" Panic floods his face. "Is Mom okay?"

"She's fine. I called Dad on my way here. They're settling her into her room now."

He visibly relaxes. Then grows suspicious. "So why are you here again?"

"I—I need your shower. And some clothes."

He stares down at me, eyes narrowed. "But you have a shower at your house..." he says slowly, as if I'm trying to trick him somehow. "And clothes."

"Zenny's at my place right now. Getting her things. She doesn't want me there. And I can't go back to Mom and Dad like this."

"Like what?"

I gesture impatiently at my rumpled clothes. "All post-fuck."

"So wait, you fucked and *then* you broke up?"

"God*dammit*, Aiden, can you just like—I don't know, shut up for half a second and let me use your shower?"

"Ah," Aiden says sagely, leaning against the staircase wall. "You're hurting." And then in the voice of someone in the throes of a dawning realization. "You're in love with Zenny Iverson."

The sudden, sharp urge to kill Aiden and bury him in his bucolic paradise outside nearly overwhelms me; I'm still fighting it off when a third voice comes from Aiden's bedroom.

"Who's in love with who now?"

"He's in love with Zenny—*oh shit*—" Aiden's face goes pale as Elijah comes out of Aiden's bedroom, shirtless and very obviously in the throes of his own dawning realization once he sees me standing at the foot of the stairs. I am also being dawned upon. Because Elijah and Aiden may have been peripheral friends for a long time, but peripheral friends don't wander out of each other's bedrooms shirtless at night.

"What's happening with Zenny?" Elijah asks.

Aiden looks nothing short of panicked, and I'm panicked too—but I'm also heartbroken and exhausted and too torn up to lie.

"Zenny and I have been...seeing each other," I say.

"And I love her," I add, knowing this absolutely makes nothing better in Elijah's eyes.

"*You've been dating my sister?*"

I'm too raw for this. "You've been fucking my brother?" I demand back.

Aiden flinches. "Guys, please."

"No, no *guys please*," Elijah says, livid. "I asked you to do one thing, Sean, one fucking thing, and that was to protect her. Not to fuck her! Obviously!"

"Well, apparently you've been fucking my little brother, so I guess we're even now."

Elijah clamps his jaw closed and I know he's fighting off the urge to fling himself down the stairs and pluck out my eyeballs. "That's different," he says, with audible strain. "You know it is."

"It doesn't matter," I say. Defeated. "She ended it."

"I still don't forgive you," Elijah says. "Not even a little."

What does it matter? Really? Zenny won't love me, my best friend hates me, and my mother is about to be beyond the reach of love or hate. Why am I bothering to argue about any of it? I deserve the scorn, don't I? Deserve the anger? And as good as it would feel to fight right now, to sweat and to bleed and to vent my anger at *something* instead of holding all this pain inside, I love Elijah too much to make him the target of it.

Elijah makes a noise of disdain at my silence and turns

on his heel, back into Aiden's bedroom.

Now it's my turn to slump against the wall. I look up at my brother, young and bear-like in his broad body and shaggy hair. "Why didn't you tell me?" I ask quietly. "I would have understood."

Aiden sighs and comes down the stairs, sitting a few stairs up so he's more or less eye-level with me. He braces his elbows on his thighs and puts his head in his hands, scrubbing at his hair. "It's...I don't know. Lots of reasons."

I put my head against the wall. A failure as a lover and as a son and now—fourteen years after Lizzy—as a brother once again. "Fuck, Aiden. I feel like shit that I didn't—that I wasn't someone you could talk to about this."

He sighs into his palms. "It's not that, it's—" He starts over. "Remember the kiss I told you about in college?" he asks. "My freshman year?"

I do remember it. Aiden had come to my apartment one night, drunk and rattled, and when I finally got him settled down with a grilled cheese because of course he hadn't bothered to feed himself that day, this story came spilling out about the weekend before. The final trial of pledge week had been some nebulous ritual involving togas and darkness and kissing—all very Greek-sounding to me—but when Aiden kissed the brother on his left, it had been something more than chastely fraternal.

"I knew the guy," Aiden had confessed, looking down at the empty plate where his grilled cheese had been before he inhaled it. "And it was dark, and you had to keep kissing for as long as they told you to, and they made us kiss for a long time and I—"

"You liked it?" I supplied.

I'm not going to pretend that Irish Catholic boys are the experts on kissing other boys, but I'm also not going to pretend that Irish Catholic boys are *totally* ignorant, if you catch my drift, and there'd been enough fooling around at my all-boys high school and enough frank gossip with Elijah that I wasn't at all bothered by what seemed to be bothering Aiden very much.

On the other hand, I'd come out of high school knowing that I was a one on the Kinsey Scale—all my random encounters confirming my belief that I was mostly straight—and Aiden seemed to be coming out of this with a very different conclusion.

"I liked it," Aiden had whispered. "What does that mean?"

"It means that you liked it."

"But—"

"Aiden. Seriously. You know me and Mom and Dad. No one is going to give you a hard time about who you like to kiss." But he had an expression like *he* might give himself a hard time.

Which is how, I imagine, we've ended up here on his stairs with my best friend half-naked in his room.

"After I talked to you that night, I kind of came to

grips with—" he makes a vague flutter with his hands. "Being bisexual. But it seemed abstract still. Like it was okay if it was the kind of porn I watched, if maybe I flirted a bit, but *actually* dating a boy just didn't occur to me. It sounds stupid, I know, but that's how it was. The opportunity to be with another guy didn't come up again and I never thought to chase it. And it was so easy to date girls. So very easy."

I've seen Aiden's very easy life with girls, and he wasn't lying. He's got the big Bell grin and the deep Bell dimple and the kind of body that promises being swept up and carried off to some evil sex lair.

"And then, I don't even know. My firm was having an event that Elijah was planning, and all of a sudden, it didn't seem so abstract anymore. One thing led to another, and then all of a sudden, I was really doing it." He goes red in the face. "Uh, I mean being actually bisexual. Not...you know."

"But that too," I say, and I'm surprised at how warm and teasing it comes out, that I can still manage to be the big brother, the caretaker, even now when my heart is gone and pulped under Zenny's doodled-on sneakers.

"Yes, that too," he says, laughing and still blushing.

"You could have told me," I point out.

"It's so easy for you to say that. And easy for you to feel, I don't know, like wounded that I didn't tell you, feel like I didn't trust you. But can you accept—just in part—

that it's not all about you? That sharing something like this is complicated?"

"Yes," I say. "I can. And I'm sorry."

Aiden looks up, propping his chin on his fists. "You're my big brother, man, you're *Sean Bell*. I wanted to party like Sean Bell, work like Sean Bell, be like Sean Bell. Telling you this would make me…not Sean Bell."

"It makes you Aiden Bell," I say, giving him a light punch to the thigh. "Which is even better."

Elijah is still furious with me. I manage to shower and borrow some clothes, and then Aiden promises to be at the hospital in the morning. Elijah won't even look at me the entire time I'm there.

Fitting. I barely want to look at myself.

When I get to the ICU back in Kansas City, I'm ushered to Mom's room, which is walled with glass and has a large door opening to the nurse's station in the middle of a semicircle of rooms. Dad snores on the small sofa across the room, and Mom's awake, her eyes moving from the TV mounted in the corner to my face. I think she tries to smile, but the huge plastic mask over her face obscures it.

"Oh, Mom," I say, coming over to her bed.

She lifts a hand, and I give it a squeeze once I reach her. Her skin looks better—pinker, less wan—and I have a moment of real, untempered relief. The BiPAP is working, the oxygen is helping. Everything is going to be okay.

I scoot a chair over so I can sit beside her and hold her hand, and to the harsh drone of the breathing machine and the various other beeps and blips of the monitors around us, we watch people shop for tiny houses and then act surprised when the tiny houses are indeed tiny.

And with both my hands curled around hers, I drop into a murky, exhausted sleep.

Morning brings shift change, so Dad and I are nudged out of the room. I don't like it, but I've learned the hard way that it's better to have the nurses on your side—and perfect hair or not, nurses don't like family members clogging up their process. So we trundle out to the waiting room for bad coffee, and I go brush my teeth in the bathroom with the toiletry kit I keep in my car nowadays.

I call the office, leave a message with Trent the Secretary that I won't be in, and then watch with disinterest as my phone lights up five minutes later with Valdman's office line. It's only because it's shift change and I'm not needed with Mom I pick it up.

"Sean Bell," I say in greeting.

"Son," Valdman rumbles. "I need you in the office today."

"Did you get the message I left with Trent?" I ask idly, knowing that he has. I decide to make more bad coffee and walk over to the machine.

"I did, and I'm calling you to tell you that's not going to work for me."

"The Keegan deal is almost fixed," I say, stabbing at the **brew** button on the machine. "The nuns are moving in two weeks, well before the Keegan demolition schedule. We have a press release in the works, and the Reverend Mother has agreed to talk to the local media about it."

"This isn't about the Keegan deal. This is about your commitment to this company."

I stare at the amber liquid spattering into the disposable cup. "I don't understand. I've been keeping up on everything else remotely."

I hear Valdman's chair shifting. "Well, I don't know how to say this delicately, so I'll say it bluntly. When you told me last winter that your mom had cancer, I was willing to let you do your thing because I figured she'd die soon after. But it's been more than half a year of your attention being divided, and that's not the kind of drive I'm looking for in my firm." His voice goes conspiratorially low. "I know you can do better. I'm going to retire from day-to-day soon, and when I do, I want you in the chair, my boy. But I can't put you there unless I know *you'll* put the company first."

The machine finishes up with an obnoxious hiss and then clicks off.

"Are you…" the words are so insane in my mouth that I have a hard time forming them. "Are you asking me to choose between my mother and my job?"

"It sounds so stark when you say it like that. Think of it as adjusted allocation. You're going to adjust how you allocate your time back to a professional level. And once you show me you can do that, then I'm willing to show you the keys to the kingdom." His voice is fatherly, warm almost, as if he feels like he's being magnanimously paternal right now. Meanwhile, my actual father is leaning against a window and staring at a highway, his broad shoulders folded into themselves like wings.

"No," I say, and it comes out so easily, too easily maybe, given that this is the one thing I used to want above all others.

Valdman's office, Valdman's chair. To be king of the garbage people, the biggest eel in the tank.

But I don't want it anymore, and I'm shocked to realize that it's not even because of my mom, not even because of Valdman's cruel ultimatum. It's because of Zenny and the man I've become from knowing her.

"No?" Valdman sounds amused, like he thinks I'm joking. "Sean, be reasonable now—"

"I am being reasonable. My mother is dying. I'm staying with her. Thank you for the phone call."

And then I hang up. I want it to feel good, but it doesn't feel like anything.

Dad has to leave around lunchtime to tend to a few things at the warehouse, and I find myself a pale, gelatinous pot pie in the hospital cafeteria and eat without tasting it. Thinking of the pot pie I made for Zenny a lifetime ago. Of making her eat it, watching her soft lips move enticingly over her fork. Of stripping her and tasting her and holding myself still with agonizing strain so she could explore every corner of my body.

And that memory spirals into every other night we shared, every other minute. The laughing, the teasing, the arguing. The discussions about God and poverty. The way I remembered more and more of my forgotten self with her.

How she made me think of the way light falls through stained glass.

That hole in my chest is huge now. Vacant, hungry, chewing through more and more of me, spreading from my heart to my eyes and my stomach and down to my wretched, selfish toes.

You fucked up royally.

The one time something good and pure and true landed in your life, you smothered it with greed, asshole.

Asshole is too good a word for me. I'm subhuman in

my selfishness. I'm a rotting pile of shit with nothing to show for my life but an empty heart and a perfect head of hair. It's dumb that I should have to confront this here, now; it's weak and stupid that I can't stave it off any longer, but who am I kidding? How long could I really have pretended to myself that I didn't care? That I could feel nothing about the one thing in my miserable life that meant everything?

I love Zenny. And I lost her. All because I couldn't stop being Sean Bell for one minute and look outside myself. All because I couldn't put her first, not when it meant losing control. She's gone and it's my fault.

Okay, and maybe a little bit the Reverend Mother's. She did say to tell Zenny, after all.

The good thing about hospital cafeterias is that no one looks at you twice when you start crying, which is what I do now, curling over my uneaten pot pie and letting the hole chew through the last remaining shreds of my soul.

CHAPTER
TWENTY-NINE

Dr. Iverson is coming out of my mom's room when I turn the corner, and I freeze. For a very idiotic, teenage second, I assume he's here to kill me for sleeping with his daughter, and a very brainless, very adolescent panic thunders through me as the father of the woman I love walks my way.

But then reason filters in, and I see him dabbing at his eyes under his glasses with a Kleenex, and I understand. He stopped in to see Mom. To visit her.

"Sean," he says, extending a hand, and I shake it.

"Dr. Iverson."

"Can I have a few moments of your time?"

My mind flickers back to Zenny, and I wonder if he'll kill me slow or quick, but then he simply leans against the wall and takes off his glasses, cleaning them with a cloth he pulls from his coat. I breathe again—he probably wouldn't excoriate me about having sex with his daughter in front of the nurses' station, right?

Right?

"Of course," I finally answer, and I turn to face the window into Mom's room. From this angle, we can see her bed and a few of her monitors, but she can't see us. "Was she awake?" I ask, half small talk, half genuinely wanting to know.

"She was. We talked. I regret..." Dr. Iverson lets out a long breath. "I regret not talking with her before this."

And suddenly it all feels so pointless. So distant, that Sunday afternoon filled with whiskey and pain. Why had we let something so small define something so important? Why had we made our lives emptier at a time when it was already so fucking unbearable in its emptiness? Tyler was right. The Iverson-Bell schism was a mistake.

"I'm sorry," I say at the same time he says, "I'm sorry—" and then we both cut off with a little chuckle.

"You first, young man," he says, putting his glasses back on. In the bright sunshine pouring in from the skylight above, I see that his eyes are brown in the middle, glinting into copper at the edges. Just like Zenny's.

"I wanted to say that I'm sorry for...holding my distance since Lizzy's funeral. Being angry. What you said to my parents—"

Dr. Iverson looks stricken. "I shouldn't have said it. Not then, not ever."

"You had every right to say it. I'm sorry I didn't understand that before. I'm sorry we let this one thing get so big that it wedged our families apart."

He sighs. "I'm sorry for that too."

We stand for a moment, and then he says, "I work with dying people all the time, you'd think I'd know how to talk to my best friend after his daughter's funeral. But I couldn't find the right words to say, and if I'm honest, part of me felt…defensive."

"Defensive?"

"For choosing to stay at the church after it happened," he explains, looking in at my mother. "It felt like there was no right answer. Did we leave in solidarity? Did we stay and try to hold the new priest accountable? What's the right thing to do when something like this happens?"

You should come back.

That was the thing Dr. Iverson said to my parents, and now that I'm old and tired, I can see what he meant by it. He meant *this community is here for you as I am here for you.* He meant *please don't suffer alone.* He meant *let me help comfort you.*

He didn't know about the anonymous threats we'd already gotten from the parishioners, the menacing notes and ugly phone calls. He didn't know that the deacons had tried to block Lizzy's funeral from being at the church or about the brewing backlash in the police investigation. He was only trying to help, and my parents couldn't hear it inside of their own pain.

"You meant well."

"If there's anything you learn as a doctor, it's that 'meaning well' can be a very small thing indeed."

God, how depressingly true that is.

We stand there in silence for a few moments more, and then Dr. Iverson puts a hand on my shoulder. "I'm around if you need anything. Please don't hesitate to ask. Not that you were ever good at asking anyway," he adds with a smile.

"I still maintain that birthday cake needed a note on it," I laugh, and for a minute, I can taste the sweet bite of homemade frosting as Elijah and I hunched over it in the Iverson kitchen. Teenage boys like hungry wolves, devouring everything in sight—in this case, Zenny's birthday cake, which hadn't yet had her name iced on it.

Dr. Iverson shakes his head. "How you boys assumed my wife went and made a cake and put it in the fridge just for a treat, I have no idea."

"Zenny was so upset," I remember, but then saying her name out loud chases the smile from my face. I wish the biggest thing between us were a half-eaten birthday cake. And not the giant storm of hurt I conjured up last night.

"She got over it. She's a tough girl," he says, and then he squeezes my shoulder before he goes. "Goodbye, Sean."

"Goodbye, Dr. Iverson."

And then it's time to go back to Mom.

They gave her a whiteboard and a marker while I was at lunch; she's allowed to take the mask off for very brief intervals, but it seems whenever she does that her oxygen levels careen dangerously down, so they're restricting mask-off time to the occasional swab of water for her drying mouth. She's written the words **mountain dew** on the board no less than five times already; each and every time the nurse explains that the bowel obstruction still hasn't resolved, that she can only have fluids via IV, that if her mouth is dry they can swab it again with water.

So thirsty, she writes. **Please.**

They give her a mouth swab, cluck and chuckle at her when she asks for a mouth swab of Mountain Dew instead of water. I don't think she's joking, but when I mention it to the nurse, the nurse scolds me.

"It'll be bad for her. Don't you want her to get well?"

That shuts me up.

After the hustling of changing sheets and brushing her teeth is over, Mom and I are alone again. When I sit down, she narrows her eyes at me.

Crying? she writes on the board.

Ah fuck. My eyes are still red from crying over Zenny in the cafeteria. "I'm okay, promise."

A frown. **B/c of me?**

I rub my hands over my face and give a weak laugh. I've been crying so much lately that it all gets kind of mixed together. "Well, yes because you're in here," I say, and then I'm not planning on saying anything more, honestly I'm not, but the thing about heartbreak is it becomes the only thing you want to think about and talk about. In a twisted way, the only thing you want to feel. So I blurt, "Actually…well, there was a girl."

This piques her interest immediately. **Girl????** She underlines the word several times in case I don't appreciate her eagerness.

"Yeah. But I messed it up, Mom. I'm pretty sure she hates my guts now."

…

She actually writes an ellipsis on the board, gesturing for me to elaborate.

"Are you sure you want to hear this? It's not a very mom-appropriate story and also I think I might be the bad guy in it."

She writes, **tell me. it's a tiny house rerun anyway.**

And so weirdly, embarrassingly, I do. I tell her how Zenny and I met at the gala, and while she looks surprised that the girl is Zenny, she also looks thoughtful, as if she's already imagining the two of us together in her head. I try to dance around the fact that we had sex, but she rolls her eyes whenever I get cagey about it.

How do you think you got here? she writes at one point.

"Ew, Mom, ew."

I tell her how after only one night with Zenny, I knew I

was fucked with wanting her, and how the want became love, and at the same time, I found myself being quietly rearranged into a man I barely knew. A man who didn't care about money. A man who worked in a shelter for the first time and began to see the real, endless need in the world around him. A man who cared about injustice.

A man who was willing to look God in the face, if God would only look back.

I tell her about how I ruined it all last night, and when I get to that part, my words sort of shudder out into silence, like a stalled car, and Mom reaches over to take my hand.

"And the hell of it is," I mumble, "we started this by me caring for her the way I care for people—with control. And that's exactly the thing that drove her away in the end."

Love is hard, Mom writes.

"Yeah."

Do you love her enough to give up control? To let her go?

"Of course."

Then maybe there's a way.

But what that way might be is never revealed because a nurse comes in with a bright smile and announces it's time for another X-ray and I am summarily shooed from the room.

The day passes slowly. So does the next one. Aiden comes by a few times during the workday to check in and we agree he'll crash at my loft to be closer. Ryan drives in from Lawrence with a duffel bag and sets up camp in the waiting room, slouching over a textbook and highlighting certain parts, stopping every thirty seconds to check his phone. I walk him through writing emails to his professors about missing class and then end up helping him with his homework because it keeps my mind off Zenny.

I wonder what she's doing now, where she is. Maybe she's at the shelter, helping pack up supplies to move to the new location. Or maybe she's got a rare sliver of free time to squeeze in some extra studying. I close my eyes for a minute, picturing her at her desk with her hands curled around her coffee mug, or maybe she's on her tummy with her feet kicking idly in the air. I picture her face creased in concentration, her mouth just this side of a pout, her slender fingers fidgeting with a highlighter.

Fuck.

I miss her.

I miss her studying. I miss her dedication. I miss her adorable boredom.

I miss coming up behind her as she works and kissing

her neck. I miss stripping her bare and drawing maps and murals all over her back with those highlighters.

I miss fucking her and kissing her and holding her. I miss her like a physical pain. Missing her is a cancer and it's stealing my cells and breaking my bones.

It's eating me alive.

It's hard to describe how time passes like this. The hospital becomes a kind of non-reality, a limbo of time and action where nothing and everything matters. In my haze of heartbreak, it barely makes a difference. But it is jarring to have the outside world intrude. Like when I look up to see Charles Northcutt strolling into the family waiting room.

Even with all the times I've fantasized about Zenny visiting, even if it was just to distribute some prayer or a blessing, it's still strange to see someone from my real life here, among all the beige walls and beeping machines.

But still. *Why is it Northcutt here and not her?*

Surely her father told her about Mom…so why hasn't she come?

Does she hate me that much?

"Sean, darling," Northcutt greets me, flopping down next to me on the vinyl sofa. He takes a look around the room, as if realizing where he is for the first time, and wrinkles his nose. "How can you stand it here?"

And then he takes a good look at me, with scruff that's definitely graduated to a full-on beard and my wrinkled clothes.

"Never mind. I guess you fit."

I don't answer him. There's no point.

"Anyway, you're fired." He cheerfully hands me a folder that I don't bother to open. I know what it will be. The usual HR bullshit. A description of stock options and retirement funds held within the company and how to transfer the accounts.

I stare at him. "Is that all?"

"Well, and Valdman has tapped me to take over the firm when he retires." Northcutt looks ready to gloat in full, but he pauses and tilts his head at me. "Doesn't that piss you off?"

I stand up. I'm in a rumpled T-shirt and jeans and he's in a five-thousand-dollar suit and I don't even care. "Come here, Northcutt. Let me show you something." And he follows because he's a curious douchebag and still wants his chance to lord this new turn over me.

We get to my mom's room and stop outside the glass, and I don't say anything at first, I just let him take it in. The seven different monitors, the uncountable tubes and IVs, the mask. The small, sunken body.

"I don't give a shit about you," I say very clearly. "Or

about Valdman. Or about that job. I worked my ass off to have all that money, and all that money couldn't do shit when it mattered."

Uncharacteristically, Northcutt doesn't answer. He's looking at my mother with real discomfort.

"Well, they'll fix her up and everything," Northcutt says eventually. He seems to be saying it for himself and once he says it, he gives a little relieved breath, like he believes it. "Yes, she'll be just fine. But you won't."

I could tell him he's an idiot if he thinks my mom is going to be patched up and sent home, good as new. I could tell him every single ugly truth about watching a body fail—watching a body fail as it still holds a person you love beyond measure.

But why? I don't care enough. I don't even care enough to hate Northcutt any longer. Let him have his empty life and his empty money, let him sit in Valdman's chair. It won't change the fact that one day he'll be in an ICU bed of his own and there won't be anyone there to sit next to his bed. There won't be anyone to swab his mouth when the nurses are too busy or change the channel when it's an episode of *Fixer Upper* he's already seen.

No one will be there to keep watch with him through the night. Which begs the uncomfortable, lonely question: will anyone be there to keep watch with me? When it's my time?

"Thank you for delivering the news," I tell Northcutt,

taking his shoulders and turning him toward the exit. "You can go back to the office and tell everyone I've become a bearded slob."

Northcutt allows me to move him, push him, and it's shocking to me that after several years of wanting to beat the shit out of him, my movements aren't rougher than they are. He moves like butter anyway, like a soft man does, and I do tuck away a bit of smugness at that. If someone tried to literally push me out the door, I'd go Kansas City Irish on him in a heartbeat, I wouldn't even need the whiskey to get started. But he's nothing but a smirking pushover and utterly undeserving of all the time I've spent hating him.

"You know, this wasn't as satisfying as I thought it would be," he says as I finally let him go.

"Funny," I say. "Feels plenty satisfying to me."

I'm lying of course. There's a quiet, clinical part of my mind that feels relieved: no more dealing with Valdman, no more dealing with that world at all. But I'm still that walking, breathing, bleeding hole—I'm just also a hole that's unemployed now.

Sisterless, jobless, Zenniless and about to be motherless. Satisfaction is as far away from me as the North Star.

The clouds are back. The clouds are worse.

We stand in the room with the X-rays on an old-fashioned lightbox mounted on a wall. Mom is awake behind us, which I'm painfully aware of as the ICU doctor walks us through the progression of her pneumonia over the last few days. It's like time-lapsed snowfall, like the spread of fog. But fog and snow are quiet and peaceful...beautiful. This white sprawl on my mother's lungs is exudative effusion at work—or put simply, Mom's lungs filling with fluid. It started at the bottom cove of one lung and now both lungs are covered with a smoky and thick white—nearly opaque with fluid and inflammation—with only the top part of one lung still black and clear.

"Her vitals are worrying," Dr. McNamara says. She shows us charts on her iPad. "You can see here—starting two days ago—oximetry, blood pressure, and body temperature are down. The blood counts and gases show the infection overwhelming her systems. Her hypoxemia—dipping below 90% oxygen saturation—is bad enough now that it's clear the BiPAP can't keep up."

"What does that mean, can't keep up?" Aiden asks. He has his arm slung around Ryan's shoulders, who is also being held by my dad. Both Business Brothers and the Baby Bell—I feel Tyler's absence like a sudden kick to the stomach.

"Well," the doctor says gently. "It means in normal circumstances, this is the time to move to intubation and a ventilator."

She doesn't finish her sentence. Because this is not normal circumstances.

You know how every time you check into a hospital, whether for a broken toe or a heart attack, they ask, "Do you have a living will or advanced directive?" And you think to yourself, *I should really make one of those sometime*? Well, when you have cancer, they stop asking and flat-out tell you to make one. Mom made hers eight months ago, and I know for a fact it's on file here at this hospital. I know it's on Dr. McNamara's iPad. I know it by heart. It requests for her not to be resuscitated, and it also requests for her not to be intubated. A DNR and a DNI.

Dad and I are the first to meet eyes, and then we look away. Aiden takes a moment, then says, "Wait, that directive thing? No, this is different—that was for cancer, and she has *pneumonia*." He looks at us like we're kindergarten students, like we're too simple to grasp this. "She didn't mean for that to count now."

"If she were ventilated," I ask the doctor, giving Aiden a look that means *we'll talk in a minute, after we get all the information*, "what would happen?"

"You mean, do I think she'd recover?"

"Yes."

Dr. McNamara looks back at the X-rays, but I know she doesn't need to look at them again. She's simply staring at something while she gets her thoughts together.

"There's no way to tell for sure, ever. But I can tell you that her CT scan yesterday showed new tumors around her liver and in her intestines, and only a month ago, there weren't any there. The odds of her surviving this pneumonia on a ventilator are low...but real. But if she survives, I'm not sure she won't be needing that NG tube indefinitely, and I'm not sure that she won't be back in the ICU within a matter of days. Her cancer is moving too fast for the treatments to keep up."

I squeeze my eyes closed, open them again. None of the Bell men are saying anything, which means it's up to me, I suppose. "And there's nothing more we can throw at the pneumonia?"

"We're throwing everything we can at it," the doctor says, giving me a weak smile. "It's overwhelming her lungs anyway."

I take a breath, press my eyes closed again. All I want on this earth is for Zenny to be holding my hand right now, to be rubbing my back. To be in my arms so I can smell the sweet rose smell of her and bury my face in her hair.

"If we talk to her and she says the directive still stands," my voice is a charred nothing of a whisper, just dead air saying dead words, "what does that look like?"

"She can keep the mask on," Dr. McNamara says softly. "And it will still help. A couple days, maybe. Or if she'd like, she can take the mask off."

I swallow. I wish for Zenny like I've never wished for anything before, but she's not here, she's not here to hold me or to comfort me or even just to stand next to me. I'm alone, because even with my brothers here and my father here, I have to be the strong one. The one leading the way. "And then what?" I ask in a raspy voice.

"She'll be more comfortable. We'll take out the NG tube and she can drink to thirst. We'll also be able to provide morphine. It will help with the air hunger."

"Air hunger?" Aiden repeats, looking stricken.

Another weak smile from Dr. McNamara. "It's what it sounds like. It's very uncomfortable, but the morphine muffles the sensation almost to nothing. We can start out low, so she will be lucid at first, and then increase it as needed."

"And if she'd make it a couple days *with* the mask, how long could she make it without one?"

"It wouldn't be long," Dr. McNamara admits. "And if this is something you talk to your mother and she wants to pursue, then we'll bring in her palliative care doctor for a more in-depth discussion. But I will say this, as an ICU doctor and as a daughter myself: life isn't measured in days. It's measured in moments. When you decide with her what happens next, consider what moments you want to create for her now."

I turn back to Mom, I don't know why, but I just need to see her right now, reassure myself that she's still here.

And she's holding up her whiteboard.

It says, **mountain dew?**

CHAPTER THIRTY

We take off the mask and swab Mom's mouth with ice water, not Mountain Dew, which earns us a fuss from her.

She's tired but lucid, and we talk. Alone as a family, and then again with the doctors at her bedside.

The DNI stays.

She wants to take the mask off for good in the morning.

I make the phone calls I have to make, and then I stare at my phone for a long time before letting out a mumbled *fuck it* and sending a text to a number I have memorized by heart after only a month.

hey. it's sean. i know things ended badly between us, and i know you probably have real reasons for staying away. that's my fault, and i don't deserve anything from you right now, but mom is coming off her ventilator tomorrow morning and i just miss you so fucking much. i keep trying to pray—for mom, for me, for everyone—but i think i've forgotten how.

when I try to pray, all i can hear is your voice.

Tyler's somewhere over Illinois when Mom starts insisting on removing the mask, or "getting started" as she calls it. Overnight, she had a final X-ray and it became clear to everyone—even Aiden—that the pneumonia has her in its snowy claws; there's barely any clear part of her lungs left. There was never going to be time for the cancer to finish eating up her insides, there was never even going to be a trip back downstairs to the regular rooms.

This was always going to be it.

It's reassuring, in a grim kind of way. And there's a sense of relief and levity as Mom's care begins to transition to strictly palliative. The doctor comes in with a tender smile, going straight to Mom's bed and holding her hand. They talk for a few minutes—the doctor taking off the mask to hear Mom's answers—and then the doctor gives a serious nod and puts the mask back on.

The morphine is ordered and hung on the pole. Soon it will be flowing through her system enough to keep her air hunger at bay, and then we can take off the mask.

The nurses are chatty, and they ask Mom if she'd like to brush her teeth and comb her hair—and then looking at the room full of clueless men—they grin and offer to do it themselves. They bring in extra blankets, and most bizarrely, some kind of gift basket from the hospital full of Shasta soda and off-brand potato chips.

"We bring it in for every family transitioning to palliative care," a respiratory tech explains, like it's a door prize and not a *congratulations on choosing death* box filled with cheap snacks.

It's somehow more depressing than anything else, that box. None of us touches it, and when Mom discovers there's no Mountain Dew inside, she eyes it like it's personally betrayed her.

They take out her NG tube, which is met with applause from everyone in the room, myself included, and then Mom wheezes something to the nurse who did it, and the nurse smiles and nods. Disappears and reappears with her purse. And with the respiratory tech's help, they take off the mask for a few minutes at a time and put makeup on my mom's face. Concealer and mascara. Dabs of blush and red lipstick. And after they comb and pin back a section of her hair, it's almost the real Carolyn Bell again. Fierce and friendly and ready to laugh.

My dad bursts into tears.

The palliative care doctor gives the okay, and we take

off the mask.

Mom takes a breath without it, and right away the monitors start binging and bonging, complaining noisily about her oxygen levels, but one of the nurses reaches up and mutes them. "Mountain Dew…please?" she asks, and we dispatch Ryan to go get it. Which is when I get a text from Tyler that he's landed and he's going to grab a cab as fast as he can.

Mom reaches for me and Dad and Aiden. "Want…to pray…"

"We can call for the hospital chaplain," I start but she shakes her head. I notice with some dismay that there's already a certain kind of paleness blooming around her lips and eyes.

"Don't want chaplain," she pants. "Want…family prayer."

Dad, Aiden and I share a look of mutual panic.

"Babe, Tyler will be here very soon," my dad pleads. "He can pray for you."

"No," she insists. "Now." Her eyes dart to mine and there's an urgency to them that can't be denied—not now.

"We can pray until Tyler gets here," I assure her. "Um. If I can remember how."

Aiden laughs awkwardly, but I'm not actually kidding. My last successful prayer was an *I hate you* directed up at my bedroom ceiling, and all the times I've tried to pray since have slid sideways into wordlessness, a flat wall of failure. And, to be brutally, grossly honest, I almost don't want to do it. Despite the fact that it's her wish, despite my slowly shifting relationship with God, there's a part of me that still balks. There's a part of me that still thinks, *I'll do anything for my mom, but I'll be damned before I pray.*

Except, when I open my mouth, words *do* come out. They come out even though I'm surly, even though I'm panicked. They're not my words, they're thousands of years old, and at first I feel stupid, because I've always seen it as a sort of filler prayer, the kind you mutter while your thoughts wander away to sports and girls. But as I pray it now, each and every word feels painfully fitted to this moment, a bespoke chant of motherhood and compassion.

"Hail Mary, full of grace, the Lord is with thee.

Blessed art thou among women, and blessed is the fruit of thy womb, Jesus.

Holy Mary, Mother of God, pray for us sinners,

now and at the hour of our death. Amen."

To my shock, other voices are praying with me at the end. My father and Aiden and even Ryan, hovering at the foot of the bed with his elixir of Mountain Dew.

"Perfect," Mom says breathlessly. "Again, please?"

She doesn't have enough air to pray it along with us, but she mouths the familiar words as we go, holding my hand tightly, and something starts to break open inside of me, something aside from the poignant pre-grief permeating the room.

I'd always thought *real* prayer, *real* religious expression, had to be unique. Individualistic. New and tailored for the person expressing it because otherwise what's the point?

But for the first time, I feel the power of praying words alongside someone else, the power of praying words so familiar and ancient they come from some hitherto unknown part of my mind. The part of my mind that isn't consumed with accounting and finance, the part that isn't even rational or entirely civilized. It's a part of me so deep, so elemental, I can't even name it. But it responds to the old words like trees to wind, rustling awake, stretching roots deep, deep down. The words don't care about my *feelings*, about my petty sulks and mortal frustrations. The words are there anyway, just as the humanness inside me is there anyway, and for one clear, shimmering moment, I understand.

I understand how you can convict God of terrible crimes and then go to evening prayer.

I understand that hate was never, ever the opposite of belief.

I understand that belief isn't a coat to be put on and worn in all kinds of weather, even the blistering sun.

Belief is this. Praying when you don't feel like it, when you don't know who or what is listening; it's doing the actions with the trust that something about it matters. That something about it makes you more human, a better human, a human able to love and trust and hope in a world where those things are hard.

That is belief. That is the point of prayer. Not logging a wish list inside a cosmic ledger, not bartering for transactional services. You do it for the change it works on you and on those around you; the point of it is...itself. Nothing more and nothing less.

We pray together, mumbling, muttering, a chorus of men praying for a woman, to a woman, about a woman. A chorus of men praying for prayers. And with each and every turn of the words, something inside me loosens and loosens. A screw unscrewing itself and falling dead to the ground, leaving nothing but a buzzing, tingling awareness in its stead.

Mom pumps my hand as we finish another prayer, and I look down at her, expecting she'll say *enough prayer, it's Mountain Dew time*, but then the door whooshes open and I'm looking up because I'm sure it's Tyler, but it's not Tyler.

It's Zenny.

Zenny in her jumper, Zenny with her large dark eyes and soft loving mouth and her nose ring winking cheekily in the sunlight.

It's Zenny, here, and I forget how to breathe.

"I don't mean to intrude," she says. But she doesn't get to what she does mean to do because my mom is waving for her to come up to the bed, waving with a trembling hand and a heaving chest. The Bell men part to let her through, and Mom gestures at Zenny to lean in close, which Zenny does.

Whatever she says, she says in a stertorous whisper that I can't make out from my position on the other side of the bed. Zenny says something back, low and musical, and my mother nods, smiles, puts a dry, gray hand to Zenny's cheek. Another hoarse murmur, something that makes Zenny's mouth pinch and crumple and tremble, and I watch as tears spill out of her eyes and she and my mom pull each other into a hug.

And that I can see this, just this once, the woman I love hugging my mother like she's family—I'm speechless with it. It's a gift I never expected to have. It's a miracle.

Thank you.

The words flutter out, easily and without labor, flying up to the ceiling. That I would be thanking God for anything at my mother's deathbed would have struck me as impossible a mere hour ago, but somehow it's true and right that it's happening now. That there would be small moments of joy tucked into this hulking, bashing loss.

Zenny straightens up, tucking some of my mom's hair behind her ear, and for a minute I think she's going to go, and I can't let her. It's selfish and horrible and a garbage thing to do, to ask her to stay here and witness this. To stay and be strong for me because I can't be strong for myself.

I don't care. It makes me awful but I can't be otherwise

right now. I need her, and she can leave me all she wants later, but for now—for now I need her.

I reach out for my little nun, and she doesn't hesitate, coming to my side of the bed and sliding her arms around my waist like she belongs there, which she does. I bury my face in her hair, holding onto her like a man holds on to the edge of a cliff. And just once—it's terrible I know, clingy and entitled and unwanted—I kiss the top of her head, letting my lips feel the ticklish brush of her curls, letting myself have that one small comfort.

"I'm sorry I didn't come earlier." Zenny says it in a barely audible whisper. "I…I wasn't sure if you would want me here. After what happened."

"I'll always want you," I say, because I'm too raw to be anything but honest. "Always."

When I look back to my mother, she's looking up at Zenny and me holding each other close. My mother lays her head back and smiles, as if this were more than she could have asked for, as if her work as a mother is done. And then she wheeze-asks for the Mountain Dew, and at long last, she gets to drink it.

Thank you.

Thank you.

Thank you.

CHAPTER THIRTY-ONE

I'll spare you the gritty details of what comes next. Death, even surrounded by family, even with prayer and morphine working in tandem, is hard. There's no do-overs, there's no rehearsals.

Tyler arrives in more than enough time to have a moment with Mom. He does a better job of leading us through prayers than I did, and I gratefully relinquish the role to him, so relieved to have at least one thing off my shoulders.

At one point, Zenny whispers to me that this is like birth in a way, and she shows us Bell men how to lovingly doula Carolyn Bell through a different kind of labor. We rub her hands and feet, we stroke her hair. We pray and talk constantly, even when her eyes start drifting closed and her breathing shudders into a series of jagged moans and gasps. We never want her to feel alone, not even for a second.

The sun beams in, and without the constant drone of the ventilator and the incessant pinging of the monitors, we can hear the September wind whipping warmly by, a comforting late-summer sound.

It takes less than three hours, all told.

At the very last, the room lights on fire. It quartzes itself into an infinite glittering moment. It floods with vivid pain and joy and love and grief and I am opened up, I am melted away, and I feel God. For a blinding, breathless, reckless moment, I touch my fingertips to eternity.

And as I do, I also touch my fingertips to Mom in this place. As she is hovering, flashing, brilliant, a soul on her way to wherever bright souls go.

I'm shaking after. Shaking like a leaf and so is Tyler, and he meets my wet eyes with wet eyes of his own and says, "Did you feel it too?"

I nod and then look up at the monitors.

Mom is gone. It's over and Mom is gone.

No one ever does drink the Shasta soda.

There's a lot of shuffling around next. They clean up the body and do whatever medical things they need to do to verify her death, then they invite us back in for a last viewing. She looks peaceful now, nothing like the laboring woman earlier, and we look at her for a long time. Dad kisses her hair and her face and her lips for a final time. The rest of us stand around like men in shell shock.

Zenny's gone and I don't know when she left, and all of a sudden the strange rapture that came with Mom's death pops like a pricked balloon, and I'm left flattened.

And yet there's more to do.

There are the arrangements to make, what funeral home will take her and the remaining hospital business to finish up. There are the phone calls, three or four of them, different organizations asking for pieces of Mom. Her corneas. Her tendons. Her skin and heart valves.

It was her wish to donate as much as possible after her death and of course it's logical—she doesn't need any of those parts of her anymore—but it still makes my throat close with anger and tears. It's like beating back carrion, being swarmed by vultures, and part of me just wants to scream *she only just died, can we have a fucking minute before her body is stripped down for parts?*

I don't scream that. I follow her wishes, and try to take some comfort in knowing that there's still something Carolyn Bell is doing for the world. That there's another pocket of joy tucked into this day, and it's that someone's life will be materially better because my mom was here on this planet.

It's still not easy.

After the hospital, we go back to Mom and Dad's house and all of the Bell brothers proceed to get rip-roaringly, staggeringly drunk, sitting around the kitchen table and telling stories. Tomorrow, the funeral director will visit and all the arrangements will be finalized, tomorrow we'll have to start calling and emailing and responding to condolences.

But tonight we grieve and laugh. Tonight we remember.

Later, as I lay in my childhood room, listening to Aiden and Tyler singing in the kitchen, the hole in my chest slowly stretches out beyond the borders of my body, it fills the entire room. It becomes a dark and massive mirror that beckons me to look inside. And inside I see my mother and sister, I see Zenny. I see God.

For the first time in my life, I look at the inside of myself. The ugly parts, the good parts, the parts in between. The grief both old and new, and the love for Zenny that flashes like a pulsar, a lighthouse for my soul, and the blue, swollen bruise of wanting her and the toothache-sweet feeling of loving her in spite of her leaving me.

For the first time in my life, I look inside myself and I just accept what's there. I accept what I can't control and what I can, I accept the parts of Sean Bell that simply are and the parts of Sean Bell that need to change. And the prayer I offer up isn't one born out of anger or grief or gratitude or some other wild, fevered feeling. It's simply an invitation for God to come sit at the mirror with me.

God does.

And that night, the warm September wind brings me a storm. A real one, with forcing gusts of wind and silver-black sheets of rain, and lightning fissuring the sky like it's trying to pry it apart. Thunder rolls through the house, rattling the window, and I get out of bed, I pull on a pair of pajama pants, I go downstairs and out to the backyard.

I stand in the storm for what feels like hours, letting the rain sluice over my bare chest and back, letting it dance over my closed eyelids and against my parted lips. I let it fill up the hole inside me, I let it find every ridge and valley and vault of my body and my heart.

I hope Mom is dancing between the raindrops now, I hope she's somewhere laughing and dancing with God.

And it comes to me like a clap of thunder that Zenny is under the same rain now, that somewhere this very same lightning-light is touching her face, and I can almost imagine it's me touching her face. I can almost imagine the rain on my lips is her lips, the drops sliding down to my navel and over my hips are her fingers and her tongue. I can almost imagine she's here with me now and I can say *I'm sorry I wanted you to choose me, I'm sorry, I'm sorry.*

I can say *But have you ever seen yourself? Heard yourself? How could I ever want any different when you are who you are?*

But she's not here.

I'm utterly alone, except for—ironically enough—God.

CHAPTER THIRTY-TWO

VOICE MESSAGE 11:34 A.M.

Sean—

After I left the hospital yesterday, it was time to begin the short retreat that postulants take before receiving their veil. Which means no outside contact, no technology, nothing but three days of contemplation and prayer. But I couldn't have you noticing my absence at your mother's funeral and thinking it was because I didn't want to be there.

I wish I could be there. I wish I could hold your hand during it. You deserve that, and I'm sorry if I ever made you feel like you didn't. You deserve a girl who will give you everything.

Before your mom died, she told me...well, it doesn't matter now, I guess. But I wanted you to know that those words are lodged in my heart like shrapnel, just like you are.

Just like you are, Sean.

There's no sanctuary free of you and the memories you gave me, there's no part of me that isn't splintered with you. I still don't know how to feel about that—angry? Melancholy? Lucky?

Happy?

Blessed?

There was a reason I didn't answer you when you asked me if I loved you back. And there's a reason I'm sneaking a phone call and not sneaking out to tell you these things face to face. Because if I told you face to face, you'd see, and you'd know and then—

God, you'd be right and I hate it when you're right. It's so funny that I ended it because you can't give up having control...and now I'm finding I have the same problem. It's not that I can't give up God or my sisters or even my vocation, because I know I could still have these things in another life. I'm not so categorical and stubborn that I can't see that. But I can't give up control over my life, because if I don't have that, then what do I have left? If I don't get what I've been working so hard for, hurting for, and sweating for—then what will all those sacrifices have been worth? It would feel cowardly, and I'm no coward.

I started this with you to find out what I'd be missing, and I did find out. It's you. I'll be missing you.

I hope my saying that counts for something. Somehow. In the end.

<END MESSAGE>

433

CHAPTER
THIRTY-THREE

Zenny's monastery is an old stone house, sprawled lion-lazy over the block and surrounded by trees. I'm surprised at how intimidating it looks to me right now—big and venerable and almost castle-like—and even the trees seem to guard the women inside, fretting at me with leaves like hands flapping in warning.

I ignore them. If God Himself couldn't stop me right now, then I'm certainly not going to let the trees do it.

I'm only here to say goodbye to her, I tell the trees. *Calm down.*

I glance down at my watch and then at the invitation I've got clutched in my hand. Elijah had wordlessly handed it to me during my mom's funeral, and I don't know what he wanted me to do with it—or if he simply wanted me to know that Zenny was still going to be a nun, despite *le detour de Sean Bell.* But I'd known what I needed to do the moment I saw it.

The monastery door is open, and I step inside the wide foyer, following the muffled, hymning sonance down the hall to the small chapel, slowing my steps the closer I get. And the slower I walk, the faster my heart hammers.

I tell my stupid heart to stop. That we're only here to say goodbye. If Zenny can be brave enough to reveal how she feels in the face of this, then I can be too. I can set her free. And I'll never recover, sure, because she's it for me, she's all a sinner like me gets—my one and only chance flashing like a firefly in the dark, too high up to catch. I'll spend the rest of my life hurting with wanting her, missing her with swift and fierce aches. I'll spend the rest of my life jealous of God, no matter what fledgling truces He and I have struck.

But I don't want that for her; I don't want her to waste any of her precious heart on an old sinner like me. I want her to live free and happy and full.

Without me.

It's been two days since Mom's funeral, and it's weird to be approaching the chapel now, since it's my second time in a religious space in almost as many days. Or maybe it's weird how not-weird it feels.

Maybe I'm reformed.

The chapel doors are closed, and I have an uncomfortable foreboding that I might be too late, a foreboding that turns into a metallic panic I can taste in my mouth.

You can say goodbye just as easily after her vows as before, I remind myself, but it's about more than that. I wanted her to feel free as she walked down the aisle to meet God, I wanted her to walk to God without any other claim on her heart. She deserved that at least, that final unmooring, that final atonement. She deserved that from me. And I'm too late to give it to her.

But then I hear a small hiccup coming from somewhere in the hallway, followed by a nose being blown. Curious, I follow the sound to its source: a small room off the side of the hallway and around the corner from the chapel's entrance.

Inside, wearing the wedding gown she should have been wearing for me, is Zenny.

Crying.

Pacing.

Fucking gorgeous.

I had a thousand things I was going to say in this moment, a thousand smooth apologies and pretty speeches, but they all fly out the window the moment I see her crying. I can't see it without wanting to make it better; I can't bear the thought of anything making her sad, ever. It's like physical pain.

"Zenny-bug," I whisper and she starts, turning around to face me.

"Sean?" she asks…and then promptly bursts into a fresh round of tears.

I don't care that we're in the monastery, I don't care what's happened before this moment, there's only her and her tears and doing whatever I can to stop them. I stride forward and sweep her up into my arms, like she's my bride in truth, and then I carry her to the bench on the side of the room, sitting down with her cradled in my arms.

She buries her face in my chest, her slender body hitching with sob after sob, and there's the silk and tulle of her bridal skirt everywhere around us, clouds of it. And I hold her close, crooning low and wordless at her ear as I rock her, as I stroke her hair away from her face and band her snugly against my torso and chest, holding her as I've wanted to hold her for the last week. Tight and close, with my face in her hair and her hands clutching at my chest.

"What is it, Zenny-bug?" I murmur. "What makes you so sad?"

She shakes her head against my chest, crying even harder, her hands now holding on to my T-shirt hard enough that the fabric is bunched in her palms, as if she is worried I'll try to let her go.

Silly Zenny. As if I'd ever let her go.

I'll hold her as long as she lets me. I'll hold her for the rest of my life.

"I can't tell what I'm supposed to do anymore," she says tearfully into my chest. "I can't tell what I want and what God wants and whether the two are the same thing."

I don't speak—I definitely have not built myself up to be the authority on what Zenny should do when it comes to taking her vows. So I just hold her and cradle her and kiss her head. I stroke her arm and make a deep, tuneless hum in my chest.

Slowly, so slowly that I don't even take note of it at first, her sobs turn into muffled tears and the muffled tears turn into tired sniffs, until she's slumped against me, enervated and quiet.

By degrees, I become aware of her body nestled against mine. The slender curve of her waist under my hand. The tickle of her curls against my throat. The firm curves of her ass cradled in my lap, the hook of her knees over my thigh.

Heat—unwelcome but unstoppable all the same—floods me, inflames me. I shift, trying to keep her innocent of my hardening cock.

"How long do you have?" I ask, wondering if I should make myself scarce before someone finds their newest novice in a man's arms, in her Jesus wedding dress no less.

I feel her head turn to glance at the clock. "Thirty minutes. They're praying about accepting me into the order, and then the rite will begin."

I finger the beading on her wedding gown. It's a few years out of fashion, and I have the feeling it was bought secondhand. Donated maybe. She still looks stunning, though, a vision right out of my reckless, unguarded dreams. The dress has straps draped across her shoulders, like Belle's gown in *Beauty and the Beast*, a close-fitting silhouette of silk from her small, sweet breasts down to the tempered flare of her hips, and from there it spills into a kind of frothy madness that is very enchanting. I run my hand through the froth, closing my eyes and imagining—just for minute—that she really is my bride, that this is our wedding, that she's in my arms because she wants to be there and not because I was an available chest to cry into.

I imagine that I can kiss her.

I imagine that I can love her.

Her hands have loosened in my T-shirt, and a finger now scrolls idly over my chest, up around the collar of my shirt to the bare skin of my neck.

"You shaved," she murmurs.

"For the funeral," I explain. That morning I could practically hear my mom clucking about what a ruffian I looked like, so I finally took a razor to the beard. I'd barely recognized the man in the mirror when I was done—the week of hospital life had carved fresh hollows under my cheekbones and smudged grief under my eyes. (My hair hadn't suffered though. I was spared that at least.)

Zenny clears her throat and tilts her head up at me. "Why are you here, Sean?" she whispers. "Why today?"

"I came to make things right," I say honestly. "I messed up. And I didn't want you dragging that down the aisle with you."

Her long eyelashes are still threaded with tears and they sparkle as she blinks. "You messed up," she repeats carefully. "So you came here. Today. Right before I took my vows."

"I don't want a single part of what you do today to be tainted with anger or bitterness." I tuck a curl behind her ear, watch as it ignores my fingers and springs back. "This is what you wanted. This is what you've worked so hard for. You deserve to have it be exactly what you dreamed."

"And it didn't occur to you that showing up would make it all about you, again? That it would stir up bad feelings for me? That it might make things worse?"

"Oh." Fuck. I hadn't.

Shit.

My head drops down as I loosen my arms around Zenny to let her go. All I'd wanted was to make things better—take a page from all the pirates and peers in the Wakefield books and make a grand gesture, but a grand gesture to support *her*, not to win her back. To show her that she and her life as she planned it meant miles and miles more than whatever my pulpy idiot heart still longed for.

And once again, I'd fucked it up.

Zenny moves, and I sure it's to get off my lap, to get away from me, but hot relief and confusion flood through my veins when I realize she's not climbing off of me, she's rearranging herself. She's straddling my lap so she can look me easily in the face, and as her knees nestle on either side of my hips, her dress surges up around us in white, silk waves.

"Sean," she says quietly, cupping my face. "I'm glad you're here."

"But—"

She presses her fingertips to my lips. "I know what I said. It's true. *And* I'm still glad you're here."

A month ago, I wouldn't have understood this, how something could have an *and*. How something could be flawed but still good, how something could be imperfect but still worth loving.

I'm beginning to understand now.

"I was crying because I missed you," she says. "I was crying because I love you."

My heart is flinging itself madly around my chest now, pounding at its prison and choking me. "Zenny."

That's all I can get out. It's all I have.

"You were right," she says, looking away from me. "I'd begun to want this for all the wrong reasons. I was going to do this for all the wrong reasons. It wasn't about God any longer—it was about proving something to the people who doubted me. Everyone who thought my becoming a nun was ridiculous or wasteful, everyone who thought I wasn't strong enough to give up money and sex."

"Oh," I say again. My tone says it all—that one noise is filled with a foolish hope the kind I've never dared to feel.

"Oh, Sean," she says, and something like pity enters her voice.

My heart freezes.

"I still think I have to do this," she whispers. "Just…for the right reasons now."

"Oh." That word again, like it's the only word I know anymore.

"But you were the one who showed me that," Zenny says gently—and dare I dream—sadly? Longingly? "I'll always be thankful to you, not only for teaching me love, but for pointing me in the right direction. You're right: I would have always regretted walking down that aisle and taking an oath with all the wrong intentions."

I suppose this isn't any worse than I'd initially feared and planned on, but somehow it feels like it. I try to regain control of my heart and fail; it's vanished once again inside that hole in my chest. "I'm glad. I want you to have the life you want; I want all your choices to be yours. Always."

"And you?" she asks, a little furrow appearing between her eyebrows. "What is the life you want? Are you going to be…"

She can't finish, and I don't need her to. She wants reassurance that I'm going to be okay without her, and I can't unequivocally give it. I'm not going to be okay. But I guess that's what I've learned over the past month: my being okay is not the most important thing in the world.

"God and I are on speaking terms now," I offer,

hoping to distract her from her question. "And for that, I have *you* to thank. You said belief was giving my heart and trusting that understanding would come later. And I realized at some point I've already given my heart without understanding—to you, Zenny. It wasn't so hard to do it a second time with God."

Her eyes flash anew with tears and she pulls me close. "Sean," she breathes against my neck, and her breasts are flat against my chest and her thighs are tight around my hips and her ass is—

"Sweetheart," I say, in a strained voice. "I need you to let go."

"No," she says, squirming even closer, trapping my rigid length between her mound and my own stomach. "That was beautiful."

I endure this with as much forbearance as I can muster, although my voice is gravelled and harsh when I say, "Zenny, you have to stop moving around on my lap."

This does make her pull away, just enough to straighten up and look at me, but the act of straightening brings her cunt squarely against my erection and her eyes flare with understanding. She swallows at the same time, warmth coming to her face.

"Oh," she says. She's been infected with that word too.

"Yes, *oh*," I tease, trying to make light of it, make light of a very sad and aching cock. A sad and aching heart. "It would be better if you moved, darling."

She doesn't move. Instead she sits on my lap, regarding me, her breathing moving fast and hard and pushing her perfect tits against her Jesus wedding dress.

My thighs are actually shaking with restraint now, my stomach is clenched with it. It is taking every shred of decency inside me not to reach under her skirt and pull myself free, not to find her slit and pierce her with my fingers and then with my cock. Not to piston into her with her wedding dress billowing around us all while I trap her to my chest and dig my teeth into her neck. I can actually feel my lust like a physical thing, a fire or a pool of molten metal creeping up my legs to my belly.

"Baby," I rasp. My hands are shaking as I put them to her waist to gently ease her off. "It's—you're—" I can't make words.

"I'm what?" she whispers.

"I'll always want to hold you, but I'm thinking about more than just holding you right now, which I know you don't want."

She looks at me with an expression torn between curiosity and responsibility. Air quavers in and out of her lungs as she asks, "What if I do want it?"

My head falls back against the wall. "Zenny," I beg in a hoarse voice.

"Maybe...we could...just one last time?"

I have no response to this. None. Because if she's asking if I want to fuck her one last time before she gives her life to God, then of course the answer is yes. Yes, and I'll plunge inside of her this very second.

But I don't know that it's a good idea. And I don't know that I won't go to hell for it.

"It wouldn't be smart," I say, sliding my hands under her skirt and finding her thighs.

"No," she agrees.

"And it would be crazy, here in this room, so close to the chapel." I stand up, taking her with me.

"Yes," she says, her legs wrapping around my waist and her arms sliding around my neck. "Crazy."

I walk over to the door to the side room and close and lock it. I don't know what I'm feeling—or I do, but it's too much of everything to keep hold of at once. I should stop this, it's going to hurt us both even more, I should be the older one and the wiser one and put her down.

I don't want to put her down.

I don't want to stop.

If this is my last taste of her, I'll take it, weeping all the while.

"Does this little nun need to be fucked?" I growl into her ear as I pin her against the wall. "Is that pretty pussy feeling empty already?"

Her head rolls back as I nip softly at her neck—careful not to leave marks she'd have to explain away later—but hard enough to make her gasp and shudder. Under the skirt of her wedding dress, my hand finds the crotch of her panties and moves it aside, plunging two fingers into her split. She's wet, so fucking wet, and so fucking soft, and suddenly I have to eat her, I have to have her on my tongue.

I let her legs slide away from my hips and I set her on the floor. Her whimper of dismay when my fingers leave her cunt is replaced by a jagged inhale as I reach for the hem of her skirt. With my other hand, I take her wrist and press her palm to her mouth, giving her a stern look. "Quiet, darling. You don't want everyone to know that you're in here getting fucked in your pretty dress, do you?"

She shakes her head, eyes wide, hand clapped tight over her mouth.

Which is a good thing, because the moment I get to my knees in front of her, a low belly moan of anticipation comes from around her hand. A moan I feel all the way to the tip of my cock.

My tongue runs along the rim of my lower lip as I push up the skirt of her dress and ease off her plain white panties. I need to taste. Need to lick. Need to suck.

Then she's bared to me, that precious part of her. The neat nest of dark curls, the ripe bud of her clit peeping out from under the vulnerable hood. And when I open her up to me with my thumbs, I see the soft petals I love so much unfurling to reveal her slick, tight secrets.

"You weren't feeling good, were you?" I murmur, rubbing thoughtfully at her clit. "Put your leg over my shoulder, sweetheart. Sean's going to make you feel all better now."

A noise comes out from under her palm—a noise that sounds a lot like *oh God oh God*—but she slides her leg over my shoulder anyway, allowing me access to the heart of her. I press my nose into her curls and breathe in deep, trying to memorize the sour-sweet-earth of her scent. I try to memorize everything—that first blooming taste of her on my tongue, her hips tilting and searching for my mouth, the jerk and quiver of her breathing as I begin eating her in earnest.

Everything is so *soft*. So soft. Like she might melt right onto my tongue, and I do my very level best to make her melt, I do. I suckle her clit and lick it, I swirl at her entrance and spear her opening with my tongue. I slowly introduce fingers and thumbs. I growl in appreciation as her hands lace through my hair and yank me closer; I moan and reach down to squeeze my cock as she starts fucking herself against my face because I'm going to come, *I'm going to come* just like this if I don't suffocate my cock for a second.

Okay, maybe more like a minute.

And all the while, she's fucking my face like it's the last time she'll ever have a face to fuck her pussy against— which it is.

"Sean," she breathes around her finger. "Oh, fuck. *Sean*."

She comes beautifully. Magnificently. A writhing, wet, gasping, happy little nun.

I wait for her to come down, nursing her through the peaks and valleys until her body goes completely soft and pliant under my lips, and then I stand up, wiping at my mouth with my arm. Her eyes blaze as they follow my movement, locking in on the sight of my wet lips. I curve them in a smirk.

"Did you like that?" I ask, leaning in close and circling the tip of my nose around hers. "Did you like having that poor pussy taken care of?"

"Yes," she sighs happily. "Oh, yes. Please—" she pulls at my shirt, trying to chase me for a kiss, and I tease her by not granting it, moving my head whenever she moves so she can't quite reach my lips. "Sean, please, I need you."

For that, I let her kiss me, let her lick curiously at her own taste and clean it from my lips. "Say you love me," I mumble against her mouth. "Say it again."

"I love you," she gasps out—gasping because before she can finish, I'm lifting her back up against the wall, my other hand fishing out my cock. Hearing her say it makes me crazed and tame all at once, feral and serene. I could listen to her say it for the rest of my life, I could survive just on the sound of those words alone, I could—

Wait.

Shit.

"I don't have a condom, baby. I'm sorry." I start to set Zenny down, and she clings to me.

"Don't stop," she pleads. "We've already been bare together before, so what does it matter?"

"Being bare inside your cunt carries a different set of problems."

"I'm on birth control," she argues.

"I'm not going to risk your future over this," I tell her firmly. Between the teeth of my zipper, my cock gives a protesting throb. I ignore it. "You're worth more than that. You're worth everything."

"Sean Bell," she says, and her voice is sharp suddenly, not a little bit stern. I meet her eyes. "If I'm worth everything, then I'm worth listening to. I'm comfortable with the risks."

"Fuck, Zenny. God knows I want to pin you flat to the wall and fuck you until neither us remember our names." I'm shaking again, still holding her tight in my arms, and when she moves to hike herself more comfortably, the head of my cock drags through her wet center. I suck in a wounded breath through my teeth, my head falling onto her shoulder.

She bites my earlobe. "I want you," she says. "I want you more than I've ever wanted anything."

I pull away so I can search her face. Her eyes are warm and urgent, her mouth drawn into a pout of tormented need.

Who the fuck am I kidding? I can't resist her; I can't resist giving her anything she wants, ever.

"Honest girl thing?" I ask, needing to be sure.

"Honest girl thing."

I notch the naked head of me into her cunt and meet her gaze. "Kiss me," I beg. "Kiss me while you let me inside you."

She kisses me with the eagerness of a schoolgirl, her mouth open and her tongue seeking, and for a minute we are poised just on the edge of sin, our tongues meeting and mating and my penis only just breaching her. "You make me come apart," she says against my mouth. "You make me more like myself."

And that does it for me. I'm gone with loving her, gone with this tumbling, heedless fall with her.

I thrust inside.

There's nothing between us.

Nothing at all, except for God and broken promises and two grasping, reaching hearts.

My teeth sink into the delicate slope between neck and shoulder, and she moans low and pleased. "I can feel you," she says in some wonder. "I can feel your skin. Your heat."

My knees are close to buckling as I work my way into her belly; static and sparks flash across my eyes; I'm airless, airless, taut as a bowstring and perishing right here in front of God, with His nun pinned up against the wall and my pants down around my hips.

Gentle and invasive all at once, the bold tip of my cock kisses against Zenny's womb, and I nearly stagger with the feeling and with the idea, and all that's left to me are smashcuts of sensation—

her pussy in a wet, unrelenting squeeze

and

the hidden corrugations and patterns of her body, all soft, all tight, all wet

and

the plump rub of her clit above my cock

and

silk everywhere, her frothy skirt overflowing my arms and rustling and waving and the lush mounds of her breasts heaving under the silk bodice.

"Does it feel good?" I say huskily, looking up into her face as she looks down into mine with a faint red hue to her cheeks and her mouth parted. "Did you need to ride on my cock, baby?"

"Yes," she pants out, her hips moving with me, angling and squirming. "God. I needed it so much."

"Why?"

"I needed to be full—*fuck yes God*—you make me so full."

"Shit," I groan, flexing my cock inside her just to feel the stretch and hug of her tight body. "Shit yeah, I do."

She squirms in my arms again, seeking, seeking, her head falling back and exposing a slender, delicate throat.

"That's it, sweetheart," I encourage her, watching with fascination as that delicate throat flutters with her lust-frenzied pulse. "Take what you need. Use my cock to make yourself feel all nice and good again."

Her mouth opens once more, a silent cry, and she's a writhing angel in my arms, falling from heaven and touching ecstasy all at once, and she sobs out a broken *I love you* as her body flings itself right into the mouth of hell, shuddering with illicit sin in the arms of a sinner, right in the very dress she wore to meet God.

Did I say I was reformed earlier?

I lied.

I'm about to fill up a nun with a week's worth of pain and anger and loneliness. I'm going to put the tip of my cock right to the firmness of her womb and claim her from the inside out. I'm going to fuck her in this wedding dress that's not meant for me, and fuck her until we're sweaty and desperate and spent.

And I do.

I bounce her hard on my cock, I stretch that pussy around my thick, heavy erection until she's shaking in my arms with her third climax, and then I let it go, all of it.

I let go of the loneliness and the loss.

I let go of the control and the chaos.

And with a juddering moan, I spend into her with several long, hot pulses, an entire week's worth saved up for her. There's enough that I feel it leaving me, that I feel it smearing between us, and I imagine the crudest, crudest things: making her drip with me, making her pregnant. It's awful, but it's all I can think of as I throb and release deep into her belly. It's all that crowds my mind—that and the rose-scent of her throat, where my face is buried.

It ended too fast, I realize unhappily. My last intimate moments with Zenny, and they passed faster than I could grab at them, slipping right through my fingers.

Zenny seems to think this too, clinging tight to me, her hands twisting in my shirt and her heels still locked against my back. And we come down together like this, wet and shaky and temporarily whole. I could cry with the unfairness of it.

"It's time, baby," I reluctantly murmur, helping her to her feet. It's heaven to hold her, but she has a different heaven waiting for her and I can't be the one who ruins it.

I help her clean up with some Kleenex, and I help her rearrange her panties, her dress, her hair, until the only evidence of what just happened is the barely perceptible blush on her cheeks and chest, and the spill of me inside her, invisible to everyone except God.

And then there are no more excuses. It's time for her to go to her vows, and it's time for me to leave.

I give her a final kiss, long and lingering, her soft lips yielding under mine and then I straighten up. "I love you," I tell her. "I'll always love you."

"You're not staying?" she asks, her lips trembling.

"You won't stay?"

"I think I've been very patient, all things considering," I say. "But watch you forswear your love for me and pledge your heart to another? Even if that other person is God? I can't bear it, Zenny. I can't do it."

A tear spills over, followed by another and another. "I haven't been good to you, have I?"

I look away. "You've been very good—"

She shakes her head, forcing a rueful smile through her tears. "No. I haven't. I don't know if I can say sorry for all of the times—I don't believe they were wrong—but I know sometimes I was…deeply inconsistent. Hot and cold."

"You had reasons to be wary," I say tiredly. "You wanted something transactional between us, and I broke that."

"But I broke it too," she confesses. "I couldn't tell you because I was terrified of feeding it…this fire inside my chest. But, oh Sean, every time you said one of those *things*—"

"Things?"

She waves a hand. "You know what I mean. Or whenever your voice would get low and rough, or whenever your eyes would get so big and open, like a sky after rain… Every time, I would feel that fire trying to burn and claw its way free. You do that to me. You tear me open and it was all I could do to hold on to the edges of my soul as you did. I loved you and I was scared, and if I had been honest…well." She sucks in a deep breath and takes my hand in hers, pressing it to her heart. "Maybe this wouldn't hurt so much."

Her heart thumps quietly inside her chest, a tired and mournful bird, and I can't help it, just one more kiss, one final brush of lips and one final taste of her.

"It was always going to hurt, Zenny-bug," I whisper against her lips. "Always."

I soak in a last vision—dark, shining eyes and a tart little nose and a sweep of lush, ticklish curls—and then I surrender her to the hands of God and her sisters. I close the door to the waiting room behind me, effectively slicing our love apart for good, and as I do, my heart breaks

one

last

time.

CHAPTER
THIRTY-FOUR

I can't get out of the monastery fast enough, half-running through the central hallway to the front door and pushing through that as if I were running out of air.

I am. I am running out. I'm choking on my own pain, my own bittersweet regrets. And I can't even summon the strength to listen to the singing and praying echoing from inside; I hurl myself down the stairs and onto the old, broken sidewalk, willing the city noise of traffic and wind to drown out the melody of Zenny's marriage to Christ.

Why did you do this to me? I demand of God. *What possible reason could there be for this?*

There's no answer, and of course there's not. If there's anything I've learned during my detente with God this week it's that He very rarely answers fussy prayers right away.

Although He better get used to them. I'm much more

Jacob than I am Abraham, ready to fight and wrestle with God at a moment's notice; I'm much more Jonah with his dead plant and his surly *I'm so angry I wish I were dead.* But I'm beginning to think that's okay now. That honesty and angst and rage and all the other messy human feelings are preferable to lifeless piety.

So I think sullen, hurting thoughts up to God, which turn into sad, lonely thoughts as I get closer to my car at the edge of the block.

I'm never not going to love her, I think with sorrow. *She's the only one my heart will ever hold inside itself, for as long as I'm alive.*

God finally sees fit to answer, and Kesha erupts noisily from my phone. I don't recognize the number offhand, and my chest deflates so fast my ribs crack, which is stupid. Like I really thought Zenny was going to call me in the middle of her ceremony? What kind of sad idiot am I?

I answer, not bothering to muffle my mopeful tone. "Sean Bell."

"Sean Bell," a creaky voice says back. An old woman's voice. A familiar voice. "I think you'd better slow down."

"I—what?"

"Slow. Down," the voice repeats as if I'm maybe not all that bright, which maybe I'm not, because I still don't understand what she means until I turn around to face the monastery, and I'm very strangely certain now that this is the Reverend Mother talking to me, and why would she be talking to me—

A flash of white flutters out of the front door of the monastery and I freeze.

And then the flutters resolve into froth, and the froth resolves into a nun in a wedding dress, her hands balled up in the skirt and holding it up as she runs toward me.

She looks like something out of a movie—or a dream. The sun gleams along her skin and catches the silk in shimmering flashes, her hair bounces and spills around her neck and face, and the wind strokes her affectionately, making the dress billow behind her.

I am rooted to the spot, emptied out of everything, even hope, as she runs breathlessly up to me.

"That ought to do it," comes the satisfied voice of the Reverend Mother through the phone, and I hear her hang up.

Wordlessly, I let my phone drop to my side and stare.

"Don't lose your joy," Zenny says, coming to a stop in front of me.

"What?" I ask dumbly.

"It's what your mom said to me before she died." Zenny takes a deep breath, stepping forward. "She said we made joy in one another, that she could tell just from the way you'd talked about me."

"Zenny—"

She shakes her head—not at me, but at herself. "I even said it. *I'm more myself when I'm with you.* I got to the front of that aisle and I realized that I wasn't more myself there, not like when I'm with you. I realized the walk down to the altar wasn't going to be a walk of joy." She looks up at me, her eyes meeting mine. "You give me joy, Sean. You give me the space to be strong and to be safe and loved and please say it isn't too late, please say I'm not too late for us—"

But I'm already gathering her into my chest, I'm already kissing her. I take her by her upper arms and hold her apart from me after a moment, trembling. "You're not taking your vows? Truly?"

She nods bashfully, a slow smile on those perfect lips, and I yank her back into me for more kisses. "Oh Zenny," I breathe, my lips everywhere in gratitude—across the bridge of her nose and her jaw and her collarbone. "I'll make you every vow in the world in exchange, I promise. I'll be everything for you."

"Everything is tempting," she laughs under my kisses. "But I think Sean Bell is quite enough for one girl to handle all on his own."

EPILOGUE

One Year Later

"Again?" I ask, amused.

"I'll have you know," Zenny says, crawling into my lap, "that it's very common for a woman in my condition."

My cock—sleepy from the two-round quickie just an hour ago—wakes the fuck up right away. Zenny's wearing some kind of loose tank top thing that allows me to see right down her shirt and she's in shorts so short that I can't believe I let her out of the house, because I'm a jealous, possessive bastard like that.

(Okay, I do know why I let her out of the house. It's because we were going to the same place together.)

"Everyone's out of the office," she purrs, her hands finding my tie and yanking at it. "We're alone."

"All of our *one* employees is gone, hmm?" I tease, but I

let her pull me into a slow, deep kiss. Emmett only comes in two mornings a week to help us sort mail and work on filing—he's working part-time to save up money for his new twin great-grandchildren. (And one time he brought them into the office, and I held one of the little lumps for three hours while the lump dozed and I made some phone calls. Don't you dare tell anyone that.)

I run my hands up Zenny's legs and grip the curve of her ass. "These shorts of yours are killing me," I say against her lips. "Are you trying to murder your husband?"

"No," Zenny says briskly, her hands dropping to my zipper and exposing me with hurried movements. "I need his dick too much for that."

"That's reassuring. *Ah, fuck*, baby, just like that. God, that's good."

She's got my thickening length in her slender fingers, jacking me slowly and tauntingly. Outside my ground-floor office, I see the humdrum roll of a delivery truck to the tire repair warehouse next door. And okay, did I ever imagine myself working on the ground floor of a forgotten building under an overpass in an office carpeted in nubby gray-blue bullshit, and oh, it just happens to be next to the Kansas City franchise of Tires, Tires, Tires?

No. No, I did not imagine this. And I wouldn't trade it for the fucking world.

Because I also didn't imagine myself married, and now I'm married to the smartest, sweetest, bravest, and most

461

beautiful woman I know. And because I also didn't ever imagine myself a father, and yet here's Zenny perched in my lap with a naughty glint in her eye and a swollen belly pushing at her tank top.

(I know, I know, she's too young to be pregnant. But let's be real—her being too young has never stopped me before.)

So I actually don't mind that I'm now the owner of a new nonprofit in an office that's as far away from glamorous as possible. I love it. I provide and source additional funding for charities across the Metro—charities like the shelter belonging to the Servants of the Good Shepherd—and what I do actually helps people.

Can you imagine?

Sean Bell, philanthropist?

But it's no less likely than Sean Bell, husband.

Or Sean Bell, father.

And all of those things are blessedly, happily true.

As for Zenny—my sweet little wife is halfway through her Nurse-Midwifery degree. She'll still anchor the shelter's birth center when both she and it are ready, and I'm going to give her the best birth center known to man. I'm going to give her the best of everything, always, until the day I die. (Longer, if I can help it. That's what good estate planning will do for you.)

Zenny divests herself of those tempting shorts and her tank top, and climbs back onto my lap, kissing my neck and rubbing against me, naked and soft and curved. Unable to take it any longer, I fist my hands in her hair and use my other hand to probe at her tight folds until the head of my sex is firmly lodged inside. She impales herself on me with no prompting, no coaching, simply seeking out the friction and the fullness and rocking herself to an orgasm, oblivious to me.

Some men might object, but I've got no complaints about being my pregnant wife's sex toy. Instead, I lean back in my chair and play lazily with her plumped breasts as she fucks me.

"So good," I croon in praise to her. "You ride me so good. Does that feel nice? Is that what you need?"

Her eyes closed and her throat working, she nods, her hips grinding against me, and I feel the moment she comes, I feel it clench and milk at my cock, and I also feel her ripened womb going tight under my fingers. It's fucking heaven to feel, like a secret finally made visible. I trace fascinated circles over the contracting muscles and over the new dark line stretching from her sternum to her pussy. I let her take all the time she needs, I let her slowly unwind into shivering, deep satisfaction and I smile as she curls into a worn-out slump against my chest.

"All better?" I murmur, rubbing at the sudden goose bumps erupting all over her back.

"For now," she says contentedly. "I might need you again in an hour."

I wrap my arms around her and hold her tight as I stroke the hard part of me inside the soft part of her. It doesn't take long—not like this, with her so warm and curvy and ripe—until I'm pulsing my wet heat into her. My breath is a series of fierce grunts and my stomach and thighs are rock-hard tensed in tandem, flexing and pushing all the cum out, out, out of me, until I'm completely drained and relaxed.

"Do we have to get back to work?" she asks drowsily, her head on my shoulder. "I just want to stay like this forever."

"We can do whatever you like, Zenny-bug. Just say the word."

"Whatever I like?"

"Whatever you like."

"Honest guy thing?"

"Honest guy thing."

She makes a happy noise and burrows closer to me, and I cradle her for as long as she lets me, holding our unborn baby between us and reflecting on a very different Sean Bell from once upon a time. A Sean Bell who wanted money and power and sex, who was willing to do whatever he had to in order to get it. Now he runs a nonprofit from a dingy office next to Tires, Tires, Tires, and he couldn't be happier. And it's all because of the angel in his lap, his little nun, his little Zenny-bug.

It's because of her, every bit of it.

Pray for us sinners, the prayer goes, and dammit if someone didn't pray for me and scoop me up into a life of joy and giving. Dammit if I haven't been circled with love by the most extraordinary people I'll ever have the honor to know. The least I can do is say *hail* back.

Hail Elijah. Hail Reverend Mother. Hail Tyler, Aiden, Ryan, and Dad.

Hail Mom.

Hail Zenny, the Lord is with thee.

Pray for us sinners.

Amen.

Author's Note:

Well, here we are again, dear reader, at the nexus of God and sex. I didn't want to leave you without clearing up a couple things.

The Servants of the Good Shepherd are a fictitious order, although there are orders throughout the world with similar names. The practices and missions you see in these pages are cobbled together from various monastic groups; every group has its own rules regarding habits, solitude, service and vows, and the rules I gathered together for SotGS of Kansas City, I stole with an author's eye. That is to say that everything Zenny does and encounters is real somewhere, but like the magpie I am, I shamelessly stitched together the things I found the most pageworthy. For further reading about the lives of modern American nuns, I cannot recommend highly enough *Unveiled: The Hidden Lives of Nuns* by Cheryl L. Reed. And when it comes to Christianity at large, *Wearing God* by Lauren F. Winner as well as an old favorite, *Unprotected Texts* by Jennifer Wright Knust, were huge influences in my composition of Zenny's faith and Sean's journey back to it.

Sean's mother dies in very similar circumstances to my

own mother's death in 2014—that being said, my knowledge of medical practice is as limited as you might imagine a full-time writer's would be, and I take full responsibility for any places where my memory and research fall short. I have to credit a few books for helping me grapple with the stark reality of ICU death and what comes after—*Modern Death* by Haider Warraich, *Cancer: The Emperor of All Maladies* by Siddhartha Mukherjee, *Smoke Gets in Your Eyes* by Caitlin Doughty, and *Being Mortal* by Atul Gawande.

The Wakefield Saga, alas, is not real, although you might recognize the Wakefield name from one of my childhood pleasures, the *Sweet Valley High* series.

The Maison De Naissance is real, however, and amazing and beautiful and an excellent reminder of hope and hard work in our world, which too often seems filled with pain.

Thank you, reader, for walking down this path with me. I threw God, sex, death, belief and unbelief at you, and while I know perspectives on those things differ wildly for every person, I'm grateful you were willing to see what they looked like for Sean. I would promise to start taking it easier on those Bell brothers, but, well, we all know how untrustworthy I am when it comes to being nice to my characters…

ACKNOWLEDGMENTS

Sinner is the kind of book that needed multiple midwives and doulas in order to be born.

My critique partners: Laurelin Paige, who gets me, who gives me unwavering encouragement, who told me on a dark November day in 2014 that if I couldn't believe in heaven that she'd believe in it enough for the both of us. Kayti McGee, who is strangely resistant to my sullen sarcasm and is willing to talk plot at the drop of a hat. Melanie Harlow, who is the prettiest, gin-iest beacon of support a girl could ask for.

My betas: Nana Malone, Tijuana Turner, Olive Teagan, Dylan Allen, Syreeta Jennings, Amie Moore, Jana Aston and Kennedy Ryan. There's absolutely no way I could have worked to form and refine Zenny and Sean's relationship without your insight and there are no words to convey how much I appreciate your help! Especially Nana Malone, who spent hours on the phone with me, and doubled as a writing coach as well as a beta…as well as my confessor for all the times it got hard.

My Ashley Lindemann, who is also my wizard, my ENFJ, my ride or die. No book has ever gotten written without her, since book number one to Sinner, and I'll owe her everything, always. To Melissa Gaston, Serena McDonald, and Candi Kane, who tend to the fires while I go off and dance—every word I write is because you help me, thank you.

My Julie Murphy, my INTJ Unseelie faerie queen, who claps at darkness and functions as my second brain. My Natalie and my Tess, who somehow still like me after all these years of stealing their beer and keeping them up late.

To Rebecca Friedman, my agent and unflagging champion. There's no book that doesn't bear the mark of your support and love and advice. To Flavia Viotti and Meire Dias of Bookcase Literary, who spread my words everywhere, thank you, thank you.

To Nancy Smay, my very patient editor, and Erica Russikoff and Michele Ficht, my very patient proofers. I'm sorry I make your search histories so…interesting.

To Vitaly Dorokhov, who made an amazing cover image, and to Letitia Hasser of RBA Designs, who was more than gorgeously accommodating when I popped up out of nowhere to beg for a cover. This cover is more than I ever could have hoped for!

To all the other authors I'm lucky enough to count as friends: Jade West, CD Reiss, Becca Mysoor, Robin

Murphy, Sarah MacLean, Zoraida Cordova, Amy Daws, Sara Ney, Tamsen Parker, Lena Hart, Ellie Cahill, Ruth Clampett, Liv Morris, Aly Martinez, Willow Winters, Ilsa Madden-Mills, Tia Louise, Nikki Sloane, Karla Sorenson, Kandi Steiner, Kyla Linde, Meghan March, Katana Collins, Jessica Hawkins, Stacy Kestwick, Penelope Reid, Giana Darling, Staci Brillhart, Gretchen McNeil, Megan Bannen, Jean Siska, Lex Martin, and Louise Bay. It takes a village and I wouldn't have made it through the dim months of winter without your love and pms and retreat toasts!

To all the bloggers on Facebook and Instagram—there's nothing I can do or say to express how much your energy and love mean to me. Thank you!

And to all of my readers—thank you, thank you, for being willing to put up with all the crazy, unexpected rides I put you through. I can't even begin to tell you how much it means that you'll roll with whatever perverted story I'm in the mood to tell.

Let's sin together always.

ALSO BY SIERRA SIMONE

Misadventures:
Misadventures with a Professor (Coming November 2018)

The New Camelot Trilogy:
American Queen
American Prince
American King

The Priest Series:
Priest
Midnight Mass: A Priest Novella
Sinner

Co-Written with Laurelin Paige
Porn Star
Hot Cop

The Markham Hall Series:
The Awakening of Ivy Leavold
The Education of Ivy Leavold
The Punishment of Ivy Leavold
The Reclaiming of Ivy Leavold

The London Lovers:
The Seduction of Molly O'Flaherty
The Persuasion of Molly O'Flaherty
The Wedding of Molly O'Flaherty

ABOUT THE AUTHOR

Sierra Simone is a USA Today bestselling former librarian who spent too much time reading romance novels at the information desk. She lives with her husband and family in Kansas City.

Sign up for her newsletter to be notified of releases, books going on sale, events, and other news!

www.authorsierrasimone.com
thesierrasimone@gmail.com